TRAP DOORS

A Novel of FBI International Intrigue

Ron Cleaver

Copyright © 2006 by Ronald Cleaver

ISBN 0-7414-3500-4

Published by:

INFINITY
PUBLISHING.COM

1094 New DeHaven Street, Suite 100
West Conshohocken, PA 19428-2713
Info@buybooksontheweb.com
www.buybooksontheweb.com
Toll-free (877) BUY BOOK
Local Phone (610) 941-9999
Fax (610) 941-9959

Printed in the United States of America

Printed on Recycled Paper

Published November 2006

ACKNOWLEDGMENTS

I wish to thank all of those who gave me encouragement throughout the writing of this, my first novel. A special thanks to my wife, Caroline, and daughters, Cheryl, Cathie, and Christie for their suggestions, and to my son, Matt, and FBI Academy co-instructor Gary Kruchten and his wife, Susan for their support.

I also very much appreciate my FBI colleagues and the many other friends located across the United States and around the world that I have had the privilege to know, learn from, and work with.

Thanks to all of you.

PREFACE

The end of the Cold War in the USSR had not brought about the hoped-for wealth and prosperity. Residents had relied on the old communist regime for most of their well-being, and although their Cold War lifestyles were far from luxurious by most western standards, their basic needs were met. They had jobs, places to live, and most were able to afford life's necessities. Many had even managed to set aside a few rubles for their old age.

Now, half-a-decade later, with a crumbling economy and skyrocketing inflation, millions of Russians, especially those caught at opposite ends of the age spectrum seem to be struggling as never before. Swelling populations over-run the capacities of Russian orphanages and gut-wrenching photos of malnourished, abandoned children are shown on media clips and circulated in newspapers around the world. Millions of forsaken retirees no longer receive their monthly pensions and are having to survive this mid-1990's rebuff any way they can.

Part of the blame can be placed squarely on the shoulders of a new economic system for which most are ill prepared, but a disproportionate amount of the culpability falls at the feet of an ever-expanding underworld menace. Power struggles play out daily with organized crime groups numbering over five thousand. Trails of bloodshed and carnage stretch across much of a continent whose streets only a decade before were considered relatively safe and reasonably crime free.

CHAPTER ONE

Bored with pouring over yet another endless string of code, Darren Kroft closed that program and launched the Internet.

Quickly scrolling down one website after another devoted to the subject of computer dating, he leaned back in his chair and asked, "Might some of these beauties be different?"

A self-centered middle-aged egotist with an expanding paunch, receding hairline, and chauvinistic attitude, Kroft had long enjoyed a success in programming that he had never achieved when it came to establishing long-term relationships with women. Neither his ex-wife nor any of the other women in his past seemed to understand either him or his needs. All had eventually accused him of being a control freak, saying he was demanding and overbearing. His response to each had been one of indignation. After all, why shouldn't these women be expected to do what he said? He was the man, and yes, that was the way things were supposed to be.

As far as Kroft was concerned, women had been given way too much authority and independence, and as a result they were no longer responsive to the men they served. From his perspective, that was one of the biggest failures with American society today, and he was tired of it.

Continuing his web search, Darren suddenly stopped at a site reading, "Beautiful women in search of western husbands." A click onto the link revealed an alluring array of provocatively clad, young Russian women, enticing seekers to come to Moscow and meet the women of their dreams.

Theorizing that the minds of these Russian babes had not yet been corrupted by the propaganda being dished out to American women, Kroft believed this site might merit further study. Not only did the women look even more tempting the second time, but a closer look at the text generously sprinkled with words like "seductive," "voluptuous," and "submissive" made them even more enticing.

Additional links took him to an assortment of options. These ranged from an all-inclusive trip with guaranteed invitations to no less than half-a-dozen "meet a Russian bride get-togethers," to less restrictive arrangements put together by travel agents providing only transportation and hotel accommodations.

Darren Kroft was hooked. The only decision for him to now make was simply when.

CHAPTER TWO

Exhausted and allowing her mind to wander, Natasha wiped the condensation from the windowpane and peered out. As she stood there, her mind jumping from one thought to another, a swirl of snowflakes temporarily blurred the glow emanating from a nearby streetlight. On the ground below, several sets of fresh footprints trailed into the darkness.

When her grandmother, Elena, left their upper-floor apartment to go shopping, she told Natasha that she expected to be gone for only a couple of hours. That was two days ago, and Natasha had been searching for her grandmother almost non-stop since, but to no avail.

As her breath continued to fog the glass, Natasha placed her finger on another pane and drew a frowning face. Then, with tears in her eyes, she whispered, "Please, God, protect her. Lead me to her."

A career schoolteacher in the former USSR, Elena Federova retired only a short time before the onset of Perestroika and Glasnost. At first glance, she reminded the casual onlooker of an artist's depiction of a babushka. A woman of small stature, Elena had rounded shoulders, a slumping posture, and shoulder-length, silver gray hair, which she usually pulled tightly into a chignon and kept covered with a triangularly folded headscarf. She wore oval, silver-rimmed glasses that were petite and tasteful. Her lips were thin and her face was wrinkled and drawn.

The feistiness that had brought smiles to the faces of her students, however, was now absent. It was replaced by feelings of helplessness and despair created by the staggering inflation that followed the dissolution of the Soviet Union and now besieged the fledgling Russian economy. There was also the problem of the government's failure to meet its pension obligations and pay her promised monthly stipends. Elena had first exhausted her savings, and being too proud to beg, she finally resorted to selling most of her personal effects. The most devastating loss was only a few days before when she bartered the wedding ring that had been in her deceased husband's family for over one hundred years. Elena had planned to pass it on to her granddaughter. Now, that was not to be. Through it all, though, Elena remained strong, guided by her own moral compass and an unwavering faith in God.

Natasha was Elena's only grandchild, and when her parents deserted her more than a quarter of a century before, Elena adopted Natasha and gave her the Federova name. First, there was the mysterious disappearance of Natasha's father. Shortly thereafter, her mother walked out on both her own mother and her toddler daughter. Natasha had no recollection of either parent, and when she asked about them, her grandmother quickly changed the subject. From an occasional comment here and there, though, Natasha suspected that either one or both of her parents were extremely loyal party communists, and it was this loyalty, she believed, that had caused a rift in their relationship with her grandmother. She remembered hearing her grandmother spout the party line only to the extent that was required for her to keep her teaching position, and even then, it was with some disdain.

Natasha tugged at her sleeve and used it once again to clear one of the fogged panes so she could see out. As she stood there, a dark sedan pulled up and parked under a streetlight near the front of the complex. Two men climbed out and walked toward the apartments.

Seeing them reminded her of that morning only a few days earlier when a loud pounding on the apartment door had abruptly awakened her. Wearing the layered clothing that had become her standard sleepwear, since the heat was turned down, she had gotten up and opened the door as far as the chain lock would allow. Standing in the hallway were two well-dressed, middle-aged men carrying briefcases. One was quite tall and the other somewhat shorter.

Surprised and still not quite awake, Natasha had stood behind the door and squinted through the slight opening, "What do you want?" she had asked them.

The taller of the two answered in a respectful tone, "We are here to speak with Mrs. Elena Federova."

"Why?" asked Natasha, as she had placed her knee a bit more firmly against the cracked door.

"We heard Mrs. Federova might be in need of some financial assistance, and we are here to help," the taller man answered.

"We don't need your help," Natasha had curtly replied.

However, before she had been able to shut the door, her grandmother had moved up beside her. Desperate, she'd said, "Let us hear what they have to say, Natasha. Maybe they can help."

Natasha had not been comfortable doing this, but her grandmother had insisted. Since the two men did look more like businessmen than the typical street thugs she had become accustomed to seeing hanging around the neighborhood, Natasha had finally given in to her

5

grandmother's wishes. She had taken their dark fur hats, long leather coats and gloves, and set them aside. Her grandmother had invited them to sit down on the wooden chairs around a table in the far corner of the room, near the frost-covered window. As they had walked toward the table, Elena had apologized for the chilled conditions in the room.

When they were seated, Elena had once again apologized, this time telling them that she was sorry about not having anything in the apartment to offer them to eat or drink.

"We understand, and it is for situations like yours that we believe we can be of assistance," replied the taller man.

With a perplexed look on her face, Elena had asked, "How is that?"

"Because you were fortunate and acquired your Moscow apartment through the privatization reforms, we have a proposal for you."

He had gone on to explain, "For the right to become the beneficiary of your apartment at the time of your death, we are willing to begin paying you, now."

"Today!" his associate had enthusiastically interrupted.

The taller man had continued, "You see, you will receive a very generous monthly payment from us for as long as you live." Gesturing, first in the direction of the old steel radiator standing along the wall, and then toward the cupboards and telephone, he had added, "There will be plenty of money to pay for fuel to heat the apartment, give you and your granddaughter plenty to eat and drink, and yes, even plenty to pay for your telephone. You will be living very comfortably."

In the interim, his associate had pulled a wad of rubles from his pocket and waved them in Elena's face. "See, all of these can be yours. This is only the first month's payment.

Just think, no more freezing, no more hunger, and no more having to sell your treasured possessions on the streets."

In the meantime, the taller man had taken two folded sheets of paper from his jacket pocket and flattened them out on the table in front of her grandmother. One appeared to have been a sheet he didn't want, and was immediately crumpled up and tossed aside. The other was placed in front of Elena. As Natasha continued to watch, the man took a pen from his pocket and handed it to her grandmother.

He had said, "All you need to do, Mrs. Federova, is sign this piece of paper and all of these rubles can be yours."

While he talked, his associate had continued to fan his thumb across the edge of the bills.

As Elena had stared at the sheet of paper, the two men anxiously waited to see if she would accept their offer.

Natasha remembered her grandmother had looked up from the paper, first at her, and then toward the two men, before finally replying, "Okay," and signing on the line identified with an "x."

Now, shaking her head in an effort to clear her mind of the flashback, Natasha continued to watch intently as the two men below made their way from the dark sedan and into the apartment complex. The shadows and darkness, however, prevented her from being able to tell whether this was the same pair who had been waving the handful of rubles in her grandmother's face only days earlier.

CHAPTER THREE

Throughout the early part of the changeover, and now continuing into the mid-1990's, headlines screaming words akin to **MURDER, MONEY,** and the **MAFIA** were becoming so commonplace on the front pages of Moscow's daily newspapers that they rarely received second glances.

Vicious underworld gangs, nicknamed the "Russian Mafia," had taken over, and were spinning out of control. Showing no fear, and little regard for human life, their brutal members targeted anyone who got in their way or had something they wanted.

Victims included prominent television personalities, bankers, politicians, investigative reporters, local and foreign businessmen, and an ever-increasing number of Russian police officers. No one was exempt.

Now, with tentacles extending more deeply into the West than ever before, efforts were quickly being made to thwart the surge.

Senior officials from both the FBI and the Russian police, the MVD, had recently concluded an emergency meeting at the Moscow Headquarters for Russia's Ministry of the Interior. At that meeting, an agreement was reached launching joint training and investigative activities between the two agencies.

Shortly thereafter, the FBI's Legal Attaché, also known as the LEGAT for Moscow, received the MVD's initial request. It was for training and assistance in the area of money laundering.

A high priority message was sent to Quantico, where the FBI Academy's Assistant Director called Supervisory Special Agents Nick Costigan and Matt Kelly into his office and told them to prepare to leave for Moscow as soon as possible.

In addition to asking for the specialized training, the Russians also invited Costigan and Kelly to work hand in hand with some of their top MVD officers in conducting active investigations. These Russian investigators were part of a newly created elite MVD unit tasked with the unenviable job of trying to break the backs of these ruthless organized crime gangs.

CHAPTER FOUR

Now in his mid-thirties, Matt Kelly would soon begin his eighth year in the Bureau. He was quickly becoming known as one of the FBI's experts in organized crime, and loved his life as both an FBI agent and eligible bachelor. After graduating from the United States Air Force Academy at Colorado Springs, Matt went to Goodfellow Air Force Base where he completed training as an Intelligence Officer. Following several overseas deployments and a tour with Special Ops at Hurlburt Field, he decided that he wanted to follow in the footsteps of his father who had been a longtime FBI bank robbery agent in Los Angeles. Taking a path similar to many other Service Academy graduates over the years, he started his FBI application processing about a year before completing his military obligation. Fortunately, he did not encounter any glitches and when a small window of opportunity opened between hiring freezes, he received his Bureau appointment letter. After completing sixteen weeks of New Agent Training at the FBI Academy in Quantico, Virginia, he reported to his first office in Chicago.

During his next six years in the field, Matt received several letters of commendation. One such letter was for making a life saving rescue while serving as a SWAT Team member, and another was for implementing innovative investigative techniques that eventually culminated in the Bureau convicting a group of long-time mob figures. It was successes like these that had brought him to the attention of Quantico and led to his transfer to the Academy.

During most of his nearly two years as a member of the FBI Academy faculty, Matt was assigned to the New Agent program. The New Agents appreciated his casual, easygoing demeanor and carefree mannerisms, and many of the single female agents seemed to be especially attracted to his sexy, good looks. At 6' 2" and 185 pounds, talk of his broad shoulders and tall, athletic build, coupled with those piercing blue eyes, short black wavy hair, and a dark heavy growth beard was known to have made its way into more than one after hour's conversation.

Things had changed, though. A series of new, high-priority initiatives had come down from Headquarters and were passed along to the Academy's International and Investigative Training Units for implementation. As a result, Matt was re-assigned to the ITU, and became the younger half of a Quantico instructor team assigned to concentrate on conducting international training and consulting.

Now on the ground in Moscow, Matt was already working with his MVD counterpart while awaiting the arrival of fellow FBI agent, Nick Costigan. As he trudged through the ice and snow on his return to the Moscow hotel, Matt decided to take a detour. An earlier walk had provided him with a glimpse of the Russian Olympic Swimming and Diving Center used in the 1980 Olympics. That was the one the United States did not participate in, due to the USSR's invasion of Afghanistan. As he peered through the frosted, fogged windows, he was reminded of his own Olympic dream. Although he had gained All-American status as a swimmer while attending the Air Force Academy, and qualified for the Olympic Trials, that was as far as he had made it. Any competition since had been limited to meets in the Master's ranks.

When he arrived back at the hotel, Matt stopped at the front desk and checked with one of the receptionists for any messages. There was one.

MESSAGE FOR: *Mr. Matt Kelly*
FROM: *Sergei*
MESSAGE: *Call Me*

He knew that the call had to be from Sergei Malkin, the investigator from the elite MVD unit with whom he had been working. Sergei made it a practice to never leave his last name nor phone number when he called Matt. He didn't want to place him in any greater danger than he already was. Alerting the hotel personnel to the fact that Matt was an FBI agent would be bad enough, but to alert them to his association with the MVD's anti-mafia unit could place him directly in harm's way. The mafia had sources everywhere: financial institutions, restaurants, hotels, wherever there was money. As far as the hotel knew, Matt was just another American government employee working there on one of many U.S. assistance jobs.

Matt went to the elevator bank and pressed the button for his floor. He needed to return Sergei's call. Since he assumed his telephone conversations were monitored, he knew that he had to be very careful about what he said.

Matt dialed a special unlisted number Sergei had given him to use when calling from the hotel. The phone was picked up on the third ring and answered, "*Da.*"

"Sergei, it's me."

Recognizing Matt's voice, Sergei responded, "I will pick you up in twenty minutes."

"Okay," replied Matt, curiously, "I'll be waiting in the lobby."

After hanging up the phone, Matt went to where he had placed his bags. Even though both he and Nick Costigan were relatively new to this international work, they had already learned several tricks of the trade. One was to have neither their true home addresses nor phone numbers on their bag tags. They always used addresses and phone numbers provided by the Bureau. This was done so that the bags, if lost, could be taken care of appropriately, since it was not expected that anyone would be at their homes while they were away on the road. It also kept any foreign snoops from having immediate access to their personal information.

Matt picked up a large briefcase stuffed with training materials he had brought with him to Moscow, and after lying it on the bed, opened it to see if any of the paper slips and clips he had inconspicuously inserted throughout its contents had been disturbed. Everything seemed to be in its place.

Walking over to the dresser, he glanced down at the drawers to see if any of the broken toothpicks he had slipped into several of the cracks were either missing or on the floor. All were still there.

Old-fashioned detection devices like these dated back to the days of agents stuffing matches from matchbooks into the sides or tops of door jams, so they would not be surprised if someone were waiting for them on the other side. Although dated, many of these methods remained tried and true, even today. In addition, these techniques were not subject to detection by electronic devices.

No, Matt wasn't paranoid, but common sense ruled. It also reminded him that he had to be alert to the possibilities of both phone taps and constant video monitoring of his activities while in his room. It was that possibility of video taping that had bothered both Nick and him the most. Matt assumed that he had already been videotaped, both in and out of his room, during more than one of these international trips. Whether he was in bed, getting dressed, using the bathroom, or showering, there was no assurance of privacy. He was also very aware that with today's high speed photo imagery technology requiring little light, that significant alteration could be made to any of these still or video images. There could be scenes created depicting situations or activities that either never occurred or else occurred very differently from the way they were shown in photos or on a video. The two agents had always been concerned that someday the mafia or a foreign intelligence service might alter and use the videos in an effort to embarrass them or the Bureau.

Before going back down to the lobby, Matt took one last look around the room. He didn't notice any cameras but knew that didn't mean much. With the sophistication of today's lenses measuring less than 1/32 of an inch, and electronic bugs so small that they could be placed on a pinhead, these devices could be anywhere. Looking toward the ceiling, he noted a smoke detector and a sprinkler head. On the walls were framed pictures and light fixtures. A television sat on a built-in dresser, and a remote control and clock were located on the nightstand next to the bed. There were wires, plugs, and outlets. On the desk were a telephone and a permanently attached vase containing three plastic flowers. There was also the closet and a bathroom, and one could only imagine what snooping devices might be found in the walls or spaces connecting the rooms on either side.

Although Matt would likely never know what, if any, electronic surveillance devices were being utilized in these hotel rooms he had stayed in around the world, he remained undeterred in continuing to inconspicuously place those old-fashioned traditional detection devices in his room, as possible alerts, whenever he felt it prudent to do so. And, if foreign snoops or others detected his actions, so be it.

As he waited in the downstairs lobby taking in the sights, Matt found himself paying particular attention to some of the seductively clad call girls as they made their rounds, wandering through the lobby and over to the elevators. Their pimps were left to go into the adjoining bar and guzzle vodkas or hang out near the bellmen's station while they waited for their girls to return. He also noticed some local thugs leaning against the huge, decorative columns. These young and middle-aged toughs wore long black leather coats, had slicked-back, black hair, and smoked unfiltered cigarettes—a scene reminiscent of wiseguys hanging out in an American gangster movie.

Sergei entered through the hotel's revolving door. Matt saw him and just nodded in his direction, not wanting to arouse any undue attention. Matt could tell by looking at Sergei that the temperature must have dropped even more since he had returned to the hotel. Sergei's ruddy complexion seemed to have taken on a deeper than usual red color and his bushy brown mustache looked stiff with ice. Remaining near the entrance, Sergei kept his dark fur hat on, but unzipped his heavy winter coat, still keeping his gun concealed. He took his gloves off and reached into his pocket, pulling out one of his favorite brands of cigarettes. Tapping it lightly against a tarnished silver lighter, he lit up and took a look around.

Meanwhile, Matt tried to remain as inconspicuous as possible. He had quickly learned that razor-sharp creases in his pants, freshly starched shirts, and highly shined shoes immediately singled him out him as a foreigner. That spit and polish was expected at the Air Force Academy and was also fine for the FBI when in the U.S., but not while working in Russia. Matt also knew that in order to blend in with the typical Moscow man on the street during the dead of winter, he needed to wear a fur hat.

After finishing his cigarette in the warmth of the hotel lobby, Sergei again glanced at Matt before ducking outside.

Matt waited about two minutes before quietly following.

Linking up in a dimly lit parking spot near the far corner of the hotel lot, Sergei unlocked the doors of his black Volga, and the two of them quickly slid in.

Sergei immediately filled Matt in on events transpiring late that afternoon. "Shortly after you left the office, I received a call from the morgue. They have what looks like another mafia hit, and I thought that you might want to go to the morgue with me. That was why I left the message."

Matt nodded, "Glad you did."

Conditions on the streets had become extremely icy and as Sergei hit the accelerator and fishtailed out of the parking lot and onto the street, he let out with a hearty laugh.

Matt responded with a less than reassuring sigh, hoping they would make it to the morgue as visitors and not as accident victims.

Upon their arrival, they were taken to the area where the body in question was being kept. Matt stared at an elderly woman who looked like she could be anybody's grand-mother.

As the two of them stood over her, Sergei remarked, "It was a hit. I have no question about it."

"Are you sure? A hit? On her? It makes no sense."

"I am sure," nodded Sergei. "She is not the first I have seen."

"But why? Any idea who she is, Sergei?"

Sergei shrugged, "There was no identification."

CHAPTER FIVE

A continent and ocean away from Moscow, the Washington, D.C. skies remained overcast. Biting wind with light snow and bitter cold had been the standard for much of this January, and today was no different. Nick Costigan's recently acquired status as an international agent had once again put him on the road to Dulles International Airport. As D.C. area residents know, light snow, blustery wind, ice, and bitter cold can virtually paralyze the nation's capital. With a litter of fender benders nearly everywhere he looked, Nick's trip from his Quantico office to the airport had not been an easy one. After leaving I-95, the I-495 beltway between the mixing bowl interchange at Springfield and I-66 looked more like a demolition derby than just an afternoon drive down a metropolitan freeway. Nick thought he had left in plenty of time to make his early evening flight, but it was now beginning to look like he might be wrong. Finally, after several slips, slides, and near misses, he was on the Dulles Only Access Road, and his white-knuckled grip on the steering wheel loosened slightly.

Traffic on the Dulles Access Road was light and the long, distinctive, white, arched roofline looming over the terminal was beginning to come into sight. It was none too soon as far as Nick was concerned. The snow was coming down harder, and the roads were becoming more treacherous. He finally arrived at the Blue Lot for long-term parking and pulled his parking ticket from the machine. Because the lines were no longer visible on the snow-covered pavement,

Nick had to hope that the spot he had just slid into was really a parking place. Even if it weren't, he didn't plan to move. Lights off, alarm set, and bags in hand, he made his way to the pick-up shelter, only to find that the weather had also slowed the shuttle service. Finally, a full-to-capacity Blue Lot bus arrived. Having neither the time to stand there, nor the inclination to freeze to death, Nick decided that he would do whatever it took. Push, shove, squeeze, he was going to find a way to get himself, a carry-on, and his suit and cargo bags onto this shuttle. With less than sympathetic looks from the other passengers, he made it on and stood straddling his luggage on the step.

At the terminal, he went directly to the International Counter and noticed, much to his dismay, that there was no time listed beside his scheduled overnight flight to Frankfurt. He knew that a cancellation or delay could mean missed connections and perhaps lost luggage. He figured his consolation for lost luggage would be that he'd get plenty of personal space if he had to wear the same stale, well-traveled clothes for the entire trip.

Despite arriving at the ticket counter on time, even after the treacherous drive and the parking shuttle hassle, Nick was still not on his way. He would sit here and wait until the weather, the airlines, and the air traffic controllers decided otherwise.

Spotting a couple of TVs nearby, he glanced back and forth between them, waiting for an updated weather report. All of the stations seemed focused, however, on the President's upcoming State of the Union address, scheduled for later that evening. Nick thought to himself, "I sure hope we get out of here before that. If I have to sit through one more of those long-winded partisan political speeches with newscasters telling me how many times a bunch of politicians interrupted a President's speech with applause, I'll be nauseous before we ever make it into the air."

Now approaching fifty, "Nick" Costigan had spent over twenty of those years as a tough, no-nonsense, FBI agent. Early in his career, while working public corruption cases, he had earned a reputation as a hard-charging, tenacious agent who did not back down, and that reputation remained with him today.

In addition, Nick had also tended to be somewhat of a maverick, and that tendency had on occasion caused him some problems. During one of those corruption cases, he gave an unauthorized interview to the press which led to a "Letter of Censure," a delayed pay raise, and temporary loss of opportunity for transfer and promotion consideration.

After having paid his penance to the Bureau for that earlier vocal indiscretion, however, Nick went on to become one of the FBI's top major case agents and field supervisors. From there he was drafted to FBIHQ, where he was an FBI Headquarters supervisor, assigned to the White-Collar Crime Section, and then on to the FBI Academy at Quantico. Fortunately, those years at the J. Edgar Hoover Building in Washington D.C., were now only fading images in his rearview mirror.

Earlier in his career, Nick had tried to be assigned to the FBI's "Club Fed," at Quantico, but the timing wasn't right. The faculty of the FBI Academy is a mixture of some of the top talents of the Bureau and is composed of both seasoned younger agents who are in the middle of their careers, and a group of specially selected senior FBI agents, like Nick. The younger agents often use the assignment as a career development stepping-stone. The older agents, normally selected for a particular expertise, have usually accepted the notion that by going to the Academy at this stage in their careers, they are placing themselves in what has been aptly nicknamed "the cul-de-sac of the FBI's career development program," and as a result will likely go no further. Nick had made his decision and opted for a Quantico assignment rather than pursuing further career advancement opportunities.

With this assignment to the Academy had come several other changes. Nick's FBI Credentials still bearing a vintage photo taken when he was a new agent, his gold-colored FBI badge, and his old trusty .357 revolver, now replaced with a Glock, .40 caliber, semi-automatic pistol, were no longer all that was required for him to start work each day.

Now, he also needed an "Official" brown-jacketed United States Passport with a more current photo, travel credit cards, a fully packed bag stuffed with a variety of training materials, and of course, his laptop computer.

In addition, traveling extensively no longer posed the problem for Nick that it had been previously. After the death of his wife from cancer a number of years before, he was forced to assume sole responsibility for the upbringing of his two children. Now that they were grown, he was free to travel as much as the job required.

CHAPTER SIX

Darren Kroft was becoming frustrated as he glared at the monitor. The word "Delayed" was posted on the screen beside his overnight flight to Frankfurt. He had purposely taken an early morning flight to Washington to ensure that he would not have any problem making his connecting flight, and here he was sitting and waiting. Having already worked the crossword puzzle on his flight from Denver, he re-read the comics and again scanned the news and local sections of the newspaper, before taking one more look at his stocks and the computer-related job opportunities listed in the business section. Unfortunately, nothing new had miraculously appeared on those pages. The closing prices on his stock holdings were still showing only the same modest gains he had seen during his earlier perusal and there were no six or seven figure CEO positions noted on the pages. It really didn't matter, though, since he already had a good job, but like most, he was always keeping his eyes open for something better. With a sigh, Darren tossed this stale news into the recycling container.

While working his way back from the newspaper trash receptacle, he took a detour by the ticket counter area. As he glanced up at the information screen, it was changing. His Frankfurt flight had changed from a delayed status to a new departure time. Although two hours later than originally scheduled, it now looked like the flight would at least be getting off the ground.

He boarded one of the mobile lounges used to shuttle passengers between the main terminal and other concourses. When he reached his concourse, he walked directly to his gate. Once there, he again sat and waited until the boarding announcement was finally made.

His flight to Frankfurt would be on a 747 and the loading onto the jumbo jet seemed to be taking forever. It began with pre-boarding for those with special needs. Next, came the call for First and Business Classes. These were followed by calls for special frequent flyer category passengers.

Once all of those had boarded, it was time for those in the Economy Class to have their turn. An announcement was made that this section would be boarded by rows. Rather than going along with the program though, many of Darren's fellow Economy Class passengers immediately rushed to the gateway and boarded. Waiting his turn, Darren finally made his way onto the plane and to his window seat located directly over the left wing. The man following immediately behind him was directed by a flight attendant to the same aisle, and the aisle seat in that same row. Fortunately, for the two of them, the middle seat in their row remained open.

Darren anxiously watched every boarding passenger, hoping no one would occupy that center seat. Finally, the time came for the flight attendants to close the doors. An announcement followed over the intercom, "All passengers please take your seats and fasten your seatbelts." As they glanced toward each other, a look of relief came over the faces of Darren and the man sitting in the aisle seat. Both nodded and smiled as though they had just managed to pull off a coup.

The snow was now falling at an even heavier rate and the wind continued to blow. Peering out the small, porthole-sized window, Darren watched, as a man bundled in a heavy, hooded parka, and wearing an orange safety vest overtop, operated de-icing equipment from an elevated yellow bucket hanging over the wings. Noting the man's ice-covered beard, he thought to himself, "What a job that must be. I'm sure glad he's the one spraying that green stuff on the wings and not me." In the distance, he could also see lines of yellow snowplows with flashing lights blowing snow high into the air.

With preparations outside now complete, the giant 747 was pushed back and began to slowly lumber toward the runway. The captain asked the flight attendants to be seated for take-off, and moments later, there was a loud roar from the engines and the jumbo aircraft lifted off the ground. As the plane climbed through the heavy cloud cover, Darren caught glimpses of flickering lights emanating from the nation's capital.

As it turned out, theirs was the last flight to leave Dulles that night. The airport was closed shortly thereafter.

Turning to the passenger in the aisle seat, Darren commented, "I'm sure glad we made it out. I was beginning to wonder if I was going to be staying overnight in D.C."

"Yeah. It was beginning to look that way for all of us," his fellow passenger replied.

"Have you been to the Frankfurt airport before?" asked Darren.

"A couple of times."

"Is it easy to find your way around? I speak only English."

"You shouldn't have any trouble," the man responded. "There are directions and signs posted in English everywhere. Besides, most of the airline people speak English. Just ask one of them if you run into any problems."

Darren Kroft was not just making idle conversation, as many passengers do. Rather, he was very concerned about making his connecting flight. He asked, "Have you ever had a delayed flight into Frankfurt, like this one will be?" But, before the man could answer, Darren continued, "Will they hold my connecting flight?"

"I don't know, maybe. I've never arrived this late. They did hold a connecting flight for several of us a couple of months ago, though," the man replied.

"Thanks," responded Darren, before turning and staring back out of the window. He would pursue more answers to his questions as the flight progressed.

Always maintaining an extremely high opinion of himself, Darren was usually very reluctant to ask questions, but this was different. Until now, his travel had been confined to the U.S., with his longest flight being the five-hour stretch from Los Angeles to New York. This time, however, he was flying international and was required to have both his new blue passport and a visa, so it was important for him to get a feel for foreign travel. Besides, he didn't need to impress this guy. Once they landed, this contact would be history.

When the jet reached a cruising altitude of 33,000 feet, the captain came over the intercom and advised the passengers that he expected their overwater, overnight, seven-hour international flight across the Atlantic to be a smooth ride. He also anticipated that they would be able to make up a little of the time lost at Dulles.

As the flight progressed and dinner was served, Darren again struck up a conversation. Leaning over, he extended his hand, "I'm Darren Kroft."

"Nick Costigan," responded the man sitting in the aisle seat, giving a perfunctory smile and shaking Darren's hand.

With these brief introductions now complete, Nick set his knife and fork aside, and unrolled his napkin and laid it across his lap. Next, he removed the foil cover from the main course to see if it was a gourmet surprise or something actually resembling the selection he had made.

Even though the food might not be any better on a 747, the seats usually seemed a bit more padded and the aisles were a little wider. No matter what type of airplane it was, though, the leg and foot space in economy class was always at a premium. His two-hundred pound, six-foot, one-inch frame, and size twelve feet were not particularly compatible with the space usually available. He always grimaced when he heard the flight attendant announce to the passengers, "Put your seat back, and get comfortable." As far as he was concerned, none of the seatbacks should recline, except for those in the Business and First Class Sections, where there was enough legroom for everyone.

He did, however, realize that things could be worse. Another senior agent who spent almost as much time in the air as he did was over six-feet, four-inches tall, and twenty-five pounds heavier. He could only imagine what it must be like for that agent to have the person sitting in the seat in front of him recline his seat as far back as possible.

Even with Nick, the tray table would sometimes barely come down level, because his knees were almost too high. And, the back of the seat in front of him would occasionally serve as an obstacle to getting the food from his tray to his mouth. Fortunately, this time, however, there was the vacant seat between the two of them and that space had at least provided for some extra elbowroom and an empty tray table for them to use to put their drinks on.

Although Kroft was somewhat overweight, he was also several inches shorter than Nick, and as a result, a reclined seat and lowered tray table did not appear to pose a significant impediment.

By now, the two had consumed about all of this gourmet dinner they could manage and were awaiting coffee.

Looking over at Nick Costigan, Darren asked, "Do you live in D.C.?"

"No, but I'm from the area. I live fifty miles south, in Fredericksburg, Virginia," answered Nick.

Darren volunteered, "I'm from Denver. Have you ever been there?"

Nick nodded he had, just as the flight attendant was arriving with coffee. He was certainly no psychic or behavioral scientist, but he had sat next to enough people on airplanes to know that the next question would be either, "What do you do?" or "Who do you work for?" Experience taught him to be rather evasive whenever that subject came up. More than once, he had regretted telling another passenger that he was an FBI agent when the subsequent conversation resulted in his being either peppered with questions and opinions about the FBI and its activities, or them ranting to him about some social agenda issue they believed the FBI should be taking on.

Darren picked up his cup, sipped the lukewarm coffee, and as he was putting the cup back onto the tray, looked over at Nick and asked, "What kind of business are you in?"

Nick responded with his standard reply, "I work for the government." That response quite often sufficed; however, sometimes the question was expanded, and that turned out to be the case this time.

"What part of the government?"

"The Justice Department"

"Oh, I guess that must be interesting," Darren matter-of-factly replied.

Fortunately for Nick, this game of twenty questions was about to end. What he didn't realize was the low regard Kroft held for anyone who worked for the federal government. Kroft figured they worked there because they couldn't get a real job anywhere else, and held them in about the same esteem as those "suckers" he believed were conned into doing volunteer work. He had gotten sick and tired of listening to co-workers complaining about how tired or busy they were, only to learn they were spending much of their free time volunteering. As far as he was concerned, if something is worth doing, it was worth getting paid for.

It was now Kroft's turn to tell about himself. He boasted, "I'm a programmer and computer consultant. My company recently promoted me to an executive management position." Pulling a card from his jacket pocket, he offered, "This is one of my old cards. It doesn't have my new title on it, but the company name, address, and phone number are still the same."

Nick asked, "Where is your company sending you on this trip?"

"Oh, they're not sending me," Darren noted, "This is strictly pleasure. I'm going to Moscow."

After the flight attendants collected the dinner trays, the cabin lights dimmed and the movie started. Nick folded his glasses and put them into his pocket before attempting to get a little sleep.

As they were passing over the United Kingdom, the cabin lights were brought back up and Nick again experienced that uncomfortable feeling of traveling through five or six time zones and wondering where the night had gone. Kroft also came alive, and pushed up the porthole window cover. The sun was providing a spectacular multi-color display as it reflected off the clouds just below their 33,000-foot altitude.

Shortly thereafter, the flight attendants were back in the aisles serving another of Nick's "favorite" breakfasts. On his tray was the usual tinfoil-covered cup of juice, yogurt, a cold roll with butter and jelly, and yes, finally a cup of coffee. He also knew that before long the captain would come over the speaker to tell everyone that they were about one hour from Frankfurt.

As the flight approached the Frankfurt Airport, the two anxiously awaited the connecting flight information, both hoping their continuation flights had not already departed. The first group of announcements included Kroft's connection to Moscow. That flight had also been delayed, so Darren should be able to make it without any problem. There was no such information regarding Nick's connection to Budapest. It was likely that he would have to make alternate arrangements for his flight into Hungary.

Once inside the Frankfurt Main Airport, the two rushed to the departure screens. There, they exchanged brief good-byes, and Nick pointed Darren in the direction of the concourse where he would catch his next flight.

After waiting in a long, slow "in-transit" line, Nick was able to get re-ticketed on a late afternoon - early evening connection that should hopefully have him arriving into Budapest and to his hotel in time for dinner. He also verified with the airline customer service representative that his bags would be transferred to the new flight.

When his flight was called, the Budapest passengers boarded a bus outside the gate holding area. From there, they were driven to the area on the tarmac where the 737 was parked. As a security precaution, all of the bags were placed beside the plane, and as each passenger walked toward the mobile steps leading up and into the plane, he pointed to his bags and those were set aside so they could be loaded into the cargo hold.

CHAPTER SEVEN

"Welcome to Budapest, Mr. Costigan. It is good to have you staying with us again," greeted the hotel's gregarious general manager.

"Good to be here," responded Nick, telling the GM and registration clerk how much he had enjoyed his previous stays and looked forward to this visit.

"Will you be teaching at the ILEA again?" he asked.

Nick smiled and nodded that he would.

"Please give your friend, the Director, my best," the GM told Nick, as he was being paged to return to his office.

"I will," Nick assured him.

While awaiting delivery of his bags to the room, Nick placed calls to both the Director of the International Law Enforcement Academy (ILEA) and the Regional Security Officer (RSO) at the American Embassy, where he left messages telling them that he had been delayed, but was now in his room at the hotel. His original intention had been to meet them for an early dinner, but due to the late hour, he would now be on his own.

Located only a few blocks from the hotel was Nick's favorite Budapest restaurant. It was a the little out-of-the-way Hungarian café that offered local brews, delicious, mouth watering goulash soup, and steaming plates of paprika chicken and dumplings. In addition to the food, there was also usually a gypsy ensemble roving around providing entertainment. Everything at the café, the beer, the food, the music, all were even better than he had remembered.

While returning to the hotel, Nick was approached by a young hustler standing on a nearby street corner. The man handed him a flyer and started pointing down the street, saying, "Beautiful girls, beautiful girls, come with me. See." Nick shook his head and started walking away.

The man continued to walk beside him, talking all the while, as he tried to steer him back in the other direction. Nick stopped, looked at him, and acted as though he didn't understand English. The guy started speaking in what sounded to Nick like German. Again, Nick shrugged, and continued to walk. Not being one to give up, the guy did something Nick had never seen before. He began performing a pantomime act, going through a series of wild gyrations, using his hands and body in an effort to describe the strippers and what they did. This was quickly followed by a nod and a wink.

Nick decided it was time to respond with a bit of the Spanish he still remembered from high school. *"No comprendo,"* he said while at the same time shaking his head and shrugging his shoulders, indicating he did not understand.

Knowing no Spanish, the hustler gave Nick a quizzical look and he, too, shrugged his shoulders. Talking to himself, the guy shuffled off back to his corner post in search of another mark. Success at last, Nick thought, as he laughed to himself.

After several trips to Budapest, he was now beginning to recognize a few of these hustlers. Some had been standing on the same corners since his very first trip, hawking business for bars and strip joints every night, but always in a non-threatening manner. His sense was that the streets of Budapest posed no greater threat than one would find in any major U.S. city. In fact, he believed there was probably less need for concern here than in some of those locales.

That same feeling did not prevail, however, when it came to pick pockets and scammers. These criminals had definitely prospered in the post-Soviet era. The U.S. Embassy briefing team had warned him of the pickpocket problem during his first trip, and on each subsequent visit, the RSO always made it a point to alert him to any new trends or ploys. There always seemed to be new twists, but one common denominator ruled. That goal, was to separate the foreigner from his or her money. On Nick's last trip, the prevailing ruse was a variation of the "phony cop scam."

This particular scheme evolved with the foreign visitor being approached on the street by an individual offering a great rate to exchange dollars, pounds, and other currencies for Hungarian Forints. Whether or not any currency actually changed hands didn't really matter, because either way, at the conclusion of that contact both parties went their separate ways.

Shortly thereafter, the foreigner was again approached, but this time by two men, both flashing what appeared to be badges and both identifying themselves as police officers. They asked the foreigner if he or she had just exchanged any currency with the man. No matter what the response, the foreigner was told by these two men wearing plain clothes to let them see any currency that he or she had.

Once the men had the currency in hand, they had two options. The first was to tell the visitor that the money looked suspicious or counterfeit and must be confiscated until a further determination can be made. The "officers" then told the victim they would have to take it back to the police station for further examination.

Their second option which was a bit more brazen, but still brought about the same result, had the phony cops taking the victim's currency and without further explanation running off in opposite directions. Either way, the foreigner is separated from his or her money, and the scammers have disappeared.

When Nick related the scheme to his last ILEA class, one of the officers said he had been approached by one of those teams. When the two phony cops spoke to him in broken English and showed their badges, this officer showed his badge and identified himself as an officer attending the ILEA. With that, the phony cops turned and ran, never asking to see his currency. The ILEA attendee didn't know what was going on at the time, but figured they must have been running some kind of a fraud scheme.

Back in his room, Nick unpacked everything in preparation for his 8:00 AM presentation at the International Law Enforcement Academy. Dead tired, he slumped into bed. It had been a long twenty-four plus hours since he had any real sleep.

No matter how much international travel he did, sleeping continued to be difficult and this trip proved to be no different. A couple of hours later, he was wide-awake and staring at the ceiling. The lighted clock on the nightstand read 1:20 AM. This time it was a hotel room in Budapest, but it could just as easily have been a room in Abidjan, Berlin, or Helsinki. With all of the time zone differences, and having already missed one night's sleep while flying, everything had become one big blur. In just one night, his body couldn't seem to adjust to these five, six, seven or whatever hour time differences there were.

On previous trips, he had tried the standard remedies of counting sheep until there were just no more sheep to be counted, and staying up until he was almost ready to pass out before crashing onto the pillow, but nothing seemed to help.

One thing was for certain, however, morning was coming, and it was essential that he get some rest.

The wake-up call came at 5:00 AM, just as he had requested. Nick mumbled something into the receiver, not initially realizing that he was talking to a recorded message. He slowly crawled out of bed.

"Damn," he said, as he stubbed his toe on a table leg while he was trying to find a light switch.

This was another all too familiar scene and a downside to his frequent travels. It had gotten so bad, in fact, that on more than one occasion he had awaken, looked around at another unfamiliar hotel room, and had to find the phone book to double check to see what city he was in or, even worse, what country.

Following his normal routine, he walked over to the window and pulled back the edge of the drape to peer out and check the weather. Unfortunately, it was still too dark to see much, but from what he could tell there was a heavy layer of fog hanging over the Danube.

While showering, shaving, and getting dressed, he turned on the TV to the international news channel so he could catch up on what had been happening in the world during the past twenty-four hours. There were several clips from the President's State of the Union address, and a couple of weather related stories, but beyond those it appeared to have been a relatively slow news day.

Later, at the breakfast buffet in the hotel dining room, Nick picked-up an international news summary and in it were two brief organized crime stories, which caught his eye, both out of Moscow. Glancing up from his reading, he noticed a waitress directing a patron's attention to a display card slipped into a small plastic stand on the table. Imprinted on the card was a cellular phone in a red circle with a slash through it. The man quickly put his phone away and appeared embarrassed by the faux pas.

"Interesting," Nick thought to himself. "No Smoking" signs are commonplace in U.S. restaurants, but "No Cell Phones?"

Nick returned to his room to get his overcoat and double check to make sure that he had everything he was going to need for the day. He opened the drapes and looked out. The fog had started to lift, and there, rising in the distance, were the lights from the Chain and Elizabeth Bridges. The beauty of those illuminated majestic structures continued to amaze him as they spanned the Danube River.

Taking a closer look, he tried to spot a pathway that ran beside the Danube, but that proved difficult. Although the heavy fog was lifting, it was still not quite clear enough for the path to be visible. During his earlier visits, when conditions were more conducive to jogging, Nick followed that pathway under the Chain Bridge, past the towering Parliament Building and onto Margit Island Park. In addition to offering views of topless sunbathers on its lower beach during sunny summer days, this beautiful park, located on an island in the middle of the Danube, was also a destination for his morning jog.

Margit Island Park was a particularly enjoyable place to spend a Sunday afternoon as families with children and dogs in-tow, strolled about. Everyone seemed to be neat, well-behaved, and just having a good time. There were popcorn carts, balloon vendors, soft drink stands, and musicians situated throughout the area. In addition to the green parklands, there was a large eight-lane swimming pool facility with plaques on the walls honoring Hungary's world-class swimming accomplishments. There were also several soccer fields, clay tennis courts, and playgrounds full of children. Trips to this delightful park had become memorable experiences for the local Hungarians and visitors alike.

On his way out, Nick stopped to talk with the doorman. During his first visit to the hotel, Nick and the doorman had become casually acquainted, and now the doorman always made it a point to tell Nick a joke each morning. Nick would laugh, but as is the case with many jokes when put into another language, something usually seemed to get lost in the translation.

The sky was the same dreary January gray that hangs over Budapest for much of the winter, and there was a damp chill in the air, as Nick walked out of the hotel and into the taxi. Patches of snow remained on the ground from storms that had dumped over a foot of snow during the Christmas and New Year's Day holiday periods.

The taxi would take him from his Pest side hotel, across the Chain Bridge and into Buda. It was not until his first trip there that Nick realized that Buda and Pest were actually separate entities divided by the Danube.

At the Chain Bridge approach, guarded by huge lion statues, Nick looked out over the river. Two sleek hydrofoils were docked nearby, ready to make daily runs to Vienna. Nick hoped to someday take the hydrofoil to Vienna and return to Budapest by train through the Hungarian countryside, but that would have to wait for another trip. As the taxi crossed over the bridge, he could see the strings of headlights and taillights passing in the tunnel straight ahead.

This tunnel was at the edge of Buda and was built as a passageway under the historic Castle Hill area, which rose 180 feet above the Danube and was about a mile long. Accessible by footpath, car, or cable tram, the hilltop was home to the Royal Palace, the National Art Gallery, and Trinity Square, with the beautiful steeple of Matthias Church towering high above. From its crest, visitors could survey Buda on one side and Pest on the other and on each trip Nick tried to make a stop there. In spite of the devastation that impacted Hungary during WWII, and the additional damage inflicted by Soviet tanks when they rumbled through the city in 1956 to put down the Revolution, the Budapest architecture remained as imposing as it is beautiful.

Now that he was through the tunnel and into Buda, it would only be a matter of minutes before his arrival at the ILEA complex.

As the taxi pulled up to the iron gates and gatehouse that secured the entrance to the Academy, Nick briefly reflected on how rapidly everything had changed there. Before becoming the new home for ILEA, this compound was a training center for the Hungarian National Police. Still in place were the old buildings, high brick walls, and a huge center courtyard. It was behind that classic exterior, however, where things had really changed. Most of the buildings had been gutted and the interiors replaced with expanded dormitory space and state of the art classrooms. It was truly an impressive training facility.

Established through the cooperative efforts of the U.S. State Department, the Hungarian government, and U.S. Federal Law Enforcement Agencies, the ILEA at Budapest serves primarily as an international law enforcement training facility for countries which were previously part of the old Warsaw Pact and USSR.

At the ILEA there are both multi-country, eight-week training sessions and specialized shorter courses. During this trip, Nick would present a financial crimes program to nearly fifty officers from Poland, the Czech Republic, and Russia. These officers were all attending the 8-week multi-country program. He had instructed officers from the Czech Republic in the inaugural session, but this was his first opportunity to work with officers from either Poland or Russia.

From what he had already heard, though, this was going to be a challenge. Many of them were getting tired of sitting in the classroom eight hours a day and he could certainly understand that. As a result, he would adhere to one of the oldest of the teaching axioms: "The mind can only absorb what the posterior can endure." There would need to be an adequate number of breaks included.

Teaching at the ILEA provided Nick with many challenges, particularly since the classes usually had officers from three different countries, receiving simultaneous instruction in their native languages, through three different interpreters. To say the least, that was a bit different from his teaching assignments at Quantico. He enjoyed the ILEA, though, and it was a good opportunity for him to pick up on some issues of interest they would openly discuss at the breaks and in after-classes evening sessions. During the summer many of the students sat with instructors outside and enjoyed a cold one, as they argued about which country had the best local brews. In the winter, they moved inside to the cigarette smoke filled Buf'e and drank cups of strong, hot, Hungarian coffee.

Although these sessions usually began with entertaining stories pitting the officers against the bad guys, they inevitably ended with a discussion centering on two universal concerns: poor pay and the threat of danger for themselves and their families. From what Nick had learned, their salaries were generally quite low, and in some cases non-existent. One group of officers described how some of the police in their country were not paid in over four months. Nick remembered reading like newspaper accounts about miners in Siberia, and their strikes and railway blockages, but what he hadn't realized was that similar plights had also been plaguing numerous police officers and their families.

"What a sad state of affairs," he thought. "What kind of societies would exist in the United States and other western countries, if our police officers went months and months without being paid?"

CHAPTER EIGHT

Unable to get the images of that poor elderly woman out of his mind, Matt Kelly remained wide-awake for the rest of the night. At the first sign of daybreak, he got up, left his Moscow hotel room, and took the subway to the Embassy for an early morning breakfast, before finishing preparations for a series of meetings scheduled for that day.

All went slower than planned, so by the time he was able to leave the Embassy compound and arrive at Sergei's MVD office late that afternoon, the winter sun was already setting. Inside, he found Sergei in his standard office posture. He had both feet propped up on the desk, a cigarette dangling from his lower lip, and the phone receiver resting on his shoulder next to his ear.

"Got delayed," Matt silently mouthed.

Sergei acknowledged that he understood and pointed for Matt to take a seat on one of the two unpadded, straight-backed wooden chairs that were directly in front of his desk. Having sat most of the day, Matt was already suffering from a severe case of tired-butt syndrome, so he motioned that he was okay.

While Sergei remained engaged in conversation, Matt waited, resting his hand against the back of one of the chairs, and reviewing the day's events in his mind. His first meeting that morning had been with the Embassy's Regional Security Officer. The RSO alerted him to an alarming increase in death threats and extortion demands being made against a growing corps of American entrepreneurs now working in Moscow, and there appeared to be little the U.S. could do about it. At the conclusion of that briefing, there had been more meetings with other Embassy staff, and finally a short stop at the LEGAT Office, before he was able to make his escape to the MVD office.

When Sergei hung-up the phone, he looked over at Matt, "You all right?" he asked.

"Fine," answered Matt. "Just a little too much sitting. I thought I'd stand for a while. What's up?"

"Maybe nothing. Who knows? That call was from a man who got my name from a patrol officer."

"What did he want?"

"Something about an old woman missing. She lives in his apartment building."

"Why call you?" questioned Matt.

After taking another drag off his unfiltered cigarette, Sergei continued. "I asked him that. He said she was very poor. She had sold many of the things from her apartment in order to live. Now she seems to have all the money she needs. He could not understand it. That was, until he heard she contracted her apartment."

"What do you think?" Matt asked.

"I think there might be something to it."

"Did he say anything else?"

"Not much. He gave me the address and apartment number where she lives. Oh yes, something else, he said her granddaughter lives with her."

"What about the man who called, who's he?"

"He would not give me his name. He said he was a concerned friend. That was all. Then, he quickly hung-up. He sounded scared."

"Do you think he's talking about the same woman we saw at the morgue?" asked Matt.

Sergei shrugged, "We will drive to the apartment building and ask questions."

"I'm ready to go," Matt replied.

Sergei motioned, and the two of them headed out the door and to his car.

At the address was a boxy, gray, nondescript, multi-story apartment building, similar to many others Matt had seen in the city. They seemed to stretch kilometer after kilometer across the Moscow landscape.

Sergei parked the black Volga under a shining streetlight near the front of the building.

Watching through the frosted window, Natasha could not help but wonder if these two men now entering her apartment building were the same two who had awakened Elena and her only a few days before and waved the wad of rubles in her grandmother's face, but it was too dark and they were too far away for her to tell.

Sergei pointed in the direction they needed to go. Matt followed him through the snow and into the building. The two walked up several flights of stairs and down a long narrow hallway. Paint on the mustard colored walls was peeling and a couple of low-watt light bulbs dangling from the ceiling lit their way. Other bulbs were in place, but one could only assume they must have burned out. Their first knock on the apartment door brought no response, but they were not surprised since darkness had already set in, and they were not expected. Sergei knocked again, this time identifying them as being from the MVD. The lock inside rattled, and the door opened slightly. Near the outstretched chain they could see an eye peering through the crack. Sergei held out his badge, and asked, "May we come in?"

The door closed, and after more rattling from the inside, it was once again opened, very slowly, and this time wide enough for them to see a tall, striking, figure standing in the doorway. She appeared to be in her mid-twenties, with shoulder length, silky, dark auburn hair. Her green eyes were red and puffy, indicating she had been crying. Matt's attention was immediately drawn to her beauty. She gestured, inviting the two of them to come in, but her invitation appeared to go unnoticed. Sergei smiled to himself and gave Matt a nudge. Startled, Matt refocused and stepped into the room. Sergei followed, and the young woman quickly closed the door behind them.

Sergei identified himself and Matt. He did not mention that Matt was from the FBI, nor that he did not speak Russian. Later, he would fill Matt in on what was being said.

"What is your name?" Sergei asked.

"Natasha," she hesitatingly responded, in a soft, quiet voice.

Noticing that she was obviously frightened, Sergei tried to put her at ease and assure her that the two of them were no threat.

"Don't be afraid. We are not here to cause you any harm," he told her.

Her apprehension was understandable. In addition to being very concerned about her grandmother, there were now two police officers in her apartment asking questions.

Decades of distrust and fear of the Russian police had made many of Moscow's residents extremely wary and she was no different.

Natasha finally nodded that she was okay.

"Is anyone here with you?" Sergei asked.

"Not now, but I do live here with my grandmother."

"Do you expect her back soon?"

"Yes," she replied.

"Where is she?" asked Sergei.

The young woman lowered her head and shrugged her shoulders.

"How long has she been gone?"

"Two days," Natasha answered.

"Where was she going?"

"Out shopping and she never returned."

"Has anyone seen or heard from her?"

"No, no one. I asked the neighbors and then the police patrols. No one has seen her."

"Has she ever disappeared like this before?"

"Never," Natasha answered.

Suddenly realizing that these two men had not knocked on her door without reason and noting the direction and tone of Sergei's questioning, she began drawing conclusions. "Where is she?" Natasha asked in an almost hysterical tone.

Sergei and Matt just looked at her, their eyes telling the story.

Tears came to her eyes, and she screamed, "What has happened to my grandmother? Where is she?"

Matt didn't need to know Russian to understand what was being said. Natasha's actions made it clear.

The two of them sat quietly while Natasha looked toward the ceiling. She took a deep breath, wiped away the tears, and slowly regained some composure.

Sergei calmly explained, "There is a woman at the morgue. We do not know her identity, but we would like to ask you to please go there with us to see if you can identify her." He went on, telling her about the call he received, and that the caller identified himself only as a concerned friend who was disturbed about the disappearance of her grandmother. The caller agreed to give Sergei the apartment address and number, but that was all, and that is how he and Matt arrived at Natasha's.

"Will you go with us?" Sergei asked.

Natasha nodded that she would.

As they got up and walked toward the door, Matt helped Natasha with her coat. Sergei opened and locked the door behind them, and the three of them quietly made their way down the stairs, out of the apartment complex, and into the black Volga.

All of the way to the morgue, Natasha sat solemnly in the back seat, staring straight ahead. Her face was consumed with worry. Matt wished he could say something to help, but since he didn't speak Russian, there seemed little he could do.

When they finally arrived at the morgue, Sergei pulled into a parking spot with a sign that Matt assumed read, "Reserved." It was obviously reserved for someone else, but Sergei cynically concluded that it was left vacant for him, especially since it was only a few meters from the entrance.

While Matt got out and opened the rear door for Natasha, Sergei opened his door, took a final drag off his cigarette, and tossed the butt on the ground. Even though he had parked nearby, there was still the problem of the entrance doors being locked. It was late and it could be a long wait in the bitter cold before someone came by to let them in.

Fortunately, their wait was a short one. Sergei spotted someone walking inside and pounded on the door. When he drew the attention of the attendant, he pulled out his badge from his pocket and held it up to the glass, motioning for her to come over and let them in.

Sergei told the attendant why they were there, and the three of them followed her to the elevator. The unidentified body they were there to view was on the third floor.

No one was sitting at the attendant station on the third floor when they arrived, so Sergei yelled out for someone to come over.

After a short wait, another attendant, dressed in a white cap, white slip-on sandals, ankle length white socks, and a long white coat, slowly shuffled over to the desk. She seemed to be mumbling something under her breath. Sergei held out his MVD badge, and told her, "We are here to view that unidentified body, the elderly woman."

The attendant motioned for them to follow as she shuffled over to the stainless steel refrigeration unit and pulled out the silver colored table so the body could be viewed. Still looking down at the floor, she muttered something else, again barely audible, and left the room.

Natasha's immediate reaction made the identification obvious. This was indeed her grandmother. Breaking down into tears and crying out, she turned. Matt opened his arms and she grabbed onto him, burying her head in his chest and shoulder. As she stood sobbing, Matt offered what comfort he could.

In the meantime, Sergei had already begun identifying the characteristics of this particular execution. He had seen the results of many notorious Russian mafia murders and this one, carried out with a single bullet to the side of the head, matched the modus operandi of many others. Because the small caliber bullet entered the side of her head and appeared to have exited through the other side, toward the rear, her face had been left virtually intact, and that made it easy for Natasha's positive ID. From the earlier anonymous phone call, Sergei had a good idea as to the motive, but he knew it might be difficult to prove.

Sergei called for the attendant, and when she shuffled back in, he instructed her to return the body to the refrigeration unit, where it would remain for an MVD forensics examination and autopsy.

Matt tried to console Natasha as best he could while they returned to the main floor where Sergei lit up another unfiltered cigarette and continued to jot notes onto a pad.

Sergei briefly explained to Matt what he had found, and because it was getting late, and with Natasha in no condition for further interview, thought it would now be best for them to all get some rest before continuing.

When they returned to Natasha's apartment, Matt motioned to her for the key. He wanted to unlock the door and go in first to check things out. After turning on the light switch, he walked into each room to make sure everything was okay. All appeared to be as it was when they left.

In the meantime, Sergei stayed at the doorway with Natasha and told her he would call to arrange a time for the three of them to get together.

Natasha nodded that she understood, and Sergei handed her a card with his name, MVD address, and phone number printed on it.

As Sergei and Matt were leaving, Natasha stood in the doorway with tears in her eyes and a look of fear and uncertainty spread across her face.

CHAPTER NINE

As he passed through the lobby, Matt made his usual stop at the front desk to flirt with another of the eye-catching receptionists and check for messages. The American Embassy in Moscow had called earlier that evening and left a message for him to call in the morning. He recognized the extension as being that of the office for the FBI Legal Attaché.

Upon returning to his room, Matt was unable to stop thinking about the look on Natasha's face as they were leaving her apartment, and the sight of her grandmother lying in the stainless steel container. There was also something else going-on that Matt didn't understand, a strange feeling within, and it was more than just Natasha's peril and his instinctive nature to protect her. After all, he had come to the aid of beautiful young women before, but those chance encounters had never produced this sensation. Continuing to ponder these thoughts, he finally fell asleep in the chair, with the lights on, and the TV playing an old English movie with Russian subtitles. Later, he woke up to a test pattern on the screen and groggily crawled into bed.

Four years of reveille at the Air Force Academy had still not prepared Matt for the shock of these early morning wake-up calls, and although it had come at the requested time, this morning's call seemed to startle him even more than usual. Maybe it was because he fell asleep so late, or that he didn't sleep soundly because of the thoughts he had been mulling over in his mind. Whatever it was, though, he knew that if he was to make it to the MVD office on time, he had better get going.

Grabbing a quick cup of coffee and a roll at the hotel bakery shop, he went out into the semi-blizzard condition of the morning for his half-mile walk to the subway station. After experiencing a Moscow winter, Matt now understood what his Academy military history instructor had meant when he talked about the role the weather played in the outcome of battles on the Russian Front during WWII.

Moscow winters provided one bleak, dreary day after another. The darkest of them seemed to be accompanied by a bone-chilling cold that Matt had never before experienced. He felt miserable most of the time, and didn't see many Russians looking much more comfortable. During his first few days of walking to and from the subway, he would occasionally smile when his eyes met those of another, and spoke a Russian greeting he had learned from Sergei, but he found these greetings were rarely, if ever, returned. At first, he thought it was due to their recognizing him as a foreigner, and surmised that people might be afraid to respond because of years of secret police intimidation and KGB watching and reporting. That concern could certainly be the case with some, but after a few more days, a few more walks, and even fewer smiles, he concluded that it wasn't just him. It was a rare instance when he noticed anyone greeting another with a smile or even a nod.

He usually took the subway when going to and from Sergei's office. This vast underground system allowed him to not only escape the frigid and sometimes blustery conditions outside, but also provided for an efficient, convenient, and very cheap way to get around. Included in its numerous stations were huge, well-maintained centers with polished marble walls, beautiful murals, and detailed statues. The letter "M" was posted at each of the subway entrances. Inside the passageways were kiosks, street vendors, panhandlers, musicians, and of course, varying numbers of well-endowed, leggy prostitutes seeking out prospective johns interested in a little action.

The subway remained one of the best deals in Moscow, and two things that impressed Matt most about the system, in addition to the minimal cost, were first, the consequences for failure to pay, and second, the depth at which the system ran under the city. In the first instance, he noted that if anyone tried to slip through without paying, an arm would pop-out and hit the rider in the leg. Matt couldn't imagine the magnitude of personal injury litigation that would result if this deterrent were implemented in an American subway system. The second related to the steep climb back to the street should these very, very long escalators fail. He was told these deep tunnel subway platforms could also be used for emergency shelters in case of air or missile attack.

With the directional signs containing Cyrillic letters and Russian words that Matt could not read, he often relied on a technique whereby he memorized the number of subway stops between locations to which he was traveling. So far this had worked well, but should it fail him for one reason or another, he did have a couple of fallback options. One was to reach into his pocket and pull out a piece of paper on which he had carefully copied *"Krasnopresnenskaya."* He knew that particular stop on the Ring Line was located within about a half-mile walk of the American Embassy. There, he could always get help. Another option was to hail a taxi and show the driver a matchbook cover from the hotel where he was staying. Carrying a matchbook from his hotel was a practice he learned early in his international travels. Otherwise, getting assistance and directions in Moscow was not very easy. Few Russians spoke any English, and even some of those who did were reluctant to help because of a general distrust of foreigners.

Matt again successfully made his way to the MVD office by counting stops. Sergei hadn't yet arrived, so Matt decided to use this opportunity to return the call that had been left for him the previous evening.

"American Embassy," answered the operator.

"LEGAT office, please," Matt responded.

The Legal Attaché's secretary was at her desk when the call came in and she read him a message that had been received. "Nick Costigan called from Budapest. He said that he might be delayed a day or two, and wants to know if that is going to create any problem? He also asked if there is anything you want him to bring from the ILEA for the upcoming program in Moscow."

"Will you please call Nick back and tell him that as far as I know, there won't be a problem with the delay, and that there isn't anything additional that I can think of that he will need to bring," Matt replied. "Oh, one other thing, the investigator I've been working with here is named Sergei Malkin. His MVD partner, Vladimir Panilov, is there in Nick's class at the ILEA and Sergei wants Vladimir to bring him back an ILEA application."

Matt didn't bother to mention to her that he thought Sergei might be more interested in the Hungarian women than the ILEA education. Sergei frequently talked about the allure of the beautiful women of Budapest and his desire to go there, one day. Matt wasn't sure that a visit to Budapest would be such a good idea, however. Sergei's wife of over twenty years might do him serious harm if she learned about his running around. To listen to Sergei, she was one very large, tough, Russian woman who was light on lovemaking and heavy on the coercion side of things. He usually referred to her as the "intimidator." It was, "the 'intimidator' did this last night," or "the 'intimidator' did that yesterday." The stories made for lively conversation, but Matt suspected there was probably much more fiction than fact in most of Sergei's wild tales concerning his wife.

Having heard similar absurd accounts from several other officers and agents over the years, and then meeting their wives, Matt had grown to realize that most of the stories were just that --- nonsensical tales. He would smirk, "if the wives only knew about all of these wisecracks, those guys would likely be in for some times with real intimidators."

As soon as Sergei arrived, the two of them went out for their usual morning coffee. After grumbling a bit about the grief the "intimidator" had given him for not arriving home until the early morning, Sergei got down to business.

"From that anonymous call, I think the grandmother's murder was the result of a real estate contract arrangement. Our unit has recently investigated a number of several similar homicides," Sergei told Matt.

Matt recalled the "contracted her apartment" comment made during that earlier telephone call and assumed Sergei would explain what was meant by that remark in time.

Sergei continued, "During Soviet times, most of our properties were owned by the State. All of that changed when privatization came in. Now we can own our homes. Just as the 'intimidator' and I now own our residence, I think Elena Federova also owned the apartment where she and Natasha live."

Matt nodded that he understood.

"I have been told that personally owned apartments in some of your big U.S. cities can cost much. Is that true?"

"It is. Some cost millions," answered Matt.

"In Moscow it seems to depend on where they are located in the city."

"Same is true in the United States," responded Matt. "American realtors say the three most important things to consider in real estate are location, location, and location."

Sergei laughed at Matt's American analysis.

"What about the grandmother's apartment?" Matt asked.

"That location is good," answered Sergei.

After finishing their coffee, the two returned to the office where Sergei followed-up on a couple of other cases before calling Natasha to set up a time for them to meet.

"Natasha Federova?" Sergei asked.

"Yes," Natasha replied.

"This is Sergei Malkin, from the MVD. Are you doing all right?"

Although still sounding upset, she responded softly and hesitatingly, "Better now."

"Natasha, can you meet with us today?"

"Yes, certainly. What time?"

"We can be at your apartment in one hour."

"That will be fine."

"We will see you then," and Sergei hung-up the receiver.

He had to attend a meeting at MVD Headquarters later in the day, but there should still be time for them to meet with Natasha now.

CHAPTER TEN

Shortly after their leaving the MVD office, Matt asked Sergei to stop at a local bakery. He bought some rolls, meat pies, and drinks to take with them. In all likelihood, Natasha had not had anything to eat since they had dropped her off at the apartment.

Moscow's mid-day traffic congestion seemed to be even heavier than usual, and from where Matt sat, the fuel gauge looked like it was on empty. The last thing he wanted to do was to have to get out in this bitter cold and push Sergei's Volga. Sergei noticed Matt glancing at the gauge and in his normal boisterous voice assured Matt there was nothing to worry about. Relief came shortly however; as Sergei spotted a gasoline truck parked along the side of the highway and pulled over to fill up.

Getting gasoline in Moscow was just another one of the many experiences that intrigued Matt. At home, he was used to going to get gas, oil, a car wash, and even food from a nearby gas station or convenience store. In Russia, the fuel stop might be at a station or it might be where a lone gasoline truck is stopped along the side of the road and pumping gas directly into your car. Why it was done this way, Matt didn't know, but at least the gas tank in the Volga was now filled. After Sergei paid the truck driver, they drove on to Natasha's apartment complex.

The surroundings certainly looked much different in the daylight. The apartments appeared less bleak, and Matt could now better understand why the location might be considered desirable. After parking the car, they grabbed the meat pies, rolls, and drinks from the back seat, and walked through the main entrance, up the stairs and down the hall to Natasha's apartment. They knocked on the door and immediately identified themselves.

Natasha opened the door and invited them in.

As they sat around the table, Sergei started some small talk and set the bags of food and drinks on the table.

"Anyone interested in something to eat or drink?" he asked.

Everyone wanted something to drink, but nothing to eat. Natasha put the food away and got glasses from the cupboard for the drinks.

Since Matt knew virtually no Russian, the MVD had assigned Sergei to work with him while he was in Moscow. Sergei had studied English for nearly two years at the Russian Language Institute, and even though that was during the Soviet times, he had managed to maintain much of his skill level through reading books and publications and conversing with several other English language trained investigators assigned to MVD units. Also, this opportunity to work with Matt was serving as a quick and intense refresher. He was already feeling much more comfortable when he spoke English. From time to time, he would ask Matt to explain the meaning of a word or to give him a word that he might use to better express a thought, and when he did, Matt was more than happy to oblige. At the same time, Matt was also making an effort to learn a few words of survival Russian.

Before a typical interview, Sergei would tell Matt what it was about. He would conduct the questioning in Russian, and later explain to Matt what had been said. On these occasions, Matt would sit there and try to make it appear that he did have some understanding of what was being said, although he often didn't have a clue, other than what he might be able to pick up from some of the non-verbals.

As Sergei began asking questions and gathering more details about Natasha and her grandmother, he was stopped in mid-sentence.

"Mister Malkin," Natasha asked, "Would it be better if we all spoke in English? Last night when you were talking to Mister Kelly, I did not mention that I speak English because I was frightened and upset. I now feel more comfortable. I do not know how much Russian Mister Kelly understands, but you were doing very well with English, and I thought this way we might all be able to talk together."

That brought a grin to Sergei's hard face, as he replied to her in English with a hearty, "That would be fine, and please call me, Sergei."

Matt also smiled, adding, "And, please call me, Matt."

"Matt is from the FBI and does not speak Russian." Sergei went on to explain, "He is in Moscow to work with us and to conduct a training program."

Natasha smiled as she replied, "I did not realize he was from the FBI, but I did guess that he was from the United States."

"Is it that obvious?" Matt asked, jokingly.

Natasha again smiled, and nodded indicating that it was.

Continuing to add to what Sergei had been asking her before, Natasha began by telling them about the serious financial troubles that had been plaguing her and her grandmother. "For some time we have not been able to count on receiving anything from my grandmother's pension. I was working at a little kiosk near the subway station. The owner paid me a small percentage of what we took in. Although it was not much, it was something and it did help to provide us with food. That was, until a couple of months ago."

She paused, and Sergei and Matt could tell something was the matter. "Are you all right?" Sergei asked.

Her eyes welled. "I will be. Just give me a minute."

"Take your time," Sergei told her, as he and Matt sat quietly.

Natasha nodded, "As business declined at the kiosk, we were reaching a point where we were no longer making enough money to pay the local mafia what they were demanding. Although the owner kept the kiosk open and I gave them everything we received, it was still not enough. A couple of more weeks went by and when I could not pay..."

At this point, she again broke down and Sergei and Matt tried to comfort her as best they could. Sergei told her, "It is okay, Natasha."

After a brief pause, she continued, "When I left the kiosk late one evening, I saw two big men wearing long black leather coats coming out of the darkness. I did not want to go near them, so I started walking in the opposite direction. They turned and started following me. When I walked faster, they did, too. When I started to run, they chased me. They caught me and threw me to the ground. I screamed for help, but no one came. Either no one heard me or else they were afraid and did not want to get involved. One of the men held me down while the other hit me again and again. They yelled at me and called me bad names. After they finished beating me with their fists, they each kicked me and left me in the snow."

Pausing again before continuing, she added, "I lay there for a while. When I had enough strength to get to my knees, I wiped some of the blood from my nose and mouth and crawled back to the apartment."

Even though Sergei had heard similar stories numerous times before, he never got used to them. The brutality and pain being inflicted was often against those who did not even have enough money for food to eat, much less meet an extortion demand.

As Matt sat envisioning Natasha's pain, he became more and more incensed. He couldn't understand what kind of animals these were who would murder an elderly grandmother execution style, and nearly beat a beautiful, young Russian woman to death because she had no money to give them.

After Natasha regained her composure and wiped her eyes, Sergei asked, "Did your grandmother recently become involved in some kind of real estate transaction?"

Natasha nodded, "There were two businessmen who visited the apartment early one morning, a few days ago. They seemed to have lots of rubles and offered to give my grandmother enough to live on for the rest of her life. All she had to do was sign a paper giving this apartment to them when she died."

"Did you know them?"

"No, we did not know either of them, but they somehow knew we had no money. You have to understand, my grandmother was very upset, especially after having sold her wedding ring only days before."

"We do understand. What happened then?" asked Sergei.

"Finally, the men waved a stack of rubles in her face, and after my grandmother signed the paper, they left. They gave her the first month's payment that same morning."

"Any idea who these men were?"

"No, they introduced themselves, but I don't remember their names. That was the only time I ever saw either of them." There was a pause, "Oh, one other thing," she added, "They did not dress nor act like our local neighborhood mafia thugs."

From experience, Sergei knew that these new apartment owners would probably claim that they had given their offer to the grandmother in good faith, and that her untimely death was a mere coincidence. Unless they somehow got word that the MVD was onto them, he assumed that it would be only a short period of time before these guys would be appearing at the complex, ready to take control of the apartment.

"I am going to have to leave soon," Sergei said. "When these guys contact you again, Natasha, I want you to call me immediately. You have my number. Do not tell these vultures that we have talked. Do not try to do anything yourself. We do not want anything to happen to you."

"I will call," Natasha assured him.

"Do you want me to drop you off at your hotel, on my way, Matt?"

"No need," Kelly replied. "That's out of your way. I know you don't have much time before your meeting, especially with all of the traffic. I can take a taxi or maybe Natasha can give me directions on how to get there on the subway."

"I should be able to give you directions, or call for a taxi, either one," replied Natasha.

Matt smiled, "I'll be okay, Sergei."

Sergei nodded, and left for his MVD meeting.

What Matt failed to mention to Sergei was that he was secretly hoping that by offering to take the subway or a taxi back to the hotel, it would give him the opportunity to see if Natasha might be interested in going to dinner with him.

Hands in his pockets, Matt stood there looking at Natasha. "I would like to take you to dinner, that is, if you would be interested."

Natasha hesitated before answering, then nodded, "Yes, dinner sounds nice. It will allow me to get away from here for a while, and I should be able to direct you to the subway and your hotel stop."

"Great," Matt smiled, "But if we're going to dinner, you'll have to choose the place."

"I can do that," Natasha agreed. "You will need to give me a few minutes to get ready, though."

While she was out of the room, Matt took a look around to see if there was anything that might help in the investigation of her grandmother's death. Because she and her grandmother had already sold many of the furnishings, the apartment was left with only the bare essentials. Nothing caught his eye, but after pulling the trash basket out from under the sink, he noticed a crumpled sheet of paper in the corner. Reaching back and stretching, he was able to pull it out. Then, touching it as little as possible, he pulled at the edges to get it straightened. Even though Matt could read only a few words of Russian, the format led him to believe this was some type of contract or agreement. At the top was a centered title, followed by several paragraphs, and signature lines near the bottom of the page. Unzipping a pocket inside his coat, he slid the paper in.

Shortly thereafter, Natasha came from the bedroom. She was wearing a ribbed, long-sleeved white turtleneck sweater, perfectly fitted black stretch pants, and high black leather boots. She looked stunning and the expression on Matt's face told it all.

"Are you ready to go?" he asked.

"Sure," she politely answered.

Natasha extended her arms as Matt helped her with her coat. Reaching behind her neck, she flipped her dark shiny hair so that it fell neatly into the hooded collar, and then carefully placed a Russian-style, black fur hat on her head.

He knew that the Bureau frowned on its agents having personal relationships with local foreign nationals and in most instances, that stance was considerably stronger than just a mere frown. But, as far as Matt was concerned, this wasn't a relationship --- not yet, anyway. Rather, he was rationalizing it as being just another opportunity for him to take a very attractive young woman to dinner. He had done that numerous times over the years, and considering all Natasha had been through, this was just showing her some kindness. Besides, it was time for him to get out and see how the locals live.

His days so far began with early morning trips to either the MVD or the American Embassy, and ended with evening subway rides back to the hotel. There, his evening activities were usually confined to exercising at the fitness club, showering, and eating an overpriced dinner, alone, in the dining room. After dinner, he returned to his room for a dose of international news and Russian subtitled movies on the TV, before finally dozing off to sleep.

As the two of them set out on their snowy walk to the restaurant, Natasha explained that she was taking him to a popular neighborhood restaurant that had developed a reputation over the years for its exquisite traditional Russian dishes and fine service. Adding, that it was not the type of place the typical Moscow tourist would usually visit.

Upon their arrival at the restaurant, Matt helped Natasha with her coat, and checked both of their coats and hats with the attendant at the cloak booth. The lighting inside was low and the music soft as a group of wandering minstrels played violins and made their way from table to table. On the walls hung artwork and memorabilia from the days of a Russia long past. Within earshot, over to the side, was a crowded bar area that appeared to be doing a brisk business. The host, dressed in a black tuxedo, greeted them and from what Matt could tell, asked if they had a seating preference. Natasha answered, and he followed her and the host to a table located near one of the fireplaces. With his eyes still adjusting to the low lighting, Matt hoped that he didn't trip and fall. After all, what kind of an impression would that make on his date?

Upon their arrival at the table, the host and waiter pulled their chairs out, and after being seated, opened white linen napkins and placed them on their laps. The waiter asked what they would like to drink, and after consulting with Matt, Natasha gave him their orders. Before leaving to get their drinks, he placed leather-jacketed menus in front of each of them. Matt noticed that this menu was not like those at the hotel. The hotel menu had a bold line describing each item in Russian, with an English translation, in smaller type, directly below. This menu was totally in Russian. He would have to rely entirely on Natasha.

After returning with their drinks, the waiter stood to the side of the fireplace while the two of them concentrated on the menu. As Matt looked at the menu, Natasha could not help but notice the perplexed look on his face. She grinned and asked, "What would you like to eat?"

"Select for me whatever you're having," Matt replied, adding, "The more typically Russian, the better."

"You asked for it," she smiled, and motioned for the waiter to come over so she could place their order.

Soon, the waiter arrived with their appetizers and bottled water. Fresh breads and bowls of traditional borscht soup ladled from a large kettle followed these. The main course was bear meat and potatoes. It was Matt's first experience with bear meat and he found it to be a bit greasy, but still very tasty. Their dinner was topped off with a rum-based pastry for dessert.

The restaurant's intimate atmosphere, with its crackling fireplace, wandering violinists, and flickering candlelight, was also certainly doing nothing to lessen Matt's feelings toward Natasha. As the two of them enjoyed a cup of cappuccino, one of the violinists made his way to their table.

As the violinist played, Matt's hand brushed Natasha's.

She smiled, and her enchanting gaze met his.

At the conclusion of the violinist's playing, Matt handed him a tip and motioned to the waiter. When the check arrived, Matt could tell immediately that this was a restaurant frequented by the local Russians, and not tourists. The tab, even with a generous tip included, was only a fraction of what it would have been at the hotel dining room.

Before leaving the restaurant, Matt took the receipt left by the waiter and printed the name of the hotel where he was staying and his room number on the back of it, and put it in Natasha's hand.

"You be sure and call me if you need anything at all, anytime," he told her.

She smiled and assured him that she would.

While the two were inside eating dinner, the light powdery snow that had been falling earlier stopped and the sky had cleared. A trail of footprints now followed them in the light skiff of snow that covered the ground. As they walked hand in hand and looked up to the stars, the Big Dipper and a beautiful, harvest moon were in full view. Matt extended his arm behind Natasha's back and she drew closer, resting her head against his chest and shoulder.

Suddenly, Natasha slipped on an icy spot and shrieked as she pulled Matt down into the snow with her. Lying there, she began laughing, and grabbed a handful of the light powder and rubbed it onto his face. Matt smiled and returned the favor by sprinkling flakes on her nose and lips.

As he was helping her back to her feet, Natasha clasped her hands around the back of his neck. Matt gazed into her eyes and pulled her to him, pressing his lips to hers.

CHAPTER ELEVEN

Within an hour of parting company with Nick Costigan at the Frankfurt Airport, Darren Kroft had successfully located the gate and boarded his connecting flight to Moscow, where he had found a somewhat different state of affairs than had originally been envisioned.

In place of a bright and bustling gate area, with announcements being made and people rushing in all directions to catch flights, Darren found Moscow's Sheremyetove International Airport terminal to be relatively dark, and an uneasy calm seemed to hang over everything.

Other than a few whispers here and there, and echoes resounding from leather heels striking the floor, one could hear little else from Kroft and his fellow passengers as they made their way through the corridor. Many of the travelers' faces appeared solemn, as if to be saying, "Just six more months and my contract will be up. Then, I'll be out of here."

During the flight from Frankfurt, Kroft had overheard fellow passengers relating accounts of the big bucks international contract employees were making while working in Russia and wondered why some of these people seemed to be so down on their return.

"After all, the money certainly sounded good and what else was there," Kroft thought to himself.

As he followed the crowd to what he assumed were the immigration and customs areas, Darren joined the first of several long lines he would have to deal with. After a half-hour wait, it was finally his turn. He slid his blue passport and customs form under the glass divider. The officer took the documents without comment and opened the passport to the page containing his photo. With a steely-eyed, piercing look, the officer moved his eyes from the photo to Darren's face and back to the photo before proceeding further. Next, the officer flipped through the empty pages of the new passport until he located the Russian visa stamp.

After entering data into a terminal located on the table in front of him, the officer stared straight ahead, never cracking a smile, never acknowledging Kroft's existence. Finally, Darren heard a beep and assumed the officer must have received notification that everything was okay, because both his passport and customs form were slid back under the glass. The officer nodded for him to proceed. He quickly picked up his documents and moved on to the next stop, where he gathered his checked baggage.

At the customs area, he stood patiently in yet another long line. Several of his friends who travel internationally had told him horror stories of long delays and searches of not only their bags, but also themselves when entering some countries. He had also heard stories about poles with buttons to push activating red and green lights. If there were any such poles and buttons here, Kroft had not spotted them. From what he understood of such systems, though, if you pushed the button and a green light flashed, you were allowed to proceed without any further checking. If, however, the light was red, you were required to take everything over to a table for a complete search of all of your bags. Being somewhat of a gambler, Darren favored the button system over having to look an officer in the eye and letting him make the decision. But, since there was no button and there were no lights, that option was out.

Fortunately, for Kroft, an attractive young redhead was standing directly in front of him. When it came time for him to approach the customs officer, the officer was so busy flirting with the young lady that he waved Kroft on through with little more than a glance. Kroft gave a sigh of relief and quickly moved to the exit point, where another officer collected his form. Outside, he was to meet the hotel transportation provided with his travel package.

Kroft used his shoulder and pushed open the double swinging doors. Directly in front of him was what could be best characterized as a bizarre mob scene. He gripped his bags even more tightly now, as those nearby were attempting to pull them from all directions. He assumed that they were trying to carry them to a taxi for tips. Others were yelling and motioning for him to follow them for what he figured were offers of transportation. Finally, to his relief, he saw his name printed on a large white card. Although it was not spelled correctly, the card was still a most welcome sight, and he started working his way in that direction as fast as he could.

The man holding the card could speak just enough English for Kroft to be able to discern that he was at least going to the hotel where he had a reservation. With that, the driver and Kroft made their way through the crowd and into a light gray Lada parked nearby. Having been awake for the greater part of the past two days, he was looking forward to his arrival at a luxury hotel, and after a nail-biting forty-five minute ride from the airport, they were finally there.

When he checked in at the registration desk, the receptionist asked him to initial beside the room rate. Kroft objected, telling her the amount was considerably higher than the rate his travel agent in Denver had quoted to him. The receptionist explained that this was their standard rate, and when Kroft lodged a second protest, she told him, "If you do not want the room, tell me now. There are others waiting to take this reservation if you do not want it." He looked around, took quick stock of his options and placed his initials in the space provided, agreeing to pay the inflated rate. Here he was, a foreigner, his first time in one of the larger capital cities of the world, not speaking the language, and not knowing his way around. Was there really any other choice? He decided not. Besides, after two grueling days of travel, he was now almost out on his feet. Just the thought of a bed and a place to shower and clean up made it worth staying at almost any price.

Kroft followed the bellman to his room. After the bellman left his bags beside the closet, Kroft tipped him with two greenbacks and locked the door when he left. He took a quick shower and crashed into bed.

Waking a few hours later, after what he thought was a full night's sleep; he looked at his watch and decided that it was time to get going. The only problem was that it still appeared dark outside. Noticing the side of a clock sitting on a small table beside the bed, he turned it toward him, took one glance, a closer look, and finally another. That couldn't be right. He was relatively certain that it wasn't already noon, but midnight? What about his watch, what does it show? He remembered re-setting it when he arrived at Dulles, but that was just two hours ahead of the Denver time. After that, with his trying to make the connecting flight, getting through immigration and customs and finally to the hotel, he had not made any more adjustments to his watch. Everything had been so hectic. As best he could now remember, though, Moscow was somewhere around ten hours ahead of Denver. No wonder he was so wide-awake.

It was the middle of the afternoon back home, but midnight here in Moscow.

Darren Kroft was about to experience his first attack of middle of the night insomnia. After failing to fall back asleep until shortly before daybreak, he remained in bed until nearly 10:00 AM, when he got up, dressed, and went downstairs for his next surprise. The hotel's standard fare buffet breakfast. For twenty-six dollars plus tip, he had his choice of eggs, cooked meats, breads, cold cuts, cheeses, a variety of fruits, and cereal.

After eating, he left the restaurant in search of the hotel's concierge. Kroft had several things in mind that he wanted to get done during his stay and he assumed the concierge was probably the best place to start. Upon learning what he was interested in, the concierge told him he would see what he could do, and would get back to him later. In the meantime, he suggested Kroft use part of his time to visit some of Moscow's many tourist attractions.

Kroft took the advice of the concierge and found himself taking in sights that travel restrictions, in force during the Cold War years, would have made it difficult for an American to have an opportunity to see. Standing in the middle of Red Square, he visualized TV images of May Day parades with missiles, tanks, and scores of Russian troops parading in front of the Kremlin elite. At one end of Red Square stood the world famous St. Basil's with its colorful, distinctively painted onion domes. It was just as the news pictures and postcards had depicted. Looking to his side, he saw the Kremlin. Its fortress-like structure with a history dating back to the fourteenth century was imposing. Atop the Kremlin's Spasskaya Tower, Kroft noticed a giant red star and four large, round clocks, all trimmed in gold.

Walking around the Kremlin's perimeter, he could not see over the high red brick wall, but he could get a good view of the many beautiful domes and towers rising above it. As he headed toward the main entrance, the hand of a stern-faced sentry went up and Darren was temporarily halted. He didn't understand why until an approaching black Zil limousine suddenly turned into the high, arched entrance. Noting flags on the limo's front fenders and security teams leading and trailing, Kroft suspected he'd just seen the Russian President. However, with the speed of the Zil, and darkened windows protecting the identity of any its occupants, it was impossible for him to tell.

From there he visited the Kremlin Museum where he saw the beautiful coaches of the Czars, gowns of the royalty, and unbelievable jewels. There was also a collection of those world-famous, enameled eggs whose name he could never seem to remember.

Continuing his leisurely stroll, Darren's next stop was at the Alexandrovsky Garden, which is the site of the eternal flame. The flame, rising from a brilliant golden star, honors war dead and serves as a memorial to the Unknown Soldier. Kroft watched as brides, still wearing their long white gowns, white heels, and veils, observed a Russian tradition of laying their flowers on the highly polished stones surrounding the star and flame.

Finally, after returning to his starting point in Red Square, Kroft went into Lenin's Tomb, before sauntering through the Kremlin's Honor Cemetery. It was there he had a somewhat unpleasant encounter with Russian authority. While standing near the end of the Honor Cemetery, a guard came over to him and pointed toward a sign that had a camera in a circle with a slash through it. Kroft had not seen the sign, but the guard's reaction indicated that didn't seem to matter. Dressed in highly shined boots, a long, heavy, gray wool coat with crimson trim, and a traditional dark fur hat with the red star centered on the front, the guard looked very official. Giving Kroft an intimidating look, he pointed toward the camera and indicated that he thought Darren had taken a picture of something the guard didn't think he should have. Kroft shook his head that he had not, but that didn't seem to deter the guard. The guard motioned for him to open up the back of his camera. Since this would expose the film, and thus all of the pictures Kroft had taken up to this point during his trip, he shook his head again. When that didn't seem to work and it appeared the guard was determined to take his camera if he didn't comply, Kroft decided that it was time to cut his losses and reluctantly opened up the back and removed the film. This picture-taking incident was troubling, and he wondered how much things had really changed from the Cold War days, but he was determined not to let it dampen his spirits.

Upon his return to the hotel, a message was awaiting him at the front desk.

MESSAGE FOR: Mr. Darren Kroft
FROM: Concierge
MESSAGE: Everything is ready for next week.
Final details will be available shortly.

That was what Kroft had been waiting to hear.

Now, all that was left for him to do before getting started on his real mission in going to Russia, was to keep his promise and buy some trinkets to take back to friends in Colorado and California.

Near Red Square was an internationally famous Moscow shopping store and mall that was described in some of his travel literature as the largest of its kind in the world. Having seen its famous arched glass roof and crossed its high walkways while taking in the sights, Darren had initially planned to return there to make his purchases, but reconsidered after learning from other tourists about a huge Flea Market where negotiating prices was expected and good deals could be made when purchasing souvenirs'.

Although he didn't like to shop, Kroft did enjoy the challenge of haggling with some of the kiosk operators. Using hand signs, calculators, and printing ruble amounts onto pieces of paper, he managed to negotiate his way through the purchases. By the end of his shopping spree, Darren was satisfied with his purchases and convinced he'd gotten the better of these merchants, making some real steals; if the truth were known, however, it was the kiosk operators who had really won. They always do.

In addition to the few pieces of amber containing imbedded insects from prehistoric times, Darren's purchases included a couple of Soviet-era Russian military hats, a collection of war medals, KGB watches, several hand-painted eggs and lacquered wooden pins, and a set of matryoshka nesting dolls.

With his time of playing tourist and shopper now behind him, Darren was ready to get down to business and meet the submissive Russian women who would be satisfying all of his fantasies.

CHAPTER TWELVE

When Nick told Vladimir that he had received a message from Matt Kelly telling him that Sergei Malkin wanted to attend the ILEA, Vladimir laughed, saying, "Once Sergei sees how really beautiful the women of Budapest are, I don't know if we will ever get him back."

"Why is that?" asked Nick.

Vladimir continued, "Several years ago the MVD sent Sergei to Riga, Latvia, to work on an investigation. While there, he kept calling back to Moscow and saying he needed, 'a little more time,' or 'just a little while longer.' We wondered if he would ever return. Finally, our commander got tired of it all and ordered him home. I think Sergei was probably working harder on trying to find more investigative leads than he was in getting the case solved. That way he could spend more time with some of the women he had met."

Nick gave a sly smile, indicating he understood exactly what Vladimir was talking about.

"Do I detect by that look in your eyes that you, too, might have heard about the women of Latvia."

"You might say that," Nick responded.

"You have been there, Mr. Costigan?"

Nick nodded, "I have."

"Is what we have heard about the women there, true?"

"If you're talking about lots of short skirts and attractive legs, the answer is, unquestionably yes," Nick agreed.

"After what Sergei told us when he reported back to Moscow, we all wanted a chance to go there, but our commander said, 'No more.' I do not know what he will say when Sergei tells him about wanting to come to Budapest."

Nick nodded and laughed.

CHAPTER THIRTEEN

With his portion of the ILEA program now completed, Nick and most of the class were taking a little time off to gather at the Buf'e for some traditional toasting and to say their good-byes. The Russian officers in this ILEA session had been particularly interested in his comments regarding money-laundering investigations. During the course, they met with him on two separate evenings and asked that he take a look at several cases that were giving them special problems. Their primary concerns revolved around tracing money to offshore island banking havens, particularly those located in the Caribbean Basin, where everything seemed to unravel and disappear into thin air.

Nick had managed to make some headway during these after-hour sessions, but he could tell there was a lot of catching-up to be done when he linked up with Matt and they got started on their training program with the special MVD units.

After the social hour, Nick returned to the hotel to pack. This would be a short night. He was going to have to rise well before dawn if he was going to make it to "Ferihegy One," one of the two Budapest international airport terminals, in time to catch his early morning flight to Moscow. He had already called the Legal Attaché's office at the American Embassy in Moscow and left his amended flight information for Matt. Hopefully, Matt would receive the message and be there to meet him at the airport.

Traffic was extremely light as Nick's taxi made its way through the pre-dawn darkened streets to the airport. Because of the early hour, there were no lines at either the airline check-in counters or the customs and immigration checkpoints, so Nick had no problem getting to the gate in time for this flight. In fact, it was so early that the café concession at the airport had not yet opened. As a result, he was going to have to board the plane without his morning wake-up coffee.

Shortly after take-off, the flight attendant came down the aisle with a breakfast plate with cheeses, sliced luncheon meats, hard rolls, butter and jelly, a glass of juice, and that ever-strong cup of Hungarian coffee he had been so anxiously awaiting. Although that cup, followed by another, was just the jolt he needed, it was not enough to keep him from getting a little sleep on the flight.

Fortunately for Nick, there was not one of those incessant talkers sitting next to him. In fact, the guy sitting there also appeared to be more interested in sleeping than talking, but that may have been because he apparently did not speak any English.

The flight to Moscow's Sheremyetove International Airport arrived on-time and without incident. Inside the terminal Nick followed the horde of passengers from his flight through the gateway, down a dimly lit corridor, and into the long line waiting to clear immigration. After getting his Official passport stamped, finding his bags, and clearing customs, he passed through the exit and quickly scanned the crowd for Matt. When Nick did not see him, he walked a little farther.

Suddenly, he saw several uniformed Russian police officers separating the crowd for what Nick assumed to be a VIP. As they approached, he could see a barrel-chested, middle-aged aged man sporting a big, bushy mustache and blowing smoke rings in the air. "Who is this character?" he wondered. A second glance revealed another man close behind. A smile spread across Nick's face.

"Matt!" Nick yelled.

Matt Kelly smiled and gave Nick one of his typical "it's about time you got here" responses, and introduced him to Sergei.

"Welcome to Moscow, Nick," greeted the gregarious Sergei Malkin.

"It's good to be here," replied Nick, as he and Sergei smiled and shook hands. "You certainly do arrive in style, Sergei."

"We heard that this was how the FBI does it."

"I don't know where you heard that," Nick responded.

Sergei smiled and pointed toward Matt. "Is that not what you told me?"

Matt just shook his head and laughed. Sergei motioned to the uniformed officers and the three of them were escorted back through the crowd.

As they walked toward Sergei's black Volga, Matt asked Nick, "No one tried to hijack your bags, did they?"

Nick looked at him questioningly. "No, there were lots of guys out there trying to get the passengers to let them carry their bags, but I held on to mine pretty tightly. Why?"

"They've been having problems at some of the Russian airports with gangs grabbing bags from passengers, and then holding the bags hostage in a room until the traveler comes up with money."

"That's a switch. Hijacking bags instead of people and holding them hostage, huh?"

"Yeah."

"Couldn't you imagine my trying to explain an extortion expense on my voucher to the Bureau?"

"Yeah, a two hundred dollar tip for baggage service might get more than a second look," chuckled Matt.

As they left the airport and headed toward the hotel, Nick relayed Vladimir's comments to Sergei about fears that once exposed to the beauties of Budapest, Sergei might not return to Moscow for years to come.

Sergei initially reacted with his patented, boisterous laugh. Then, he suddenly stopped laughing, almost as quickly as he had started, and looked up. Brushing his fingers downward across his bushy mustache, as though he were pondering that thought, he responded, "You know, Vladimir might be right," after which he continued to laugh even more loudly.

As Sergei provided a thrill ride through the heavy Moscow traffic, Matt briefly went over some of what he and Sergei had been doing and gave Nick an update on what he knew about their upcoming training program with the MVD.

CHAPTER FOURTEEN

Was the concierge going to be a matchmaker?

Was there to be a Russian bride in Darren Kroft's future?

Only time would tell.

Tonight would be Kroft's first opportunity to indulge, and he could only hope that it would be followed by many intimate liaisons during the remainder of his stay.

The concierge had called his room earlier in the day and left a message with the pick-up time. Kroft brushed his teeth, rinsed his mouth, slapped on a heavy dose of his favorite after-shave, and went down to the hotel bar where he had just enough time for a vodka before meeting the limousine outside the lobby entrance.

The limo arrived at the hotel entrance right on time, and as the driver opened the door, Kroft looked around to see if anyone was watching. After noticing that a couple of women were, he took a deep breath, stuck out his chest, sucked in his gut, tugged at his belt line, and strutted out and into the limo like he was someone of importance.

After settling into the limo, the driver opened the bar for Kroft and another passenger while he made several more stops. At these additional hotel stops, more bride-seekers were eagerly awaiting their pick-up. As the new participants got into the limo, Kroft and the others smiled, introduced themselves, and continued taking full advantage of the limo bar. The more everyone drank, the more they talked, and the more they talked, the greater their embellishments became regarding their conquests of the opposite sex. Topping one another proved to be no small challenge, but Kroft felt he won, even though most of what he said was total BS. Kroft told himself, they would never know the difference and, besides, they were all probably lying, too.

When they arrived at the social club, the manager and several of his associates met their limo and directed the men into the club. Another limo load had arrived ahead of theirs, and more would be coming shortly. Those earlier arrivals were already enjoying drinks and striking up conversations with some of the women.

As Kroft looked around, he could not believe the number of classy and extremely attractive women in attendance. Furthermore, he could tell that this social club was not one to scrimp when it came to providing for their female attendees. Most were professionally made up, wearing perfectly fitted dresses, dark stockings, and high heels. This was definitely not going to be one of those wild gatherings several of the braggarts in the limo had been talking about attending. So far, there were no signs of any g-strings, bare breasts, or swinging tassels. Everything he saw evidenced class and any guy who was secretly hoping to find his newest den of iniquity was likely to be in for a big surprise.

All of the women were wearing nametags similar to those given the men when they arrived, and flag pins were attached to each participant's tag identifying a country of residence. Kroft was surprised at the number of different of flags he saw the women wearing. He could tell, however, they were all from countries that had previously been a part of the former USSR. To help everyone communicate better, the nametags also bore the languages spoken by that person. Kroft's tag bore his name, a small American flag, and the word "English." This disclosure caused his ego to take a bit of a beating, though, as he looked around and noticed that most of the others had more than one language listed. In fact, there were a couple of the men with three noted and he had already seen one woman with four languages identified. This was indeed impressive.

From Kroft's perspective, however, there did seem to be a shortage of "English" notations on the women's tags so far, and as a result, he realized that his contacts would probably be limited to somewhat less than a third of those in attendance. Even so, he didn't see any serious problem since there were many more women than men, and these men were not just from the U.S.

Time to start thoroughly checking out the merchandise, Kroft thought, as he began his swaggered stroll. Trying to look cool and aloof as he walked, he held his head high, managing only a condescending smile here and a nod there. From what he could tell from his brief survey, the majority of these women were between twenty-five and thirty-five. There were exceptions, however. A couple of the younger ones looked to be no older than their late teens and several on the other end of the spectrum appeared to be well into their forties.

He noticed that none of those in their late teens and early twenties spoke English, but that was okay with Kroft. He assumed the younger group would be more likely to possess that independent attitude he so despised in women, anyway.

What Kroft failed to realize, however, was that many there were no more likely to want to be mentally and physically subjected to his whims than those back at home were. Some were so desperate, though, that they might be willing to tell him and any of the others anything they thought these guys wanted to hear. Life had dealt some of these women harsh hands during the recent years and many were just looking for a way out, any way. As such, they were grasping for anyone or anything they thought might be able to help.

These women's feelings of desperation made receiving one of these special social club invitations all the more desirable. As a result, the club owners were not shy about making special demands and taking advantage of any woman trying to secure an invitation. Most of them had already been required to provide special services to their hosts in exchange for the invitations, and their satisfactory performance of those services had also assisted in paying for the fine clothes they were wearing, and their first class appearances.

Standing over in a dimly lit corner of the social club was a tall, alluring blonde. The possibility of meeting someone like her had been one of the enticements luring Kroft to Russia. So far, he hadn't noticed anyone talking with her, but he knew that couldn't last. With nervous anticipation, he started to move in her direction. The thick layer of smoke that had settled over the room was making it difficult for him to see, but the closer he got, the more inviting and provocative she became.

Appearing to be somewhere in her forties and even more seductive than he first imagined, she was one of the most beautiful women Kroft had ever seen. But, would he be able to talk to her?

Finally, he was able to get close enough to get a good look at her nametag. It read Yekaterina "Catherine" and to his relief, printed beside the small Russian flag pin were the words "Russian" and "English." With her alluring looks and the fact that she spoke English, Kroft could see that it was time for him to step up and be a player.

As she continued to glance in his direction, Kroft contemplated a strategy. Being the suave, cool guy he knew himself to be, he couldn't be like the other guys and make his move by just going over and introducing himself. No, Kroft would wait until he could come up with something better.

Catherine had spent several hours earlier that evening making sure everything was just right. She selected a full-length gown that looked like it had been taken directly off a Paris model. It was sleek, straight, dark, and low cut, with a long slit up the side that gave her ample opportunity to show off a long, smooth, sexy, and very well-proportioned leg. She wore dark stockings and high heels, and to accent the dress, selected an expensive white gold and diamond necklace with matching earrings and bracelet. Her make-up was professionally applied, and did an excellent job of hiding any of those unwanted, unkind middle age blemishes. The eye shadow complimented her deep blue eyes, and the lip-gloss she chose gave her lips a look of luscious invitation. Even though Catherine was already fifty, she certainly didn't look it. She knew what she was doing when it came to looking beautiful and had used that beauty over the years to bring countless numbers of men under her spell.

Before Kroft could make his move, though, Catherine acted. Smiling, she looked over and gracefully extended her hand his direction. With a soft, alluring voice, she said, "Good evening. I am Catherine."

Kroft's planning evaporated. His knees buckled and his voice quivered. Trying to put three words together, he stuttered, "Hi...I...I'm Darren." Regaining some composure, he asked, "May I get you something to drink?"

She smiled and gave him a seductive look. "A vodka and tonic would be nice. Thank you."

Once again, his knees began to buckle, but he quickly recovered and made his way over to the bar. With their drinks in hand, and not wanting to embarrass himself with a trip or a spill, he cautiously returned to the dimly lit corner where she was standing. There, he gathered enough courage to start some small talk.

"Catherine. That's a pretty name. I'll bet I can guess who you were named after."

Catherine smiled, but before she could answer, Kroft blurted out, "Catherine the Great, right?"

She answered quite matter-of-factly, "That is correct. My mother was a teacher and very interested in Russian history. From the stories she told me as a child, she had an especially high regard for Catherine and decided long before she ever married my father that her first daughter would be named after the Empress. You may call me Katya though, if you prefer."

"No…no, I like Catherine just fine," Darren nervously replied.

Now that the ice was broken, it took little in the way of encouragement to get him to continue talking. He had an insatiable appetite to brag about himself, and with Catherine there to fuel it, he kept it up most of the evening. Unknown to Kroft, this was exactly what she wanted him to do. She was already making mental notes of everything he was saying.

CHAPTER FIFTEEN

Early in her Soviet education, Catherine was identified as a very bright and articulate student, with strong language skills. As a result, she was selected to attend the prestigious Soviet Language Institute in Moscow, where she was immersed in English language training. After graduating from the Institute, she was selected for assignment to become one of the feared Russian Visa ladies, and after a short time, positioned herself to take advantage of all of the power and prestige the job had to offer. These specially trained women, sometimes called "black widows" or "dragon ladies" by their detractors, possessed not only sharp minds and superb language skills, but also were masters at the art of interview and interrogation.

Shortly after she began serving in her Cold War era Visa post, the KGB approached her. They were impressed with her potential to become an effective agent, and began testing her with several minor tasks and assignments, which she passed with ease.

Having proved herself in those initial tests, the KGB gradually increased her responsibilities to the point where she became recognized as a legitimate domestic and foreign-intelligence operative. With that distinction, her days at the Visa post came to a close, and she was transferred to the KGB's Lubyanka Square Headquarters in Moscow. While there, she became intrigued with performing psychological assessments and through special training and practice developed the ability to determine whether and by what means a target might be co-opted. She seemed to have a sixth sense in doing it, and over the years this proved to be her most valuable asset.

Her brains coupled with her beauty, Catherine was the perfect foreign intelligence agent. She was one of the best ever developed by the Cold War era Soviet internal security and intelligence corps. She also managed to fare quite well for herself. Using her body and her mind, she succeeded in compromising some of the best talents the opposition forces had to offer.

Things changed, though, and it was during the early 1990's that Catherine began to reconsider her future and saw a new direction. She put aside the old communist ideology, the outdated causes, and much of the rest of what she had so thoroughly embraced. She replaced them all with the power, money, and materialism offered by a new and very violent Russian mafia.

As soon as Kroft told the hotel's concierge of his desire to meet Russian women, the wheels for him becoming a potential target were quickly placed into motion. First, there was a review of his hotel registration file folder. Included in it were his business card, the travel agent's computer generated reservation forms, and Kroft's hand printed registration card containing his name, home address, passport number, signature, and of course that all important method of payment, with imprinted credit card slip, and authorization number attached. At the bottom of the card was a separate block where the type of employment and position were to be noted. In that space, Kroft had clearly printed "Computer Consultant Executive."

With this information in hand, the concierge's next stop was with one of his social club contacts. That contact, in turn, arranged for Kroft's invitation.   His evening's entertainment would not be left to chance.

For some time, the Russian mafia had been effectively moving large sums of money throughout the world. With the rapid changes in technology, however, these movements were now becoming more and more difficult. As a result, it was imperative that they concentrate on developing new cutting-edge technology sources everywhere, and nowhere in the world were these sources becoming more important to them than in the United States.

CHAPTER SIXTEEN

After listening to some of his bragging, Catherine realized that Mr. Darren Kroft might just be one of the people their organization could use. She needed to continue gathering more details about his experience and expertise, though.

As the evening progressed, she continued to assess Darren's usefulness to their international activities. She analyzed his motivation. Was it greed, power, or something else? She also tried to learn as much as she could about his sexual drives, interests, and desires, and needed to determine the strength of his principles and ethical standards. Was he a person of integrity? During the remainder of this evening and over the next several days, if she had her way with him, Kroft would be revealing more about himself than he could have ever imagined.

Although he envisioned himself as an enlightened man of the world, in reality, Kroft was extremely naïve, especially when it came to the dark side, with its secret agents and intelligence information-gathering forces. His knowledge of foreign intelligence agents and the mafia was limited to what he had seen glorified on the movie screens or watched on TV. He would be no match for someone with the skills and cunning of the likes of Catherine.

Darren and Catherine found a table near the dance floor. Here, they could get a little more comfortable, have some drinks, and sit and talk. When the music started, he reached out for Catherine's hand and escorted her to the dance floor.

As they danced, Catherine gradually drew him closer and closer to her and Kroft once again experienced a sudden weakness in his knees. This time, though, his heart also started pounding rapidly as his cheek drew next to her silky hair and he held her tightly. Several more heart-pounding dances followed before the two of them made their way back to the table to participate in a series of evening toasts.

As the traditional Russian toasts began, Catherine made sure that their vodka glasses were always full. The toasts were numerous, and the more Kroft drank, the looser his tongue became. All the while, Catherine filed away more bits and pieces of information about him. Fortunately, for Catherine, her newest target never picked up on her old Russian toasting trick of periodically substituting water for the vodka in her glass.

After all of the toasts were completed, the last dance of the evening was announced. Having already had more than enough to drink, Darren was led onto the dance floor by Catherine. She gripped his hand and torso tightly while leading him along. As the final notes were being played, she whispered softly into his ear, "Would you like to take me back to your hotel for a nightcap?"

Somewhat startled, Kroft's face lit up with a big grin. Teetering back and forth on his feet, he unhesitatingly slurred, "Yeah, sh-sh-sure!"

Catherine gave him an alluring smile, and the two of them returned to the table so she could get her purse and go to the powder room.

After the lights brightened, Catherine took Darren by the hand and led him back through the Social Club and out into an awaiting limo.

This time it would be just the two of them sharing the back seat and Kroft could hardly wait to get the door closed.

CHAPTER SEVENTEEN

After Nick completed checking into the hotel and the bellman delivered his bags to the room, Matt took him to the American Embassy. There, they would first go to the FBI office so Nick could meet the LEGAT and his secretary, and then to the offices of the Embassy's Regional Security Officer so Nick could receive his mandatory security briefing.

As they entered the FBI office, Victor got up from behind his desk and looked in Matt's direction. "It looks like you have been surviving Moscow okay. At least you're still alive."

"So far, so good," responded Matt smugly. "I thought you said this was a dangerous city."

"Just wait," replied the LEGAT. "It'll catch up with you when you least expect."

With that, Matt directed his attention toward Nick. "Victor, this is Nick Costigan."

"Welcome to Moscow, Nick," greeted Victor with a handshake.

"Thanks, it's good to have finally arrived."

"May I get either of you some coffee?"

"Sounds great. Sugar only for me," answered Nick.

"Make mine black," replied Matt.

Victor got the coffee, and as everyone sat down, he asked Nick, "How were things at ILEA?"

"Everything seems to be going well there. Have you visited Budapest and the Academy?"

"Not yet, but I hope to go soon."

"You really should try to get there, especially since so many of the attendees are from countries you cover."

"You're right. I'll have to do that, but it seems like there's always something else to be done here."

"I can understand that," Nick nodded.

Victor asked, "What were the major concerns of the Russians in this last class?"

"They're having a lot of trouble following paper-trails. More than one of them told me that once the money leaves Russia, it's gone for all practical purposes. They describe it as vanishing into the Caribbean."

"Something like those stories we have heard over the years about the Bermuda Triangle."

"Funny you should mention that," Nick replied. "One of them said the very same thing."

"Did this following-the-money concern seem to be coming from any particular investigative group?"

"No, it didn't seem to matter. Fraud, organized crime, terrorism, corruption, they all seem to be experiencing the same kind of problems."

"Sounds familiar, doesn't it," Victor remarked, as he looked in Matt's direction.

As the three of them were well aware, this problem was not unique to Russian investigators. For years, investigators had been frustrated trying to follow these daisy chains of complex paper-trails around the world, especially when they leap-frogged from one sovereignty to another. There were a variety of causes for the difficulties, but bank secrecy and confidentiality laws, and the lack of treaties and agreements among nations for exchanging financial information, had been the primary culprits.

Nick continued, "I told the Russians in the class about your being here, and the fact that you spoke Russian. Hopefully, they will give you call a whenever they feel like the Bureau might be able to help."

Victor smiled and nodded approvingly.

"I also tried to give them insight into some of the things that have worked for us," Nick added.

Victor interrupted, "You will be going into those areas in the program you two are presenting here, right?"

"Sure," answered Matt. "Speaking of the program, have you heard anything more?"

"Almost everything seems to be going as advertised. I used the word 'almost,' because there were a couple of glitches." Noting some concern on the faces of his fellow agents, Victor shook his head. "Nothing to worry about. The main thing had to do with the fact that our Ambassador is now going to deliver the keynote address."

Nick and Matt looked at each other with some surprise, since the American Ambassador to Russia is one of the highest-ranking officials in the U.S. State Department.

Victor continued, "This is because of some new policy statement made by our President."

"Made when?" Matt asked.

"Yesterday, it's in connection with a new get-tough policy on organized crime, especially when it comes to the Russian mafia."

"That sounds pretty good for us," Nick replied.

"It is, assuming the Russians are in agreement."

"Is there some question about that?"

"I don't think so, but we should find out soon," answered Victor.

"How's that?"

"Along with the Ambassador, there will be remarks made by some top Russian officials."

Nick interrupted, "Speaking of Russian officials, what's their attitude about our being here?"

"I think it's mixed. No question, there's a degree of skepticism out there. But remember, much of both the old and new Russian hierarchy rose out of the old KGB."

"Enough said," commented Nick, as he flashed a sly smile, and added, "Isn't it interesting how it appears that many of Russia's top officials were, at one time or another, KGB agents; while at the same time I would be hard pressed to come up with the names of any high ranking U.S. officials who had been career FBI agents."

"Yeah, even most of our Directors have not come from the career agents ranks," added Matt.

Victor nodded in agreement with what both Nick and Matt were saying.

Matt then asked, "But, these officials are at least showing token support for these joint efforts, aren't they?"

"They seem to be," answered Victor. "I don't really think there's anything to worry about."

Unfortunately, for Nick and Matt, most all of this had already been leaked to the press and it was now anticipated that the Russian media would be there in force, at least for the opening ceremonies. Needless to say, Nick was less than thrilled with this revelation, especially considering how he had fared with the press earlier in his career.

It was obvious that their stay in Moscow was now going to be quite different than either Nick or Matt had anticipated. Their original intention had been to maintain a relatively low profile throughout the trip, but with the possibility of their program now getting significant TV and newspaper exposure, they would have to exercise extra caution.

Russian mafia threats had been circulating against the FBI since the Bureau first arrived in Moscow, and recently these threats seemed to be being taken more seriously. The word was out that these Russian wiseguys were bragging about teaching the FBI a lesson, but no one knew if they were bold enough to try anything. With Nick, Matt, and Victor being the only FBI agents in Moscow, though, it was only prudent that the three of them exercise extra caution. None of them was interested in finding out whether these mobsters were willing to follow through on the threats.

In spite of all this, Nick was still hoping to have the same opportunity Matt did to work with Sergei and Vladimir's elite MVD unit, and if that was going to happen, the two of them needed to get going. Matt used the LEGAT's phone to call Sergei who said he would pick the two agents up outside the main entrance to the Embassy in one hour. In the interim, Nick would receive his security briefing from the RSO.

Right on the dot, the black Volga pulled up to the curb beside the vehicle entrance gate and whisked Nick and Matt off to Sergei's MVD office.

While riding to the MVD office, Matt asked Sergei, "Have you heard anything from Natasha today?"

"Nothing, but we will give her a call as soon as we get to the office." Upon their arrival at the MVD, Sergei dialed Natasha's number. There was no answer. "We should go to her apartment," Sergei told them as he sprang up from his desk. The next thing the two agents knew, Sergei was motioning for them to close the door behind them, as they left the office and he was leading them toward the car.

At Natasha's apartment, Sergei knocked on the door. Both he and Matt identified themselves and called out her name, but there was no answer. They continued down the hallway, knocking on the doors of several neighbors, until finally finding an elderly lady at home.

She opened her door a crack and Sergei showed her his badge.

"I am from the MVD," he told her.

"Please leave me alone. I do not want to get involved," she said.

"I have not even told you why I am here," Sergei grumbled. "Now open the door, I need to ask you some questions."

She pushed the door closed enough to loosen the chain, then re-opened it, telling them in a biting tone, "Come in, if you must, but I warn you, do not be long."

"We will take no more of your time than is necessary," Sergei assured her. "Have you seen or heard from your neighbor, Natasha Federova?" he asked.

"I have not seen her today, but when I was returning from my daily walk, there were two men knocking on Natasha's door. As I walked behind them, they turned just long enough to see who I was, then turned back around. They said nothing, and I went into my apartment."

"Do you know them?"

"No, but they did look like two men I saw talking to Natasha before."

"Where?"

"Outside her apartment."

"Was that all they were doing? Just talking?"

"Well, I did later see her leave with them in a car, but mind you I was not watching her."

"Yes, I understand," responded Sergei. "That was the same day?"

"Yes."

"What did these men look like? Can you describe them to me?" Sergei pursued.

"The men today?"

"Both times," responded Sergei. "You did say that you thought they were the same two men both times, right?"

"That is correct. I think they were the same ones, but I did not get a very good look either time. I do remember though that they did look mean. Both appeared to be in their late 20's, had slicked-back hair, and were wearing long, black leather coats."

"I assume they do not live in this apartment complex?"

She shook her head, no.

"You are certain?"

Continuing to shake her head, "I am certain that they do not."

"Have you seen anyone else or heard anything unusual coming from Natasha's apartment?

"I have not," she retorted, glaring indignantly. "I mind my own business. Now, would you please try doing the same and leave me alone? I told you before, I do not want to get involved." With that, she quickly ushered the three of them out and closed her door behind them, immediately re-engaging the multiple locks.

After their return to the MVD office, Matt carefully unfolded the crumpled piece of paper he had found lying behind the trash basket in Natasha's apartment. He handed it to Sergei, explaining where he got it. Sergei took it carefully by the corners, and after reading it, confirmed Matt's suspicions.

"This is a real estate contract," he said. "I will get it into the lab."

At the lab, the MVD forensic technicians would do a complete document analysis, and try to make positive ID's on any fingerprints found on the paper. Since the names of any individual or business beneficiaries identified on these contracts were usually fictitious, Sergei believed that their best hope for identifying these guys would be through fingerprints. It had been his experience in the cases they had made to date, that true identities were only learned after these scum showed up with a signed contract in hand to take control of the property, and that was usually shortly after the deaths of the owners.

CHAPTER EIGHTEEN

So far, the seduction had gone like clockwork. Most of the foreign intelligence agents and diplomats Catherine had wooed in the past had taken considerable time and work, but not Darren Kroft. He was quick and easy. Once those tentacles reached out to him during their very first early morning rendezvous back in his hotel room, he was putty in her hands and his fate was sealed. He had fallen about as fast and hard as any target Catherine could ever remember. With each intimate session, she became increasingly passionate, and that led to her being able to gain even greater insight. Now, it appeared a certainty that he would fit the criteria established for filling a key spot in their organization's new venture. His bragging coupled with telephonic confirmations regarding his credentials and background, from their organization's U.S. sources, had definitely made him a legitimate target for both her and their concentrated attention.

Since that first night, Catherine worked to create within Darren a burning desire to be with her during his every waking hour. She was well aware of how very important it was to be able to put that feeling and desire into a man, and once attained, Catherine knew she had him. It was then just a matter of keeping the lure and doing what she referred to as "performing necessary maintenance."

She did this by seeing him just enough to keep that wanton lust and desire he had for her burning inside. In turn, he would remain vulnerable and pliable for as long as needed. Her years of experience in the art of successfully trading sex for information were once again paying off handsomely.

At every opportunity, Kroft continued to seek Catherine. When he complained about not getting to be with her as much as he wanted, Catherine gave him a little smile and knew that her tactic of "just enough" was working as planned. This was not love to her; none of her affairs had been. And, although she had been married once, and had plenty of experience in how to put that spark of interest and excitement into a relationship, she had never really experienced true love with anyone. As far as she was concerned, this thing called love really meant sex, and was nothing more than a cold, calculating business. You either met the objective or you did not, and as such you were either a success or you were a failure. It was as simple as that. When she was with Darren Kroft, Catherine concentrated on pushing those special buttons she knew would virtually guarantee success in meeting the objective.

Before each meeting, Catherine sat down and mentally reviewed her psychological assessment training. She carefully re-examined what might be the best approach for her mafia associates to use. When and how they made the pitch to Kroft would be critical.

In her old intelligence days, Catherine had been successful in employing several different techniques. She sometimes set-up the guy by videotaping the two of them in compromising situations and then blackmailing him for the desired information. Other times, the pawns had confided to her some of their innermost secrets, and when confronted with exposure of these private revelations, they would usually break down and do whatever was asked. If they did not, their marriages, as well as their careers as diplomats, intelligence agents, business executives, military officers, or whatever, would be over should these disclosures and compromising photos somehow manage to make their way to families, governments, employers, tabloids, and the like. As her associates had told her time and again, "Catherine, do whatever it takes."

Because Kroft was neither married nor the employee of an organization requiring a security clearance, he did not fit snugly into one of her typical "trick bag" positions. Instead, she had been concentrating her efforts on trying to discern whether he harbored any noticeable distaste for his government or its authority, and did he feel like he had been discriminated against or treated unfairly in employment. If so, she could try to capitalize on an anti-government, anti-system, or anti-big business attitude. In promoting this feeling, she would approach him with a "we'll show them" attitude. The other concentration she had been working on was to identify what value he placed on money and material goods, and the extent to which he would go to achieve wealth.

She had not detected any particular ideology, anti-government sentiment, or anti-business attitudes, but she had certainly observed his penchant for money. That had been apparent from their first evening at the social club. Kroft made it a point to ask Catherine if those were "real diamonds," or "just zircons," she was wearing. Based on the surprised, bug-eyed look he gave to her response when she assured him that they were in fact Russian diamonds, Catherine was able to draw some conclusions regarding his attitude toward materialism and money. As a result, she always made it a point to insure that he got a good look at any gems she was wearing when the two of them were together.

With the picture now somewhat clearer, Catherine met with Boris, their organization's equivalent of an American mafia underboss, and two of the gang's strong-arm lieutenants at the social club. The four of them discussed how they would put Catherine's plan into motion. And, because Kroft was not going to remain in Moscow indefinitely, the time was rapidly approaching for them to make their move.

During the meeting with Boris, it was agreed that these two lieutenants and one of their fellow mafia associates, who spoke English, would make the initial pitch to Kroft.

Catherine would remain in the background as his seductive mistress. She would be responsible for keeping their affair going, and act as a sounding board to which he could unwittingly express his feelings and concerns. There was little question in anyone's mind about Catherine's ability to subtly influence any of Darren Kroft's innermost thoughts.

CHAPTER NINETEEN

The opening ceremony for the FBI seminar attracted more attention than Nick, Matt, or even Victor anticipated. Along with the American Ambassador, his interpreter, and the security detail, were numerous Russian diplomats, and high-ranking officials from throughout the Ministry of the Interior. Also in attendance were those from the Russian Tax Police and the Federal Security Service, FSB, who had replaced the KGB.

Most of the Moscow-based newspapers were well represented. Their reporters were already taking seats near the front, and had pens, notepads, and mini-tape recorders in hand. As the three FBI agents glanced to the rear and both sides of the amphitheater-style auditorium, they had to temporarily shield their eyes from the bright lights being set up by the both Russian and international television news services. Also setting up equipment were photojournalists. They were strategically placing their tripods and already testing flashes.

With the red, white, and blue flags of both the United States and Russia now in place and the headsets distributed so that all could listen to the interpreters, Victor stepped to the podium. It was show time in the Russian capital and the TV cameras were ready to roll.

"*Dobroye Utro. Menya Zovut,* Victor Gorski. I am the FBI Legal Attaché, assigned to Moscow." Even though Victor spoke Russian, he usually opted to use English when making comments in large forums like this.

His good morning greeting given, Gorski formally introduced the honored guests and when he did, each one nodded to the FBI Legal Attaché.

The senior General in attendance then followed Victor Gorski's introductory remarks with opening remarks of his own on behalf of the MVD. As Nick and Matt had subsequently learned, the agreement for this training was not universally accepted. Some of the old entrenched Russian hard-liners were, in fact, quite agitated by the thought that the FBI would be invited to come onto their turf and present a program. In the interest of international relations, though, cooler heads had prevailed and the Russians agreed that it was in everyone's best interest to have the program presented, even if it was to some degree being thrust upon them. As a result, the General's comments were poignant but brief. He concentrated on addressing the growing hardships facing the Russian people as a result of the Russian mafia menace, and the efforts being made by the MVD's elite anti-mafia unit to combat them.

Next was the U.S. Ambassador's keynote address. In preparing his remarks, the Ambassador had asked the Legal Attaché to assist him in compiling the necessary information. As a result, Victor had stayed late almost every night during this past week, sending faxes, summarizing volumes of data received from the Bureau, and answering any additional requests that came up at the last minute so that the senior American diplomat had all he needed.

The Ambassador opened his speech with a typical Russian greeting followed by a brief history lesson outlining the evolution of traditional organized crime, as we know it in the United States. He went on to discuss the Russian underworld and how the "thieves-in-law," which had grown out of the Soviet era prisons had declined and were now being rapidly replaced by the new, flashy, big-spending, and extremely violent Russian gangs.

Taking advantage of this high profile, media-intense forum, the Ambassador also set forth America's new get-tough policy, emphasizing several areas that experience had taught him would make good sound bites for the evening news, both here in Moscow and back home in the U.S.

"It's not only the ten to fifteen Moscow murders every-day that concern us, but also the tens of thousands of companies, and literally hundreds of commercial banks that are now being controlled by Russian criminal organizations..."

Using gestures to emphasize each point, he continued. "If it's grip is not released, this mafia stranglehold will, just as surely as I am standing here, eliminate what life remains in your Russian economy... The task is formidable, but there is no option if we are to have safe and productive societies for all of our families... It's not only your future, but the future of many others around the world that is in your hands..."

As the Ambassador was closing his emotional plea, he paused while his eyes panned the audience. In a strong and deliberate tone, he slowly repeated, "The time is now. It is up to you."

After another pause, he briefly explained that this international financial crimes seminar was just the first step in America's increased effort to assist in eliminating this vicious international criminal menace. Thanking the audience for their attendance, the Ambassador closed his remarks with, "*Spasibo*," and nodded graciously before returning to where he had been seated.

These comments of the Ambassador were, of course, music to Nick and Matt's ears. They hoped that it was not just more rhetoric, but that everyone would in fact "get tough" and follow through. They could see, however, that their program was now high profile, and as a result, they would certainly be attracting a lot of extra attention.

A respectful, but somewhat reserved applause followed the Ambassador's speech, and those in attendance were invited for refreshments. This cigarette and refreshment break not only allowed the media access to the dignitaries for additional interview comments and sound bites, but also gave them with ample time to dismantle their equipment.

With the formalities and opening ceremony now concluded, and the media and dignitaries gone, the program began in earnest. The attendees were asked to identify themselves and give their investigative backgrounds. It was obvious all were highly experienced and undoubtedly, some of the best that the MVD and the other agencies had to offer.

As was the case with many programs of this type, the first couple of hours can be tough going, and "breaking the ice" with this Moscow group was no exception. Nick and Matt were the first FBI agents most of these Russian police officers and investigators had ever met, and it was not until the last several years that they would have even considered being in the same room with the FBI. In fact, during most of their lifetimes the FBI had been their arch adversary.

However, as the day wore on and the Russians were able to see that these two FBI agents were people like anyone else, they began to open up, especially when Nick mentioned their working together and used the word "comrades" when referring to himself and everyone else in the room. Their sly smiles and glances toward one another suddenly made him realize what he had said. To that, Nick smiled and shook his head. They all laughed. It also didn't hurt having Sergei in there to help keep things lively.

By afternoon, things were much improved. Matt and Nick were impressed with their attendees' knowledge and direct questions, sometimes to the point of being almost too pointed. Their increasing openness was refreshing and would make the information exchange much easier in the coming days.

With streetlights and headlights now shining outside, and "those minds in the classroom having absorbed about all their posteriors could endure," it was time to call it a day.

Nick gave his best shot at pronouncing *"Dobri Den,"* to which Sergei responded, "and good afternoon to you, too."

To this, everyone laughed and quickly gathered up their materials. For many, however, their day was not over. They would have to return to their offices and finish work there before going home.

The first day of any training program always seemed to be the toughest, and as Nick's final lecture for the day had come to a close, he and Matt felt relieved. Although neither was able to totally rid himself of the butterflies, both had once again counted on that tinge of uneasiness to give them an edge, and it had. As many public speaking gurus have pointed out, the notion of getting up in front of an audience of strangers and making a presentation can be one of the most frightening and difficult things a person can do. Several of Nick's FBI National Academy attendees had told him they would rather be the first one through the door to capture an armed and dangerous fugitive, than have to get up before a group of citizens or experienced law enforcement officers and make a presentation. Give 'em the door to kick in, any day.

When the two agents returned to their hotel that evening, both checked for messages before going to their rooms to freshen up prior to dinner.

"No messages," commented Nick. "So, I guess that's a good sign."

"Yeah," Matt agreed.

Shortly after getting to his room, Matt turned on the television and made his usual security checks to see if anyone had been in there snooping around. He didn't notice anything out of order. Suddenly, there on the TV was taped footage of Nick and him standing beside Victor at the opening ceremonies. Unfortunately, he couldn't understand a word of the Russian news commentary that was accompanying the video, but their faces and the FBI seal inserted into the background were readily identifiable. With this, there was no question that the three of them had indeed made the big time. They were the lead story on Moscow's nightly news.

Victor was already known as the FBI Legal Attaché in Moscow, but with this disclosure, Matt and Nick's identities as generic American bureaucrats were now history and as a result, the charade they had been playing at the hotel and other places they frequented was over. They were American FBI agents in Moscow, and their presence was no longer a secret to anyone, especially the Russian mafia.

Having returned downstairs, the agents noted several televisions hanging on the walls as they walked from the elevator to the central lobby. All appeared to be turned on, and the video segments being replayed across the screens were more pictures of them with what they assumed were their names and the letters, FBI, in Cyrillic type across the bottom.

Nick nudged Matt on the arm, "Take a look at the bellmen's station. I think we're celebrities."

The bellmen were huddled in a group and appeared to be looking in their direction. One of them held his hand up to his mouth and appeared to be whispering to the others, as he pointed toward the TV.

After a long first day, dinner at one of the hotel's upscale restaurants appealed to them much more than venturing back out on their own into the cold and blowing snow to find somewhere else to eat. They had learned on some of their earlier trips that they had to be careful where they ate, anyway. Being sick in a hotel room halfway around the world with a case of Montezuma's revenge was not fun. Nick, Matt, and most any other agents who worked internationally had experienced that feeling more than once. In fact, several of the agents and prosecutors had been forced home early because of illness, some with serious and long-lasting conditions. Finding bottled water and safe food was always a concern. They seemed to find their best success with the major hotel restaurants, but even then, there was no guarantee. If they were uncertain, they tended to rely heavily on the embassies and their host sponsors for direction. When they did elect to go outside the hotel to eat, they had to try to locate an English-speaking taxi driver who would not rip them off and at the same time get them safely to a restaurant and back to the hotel.

After dinner and an extended visit to the hotel bar where a Russian combo was playing, the two of them went to the hotel currency exchange to convert some more dollars into rubles. As they passed the reception desk, one of the young desk clerks whom Matt had gotten to know called out to him.

Matt went over to where she was standing.

"Mr. Kelly, I just received a message for you from the hotel telephone operator." While he waited, she retrieved an envelope from his key and message box and when handing it to him gave him a big smile, adding, "If you need anything else, be sure and let me know."

Matt returned the smile. "Anything?" he asked jokingly, and winked, as he opened the envelope. After quickly glancing at the folded sheet enclosed, his demeanor suddenly changed, and he thanked her and turned, immediately following Nick to the elevators.

Noting Matt's sudden turnabout, Nick remarked, "What happened back there?"

"What?" questioned Matt, his mind continuing to race as he pondered the message.

"An attractive young Russian woman flirts with you. You initially respond as I would have expected, and then all of a sudden your attention seems to be diverted away from her 180 degrees. Are you sick?"

"No, just curious."

"About her?"

"No, no. This message."

When they were in the elevator, Matt handed the envelope to Nick. The folded sheet of paper inside read:

MESSAGE FOR: Mr. Matt Kelly
FROM: Natasha
MESSAGE: You are in danger

"Any idea what she's talking about?" Nick asked.

"None," replied a very concerned Matt Kelly. "But, I'm much more worried about her than about myself."

CHAPTER TWENTY

"Go away!" grumbled Darren Kroft, reacting to a loud pounding on the door of his hotel room. Even though it was already past noon, Kroft was still in no mood to get out of bed. His head was spinning from a monumental hangover, but there were no regrets, since it had come as a result of another memorable night with Catherine.

As the pounding continued, Kroft finally gave in, yelling, "Okay, just a minute."

He threw back the covers and staggered to the door. There, he squinted through the peephole. Standing outside his room were three distorted figures. Two looked to be about his age or younger and were dressed in what appeared to be expensive suits. The third seemed older and more casually dressed.

They knocked again.

"What do you want?" Kroft asked.

To his surprise, the response came in English, "We would like to talk with you, Mr. Kroft."

"About what?"

"It is regarding a business opportunity," came the reply.

"I'm not interested. Please go away," Kroft insisted.

Seeing this approach was not working, the older man offered another option.

"Mr. Kroft, we would like to invite you for a drink, downstairs in the hotel bar."

Kroft took a quick assessment of his options. He concluded that since these three men had specifically come to his room, called him by name, and wanted to talk, they were probably not going to take "no" for an answer and just walk away. However, if he did agree to meet in a public place, like the hotel bar, he believed there would probably be less personal risk.

"Okay. I'll see you down there in one-half hour," Kroft answered.

"We will be waiting," the man replied.

Kroft continued to watch through the peephole until the three of them disappeared down the hallway.

He took a quick shower and tried to get himself into some kind of condition to make the meeting. He remained perplexed, though. Who were these guys and how did they know about him? Furthermore, why would three men he had never seen nor heard of before want to talk to him about a business opportunity? Had this been in the States, Kroft would have likely gathered up his belongings and slipped out a side door of the hotel. But, since this was Moscow, he knew that was not an option. He had nowhere to go. He thought about trying to call someone, anyone, to talk to about it or help him get away, but the only person in Moscow he really trusted was Catherine, and he was afraid there really wasn't much she would be able to do.

After re-thinking his situation for all of thirty seconds, however, he changed his mind and decided to give her a call. He didn't have much in the way of specifics to tell her though, three guys knocking on his door wanting to talk to him about a business opportunity. That was it. As her phone rang, he sat on the edge of the bed, nervously tapping his foot.

Finally, Catherine picked up on the other end, but before she could say anything, Kroft anxiously asked, "Catherine?"

"Darren, is that you?"

"Yes, yes, it's me," he said, speaking very rapidly. "Catherine, something very strange has happened. I need your advice. They knocked on the door, and called me by name."

"Who is they, Darren?"

"Three of them," he replied. "They were at my door."

"Now settle down Darren. What did they say?"

"They wanted me to let them in so we could talk. It supposedly had to do with some kind of business opportunity. I told them that I wasn't interested, but they said they still wanted to talk and would wait downstairs. I'm supposed to meet them in the hotel bar in a few minutes. What should I do, Catherine?"

"Just so I have this clear, Darren. Three men knocked on the door of your hotel and said they want to talk with you about a business opportunity. Is that it?"

His rate of speech still racing, "Yes, and they wanted to come in, but instead we are going to meet in the hotel bar."

"I don't think there is anything for you to worry about, lover. That is just the way some of our Russian businessmen do things here in Moscow. Because of harassment from the police, some of them feel much more comfortable conducting their business behind the closed doors of hotel rooms."

"Or in bars?" Darren asked.

"Oh yes, bars, too."

"You're sure it's okay?"

"I think so," Catherine answered. "Go ahead. Meet with them and listen to what they have to say. It will be all right. After your meeting, you can call me and we can get together. You can tell me all about it."

"Okay," responded Kroft, somewhat apprehensively. "I have to go, now."

"It will be all right, lover boy," she reassured him. "Remember that I will be waiting for you."

"Bye, Catherine," and Kroft put down the receiver. The tension remained, but at least he was a bit more relieved.

Already several minutes late for his meeting in the bar, Darren walked in and took a careful look around. The three men were sitting at a horseshoe shaped booth in a dimly lit corner near the back. When he nodded in their direction, they motioned for him to come over.

The oldest one extended his hand and introduced himself as Leonid. He explained that he was a professional interpreter and had been retained by the other two for their meeting. He introduced the other two men by the first names, Mikhail and Yuri. Those two then shook hands with Kroft and nodded, as Darren commented that he spoke only English.

Leonid smiled and responded, "That is why I am here."

Kroft nodded that he understood.

Leonid continued, "Mikhail and Yuri are Moscow businessmen who have learned that you profess to have an expertise as an American computer consultant and they are interested in possibly retaining your services."

Kroft questioned, "How did they learn about me?"

Leonid interpreted what Kroft had asked.

He then translated Yuri's response, as Mikhail nodded in agreement. "They would prefer to leave it at that for now, only acknowledging that they have heard of you and believe that your skills might be a good business fit with their interests."

Kroft decided not to press the issue, figuring a name might come up in their continued discussion.

"What kind of business opportunity are they talking about?" Kroft asked.

Leonid looked to the others and answered, "Computer consulting work."

"Please tell them that I am here only on a Tourist Visa, and will have to be leaving Moscow shortly. I don't think I would be of much use to them."

"They don't believe that would be a problem. You see, they are primarily interested in your working for them in the United States."

This response was obviously quite puzzling to Kroft, and as a result, he asked them to tell him more.

Through Leonid, they went on to explain that their organization had an extensive network of businesses and financial services operating throughout the United States. They were always looking for promising new talent and from what they understood, Kroft might fit in. They would not be able to go into the details, though, until they determined whether or not he was their man. If he was, he could be assured that he would be paid very well for his services.

Their mention of money suddenly tweaked Kroft's interest, but from what he had seen so far in Moscow, what was big money for a Russian might not necessarily mean big money for an American.

Kroft responded, "How much are they talking about when they say 'being paid very well?'"

Leonid looked at Mikhail and Yuri, received their response, then looked back at them for a second time as if to say, "Am I hearing correctly?" They nodded, yes.

"Mr. Kroft, they say that if you are the right man, you could be compensated in the millions."

"I'm not talking about rubles," Kroft said. "Ask them how much in dollars?"

Leonid again interpreted Kroft's remarks.

Yuri responded, as both he and Mikhail nodded.

"Mr. Kroft, Yuri said they are talking about dollars."

Kroft's jaw dropped and his eyes widened in amazement. It was obvious to all that he was impressed.

Trying to regain some of his composure, he swallowed several times and snickered, saying, "Who do I have to kill?"

Kroft's cynicism did not appear to lend itself particularly well to interpretation. Mikhail and Yuri looked at each other with somewhat surprised expressions, and commented back to Leonid. "Tell Mr. Kroft that is our job, not his."

When Leonid interpreted their response to Kroft, he suddenly felt a lump in his throat and his heart skipped a beat. There were no smiles on their faces and their cold, steely eyes reflected the seriousness of their reply.

Trying to make light of his previous question, Kroft responded, "I'm happy to hear that's not in my job description."

His quip did not seem to translate.

Seeing their reaction, Kroft paused, and in a more serious tone, asked, "What is it you want me to do?"

Adding to Yuri's earlier comment, Kroft was again told that they were an integral part of a vast international organization that operated around the world. They were growing very rapidly and felt that Kroft could be a valuable addition to their operations in the United States and elsewhere. Their organization was very interested in getting a stronger foothold in the American computer consulting business and believed he might just be the man to get that done.

Kroft nodded, indicating he might be interested.

With Leonid interpreting, Yuri looked directly into Kroft's eyes, "If you are our man, Mr. Kroft, we will make you the CEO of your own company. We will provide you with the total financing package and all of the support you will need."

"What about clients?" Kroft asked.

"You can leave that up to us, too."

The look in Kroft's eyes told Yuri and Mikhail they had likely hit their mark. The combination of money and power had definitely gathered his attention. Yuri and Mikhail were still going to have to further assess his attitude regarding a willingness to carry out criminal activity before they could be sure, but, so far, it appeared quite obvious that Catherine's analysis was right on target.

Mikhail's cell phone rang. It was the boss. Excusing himself from the table, he got up and went to another part of the bar where he could talk in privacy. Yuri then slid across the bench to get up and go to the men's room. As he was leaving, he told Leonid to order another round of drinks for everyone.

When the waitress came over to the table, Leonid ordered another round and asked if she would also bring something for them to snack on. She told him she would be right back with both their drinks and snacks. As she started walking away, she turned and gave Kroft a tempting glance and a wink. Kroft smiled at her, and looked to see if Leonid was paying attention to what was going on. He was.

In an effort to make conversation, Leonid asked Kroft how he was enjoying his visit to Moscow so far.

"It's been great! I only hope this won't be my last visit."

"That is good to hear," responded Leonid. "What have you enjoyed the most?"

"The women!" Kroft answered with a sly smile. "I really like the Russian women. They are much different than the prima donnas we have back in America. Here, the women really appreciate me. You noticed the look that waitress gave me, didn't you?"

"I did," Leonid said, with a smile and a nod. "It sounds as though the Russian women are going to miss you when you leave."

"Probably so," Kroft chuckled, "but with it being just me, I can't keep them all satisfied forever." With a cocky look on his face, he tapped Leonid on the side of the arm with the back of his hand, saying, "But you must know how it is, huh?"

Shaking his head, Leonid responded, "I wish I could say I did. It sounds as though I need to take some lessons from you."

"Maybe someday. We'll have to see what we can do about that. Maybe I can send some of my overflow your direction," Kroft quipped.

Leonid smiled.

"By the way, Leonid, how long have you been working with Mikhail and Yuri?"

"Oh, not very long," he answered. "But, I have been doing work for others within their organization for several years."

As Kroft looked up, Yuri and Mikhail were returning to the table. Following close behind was the same waitress who had attracted Kroft's attention earlier. When everyone was seated, the well-endowed waitress leaned over the table to give them their drinks and snacks. When she did, she made sure Kroft got a full and unobstructed view of at least some of what she had to offer. He didn't fail to take notice, and she gave him another tempting glance before turning to walk away. His eyes remaining glued to her body's every movement.

Reminding Mikhail that he had been unsuccessful in making a move on the waitress while the three of them were waiting for Kroft to get down to the bar, Yuri joked in Russian, "He must have something she wants."

Mikhail shot back in a somewhat jealous tone of voice, "Nothing I do not have. She just thinks he is one of those big-tipping foreigners looking for a bride. No other reason."

Not understanding a word that was being said between Yuri and Mikhail, Kroft looked at Leonid with a questioning look.

"Never mind, they were just arguing about which waitress has the biggest breasts."

"Any conclusions?" asked Kroft.

"I think our waitress is winning," replied Leonid.

Yuri gave Leonid a serious look, indicating he was ready to get back to the matter at hand.

"Yuri asked me to tell you that for the money and the position we are offering, much will be required."

"Please tell him I would have expected nothing less. I am willing to give a total commitment for the right amount of money."

Yuri responded, "Good. That is what we wanted to hear." He looked directly at Kroft, and spoke very slowly and pointedly, as Leonid interpreted, "Would you be willing to do whatever is needed to get the job done, Mr. Kroft?"

Kroft flippantly responded, "WHATEVER can have a very broad meaning. I mean, I would do a lot of things, but I don't think that I would kill someone or something like that."

Yuri paused, looked at Mikhail and back at Kroft, "We told you earlier, that is our job, not yours."

Kroft could once again see that his offhanded response was not well received. When they said, "WHATEVER," that was exactly what they meant. These guys were serious!

Trying to get himself out of a squeeze, Kroft began to back-pedal.

"Becoming a wealthy CEO has always been very appealing to me, but I will need some time," Kroft told them.

"How much time, Mr. Kroft?" asked Yuri.

"Can you give me a couple of days?"

"Two days it is. We will meet here at noon, the day after tomorrow."

Yuri summoned the waitress and ordered another round to toast their future success.

Their eyes meeting and heads nodding, Yuri announced, "Bottoms up."

Once downed, all of the glasses were slammed to the table. Yuri let out a loud belch and said something to Leonid.

To this Leonid responded, "Meeting adjourned!"

Kroft felt relieved and seeing this as his chance to make an escape, quickly shook hands with everyone and eased his way out of the booth.

CHAPTER TWENTY-ONE

Matt found himself re-living, again and again, his snowy, moonlit walk from the restaurant with Natasha. The feeling that came over him as he pulled her up and they embraced was something he could not get out of his mind. He also believed that she must have experienced similar feelings. Otherwise, why would she have left the message warning him that he was in danger?

Before class began that morning, Sergei and Matt were having coffee. "Have you heard anything from Natasha?" Matt asked.

"Nothing. I think we should go to her apartment after class, today, and make sure she is okay," suggested Sergei.

"Sounds like a good idea to me," Matt unhesitatingly agreed. "I'll tell Nick."

There were many questions asked during this day's seminar sessions, but Nick's ability to take a complex subject like money laundering and through examples simplify its many different needs and objectives so all could understand them had been most appreciated.

With class over for the day, they locked up the room and got into Sergei's Volga to go to Natasha's. Nick and Matt looked at each other and quickly fastened their seat belts as Sergei darted in and out of Moscow rush-hour traffic. It was not only his driving that concerned the two of them, but also his practice of lighting up one cigarette after another, while doing it. This was typical of Sergei, however, and it was certain that two FBI agents from Quantico were not going to change either him or his habits.

Darkness had fallen by the time they arrived at Natasha's apartment complex. As the three made their way through the entrance area and up the stairway, they saw no one. There was no answer when they knocked on the door to her apartment. Sergei and Matt both called out for her through the door, but still there was no answer.

Finally, Matt decided he would slip a note under her door.

"Natasha –
Please call me at the hotel.
If I am not in my room, leave a message and a phone number.
I will call you.
I want to see you again.
Matt"

They left her apartment.

"Are you two ready to get something to eat?" asked Sergei.

"Sounds good to me, I'm starved," Matt responded.

"Let's do it," answered Nick, as he slid into the rear left, death seat, allegedly so named by a former Bureau Director because of its supposed vulnerability when making left turns.

Sergei drove the two of them to one of his favorite MVD watering holes where he thought several others from the class might be spending the evening. Sure enough, as they walked through the door, there were a half dozen or more from the class sitting around a couple of the tables. When the group saw them, they started chanting "FBI, FBI," and waved for them to come on over. The three of them waved back, and as they started walking through the crowd, Nick, failed to duck, and bumped the top of his head on one of the low-hanging lights. That brought a rousing round of applause and good-natured howl from the group.

Through the smoke-clouded lighting, Matt and Nick could see dark wooden floors, a long bar, and groups of wooden tables and benches pushed together. A low roar of conversation echoed throughout the room. Everyone seemed to be having a good time and the game of grab-ass being played between a couple of the waitresses and several of the officers became more and more active as the night wore on. The drinks were cheap and the food, although not fancy and certainly not low in cholesterol, was good, and the price was definitely right.

By the time, Nick and Matt returned to their hotel it was nearly midnight. Matt had just dozed off when the sound of a ringing telephone nearly jolted him out of bed. As he rolled over to pick up the receiver, he wondered who in the world would be calling him at this hour.

"Hello?" he groggily answered.

"Matt, is that you?" a female voice asked.

After hesitating briefly, Matt asked, "Natasha?" as he sat up in his bed.

"I found your note. You said to call. I did try earlier, but there was no answer, so I decided to try one more time."

"Yes! Yes!" Matt exclaimed, "I'm glad that you did! Are you okay? We've been worried about you."

"I am fine," she replied somewhat unconvincingly.

"When can I see you?" he asked.

"Would tomorrow night be alright?"

"Great! We can have dinner. Anywhere you would like."

"Dinner sounds nice."

"What time?" asked Matt.

"Is six too early?"

"No, that's fine. Where would you like to meet?"

Natasha replied hesitatingly, "The lobby of your hotel?"

"That will be fine."

"I will see you there," she responded in a voice that set his heart pounding. "Good night, Matt."

Before Matt could say anything additional, the line went dead. As he lay there trying to go back to sleep he couldn't get her voice out of his head. She sounded okay, but he could tell something was bothering her.

Meeting at their usual place and time in the hotel dining room for the breakfast buffet, Matt looked over to Nick. "Guess who called me after we got back last night?"

"Natasha got your message, huh?" Nick responded confidently.

"Yeah, we're going to get together for dinner tonight."

"I guess that means I'll be dining with Sergei at one of those renowned gourmet locations frequented by the MVD."

Matt smiled and nodded, "Sounds like it."

"That's okay, though. I'll get plenty to eat and you know it'll be cheap," Nick remarked. "And you, well, you know what we have been told and have now learned about Moscow being one of the most expensive places for travelers around the world."

"Yeah, but to be with that beautiful young woman, I'll gladly bear any additional cost," Matt smugly replied.

"Touché," Nick agreed. "Now, what did she have to say when she called?"

"Not much. I think she could tell I was half-asleep. I'm sure she'll bring me up to date tonight."

Breakfast finished, Nick remarked, "Well, I guess we'd better leave if we're going to get to class in time to get things set up before everyone gets there."

The two agents returned upstairs to their rooms, and after picking up their coats and briefcases, returned to the lobby in time to meet the MVD shuttle van, which was already waiting outside the hotel's main entrance.

Several of the class members had closed the police club the previous evening and their eyes read like roadmaps, but at least they were all there. Nick started the class, and, from then on, the two agents alternated with two-hour blocks of instruction for the remainder of the morning and afternoon sessions.

When they gave examples surrounding bank secrecy, confidentiality, anonymous and numbered accounts, and bearer share and layered International Business Corporations or shell companies, it was obvious that they had clearly piqued the interest of the Russian investigators. Several acknowledged having similar situations come up in their investigations, but hadn't understood how these things worked, until now.

With another day of class complete, they were now half way through their Moscow program, and as far as Matt was concerned, it was all going to end much too quickly.

Back at the hotel, Matt went up to his room and quickly freshened up for his evening rendezvous with Natasha. Returning to the lobby a few minutes later, he awaited her arrival. Glancing at his watch, he realized it was already a couple of minutes after six. Ten minutes later Natasha rushed in, appearing to be out of breath. Matt waved to her. She flashed a big smile and walked over to the upholstered love seat where he had saved her a place. The two of them hugged and gave each other a polite peck on the cheek.

"Sorry I was late, but you know Moscow rush hours."

"No problem," Matt told her.

"I was worried you might leave."

"Never," he smiled. "Are you okay?"

Noting his concern, she smiled and nodded her head, "Yes, I am fine. It is you I am worried about. We need to talk on our way to dinner."

"All right," Matt agreed.

Natasha leaned over and whispered, "I would rather not talk about it here."

Matt nodded. "Speaking of dinner, where would you like to go?"

"I know a quiet little place about a twenty-minute walk from here. The food is good and we can sit and talk there.

Sounds good to me," Matt responded. "Shall we go?"

As they were leaving the hotel, Matt saw several young thugs hanging around the lobby, but they didn't appear to paying any particular attention to either of the two of them.

There was a crisp chill in the evening air. Holding hands as they walked along the shoveled pathway, Natasha started to tell Matt about the message she had left.

Matt interrupted, putting his finger to her lips. "We can talk about me later. First, I want to hear what you've been doing and why it has been so hard for me to get in touch with you."

"Well," she said, "I am finally working."

"You don't sound too thrilled about it," Matt replied.

"I am not, really. It is not the kind of job that I am excited about having, but it is a job and the money is good."

"Tell me about it."

She continued, "I am working at a social club, and it is strange how it all came about. Someone, I still do not know who, heard that I needed a job. Whoever it was then sent two men to the apartment. They told me about a waitress job at the club and wanted to know if I would be interested. I said that I might be and the next thing I knew they had me in their car and were taking me to be interviewed. I was hired and started working that very same day. I later learned that this was not the way things usually happen. There are many young women out there trying to get the jobs, but these men came to me."

"Why are so many women trying to get those jobs?"

"The tips, they are good!" she assured him.

"By the way," asked Matt, "What exactly is a Russian social club, anyway?"

"I don't think all social clubs are the same. This is the only one I am familiar with, and it has different things going on during different nights. Most nights it is just a place where people can go to meet and get a drink and socialize. However, one or two nights a week, they bring in women from throughout Russia, the Ukraine, Georgia, Moldova, Belarus, and other places. These women throw themselves at men arriving from the West who are supposedly looking for Russian brides."

Matt interrupted, "Are you interested in that?"

Natasha laughed, and put her finger up to his lips and said, "No, of course not, Matt. What do you think?"

Matt looked at her sheepishly.

"I am not one of those girls. I just serve food and drinks. However, several of the men..."

Matt again interrupted, "You mean lecherous old guys?"

Natasha nodded and smiled, as she continued, "have already tried to... What is it the American girls say in the movies? 'Make a move on you,' but I just tell them that I am married. So far, that has usually gotten them to start talking to one of the other girls. When that has not worked, I just look over in the direction of a couple of the young Russian tough guys, who are always hanging around the club, and it is assumed one of them is my husband. One man said something like, 'Oh, I am sorry,' and that ended it. I suspect most of these guys are not really looking for a bride, and certainly not to get beat up," she chuckled. "I think what they are really looking for is something else. What do you think, mister FBI?"

Matt agreed, "I think you're probably right."

"Oh, there is another special night, Matt. They call it 'Girls Night Out.' On that night we have male dancers wearing very little as they strut around the stage area. Interested in a part-time job?" Natasha asked, laughing. "I think you could probably get some great tips tucked in. Some of those rubles might even have phone numbers written on them."

Matt laughed and gave her a wink. "Would there be lots of lecherous, young women tugging at me?"

"Maybe, but hopefully not too many," she responded, giving him a smile and an alluring look.

Matt drew her closer.

Continuing their walk, Natasha gave Matt details regarding another strange thing that had happened recently. There had been a telephone call from the morgue telling her that the forensic work on her grandmother's body had been completed, and they were preparing it for release. Natasha was going to have to make the necessary burial arrangements and she was worried about where the money would come from. Much to her surprise, that had all been taken care of. She explained to Matt that she had received a call from the morgue telling her that someone had paid for her grandmother's casket, the funeral, and burial plot costs. When Natasha asked, "Who?" The person answered only that it was from an anonymous benefactor and the information could not be revealed.

"So, let me get this straight," Matt responded. "First, you receive the job offer from the club and now this payment has been made for your grandmother's burial."

"That is it. It has all been very strange."

Matt asked, "When are they going to have the services for your grandmother?"

"Nothing has been set. I have not been able to make the arrangements."

"Let me know when you make a decision, because I want to attend if at all possible."

Natasha smiled and nodded that she would.

"Now," she asked in a concerned tone of voice, "Can we talk about that message I left for you at the hotel?"

"Okay," Matt agreed.

"During the evening newscast when you were on TV, I overheard a remark at the Club that made me worry about you. There were a group of tough-looking guys sitting at a table. As I was serving them another round of drinks, pictures of you and one or two other FBI agents flashed across the screen. One of the men sitting there said, 'I don't like having the FBI in Moscow. We might have to make them feel unwelcome.' " The others at the table nodded in agreement, and he shouted, "*Doloi, FBI!*"

Matt gave her a quizzed look.

"I am sorry. That means, 'Down with the FBI' or 'Leave, FBI.' "

Matt gave a grin, "Oh. Is that all?"

"Matt, these men were serious! I am afraid they might try to do something to you."

"Okay, I really do appreciate your concern, Natasha. Do you know who they are?"

"I never saw them before, and one thing you do not do at the social club is ask too many questions. That is, if you value your life."

"I certainly understand. You make sure you don't do anything that might get you hurt. Okay?" Matt told her in a serious tone.

Noting his concern, Natasha answered with a smile, "Okay."

Matt smiled back and suggested, "Let's change the subject."

Natasha nodded in agreement and looked into Matt's eyes, "I always thought of FBI agents as being like James Bond."

"Isn't that me, or didn't you notice?" Matt asked.

"I noticed," she said, and winked at him. "Are you also like him when you are not working?"

Matt laughed smugly, and put his arm around her to draw her even closer. As he did, he gave her a kiss on the cheek. "I guess that will be for you to find out."

"Dare you to do that again," Natasha teased.

As Matt looked into her eyes, she put her fingertips first to his lips and then to hers. He held her tighter, and the two of them exchanged a passionate kiss. As she continued to linger in his arms, neither of them was willing to release the other.

Suddenly, their embrace was interrupted by the thundering sound of footsteps. Matt turned in time to see at least five men starting to surround them. Two of them were brandishing stainless steel pistols and yelling something that sounded to him like, "*Doloi, FBI! Doloi, FBI!*"

Recognizing the broken English sound of the letters *FBI*, Matt knew it was him they wanted. He grabbed

Natasha's hand and thought about running, but quickly realized that was not an option, as they were surrounded.

The men continued to yell more of what Matt assumed to be Russian expletives, along with "*Doloi, FBI!* The look of rage in their eyes left no question in Matt's mind about their intent. As he looked to Natasha and saw the fear on her face, he contemplated what it might take to free her. In the U.S., he would have been armed, but because he was teaching in a foreign country, his pistol had been left in the Academy's gun vault. This left him at a significant disadvantage. He had to do something before they killed both of them. Time was running out.

Sensing and hoping none of these attackers understood English, Matt stood his ground and quietly under his breath told Natasha, "Listen carefully and don't say anything. I am going to try and make a break of it. I'll start running on the path, back in the direction of the hotel. When I do, you start running as fast as you can in the direction of the restaurant. Don't stop for anything."

"But…"

Matt interrupted, "Don't say anything." He felt these guys would concentrate on trying to get to him, and hoped that in all of the commotion Natasha would be able to make good her escape. It was the only way he could see to get her out of harm's way.

There was another, "But…," from Natasha.

Matt gritted his teeth, "Now, do as I say."

Quickly turning, he bolted between two of the attackers and started sprinting toward the hotel. When all five of the young hoods pursued, Natasha took off running into the darkness in the opposite direction.

As Matt continued running down the snow-packed pathway, he was gradually putting more and more distance between himself and his pursuers. Then, suddenly, a series of shots rang out. The two thugs who had been waving their guns so vigorously in Matt's face had stopped running and one of them started shooting. One of the bullets found its mark. Matt slowed, and finally stumbled to the ground. Shortly thereafter, the taunting gang was once again upon him.

In the meantime, two beat officers were coming out of a small coffee shop a couple of blocks away when they heard the sound of the gunfire ringing out in the crisp, cold air of the evening. Hurrying on foot in the direction from which the shots came, the officers called for back up, and within seconds heard the sound of a siren echoing in the distance.

With Matt lying face down on a patch of dirty snow, and the blood starting to pool beside his shoulder, one of his attackers delivered a swift kick to his ribs. As Matt cried out in pain, another attacker quickly followed with a jarring blow to his head. These kicks continued, and the louder Matt responded to each subsequent blow, the more excited his attackers became. The five seemed to be taking extreme pleasure in seeing whose kick could inflict the most pain. Their actions had reached an almost frenzied level, and then, Matt lost consciousness.

Is he dead? Matt's attackers looked at one another. Then, throwing up their hands in an act of celebration, the five resumed their chants, *"Doloi, FBI! Doloi, FBI!"*

As the sound of the siren grew louder and the flashing blue light now loomed in the distance, all five of the attackers quickly glanced at one another and scattered into the darkness.

Shortly thereafter, a white, four-door patrol car with a wide blue stripe just below the windows, and a roof-centered flashing blue light pulled into the area where the group of young thugs had darted into the darkness. The MVD officers jumped out of their patrol car and ran over to where Matt was lying. Kneeling down and feeling a pulse, they immediately radioed for an ambulance.

The only signs of Matt's attackers were now indistinguishable forms that had faded into the darkness. And, a subsequent quick look around by the officers identified no witnesses. Even if there had been witnesses, the police knew they would probably not have stayed around long enough to answer questions. Here, cries for help had most recently been answered with drawn curtains and turned-out lights rather than helping hands. No one wanted to get involved.

Frightened and exhausted after running, Natasha finally arrived at the entrance of the quaint little neighborhood restaurant where she and Matt had been headed prior to the attack. She knew the owners and felt secure in slipping in there to use their phone. As she entered, the owners noted her condition and immediately helped her into the back, where she could sit down. They tried to give her something hot to drink, but Natasha shook her head. Her only concern at the moment was to get to a telephone.

Taking her wallet from her coat pocket and frantically rummaging through it, she finally located Sergei's card. Now, if she could only get in touch with him. She dialed the number. There was no answer on the first few rings. She realized that it was after his normal working hours, but she thought if she let it ring long enough, someone might get tired of listening to it and pick it up. Her persistence paid off. One of Sergei's fellow investigators finally answered.

As he listened, Natasha spoke rapidly, almost hysterically, saying this was an emergency and she had to get in touch with Sergei immediately. The investigator asked her to slow down, and told her that Sergei had gone out for dinner, but that he would try to contact him. First, he needed her name and the number where she could be reached. Natasha gave him her name, and looking down, she read him the number on the telephone. She told him that she would be at that number for at least the next hour or two. Still frantic, although a bit calmer now, she pleaded, "Please! I have to talk to him. It is a matter of life and death!"

Sergei and Nick were just beginning to settle in for their evening out at one of Sergei's favorite watering holes when he felt the vibrating. He had grown to loathe that feel, and because of so many recent calls, had instructed them to use it only when there was something that demanded his immediate attention. As far as he was concerned, if it could wait until the next day, so be it.

Sergei called the office and spoke with the duty investigator. "A woman had called saying it was an emergency and left a number. She said her name was Natasha Federova."

Sergei jotted down the number and as soon as he hung-up, started dialing. "Natasha, this is Sergei. What is the matter?"

She began to ramble hysterically.

"Slow down, Natasha. You are talking too fast."

"Okay. Okay."

"Now, take a deep breath," Sergei instructed her.

"All right. I did."

"Slowly, Natasha. Now, tell me again."

Still rattled, she started over. "We were attacked. They had guns! I think they shot Matt!"

"Okay, Natasha, now take another deep breath."

She sobbed, "All right."

"Now slowly, tell me where you are."

Upset and confused, she looked up from where she was sitting and asked the owner if he would take the phone and give Sergei the address. The owner agreed, and after giving him directions, handed the phone back to Natasha.

Listening to her continued sobs, Sergei could tell he was not going to be able to get much more from her over the phone. "Natasha, stay where your are. Nick and I are on our way."

"Get your coat," Sergei told Nick. "It sounds like Matt may have been shot! I will explain on the way."

Nick grabbed his coat, reached in his pocket, and quickly threw down some rubles onto the table for the drinks they had ordered, and rushed after Sergei out the door.

If Sergei's actions back at the restaurant weren't enough of a clue to Nick as to the significance of the telephone conversation, his driving surely did. Sergei's normal driving was something to take notice of, but this ride was making anything before look like practice. As he raced down the dimly lit streets, Sergei explained to Nick the substance of his brief conversation with Natasha.

Sliding into a parking place near the front of the restaurant, Sergei jumped out of the Volga and went flying through the heavy, wooden door, with Nick following close behind. Upon seeing the two of them, the owner quickly ushered them into the back where Natasha was sitting.

When Natasha saw Sergei, she jumped to her feet and held out her arms and cried, "Sergei, Sergei, it was so terrible!"

Sergei held her, and Natasha once again broke down crying. With her head on his shoulder, he gently patted her on the back and began talking quietly, trying to calm her. When he was finally able to get her seated at the table, Sergei quickly introduced Nick and asked her to tell them what happened.

Natasha explained, "While Matt and I were walking to this restaurant, a group of mean-looking guys suddenly came up from behind. They had guns. They surrounded us and started yelling, 'Down with FBI!' I thought they were going to kill both of us," she sobbed. "Matt told me he was going to try to get them to chase him, and when he made his move, I was to try and escape in the opposite direction. That was the last time I saw him." Her head dropped.

"Okay. You are doing fine," Sergei told her. "Go ahead."

After re-gaining some composure, she continued, telling them that while she was running, she heard gunshots echoing in the distance. When she glanced back into the darkness she could not see Matt, but did see what looked like their attackers standing around doing something.

"Can you take us to where you last saw Matt? Sergei asked.

"Yes! Yes!" Natasha responded, jumping up and grabbing her coat. "We must go now!"

The three of them thanked the restaurant owner for his kindness and went quickly out the door and into the car. It was only a couple of turns before they were back onto the street where Natasha and Matt had been walking.

Sitting in middle of the backseat and leaning over the front seat between where Sergei and Nick were sitting, Natasha pointed straight ahead. "I think it is where that blue light is flashing. Yes, that is about where we were attacked."

Sergei stopped in front of the dirty white and blue patrol car parked on the street. Standing in the crisp cold were officers from the beat patrol and their radio car back up. Sergei immediately identified himself and held out his badge. These officers were awaiting the arrival of a team of investigators that had been called to the scene and thought

Sergei and Nick might have been that team. Sergei quickly explained that they were not, but were very concerned about what had happened.

The two radio car officers explained that they were the first to arrive on the scene. Beat patrol officers in the area had heard what they believed were shots fired and had summoned them. As they had approached, their headlights had shown on what appeared to be a body lying in the snow, and a group of silhouettes running into the darkness. When the officers got out of their car, they found a man lying on the ground. He was still alive, but unconscious, and was bleeding from what appeared to be at least one gunshot wound. They had called for an ambulance and it had left with the victim about ten minutes earlier, taking him to the area hospital.

Sergei asked if they knew who the man was, and they responded that they did not, other than he was an American official. They could not read any of his English language identification, but they did find a card in his pocket. It read (in Russian), "This is an American official representing the government of the United States in an official capacity. Any questions should be directed to the American Embassy in Moscow."

"Any witnesses or suspects," Sergei asked.

The officers shook their heads.

Sergei gave them his card and told the officers to call him immediately with any, and he emphasized "any" additional information they might learn.

Praying that Matt was still alive, the three of them ran back to the black Volga and headed for the hospital.

CHAPTER TWENTY-TWO

It had been only a few hours since Catherine and Darren had returned to his hotel room for a passionate romp after another evening out. Catherine left in the early morning with a promise to return for the meeting with the three Russians. Her seductive ploy seemed to be working well beyond what even she had anticipated, and with each encounter, his desire for her grew more intense.

As she entered the hotel's main lobby, Catherine looked ravishing as ever, still able to turn the head and capture the eye of most every man in sight. At the restaurant, the maitre d'hôtel escorted them to a table overlooking a winter wonderland of beautifully carved ice sculptures.

Since his previous meeting with Yuri, Mikhail, and Leonid in the hotel bar, Kroft had been contemplating their offer and struggling with the decision he was going to be making very shortly. He had discussed their proposal with Catherine earlier and she had agreed to join him at this upcoming meeting.

It was almost time for the scheduled gathering. Darren and Catherine went into the bar and settled into the same booth he had previously occupied with the three men. When the others arrived, Kroft raised his hand, motioning for them to come over. He introduced Catherine to the men, and much to his surprise, they already knew her. Seeing that, he was temporarily taken aback by this familiarity, but Catherine calmly explained to him that she worked with the same organization.

When he got over the initial shock of this revelation, Darren was both relieved and hopeful. Through this business venture, he might be able to keep this affair with Catherine alive for years to come. He had come to Russia to find a bride, but now marriage did not seem so important. He knew he wanted to be with Catherine --- married or not. From what he had already observed, she seemed to have everything. Not only was she beautiful, but she also appeared to be very well off financially. She wore expensive clothes, had very fine jewelry, and drove a sleek sports car that he could only dream of owning one day. If he were to really become a CEO, and over time receive compensation in the millions of dollars, as the three Russians were suggesting, then that might be enough for him to keep her. And, he didn't care where they lived, Russia, the U.S., or some distant, out of the way island paradise, it didn't really matter. All he knew was that he wanted to be with her.

Yuri began their meeting in traditional Russian fashion by lifting his glass of vodka and making a long-winded toast. Darren noticed that there never seemed to be a shortage of vodka flowing in Moscow. Mikhail followed with a second, and now it was Kroft's turn. Because his was the third, Darren remembered this toast was to be directed to the women, present or absent. He looked into Catherine's eyes as he gave the toast, and she smiled at him approvingly. Before the toasting was concluded, they would all be responsible for proposing at least one toast. Unknown to Darren, though, he would be the only one taking all of the drinks straight. Catherine and her Russian associates were periodically substituting water for all or part of their vodka.

After a call for bottoms up was announced and Kroft downed what he thought was to be the his last vodka, Yuri looked him squarely in the eyes, and asked, "Have you come to a decision regarding our proposal, Mr. Kroft?"

As Yuri stared steadily at him, Darren began to fidget, looking first at Yuri, then over to Catherine, and then back to Yuri. He asked, nervously, "Will I be able to work with Catherine?"

Looking him in the eye, Catherine responded, "I will be able to work with you, Darren, but I must remain in Moscow."

Darren looked disappointed.

Noting his reaction, she quickly added, "But, we will still be able to talk to each other over the telephone, and when you come here on trips, we will be together."

That thought of regular business trips to Moscow was all it took. With his heart pounding, Kroft looked back to Yuri and said, "You're organization has a new partner!"

Catherine put her arm around Darren and gave him a kiss on the cheek.

Yuri and Mikhail summoned the waitress to fill the glasses again, and offered a toast welcoming their new computer guru into the business.

Darren asked, "How? When? Where will my company be started?"

Yuri answered, "The 'where' is easy. You will remain in Denver, Colorado. The 'how' and the 'when' will be coordinated through our people there. You will be contacted."

Darren nodded.

Yuri continued, "You must never tell anyone about any of this or any of us. Do you understand?"

Again, he nodded, "I understand."

"Telling anyone about our relationship could be worth your life!" Mikhail added.

As the five of them enjoyed several more rounds of vodka toasting, it was apparent Darren was becoming intoxicated.

While the others were getting up to leave, Catherine blew into Darren's ear and whispered, "Well, Mr. CEO, I think it is time for us to go to your room and celebrate."

Darren smiled and gave a slurred response, "Lesh go, pardner!"

She laughed, as they finished off what remained in their glasses and Catherine took his hand, leading him over to the hotel elevators.

CHAPTER TWENTY-THREE

Matt was lying unconscious on a gurney in the emergency room and awaiting surgery when Nick, Sergei, and Natasha arrived at the hospital. The medical staff had stopped the bleeding, but the doctors would not speculate as to a prognosis regarding his recovery and would say only that his condition was stable. Victor Gorski arrived shortly thereafter and once he had been able to sketch together details from the other three, he called the Embassy. He spoke with the Ambassador and the Press Office. He had his secretary send an immediate message to Bureau Headquarters. A special attention line was directed to the FBI Academy and its International and Investigative Training Units.

The four of them remained at the hospital throughout most of the night. Sergei requested that MVD officers be assigned to perform round-the-clock protection of Matt's room. When the first team arrived shortly before daybreak, Nick told Sergei and Natasha to go home and get some rest. He and Victor would begin taking shifts at the hospital. One of them would always be there. He would call the others if there were any change.

Initially, both Sergei and Natasha resisted this idea of leaving, but Nick pointed out there wasn't anything they could do, and they needed to get some rest. He again reassured them that he would call if there were any change.

Reluctantly, the two of them agreed, and left. Sergei told Natasha he would take her to her apartment. From there he would go home and clean up before returning to the classroom to brief those attending the training program about what had happened. The course would obviously have to be concluded at this point, but Sergei would tell them that he hoped arrangements could be made with the FBI Academy for it to be rescheduled at a later date.

Sitting prayerfully with his head in his hands, Nick took the first shift. He kept mulling over the events of the previous evening. If they had only low-keyed the program, if the Russian media hadn't shown their faces on the evening news, and if the four of them had gone to dinner together.... The "what ifs," and the "this versus that" scenarios were running rampant through his mind.

By late afternoon, Victor had returned to the hospital with sandwiches, a couple more bottles of water and a thermos of hot coffee. Nick had refused to leave the room except for the time it took for him to give blood. As a result, he was a little weak. He had had nothing but a bottle of water to drink and a hard roll to eat since the previous afternoon. The food and drinks were most welcome.

The doctor who had come into the room earlier in the day explained to Nick, through an interpreter, that the bullet had gone completely through a fleshy part of the shoulder and had fortunately missed striking any vital organ or a major blood vessel. The surgery had been relatively uncomplicated and they believed successful. The kicks to his head and torso, however, were another story. These had produced a concussion, broken ribs, numerous cuts and bruises, and other external and internal injuries. This doctor and the others who had attended to Matt were still uncertain as to the total extent of those injuries. He did explain, though, that when Matt regained consciousness, he might experience a temporary loss of memory and have blurred vision and headaches, but hopefully nothing more serious. Nick knew that only time would tell.

As the four of them sat in Matt's room somberly hoping and praying for signs of improvement, Natasha broke the silence. She told them about her new job at the social club and the conversation she overheard the night they broadcast the FBI agents' pictures across the Moscow evening news.

She had told them earlier about their attackers yelling, "Down with FBI!" as they were surrounded, but had forgotten to mention either her new employment at the social club or her note to Matt concerning the conversation she had overheard.

Sergei rattled off a series of questions. "Try to remember anything you can about what went on that evening at the social club. Exactly what did they say? Do you know any of them? Had you ever seen any of them before?"

Natasha again recounted the events as she had described them to Matt shortly before the attack. Because she did not know any of the attackers or those involved in the conversation at the social club, she could not be of much help. She did tell Sergei that she would probably recognize them if she saw them again, though.

Sergei asked, "When do you go back to work?"

"I called in sick tonight, but after this, I will probably never return. Last night was my night off and that was how I was able to meet Matt for dinner."

"Natasha, I cannot tell you to continue to work at that club, but it might be the only way for us to find out who did this to Matt. You can be my eyes and ears there. Working will also give you money to continue to live on."

Noting a look of doubt on Natasha's face, Sergei added, "If you ever again see any of those guys who were talking at the club that night or who were involved in the attack, you

142

call me immediately and I will handle it. You should not try to do anything yourself, and I promise they will never know it was you who told me."

Still holding tightly onto Matt's hand and looking down at him, tears came to her eyes as she responded, "All right, I will stay. I would do anything for Matt."

One of the nurses who had talked with Victor earlier that evening came back into the room and motioned for him to come over.

When he returned, Victor told everyone, "No more than two of us can stay in the room at a time, so I guess that means the waiting room for the others." Looking over at Sergei, Victor asked, "Can you stay here while we get Nick moved."

Both Sergei and Natasha responded simultaneously, "Yes, certainly." They both wanted to be there as long as there was any need.

With the violent attack on Matt, and Natasha's description of the events leading up to it at the social club, Victor realized that he needed to make some changes in the way the FBI was doing business in Moscow. He turned to Nick and said, "Let's get you moved out of the hotel. You can stay at my place in the Embassy compound."

Nick nodded that would be fine.

When they arrived at the hotel, Nick and Victor went to the registration desk. Nick asked the clerk to prepare the bills for himself and Matt Kelly, because they would be checking out. The clerk noted the necessary information, and with a shy smile, commented that she was going to miss seeing Mr. Kelly around the hotel. Nick nodded that he understood. She gave the keys for both rooms to Nick and assured him everything would be prepared by the time they got things packed and returned downstairs. Their first stop was Nick's room. It was obvious to them, as soon as they opened the door that someone had been in there, looking for what, he didn't know. There certainly was no need for him to go through the routine of checking out the items he had so strategically placed in his bags and clothing drawers to detect intruders. Things were strewn all over the room, and there was a large, bold-print message scrawled across the bathroom mirror that said, "*SMERTZ FBI.*" Nick and Victor hurriedly gathered up his things and went to Matt's room.

On their way, Nick turned to Victor and asked, "What did that say on the mirror?"

"Death to the FBI," Victor answered.

As expected, Matt's room had also been trashed. On the bathroom mirror was that same message, "*SMERTZ FBI,*" and his belongings were scattered in even greater disarray than were Nick's. The two agents once again gathered everything up as best they could, and called for a bellman to help them get everything downstairs and into Victor's car.

As Nick was clearing both his and Matt's bills, he heard a voice that sounded vaguely familiar. The man was checking for messages. He looked over and saw the man he had been sitting next to on the flight from Dulles to Frankfurt. At about that same time Kroft also looked over, and they proceeded to re-introduce themselves.

"Nick Costigan," he said as he extended his hand.

"Darren Kroft. Surprised I haven't seen you here before."

"It's a big hotel. I guess that's probably why. Have you enjoyed your stay?" asked Nick.

"Very much so. And, I don't expect this to be my last visit," Kroft responded, as he caught Nick's eye and gave a nod and a wink in Catherine's direction, as if to say, "You see what I mean, don't you?"

"Oh?" acknowledged Nick quizzically.

"Yes, you see, I now have a beautiful business partner here in Moscow." Looking toward Catherine and then back at Nick, Kroft introduced her. "Catherine, this is Nick Costigan. He's the man I sat beside during our flight across the Atlantic."

Nick did a double-take. "It's a pleasure to meet you," he said with a smile.

Catherine gave an alluring glance and replied, "Likewise, I am sure."

Seeing the look in her eyes as she gazed at Nick, Kroft quickly took Catherine by the hand and yelled back, "Gotta go. Maybe we'll meet again someday."

As she was being whisked off in the direction of the bar, Catherine looked back at Nick and winked as she mouthed, "I certainly hope so."

Nick asked himself, "Could this really be happening to me?" It was Matt, who was the magnet when it came to attracting women, not him, and this made him a bit suspicious. In all of his years as an FBI agent, no woman had ever come close to going out of her way to make a serious pass or come on strongly to him. Not that he had noticed anyway. Sure, he heard stories from agents about being approached by those of the opposite sex, but from his experience, most of them must have been just that, stories. With the exception of Matt and a couple of other agents Nick had known over the years, he believed that most were doing nothing more than fantasizing.

Nick couldn't say he wasn't flattered, however, by this brief bit of attention Catherine had shown toward him, but she was gone and it was now time for him to get back to the business at hand. Pen in hand and his glasses adjusted, he checked over his and Matt's hotel bills.

Being a CPA, Nick normally fancied himself as being somewhat of a financial guru, but when it came to figuring out these bills he felt he had met his match. There didn't seem to be any large discrepancies, though, and he didn't have time to wait to go over them in more detail, so he accepted them as they were. He signed the credit card receipts and Victor and he were on their way to the Embassy.

While riding in the car, Nick asked himself, "Why would a knockout like Catherine be interested in some guy like Darren Kroft? What kind of a business could she be in with him?"

Back in the hotel bar, Darren blurted out to Catherine, "I think you should know. That guy told me that he works for the U.S. Justice Department. He's probably some kind of bureaucratic mope there, but my sense is that Yuri and Mikhail would not want us to get too close to people who work in places like that."

"You are probably right, lover boy," she responded.

Catherine saw that Darren was quickly working himself into a jealous rage. She had purposely given that flirtatious look and wink in Nick's direction to see what reaction she would get from Darren, and was now enjoying every minute of the fallout it had created.

"Let's change the subject away from him and get back to us," Darren told her, asking, "What kind of work do you do for the organization?"

"I'm involved with, among other things, helping to operate the social club."

"The club, that's nice," he responded, "and what are the other things?"

"There are a variety. You see, although our organization is headquartered here in Moscow, we are a worldwide network. We and our associates are very active in areas such as banking, securities, telecommunications, real estate, hotels, casinos, and, of course, the social clubs with their bars and restaurants."

Darren asked, "Why do they need me? What is it that I can give them?"

"We are trying to get a greater foothold in American computer consulting as it relates to the financial industry. You know, businesses like banking and securities."

Darren nodded that he understood.

"We believe your expertise will be most helpful to us in our achieving that goal, and your being from Denver was also a big plus. When you return home, you will be working with a man named Alexander. All of us call him Sasha. He oversees our activities there and he will be in regular contact with you regarding the establishment of your new business. Any problems you experience should be discussed directly with him. Sasha's people will take care of everything."

"Ok-a-a-ay," Darren hesitatingly responded.

"By the way," she asked, "when is your flight back to the United States?"

"Day after tomorrow"

Catherine stuck out her lower lip and dropped her head indicating sadness. "So, I guess that means there is not much time left for us to be together here, is there?"

Darren's head dropped.

She smiled, "So, I guess we will just have to make the most of the time we have left."

He grinned as he lifted his head, and with excited anticipation, said, "It sure does!"

CHAPTER TWENTY-FOUR

Nick and Victor left their bags at the LEGAT's residence in the Embassy compound and walked to his office where they would check for any incoming messages from the Bureau.

On top of the stack was a highlighted sheet marked, "Immediate Action Required." Victor read the message and handed it to Nick. FBI Headquarters was advising them that a U.S. Air Force medical evacuation flight would be arriving in Moscow early the following morning to take Matt and Nick to an American airbase and medical treatment center in Germany.

Victor assured Nick that he would personally take care of the necessary Embassy coordination and ambulance transportation arrangements as soon as he returned from taking Nick back to the hospital.

At the hospital, Sergei reported that there was no change. The nurse did tell him that Matt's vitals appeared to be improving a little, however.

When Nick broke the news that he and Matt would be leaving for Germany early the following morning, tears came to Natasha's eyes. She excused herself and eased her way through the door and into his room. Times of crisis have always been known for bonding people together, and this was certainly no exception. Since their first contacts, Sergei and Natasha had grown especially close to Matt, and while Nick's time with them had been considerably shorter, he too, had formed an instant bond with the two of them. There was no question that they were all going to miss each other.

When Nick entered Matt's room, he found Natasha sitting at his bedside. She was holding his hand and leaning over whispering into his ear. Her feelings were obvious, and she remarked to Nick that she intended to remain there with Matt as long as she could. She certainly understood the reason for transferring him to an American hospital in Germany, but that still did not make it any easier for her.

Nick went back out and told Sergei that Victor was coordinating the final arrangements through the Embassy. He also mentioned that he had already cleared their hotel rooms and bills, and that Victor would be bringing their bags with him when they went to the airport. It looked as though everything was set.

CHAPTER TWENTY-FIVE

The nurses and ambulance transport staff had gathered outside Matt's room and told everyone they were ready. Sergei and the two MVD officers standing guard outside Matt's room would take the lead and escort them to the airport. Victor and Nick would follow in the Bureau car. This time both agents were armed, as Victor had brought along his old .357 revolver for Nick to carry.

Natasha asked if she could ride in the ambulance with Matt. The medical staff initially opposed her request, but that was, until Sergei inserted himself into the discussion. He told them that he wanted her to ride with Matt, and that she could act as his interpreter should he regain consciousness. Rather than arguing, the staff nodded in agreement.

Early morning was the best time for this type of movement. They didn't have to worry about getting bogged down in the heavy, stop-and-go traffic that was present most of the rest of the day. Knowledge of the transfer had also been kept under heavy wraps so that only those who had a need to know were provided with the details. Included were members of the American Embassy staff, the MVD, the hospital and transport staff, and of course those coordinating the movement at the airport.

Fortunately, their movement to the airport went without incident and sitting there on the tarmac was a most welcome sight. A gray and black United States Air Force plane with those beautiful stars and stripes painted on its tail.

As they were getting ready to transfer Matt from the ambulance, Natasha gave him a tender kiss. With tears streaming down her cheeks, she whispered in his ear, "I will never forget you for as long as I live," and quickly climbed out of the ambulance and ran over to where Nick and Sergei were standing nearby.

As the U.S. Air Force Medical team was moving Matt from the ambulance and onto the plane, Nick looked at Sergei and the two of them exchanged traditional Russian bear hugs, vowing to meet again, and continue the course. Natasha looked at Nick and smiled through her tears. Giving him a kiss on the cheek, she told Nick, "Take good care of him."

"You know I will," Nick assured her. "You be sure to take care of yourself, and above all, be careful!"

Natasha nodded solemnly that she would.

Nick consoled her, adding, "Sergei and Victor have our telephone numbers at the Academy. You be sure and stay in touch with them, so we know how you're doing."

"I will," she promised.

As the engines churned, the dirt and paper littering the area began to blow across the tarmac. It was time for Nick to board. He handed Victor the .357, and the two shook hands at the doorway. As soon as Victor was out of the way, Nick waved good-bye to everyone, and Natasha blew Matt a kiss. The crew chief closed the door, and Natasha, Sergei, and Victor watched as the plane moved from the taxiway to the runway and then disappeared into the clouds.

While driving them back to the hospital parking lot where Sergei had left the black Volga, Victor asked Natasha if she needed a ride back to her apartment.

She told him, "Thanks, but Sergei already offered and it is on his way."

"I will call you. We can get together," Sergei told Victor. "We have little information on the shooting, but our guys will squeeze everything they can out of their informants."

"We all appreciate that, Sergei."

"You can assure your FBI Headquarters in Washington that we in the MVD are doing everything we can, and I guarantee you that we will be successful."

"I will let them know," Victor assured him.

Sergei then added, "Other than you, Nick and Matt are the only FBI agents any of us have ever known. As you can imagine, throughout the old USSR there were so many negative jokes and stories about FBI agents that no one was really sure what the truth was. Nick and Matt have now changed much of that for us. We were able to see that you guys are much like us and the only way we can get things done is by working together. I can assure you, there isn't one MVD officer who attended that class who will forget either of them."

Shaking hands, Victor responded, "Thank you, Sergei, I'll pass that along. I know it will mean a lot to them."

CHAPTER TWENTY-SIX

During the air-evac from Moscow, Matt slowly regained consciousness, and started asking Nick about where he was and what had happened. As Nick began filling him in on the details, an announcement was made that their flight would be landing momentarily at Ramstein AFB in western Germany. From there, the agents would be taken by ambulance to the military hospital at nearby Landstuhl Regional Medical Center.

As the ambulance turned onto the road leading to the hospital, the adrenaline rush that had kept Nick going during the past couple of days seemed to have suddenly left and he was beginning to feel like warmed-over death.

Soon after entering the hospital's emergency room, Matt heard a familiar voice from the past approaching his transport bed. "Matt Kelly. This can't be the same one I know. He would have had at least two gorgeous babes hanging from each arm."

"Bill. Bill Bradshaw, is that you?" Matt groggily responded.

It was indeed, Lieutenant Colonel William Bradshaw, M.D., United States Air Force. Matt and Bill had been roommates at the Air Force Academy, and after their graduation, there had been some question as to whether things at the Academy would ever be the same. Both had Grade Point Averages (GPA's) that well exceeded their Military Performance Averages (MPA's), and each had also achieved "centurion" status while at the Academy for having had to march over one hundred, one-hour tours with a rifle, for a variety of Academy infractions. Being a model cadet was obviously a status neither of them ever achieved.

After reading the summary prepared by the medical crew on the air-evac transport and again checking Matt's vitals, Dr. Bradshaw sent him for x-rays. After those were completed, and no serious internal injuries were identified, the doctor began his comprehensive examination.

He began removing the heavy bandaging, and after checking the area around the bullet wound, commented, "So far, so good." Next, he and the nurses cleaned and re-dressed the areas around the cuts and the bullet wound. When the examination was finished, Matt was wheeled off into a room where he could finally get some much-needed rest.

Nick met with Dr. Bradshaw after Matt finally fell asleep. He wanted to get as much information as he could to pass along to Matt's parents in Los Angeles and to send back to Bureau HQ and Quantico. The doctor explained that considering all that had happened, Matt was actually doing better than he'd expected. They would continue to care for him and monitor his progress for the next few days, and, as soon as he was well enough to travel, they would transfer him back to the States. There, it was anticipated he would continue his recovery at home, with a visiting nurse checking on him daily.

After reporting all he had learned from Dr. Bradshaw to their FBI Academy unit chief, it was agreed that Nick would remain in Germany with Matt until his return home. Now, it was finally time for Nick to get some much-needed rest. This was the longest he could remember having gone without sleep since his yearlong Army tour as an MP Company Commander in Vietnam.

In the days that followed, Matt continued to improve rapidly. After finishing his latest updates to Matt's parents and those at Quantico, Nick placed calls to both Victor and Sergei in Moscow, hoping to reach them before they left their offices for the day.

Victor was out. His secretary told Nick that he had been called out on a case in Ukraine, so Nick left the information with her. When he placed the call to the MVD and asked for Sergei, Nick was told that he had gone to a funeral, but they expected him back later, and a message would be left for him to call Nick upon his return.

It was evening in Moscow before Sergei returned to his office. Seeing the message left on his desk, he returned the call and to his surprise was actually able to get through.

"Nick, this is Sergei."

Having been awakened from a much needed late afternoon nap, Nick groggily responded, "Good to hear your voice, Sergei."

"Sounds like I woke you up. Sorry about taking so long to get back to you, but I just received your message." Sergei paused to take another long drag from his cigarette before continuing, "Today I was with Natasha. Her grandmother was buried."

"How did she handle it?"

"It was difficult. She made several very emotional remarks at the cemetery, before completely breaking down. She was doing a little better when I left."

"It was good that you were able to be there with her, Sergei. I don't know what she would have done without you. From what you and Matt said, she loved her grandmother very much, and there didn't seem to be anyone else in her life."

"That was until Mister FBI came along," chuckled Sergei.

"Oh yeah, how could I ever forget that?" replied Nick. "Who else attended the funeral?"

"Only the priest and some neighbors."

"That was all?" Nick asked.

Sergei paused. "No, there was a woman standing some distance away from us in the shadow of a large tree. We could not tell for sure who she was and did not know why she was there. She was dressed very nicely and had a black mesh veil covering her face. Once we went back to the cars and were getting ready to leave, she walked over to the graveside and knelt beside it. After dropping a single rose into the grave, she got up and left. Neither of us had any idea who she was or why she was there."

"That is strange," Nick agreed. "Again, it is good you were able to be there. You are a good friend, Sergei."

"How is Matt?"

"He appears to be progressing well. The doctor seems optimistic."

"That is great news and I will pass it along to Natasha," Sergei replied. "Be sure to tell him that we were asking about him. She has already started calling me, sometimes twice a day, to find out if I have heard from you two."

"I'll be sure to pass that along," Nick chuckled. "Anything else?" he asked.

"Yes, one other thing. Tell Matt that I finally got a report back from the lab on that crumpled piece of paper he gave me, and they did get some good prints. That is the good news."

"And the bad," Nick asked.

"The bad news is we cannot identify whom they belong to. Not now, anyway. But, as you well know, once we get suspects, those prints might make the case."

"Right, I'll pass all of that along to Matt when I see him later tonight."

"It was good to talk with you, Nick. Give Matt my best. And, oh yes, Natasha's too. She would not be happy with me if I forgot to say that."

"I will. Good bye, Sergei."

CHAPTER TWENTY-SEVEN

Enjoying a cigarette while sitting on a stool at an empty bar in the social club, Catherine had just gotten off the phone with Darren Kroft. After brief stops in Frankfurt, Germany, and Washington, DC, he had arrived safely back in Denver and was awaiting a call from the man known to him only as Sasha, or Alexander.

"Another one down," she said to herself, reflecting on her most recent triumph. There was no question in her mind that Darren was smitten. He was already whining, telling her how much he missed her and how much he wanted to be with her. In fact, he told her that no sooner had he cleared the immigration and customs checkpoints upon his arrival back in the States at Washington-Dulles, than he was already trying to figure out a way to make his return to Moscow to be with her.

That was the last thing Catherine had on her mind, however. As far as she was concerned, Darren Kroft was now nothing more than another statistic; a sniveling wimp whose love handles she hoped would never again have to be clutched by her in a feigned passion. Furthermore, if having sex with him hadn't been enough to turn her stomach, his immature puppy-love antics certainly would have, but he was not the first to have acted this way toward her. Over the years, there had been numerous others.

"What putty men are in my hands," she thought. "How could these diplomats, foreign agents, military officers, business executives, and others ever consider giving up their families and everything they had worked so hard for and built their lives and reputations around just for a chance to get in the sack with me?"

Was she really that good? She did not know, but she could certainly attest to the fact that she had never been with a man who was so incredible that she would risk it all for him.

CHAPTER TWENTY-EIGHT

Dr. Bradshaw left a message at the nurses' station that he wanted to see Nick when he came in to visit Matt.

Nick knocked on the closed door.

"Come in," the doctor called out.

Nick opened the door and saw Dr. Bradshaw sitting behind his desk doing some paperwork. "Thanks for coming by, Nick. I have good news. Matt's recovery has been moving faster than any of us would have ever expected. I'm ready to release him for transport back to the States on one of our flights."

"That sounds great," responded Nick. "Does Matt know?"

"I told him late last night when I stopped by to tuck him in," the doctor quipped. "You know I'm going to miss having him around. It has been great to see him and talk about the 'good old days' when we roomed together at Camp USAFA."

"Sounds like you two really enjoyed it there," Nick remarked.

"Yeah," Dr. Bradshaw smiled and sarcastically agreed.

"Thanks, Doc. I'll see what flights I can get and be back to see Matt before he leaves."

"I'll be sending instructions with him, but just so you know. When he gets back, he should stay home to recuperate. You'll need to arrange for a doctor to see him regularly and have a nurse come by each day to check on him and change his bandages."

"I'll call the medical unit at FBI Headquarters from here before I leave, and then go into DC to see them as soon as I get back."

Nick left and caught a ride to the base commercial airline office where he was able to get his return ticketed for that same day. After that, he located a phone and called FBI Headquarters and the Academy to alert them of his and Matt's return to Washington.

In the meantime, Dr. Bradshaw went on his morning rounds. Upon entering Matt's room, he found him joking and clowning around with an audience of nurses who had gathered nearby.

The doctor smiled, "Don't let the antics deceive you. His moves date back to the days when we were cadets at the Academy and he was trying to impress the Colorado coeds. He's had a lot of practice."

The nurses laughed.

"You didn't have to tell them that, Doc."

"Oh, but I did," responded Dr. Bradshaw with a smile. "Remember, I'm responsible for protecting the welfare of our nursing staff. Besides, as I told you last night, you're okay to travel and are on your way out of here."

"When?" Matt sighed.

"The next flight home"

The nurses let out with a joint sigh, and Matt laughed. "Can't I stay around for just a few more days, Bill?" he asked. "Let me temporarily act as your Welfare and Morale Officer."

"That's all I would need," laughed the doctor.

As Nick entered Matt's room, there was no question in his mind that Matt was feeling much better.

"I'm on a flight out of here later today and I'll be seeing you as soon as we get back home," Nick told Matt.

"What then," asked Matt.

"I've already talked with the medical unit at HQ, and they, along with the Academy nurses, will be handling your recuperation. One of the Academy nurses will be going by your place to check on you and change your bandages daily. I just got off of the phone with them a few minutes ago, and they said to give you their best, and that they would be sure to take good care of you."

"Well, I guess that rules out any malingering," Matt chuckled.

"You said it," Nick agreed.

"Sounds like they're just what's going to be needed for this special case," quipped Dr. Bradshaw.

CHAPTER TWENTY-NINE

Although not working since his return to Denver, Darren remained reluctant to quit his job. He wanted to make sure that this new business opportunity was for real, first.

He had gone skiing for the day and, when he returned that evening, noticed the light on his answering machine flashing. When he pressed the button, he heard a deep male voice say in broken English, "Call the Ruble Bar and Restaurant. Ask for Sasha."

Darren had never heard of The Ruble Bar and Restaurant, but in a metropolitan area with a population approaching two million, that wasn't surprising. When he pulled out the Denver phone directory containing the "R" listings, he found page after page of restaurant listings. Running his finger down the list, he located a small print, two line, name, address, and phone listing only for "The Ruble." He went to his computer and looked up an Internet map site to see exactly where it was located.

He knew his way around the east and southeast suburban areas of Douglas and Arapahoe Counties reasonably well; however, much of the rest of the city was virtually unknown to him. Recently, he had moved from the sprawling eastern suburb of Aurora to a posh, new, yuppie singles' area that had sprouted up out on the southeast side, near the Denver Technological Center.

As the map came up on his computer screen, he could see that The Ruble Bar and Restaurant was located on the northwest side of Denver. It was in the city of Arvada, just off Wadsworth Boulevard, a main thoroughfare running through the western suburbs.

Darren called the number.

"Ruble Bar and Restaurant," answered the hostess.

"May I speak with Sasha," Kroft asked, hesitatingly.

"Just a minute, please."

"This is Sasha," a heavily accented, gruff, and gravelly voice sounded.

"This is Darren Kroft."

"Yes, Mr. Kroft. I have been waiting for your call," responded Sasha, in a somewhat friendlier tone. "We need to get together as soon as possible. Can you meet me here at the bar this evening?"

"Yes, sure," answered Kroft.

"Good. See you at eight?"

"Okay," Darren replied. "I'll be there. Good bye."

Upon entering The Ruble, Darren felt as though he were back in Moscow. The rooms were dimly lit and smoke-filled, and the atmosphere similar to that he had experienced in the Russian capital. There was traditional Russian music playing in the background and Russian photos and décor hanging on the walls. An attractive hostess approached and offered to seat him. He nodded at her and winked, all the time trying to act cool, and told her that he was there to meet with Sasha. She smiled, asking herself "is this guy for real," and escorted him to a booth near the back where Sasha was sitting. When Darren arrived at the table, a large intimidating looking man stood and extended his hand.

"Greetings, and welcome to The Ruble, Mr. Kroft. My name is Sasha."

Again, just as in Moscow, when he had met Leonid, Yuri, and Mikhail, there was no last name given, and Darren assumed that this was they way they wanted it.

Gripping his hand, Kroft responded, "I'm Darren, Darren Kroft."

Sasha gestured for him to be seated, and told the hostess to send over their waitress.

"Would you like a drink?" Sasha asked Kroft.

"Yes."

"Russian vodka?"

"That would be fine," Darren answered.

"Two vodkas," Sasha told the waitress.

She nodded and left.

Even though there was a manager assigned to run the day-to-day bar and restaurant operations, Sasha was the one who was really in charge. And, it was from this obscure and out-of-the-way ethnic bar, located in one of Denver's most western suburbs, that Sasha directed this gang of Russian mobsters in their western states' activities. Although still active in the traditional big-ticket organized crime areas of extortion, gambling, loan sharking, and drugs, their operations had now expanded into some of the more lucrative financial areas of staged accidents and insurance frauds, gasoline tax fraud, check frauds and kiting, health care fraud, and banking and securities frauds.

Sasha spoke in a very business-like tone, telling Darren, "I received word from my associates in Moscow that you met with them and are ready to begin work here."

Darren nodded that he was.

Sasha paused while the waitress set down their drinks, and waited to resume talking until after she had left. Picking right up where the conversation had left off, he continued, "Good. It is time for us to discuss business. As far as anyone will know, you are the sole owner of this business. Your name will be the one on the papers. But..." Sasha paused, "I think you know who your real partner is."

Darren once again nodded.

"Under no circumstances will you ever reveal our association to anyone. If you do..." Sasha slashed his open hand across his throat as if it were a knife.

"Do I make myself clear, Mr. Kroft?"

"You do. You have no need for concern," Darren assured him.

"Our people have been putting everything together."

Sasha didn't know all of the details, but their lawyers had been busy getting the required paperwork filed with the State, and they were also taking care of any necessary licensing. The office space was being coordinated through the real estate group that managed the organization's holdings and properties across the country. That office was also taking care of arranging for the furniture and other appointments. All of the required recordkeeping and accounting would be handled directly by one of their associated accounting operations.

"I think we have everything taken care of for you, Mr. Kroft."

Darren agreed, "I'm sure you have."

"Shortly, it will be your turn to start performing," Sasha remarked with a tone of intimidation in his voice.

"I'll be ready," Darren assured him.

Now satisfied that his new position as a CEO was secure, Darren would turn in his resignation to his current employer tomorrow morning.

CHAPTER THIRTY

Since his return to the States, the doctor had confined Matt's activities, requiring him to remain around his Occoquan village townhouse and doing nothing more strenuous than lifting a fork or glass, and scratching the neck and belly of his yellow Labrador retriever. His time was to be spent resting and relaxing.

The Academy nurses were faithfully arriving each day to change his bandages and monitor his progress. Today, the nurse told him that everything looked very good, but continued to implore him to limit his activity and get more rest. He told them he would, but this sitting around day after day was getting old, fast. Cabin fever had set in. He had no question in his mind that he was going to have to start doing more.

Opening the frost-covered, sliding glass door and walking out onto his wood deck, Matt peered out over the empty slips as they stretched across the frigid waters of the Occoquan River. His slip was located less than a block away from where he was standing, and he could hardly wait for the return of the cherry blossoms so he could take his boat out of storage.

Suddenly, the doorbell rang. Buddy rose from a sound sleep beside Matt's chair and gave a low bark.

"Just a minute," Matt yelled, as he walked from the back of the townhouse to the front door.

Matt opened the door. It was Nick. Buddy stretched up on his hind legs, his tail slapping against Matt's leg.

Nick grabbed the yellow lab by his front paws. "It's good to see you too, Buddy. I suspect if the truth were known, the real reason the nurses like to come by and check-up on Matt is to see you."

Matt sighed and reluctantly agreed, "You're probably right. Anything going on?" he asked.

"Nothing other than my trying to keep you out of trouble and get you back in the good graces of the Bureau," responded Nick.

Matt gave a quizzical look, "Why? What's happened now?" he asked.

"The Academy's security officer and the Bureau hierarchy seem to be having a little trouble understanding your after-hours involvement with a woman named Natasha Federova."

"You explained that it was 'liaison.' All for the good of the Bureau, and America's foreign relations, right?"

"I don't remember using those exact words," replied Nick, "but, yes, I hopefully got the point across."

"Well, I'm sure you did admirably. Besides, Nick, you're always up for a new challenge."

Nick smiled and shook his head. It seemed as though nothing ever bothered Matt.

"As they say, Nick, 'don't sweat the small stuff.' "

"I just hope they see it that way uptown," Nick responded.

"I'm sure they will," smirked Matt. "Remember, HQ keeps telling us this job requires sacrifice."

"Especially when that sacrifice involves coming to the aid of beautiful young women?" added Nick.

Matt smiled, "Especially then! Speaking of beautiful young women, have you heard anything from Moscow?"

"Victor called asking how you're getting along and said that the MVD has already requested our return to finish the course when you get well."

"That's good to hear."

"He's also talked with Sergei several times since we left and they're still looking for the guys who shot you."

"Do they know who they were?"

"As far as I know, no, but, they're still chasing down leads, and the Bureau has offered to help the MVD in anyway we can. With everything going down on their turf, though, that gets kind of touchy and they've indicated they'll handle it."

"I'm sure they're doing all they can. They'll get 'em."

"Oh, and by the way, Victor said that Natasha still calls him a couple of times a week to see if he has heard anything about how you're doing."

"Did he say anything about her?"

"Nothing other than she continues to work at the social club and is living in her grandmother's apartment."

"I'm thankful for that, but doesn't it seem strange those slime balls haven't come out of the woodwork and tried to kick her out yet? I'm beginning to wonder if whoever holds the paper on the apartment didn't get the word that Sergei and the MVD are snooping around and waiting for them."

"Probably so. If it hadn't been for you and Sergei, I think she would have been kicked out within days of her grandmother's death."

"Maybe even hours," shot back Matt.

"They probably figured they had better let things cool down for a while."

"I think you're right."

"Who knows. They may never try to enforce that contract."

"I sure hope they don't, for Natasha's sake. I'm worried about her, Nick."

"Me, too, but I feel a lot better knowing that Sergei is there looking out for her."

"They haven't moved our offices since I've been laid up, have they?"

"No such luck, but they did start to take down your 'love me' wall."

That bit of humor brought a rise from Matt and, along with it, a painful cough that made him grit his teeth as it still felt like his insides were tearing apart.

Over the years, their investigations had taken them into the offices of numerous high-level bureaucrats, public officials, and corporate executives. While there, they noticed that some of those officials had decorated not only their offices, but also the reception areas and sometimes even the conference rooms in what Matt and Nick had come to commonly refer to as an "I Love Me" motif. Included in this décor would be nearly every picture this particular executive had ever had taken with somebody "important." These photographs were usually signed and conspicuously placed on the walls in some sort of status hierarchy. Nick and Matt suspected the pecking order might change from time to time, depending on who was visiting or whom they were trying to impress at the time. In addition to the photos, there were also the standard diplomas, certificates, plaques, awards, and whatever else they could manage to squeeze into the space.

"No Matt, nothing's changed."

"Still no sign of daylight, either?" asked Matt.

"None. We're still residing in the upper-lower basement level of building nine.

"Any skylights in the offing, yet?"

Nick laughed, and shook his head, "None," adding, "But at least we're still above the lower-lower level and the Behavioral Science Unit, though."

The offices for the FBI Academy's Investigative Training Unit were located directly under the gun vault. Constructed at a level some ten feet below where they bury people, with no windows, a heavy steel vault-like door at the primary entrance, artificial light, and painted cinderblock walls, one might sometimes wonder which side of the law these people were on. The space had originally been designated as the emergency relocation site for J. Edgar Hoover and his executive assistants in case of national emergency. That was a long time ago, and over the years, the space had been re-allocated to meet the need for expanded office space and additional classroom requirements. It was still the place to be if a tornado ever came through, however.

When asked by officers attending the FBI National Academy and others about their office space, Matt and Nick often quipped, "We're either a very valuable Bureau commodity that needs to be protected, or else the Bureau may be just trying to hide us, keeping us out of sight and out of mind. We'll leave it up to you to draw your own conclusions."

"Well, time to go," Nick told Matt. "It looks like you're about to the point where you'll be able to start coming back into the office for at least a couple of hours each day."

Matt nodded, "That's the way I see it, too. Now, all I have to do is convince the doctor to release me."

As Nick was getting ready to leave, Buddy came to him and dropped a ball at his feet. Nick took the dog's hint and told him, "Okay, Buddy, we'll go out, but I'm going to have to leave before long."

When the door opened, Buddy saw his friend, Lieutenant Colonel Terry Draw, USMC, Ret. Buddy and his friend, the Colonel, had become very attached, as Terry let Buddy out during the day, and also kept him at his place whenever Matt was on the road.

Giving an excited wiggle, the yellow lab jumped off the porch and darted toward the driveway next door.

"Hi, Buddy," Terry said, as two front paws pounced off his chest and a bright green tennis ball dropped at his feet. Terry leaned down and rubbed Buddy's neck and front shoulders vigorously, until he rolled over on his back for his usual belly rub.

Nick looked over to Matt and laughed, "It looks like Buddy's found somebody else to play with, so I guess I'd better be getting back to the upper-lower level of building nine."

CHAPTER THIRTY-ONE

The doctors insisted that Matt work only part-time for the first week or two he was back at the Academy, but he persisted in trying to convince them he could do more. They finally gave in and told him to go ahead and do what he wanted, but that he had to be careful, and he would not be able to go back on the road until he was fully recovered. In the interim, Matt and Nick's teaching assignments would be confined to the Academy complex. They now spent most of their time co-teaching specialized In-Services and courses for the FBI National Academy Session. One course included an array of Financial Crimes, and the other Money Laundering, both areas of investigation they were intimately familiar with and included regularly in their international training programs.

The phone rang just as Matt was getting up from his desk to join some of his Academy colleagues for lunch in the Boardroom. It was his secretary. "Matt, I'm transferring a call from Moscow."

"Hello, hello, this is Matt Kelly."

"Hello, Matt, this is Sergei," the voice echoed from the other end. "I am sorry our connection is not better."

"That's okay. It's good to hear your voice, Sergei,"

"How are you feeling, Matt?"

"Great!"

"That is good to hear. Your friends here have been asking about you. We are all very concerned."

"Thanks, Sergei. Please give them my best and tell them I appreciate their concern."

"I will do that. Matt, I am sorry I have no arrest to report, but we will get who did that to you, I promise!"

"I know you will, Sergei," replied Matt.

"Matt, I also wanted to pass along something from Natasha that I thought you might be interested in."

Matt's voice perked up. "Okay!"

"Not that kind of interest," snickered Sergei, adding, "Not that she is no longer interested in you, I can assure you that she is. She does not tell me her feelings, but I can tell it in her voice. She calls me almost everyday asking if I have heard from you."

"That's good to hear, Sergei."

"But that is not the reason for this call, Matt. Last night, she overheard a conversation at the social club about an American who is working with a group of our mafia hoods. She thinks his name is 'Craft' or something like that, and that he is some kind of computer consultant. Natasha thought, from what she overheard, that he was over here about the same time as you and Nick were. It sounds like the mob is expecting this guy to steal millions from some type of computer scam he is running in Denver, Colorado. She didn't hear much more, but I thought you and Nick might like to know."

"Thanks, Sergei. I'll tell Nick."

"Remember, Matt, it might be nothing more than talk. But, I wanted you to know."

"I appreciate the call, Sergei, and we will look into it."

"Well, it is getting late here, and the 'intimidator' is expecting me home, so I had better say good-bye for now."

"Thanks again for the call, Sergei, and please tell Natasha that I am doing well, and she remains in my thoughts. Stay in touch."

"I will. Good-bye," Sergei responded.

On their way back from the Boardroom after lunch, Matt asked Nick to stop by his office. He wanted to fill him in on his conversation with Sergei. When he got to the point of telling Nick about this computer consultant named "Craft," from Denver, who was supposedly in Moscow about the same time as they were, Nick interrupted.

"There was a guy I sat next to on the flight from Dulles to Frankfurt. He told me he was some kind of computer guru, and, as best I can remember, that was his last name, and he was from Denver. In fact, I may I still have the business card he gave me. I'll look for it when I get back to my desk. Another ironical thing about this is that I ran into him, again, when I was checking us out of the hotel. He was with some knockout blonde. He introduced her as his new business partner. I thought 'business partner, sure.' The two of them just didn't fit. She didn't look like a typical hooker. She was class all the way, and to be seen with that guy? It just didn't add up."

Matt finished summarizing what Sergei had said, and Nick returned to his office to see if he could find the card.

Quickly thumbing through the group of cards he had gathered on their last trip, Nick found the one he was looking for. The name on the card read "Darren Kroft." If Kroft was now into a new business venture, the company name, address, phone and fax numbers, and e-mail address on this card were probably no longer valid, but that kind of information might still be helpful later.

He called Matt. "It's Darren Kroft, with a 'K'."

The two decided it was time for a conference call with the supervisors from both the Organized Crime and the White-Collar Crime Squads of the FBI's Denver Division. They needed to let them know what they had learned from Sergei.

"FBI, Denver," answered the operator.

"This is Nick Costigan from Quantico. Are the OC and White-Collar Supervisors in the office today?"

"Yes," responded the operator, "But their secretaries are holding their calls. They are in a meeting with the SAC (Special Agent in Charge) right now."

"Would you please try to set up a conference call for two o'clock, your time, today? Matt Kelly, who is also on the faculty here at Quantico, and I need to talk with the OC and White-Collar Supervisors."

"I'll try, Mr. Costigan," the operator replied.

"Thanks. We'll be waiting."

Promptly at four o'clock, Quantico time, the phones rang in both Nick's and Matt's offices. The operator said, "I have Supervisors Wallace and Cross on the line for a conference call."

"Thanks," responded Nick and Matt simultaneously, "Go ahead."

"Nick, this is Tom Wallace. Long time, no see."

The two of them had been classmates in New Agent Training and tried to keep in touch over the years, but their efforts had not always been successful.

"Marla Cross is on the line with me. She has just been re-assigned from HQ to be our White-Collar Supervisor. What's up, Nick?"

"While Matt Kelly and I were working in Moscow, we got to know a couple of Russian investigators pretty well.

They are assigned to an anti-mafia unit the MVD has created there."

"Sounds like mission impossible."

"Pretty much. It's tough, Tom, but they're giving it a good shot," replied Nick. "Matt received a call today from one of those MVD officers. Sergei told him about a conversation an informant of his recently overheard. The information centers around a computer consulting business that Russian OC is supposedly running in Denver. Word is they intend to steal millions."

There was a temporary interference in the line. "I don't know what that was, but we're still here, Nick. Go on."

"It sounds as though they have an American operating as their principal and, ironically, I think I may have met the guy while we were there. He introduced himself to me as Darren Kroft, that's 'D-a-r-r-e-n K-r-o-f-t.' He also gave me a business card and I'll fax a copy of that to you when we get off the phone. I doubt that he is with that company any longer, but at least you can put it into indices for reference purposes."

"Have you heard anything about this?" asked Nick.

"I haven't," answered Tom Wallace.

"Me, either," Marla Cross responded.

"We'll run his name and I'll put this out to the squad and see if any of our sources have picked up anything," Wallace assured Costigan.

"And, I'll have our squad check the on-line databases in connection with Colorado corporations, business licensing, and so forth," added the new White-Collar Crime Supervisor before hanging up.

CHAPTER THIRTY-TWO

Returning from class the following morning, Nick heard the phone ringing in his office and rushed down the hallway to get it.

"Costigan," he answered.

"Nick, Tom Wallace, in Denver."

"How are things in Paradise?" asked Nick.

Tom chuckled, "This is your paradise, not mine. But, everything is fine here."

Nick had grown up in Colorado, and during his earlier years in the Bureau he had kept his name on the Denver "OP" list as his FBI "Office of Preference." He had hoped to be re-assigned there someday, but with Bureau transfers they way they were, it hadn't happened, and likely never would.

"I have just a minute but want to let you know what we've learned so far. Marla Cross's squad did come up with something on that guy 'Darren Kroft.' Their database searches showed his name on a Colorado corporation that was created this year. The address is down in southeast Denver off I-25, near the Tech Center. We'll get it checked out today. Also, nothing has shown up in either NCIC (National Crime Information Center) or any of the criminal history checks, so it doesn't look like he has a record. Our OC databases and indices came up empty, too, under that name and DOB."

"Thanks, and let me know if you get anything else," Nick responded.

Wallace assured him that they would.

CHAPTER THIRTY-THREE

The line of tellers let out a sigh of relief as another busy payday afternoon rush was almost over. With the last customer just about out the door, the bank's security staff was moving about the lobby making sure all the doors were closed and secured. Only authorized bank employees and Darren Kroft, the bank's newly retained computer consultant, were allowed to remain behind.

This was the fifth job for Darren Kroft's infant consulting business in nearly as many months and more were already looming on the horizon. Business was booming. So far, there had been two banks, two brokerage firms and a credit union.

Kroft was not so naïve as to believe that these contracts were coming solely from his reputation as a computer expert. Sure, his resume had been used by Sasha's contacts to help sell his services to the upper management at some of these financial institutions, but there was obviously much more to it than that. Even though his credentials were quite impressive, so were those of many others he knew, and they were not enjoying that same overnight success that had so conveniently dropped into his lap. It obviously had to do with Sasha. He somehow always managed to be able to get whatever he wanted. Exactly how, was the question, but Kroft knew better than to ask. He had learned years earlier that if you aren't sure you want to know the answer, then don't ask the question. He was fairly certain that he didn't want to know.

Tilting back in his padded, black leather chair, Kroft propped his feet up on the corner of the huge mahogany desk and closed his eyes for a few seconds. Being both the CEO and sole computer consultant for his recently established company had been great. He was able to enjoy not only the money and prestige one generally associates with the title CEO, but he also didn't have to listen to the whining and headaches of employees.

Opening his eyes again, he stared toward the ceiling and began thinking about what might have been. Over the years, he had been called into numerous institutions and asked to address their computer problems. While there, he was successful in getting most of their problems taken care of with minimal disruption, and in the process was given carte blanche access into their entire computer system. Many never even followed-up to determine where he had been in their systems or what he had done. "How naïve!" he thought. And, to his amazement, that same openness had continued to remain available to him everywhere he'd been recently working.

"Perhaps," he considered, "I shouldn't be so surprised. Maybe the businesses do know what they're doing. I did tell Sasha that it would help if I could have as close to total access into their entire systems as possible, and he assured me that I would get whatever I needed."

Because of that access, Darren was confident he would now be able to penetrate each of those recently contracted financial institutions and brokerages whenever he wanted.

CHAPTER THIRTY-FOUR

Although sketchy, the information Sergei provided to Matt was certainly worth a follow-up. Supervisory Special Agent Tom Wallace opened a preliminary investigation and assigned Special Agent K.C. Woodson, one of the Denver Division's most senior agents, to the case. For years, SA Woodson had been extremely successful in keeping tabs on established local players, and spent most of his time chasing organized crime figures and drug traffickers. Recently however, a heightened Russian mafia presence was bringing new names and faces into the area, and situations such as the one at hand were forcing him to redirect much of his time and effort.

K.C.'s first lead took him to a new southeast Denver high-rise complex. Marla Cross had come up with this building as the address for Darren Kroft's new office. Inside was a huge glass-covered directory listing the buildings occupants. As his finger scrolled down one listing after another, he suddenly stopped and walked over to the elevator. Pushing the button and getting off on the twenty-third floor, K.C. looked both ways, before going down the hallway.

The office appeared to be closed, but that was fine with K.C., since he hadn't intended to go in anyway. He just wanted to know that it really existed. To his surprise, though, this was not another of those "mail-drop" businesses sharing an impressive address with numerous others behind a plain door with a single mail slot. Rather, this entrance was quite impressive with recessed spotlights shining down on a pair of beautiful wooden doors bearing the business logo and raised, gold trim, letters reading, "Darren Kroft, CEO."

K.C.'s next stop was the Colorado Division of Motor Vehicles where he obtained several copies of Darren Kroft's driver's license. With a photo, his most recent home address information, and vehicle license and registration information in hand, K.C. would attempt to learn what Kroft was up to.

Back in his office on the 18th floor of the Federal Courthouse Building, K.C. met with Tom Wallace. They arranged for the special surveillance group to set-up on and follow Kroft for a couple of days, and see how and where he was spending his time.

K.C. and the special surveillance group arrived at Darren's condominium shortly before daybreak and found Kroft's red Ford Mustang Cobra parked in front. Now, all they could do was sit and wait.

As Kroft came out of the condo and unlocked the door of his car, he took a quick look around, and didn't seem to notice members of the surveillance team as they slouched down in their cars.

Their tail of Kroft initially took them out onto I-25 and over to C-470 toward the foothills. It was obvious that Kroft thought he was something special. He cruised along sitting back and looking around with a smug expression on his face. Even though his new special model Mustang Cobra might not be quite up to the standards of Catherine's six-figure Ferrari, he still felt like he was somebody important and enjoyed all of the looks he got as he roared down the highway.

Preparing to leave C-470, Kroft pulled into an exit lane and onto the ramp. At the second traffic signal he entered the parking lot of the First Westside National Bank and Trust

Company. Continuing to observe from a distance, the surveillance team watched as Kroft gathered his laptop carrying case in one hand and briefcase in the other, and made his way into the bank. When it looked like he would probably remain there for the day, all but one of the surveillance units broke off and went to other assignments.

At nine o'clock, when the bank opened for regular business, K.C. strolled in to take a look around and see if he could figure out what Kroft was up to. The bank was in a large, nearly new building and appeared to be prospering, but that was about all he could see. There was no sign of Kroft, however. Deciding there was nothing else he could do there, K.C. got back into his Bucar (Bureau automobile) and headed downtown to the FBI field office to meet with Marla Cross.

There was no one else in Marla's office when K.C. knocked on the open door. She appeared to be intently concentrating as she shuffled through a stack of papers. "I don't want to interrupt, but may I see you for a minute?"

Looking up, Marla responded, "Sure K.C., come on in. You know my door is always open. Even to the OC Squad."

K.C. smiled to himself. There had always been a friendly rivalry in the Division between the OC and WCC squads, and with Marla's arrival from FBI Headquarters, it hadn't stopped. In fact, if anything, it had intensified. At a little over five feet-one inch, supervisor Marla Cross was a feisty, hard-nosed, blue-flamer who was committed to ensuring that the white-collar crime program, for which she was responsible, remained at the forefront of the Denver Division. "Blue-flamer" is a term used by street agents throughout the Bureau when describing agents who are obsessed with becoming Assistant Directors and Special Agents-in-Charge. In contrast, most FBI agents opt to never enter the career development mainstream and, in turn, remain street agent investigators for their entire career.

K.C. continued, "I was just at First Westside National Bank."

"The one towards Golden?" she asked.

"Yeah, that's the one. It was in connection with the information the guys from Quantico were talking with you and Tom about."

"I remember," responded Marla.

"We followed this guy, Darren Kroft, from his apartment to that bank this morning. It looks like he's doing some work there."

Marla nodded.

"Do you have any contacts there?" K.C. asked.

"Interesting you should ask. I was speaking just this past week to the area bank security managers at their monthly luncheon. After everything was over, one of the guys stayed around and came up and introduced himself. He said he was retired out of the Denver Division and I think he told me that he was the head of security for that bank. Let me see if I can find his card." She searched through her top desk drawer. "Here it is. 'Jeff Brown, Director of Security, First Westside National Bank and Trust Company.' "

"I know Jeff. He was a Denver Division re-tread. His second tour here started a couple of years after I arrived in the Division. He came in off the old 'OP' list. All together he must have worked here for at least ten years."

"On the White-Collar Squad?"

"Most of the time, yeah. He was a good agent. I'll give him a call."

As K.C. was leaving her office, Marla asked, "He wasn't one of the guys who got caught up in that 10/1/69 thing, was he?"

"No, I think he came into the Bureau in the late fifties or early sixties, so he escaped all of that."

"What was the deal with that anyway?" Marla asked. "It was a little before my time."

"It's been a while, but as I recall, it went kind of like this. The Bureau decided that any SA who came on-board after 10/1/69 and had not served in what they then called either a 'Big Ten,' or later a 'Big Twelve' field office, was to be arbitrarily transferred to one of those 'Big Ten' or 'Big Twelve' offices. It created all kinds of problems for those agents and their families."

"And probably contributed to an even higher divorce rate than agents already had?" commented the supervisor, a Bureau divorce statistic herself.

"Probably so, it was not a pretty picture," replied K.C. as he was walking out the door. "I'll give Jeff a call."

"K.C.," Marla called out, as he turned and looked back, "Feel free to call on the white-collar squad for help anytime."

"I will. I'm not proud," he said, laughing.

Back in his cubicle, K.C. dialed the number for the bank.

"First Westside National Bank and Trust," answered the operator. "To whom may I direct your call?"

"Jeff Brown in Security, please," replied K.C.

"Mr. Brown's office," a female voice answered.

"Is Jeff in?" asked K.C.

"May I ask who is calling?"

"K.C. Woodson, from the FBI"

"Just a moment, please."

The intercom buzzed, "Mr. Brown, its K.C. Woodson from the FBI."

"K.C.," Jeff jovially responded, "How are things going? I haven't heard from you in a while."

"Still surviving. You know how things are in the Bu."

"Yeah, I know," replied Jeff.

Having recently reached retirement eligibility, K.C. then anxiously asked, "How are things going in retirement?"

"It's been a mixed bag," Jeff Brown reflectively answered. "There are times when it's been great and others when I have felt like the 'R' in Retirement maybe stood for Reject."

This was not exactly the response K.C. was hoping to hear. "Why do you say that?" he asked.

"My first job out of the box lasted less than eighteen months. After that I moved from one job to another, before finally settling into this one."

"Why so many moves?"

"It works like this. There are businesses out there that want to hire you for your contacts. They use you to get their foot in the door, and after they're in, you're squeezed out. This usually happens within about eighteen months to two years."

"Why eighteen months to two years?"

"That's about all the 'shelf life' they think you have."

"Shelf life, huh?" chuckled K.C.

"Yeah," Jeff cynically responded. "That's a term they've come up with when describing post-retirement employment."

"So, what did you do between your eighteen months of 'shelf life' and now?"

"First, I got my P.I. license and did some investigative work. After that I made some pretty good money acting as an expert witness."

"A hired gun, huh?"

"Yeah, but I could never seem to get into the groove of testifying for the defense."

"I hear where you're coming from," replied K.C.

"It was while I was doing one of those P.I. jobs that I came upon this one with the bank, and this will probably be my last stop."

"Uh-huh," responded K.C.

Jeff continued, "Whenever I leave here, while my wife and I still have our health and can travel and do things, I think I'll just retire. None of us is getting any younger and the money certainly isn't worth all the hassle." Jeff then added, "Remember all of those old jokes about 'not being able to take it with you,' and 'no one having ever spotted an armored car following a hearse.' "

"Yeah," chuckled K.C., "You're making me seriously consider not even trying to find another job once I pull the pin. In fact, I've recently been thinking about doing some volunteer work."

"That doesn't sound half bad to me," Jeff concurred. "My recommendation would be not to chase the bucks, and instead, do those things you really enjoy and make you feel good about yourself. After all, at this stage in life who are you trying to impress, anyway?"

"And, moreover, who really cares?" added K.C., "I hear where you're coming from Jeff, and thanks."

"Well, enough cynicism from me on my retirement soapbox," Jeff responded. "I know that isn't why you called, so what is it I can do for the F.B.-One today?"

K.C. continued, "I was seeing if you could check something out for me. This morning, I tailed a guy we are looking at to your bank in Golden. I assume he's working there, because after parking and locking his car, he loaded up his laptop and briefcase and took them into the bank with him. A guard let him inside before the doors opened for regular business hours."

"Oka-a-a-y," Jeff responded with a questioning tone. "The Golden office is where our main computer and operations center is located. By the way, what's this guy's name?" he asked.

"Darren Kroft, and, as far as I know, he's some kind of a computer consultant," answered K.C.

"The name doesn't ring a bell," replied Jeff, "but I'll check around and see what I can find out."

"Thanks, Jeff, and please not a word of this to anybody."

CHAPTER THIRTY-FIVE

The cellular phone lying in Kroft's open briefcase was ringing. "This is Darren," he answered.

The gravely voice of the caller responded, "Meet me in the bar at seven. I have something for you."

Kroft replied, "Okay," and the line went dead.

After the call, Kroft decided to work a little longer since he saw no reason to drive all the way across town, just to turn around and return to the northwest side. Besides, he had to eat anyway, and now that he was part of the organization, the prices at The Ruble were certainly right.

As evening approached, the lone two-man surveillance unit that had remained behind at the bank followed Kroft out of the bank's lot. Surprisingly, instead of going southeast, toward his apartment, Kroft headed north, going through Lakewood and Wheat Ridge, and into Arvada. On Wadsworth Boulevard, he headed north, before pulling off into the parking lot at The Ruble Bar and Restaurant.

The surveillance agent called K.C. to alert him. K.C. told him to stay put, and that he should be there within a half-hour. That sounded good to the surveillance agents since neither of them had ever experienced traditional Russian cuisine.

In the meantime, Kroft went into the bar. When the hostess saw him, she said, "This way, Mr. Kroft. He is waiting for you."

"Sit down," Sasha instructed him. "What would you like to drink?"

"Vodka?" Kroft replied.

"Good answer," shot back Sasha.

The waitress brought over their drinks and the two of them ordered the house specialty appetizers and two thick, juicy steaks. They raised their glasses and toasted in the Russian tradition Kroft learned in Moscow.

When K.C. arrived, he and the other two agents entered The Ruble. The lights were dim and smoke was heavy. The hostess asked them if they would prefer smoking or non-smoking, as if there was a difference in this place, K.C. thought. Unsure as to whether or not Kroft was a smoker, K.C. elected smoking, and for once he guessed right.

The agents were sitting too far away to hear what was being said, but they could see that Kroft and the other guy appeared to have finished their steaks and were now talking. It was obvious these were more than just a couple of guys who had just met at the bar and decided to have dinner.

"How is our business doing?" asked the chain-smoking Sasha.

"Great," responded Darren.

"That is what we want to hear. You make sure it stays that way."

Kroft nodded that he would.

"Are there any problems or is there anything that you need?" asked Sasha.

"Nothing right now," Kroft answered.

Sasha pulled a small piece of paper out of his pocket and slid it across the table to Darren. "This came in today from Moscow. It is another number you are to start using."

"I see this bank's also down in the Caribbean," Kroft commented.

Sasha nodded affirmatively.

"Have you heard anything from Catherine?" Darren asked, with a look of anticipation.

Sasha had not heard anything and he could only imagine what she really thought of this sorry wimp, but he knew she was the best leverage he had over Kroft, so Sasha told him, "Just that she misses being with you."

That was all it took to bring a big smile to Darren's face. "Any word on when I might be returning to Moscow for a meeting?"

"Nothing yet," responded Sasha, "But your time will come."

Not soon enough thought Kroft.

With their dinner finished, Sasha told him, "That is all for now," and Darren knew that meant it was time for him to leave.

From The Ruble, the agents followed Kroft, going east on I-70 to the mousetrap interchange and south on I-25 to where he lived. After "putting him to bed," K.C. called back to the office and left a message for Marla Cross, asking her to have a financial analyst run all indices and any other database checks on a bar and restaurant in Arvada named "The Ruble."

CHAPTER THIRTY-SIX

Special Agent K.C. Woodson was definitely old school. He could use a computer, but did so only when it was absolutely necessary. As far as he was concerned, the real investigative work of the FBI got done out on the streets, not sitting in the office in front of a computer screen. That point had been brought home to him early in his career and he still remembered it as if it were yesterday.

As a newly assigned First Office Agent (FOA) he was following his new agent counselor's advice and trying to maintain a low profile until he got a feel for things in his new field office. He had spent most of the previous day meeting his new supervisor, in-processing, and finally taking his FBI handbook and a few notes from Quantico from his brown leather Bureau briefcase, and putting them into the top drawer of his single-pedestal, linoleum-topped, gray metal desk.

The supervisor made it very clear that when he was in the office, he would be allowed to have on his desk only his wooden workbox and any case files that he had checked-out from the squad rotor clerk. At day's end, all of the files were to be returned to the rotor and his workbox was to be locked-up in the workbox room. That meant everything was to be cleaned off his desk when he was not there. The only exception was the single black rotary dial telephone with an extra-long cord. That phone, shared by four agents, could remain on one of the desks.

He later heard that the supervisor had received a note of chastisement from the SAC because there was a file found on the desk of one of the agents on the squad while he was out of the office attending an In-Service training program. There seemed to be some question as to who had left it there; and even though the squad bay was secured, that still didn't seem to matter.

K.C.'s second day on the job had started with taking time to wander around the office and see if he could remember where everything was. During the previous day, he had been given a tour, but now it was his chance to find everything for himself. By 8:30 he had completed this second walk around and had made his way back to the fugitive squad's bullpen where he found himself sitting alone. Looking around and seeing no one else there would have been a clue for any experienced investigator, but K.C., an inexperienced new FOA, failed to make the connection. Suddenly, the wrath of his veteran supervisor was brought down upon him. K.C. was informed of an FBI term with which he was to become all too familiar. It was called TIO (Time in Office), and his supervisor explained to him in no uncertain terms that there had better not be very much TIO in K.C.'s life, if he planned to make a career as a Special Agent of the FBI. The FBI got the job done on the streets, not in the office, and in the future, the supervisor had better never see him sitting around the squad bay after 8:30. K.C. never forgot.

In the years that followed, issues like TIO and the Bureau's Inspection Staff concerns regarding how many pencils and paperclips were kept in an agent's desk drawer had been downplayed or removed, but they were replaced with what K.C. regarded as other nuisances. One of these was something called TURK (Time Utilization Record

Keeping). As the name implied, TURK was a management accountability tool that for several years had looked to K.C. like a variation on the old tail wagging the dog syndrome. He would ask himself, "Is the Bureau controlling TURK or is TURK controlling the Bureau?" K.C. knew what he believed, but was reasonably certain those at FBIHQ (FBI Headquarters) or the SOG (Seat of Government) as it had been known in yesteryear, did not view it the same as he did. For now, however, K.C.'s personal pet peeves regarding TURK had to be put aside, as Tom Wallace had asked him to assist in preparing paperwork for the upcoming inspection. Included in this would be a TURK summary to be interpreted and evaluated by the Inspectors and Inspection Staff Aides in eventually determining their squads overall "efficiency" and "effectiveness."

While K.C. was getting ready for another day on the streets of the Mile High City, his phone rang. It was Jeff Brown, "Can you meet for a cup of coffee?" he asked.

"Sure. You name the place. I'll be there. Anything to get away from this inspection and TURK nonsense," K.C. replied.

"TURK is one thing that we don't have here at the bank."

"You probably don't have any #3 (Locator) Cards either, do you?" asked K.C.

"Sure don't. I had almost forgotten about those. I don't know how many thousands of those Cards I must have filled out during my BU career."

"Probably about one every day."

"That sounds about right, K.C. At first, it was just writing down the file number and where we were going to be, and leaving it at the message desk. Later, that TURK stuff came in and we had to add that, too. Thinking back on it, how could I ever forget? Now all I have to do is tell my secretary where I'll be."

"Yeah, me too," K.C. responded with a laugh.

"Someday it'll be your turn, K.C. Hey, back to our getting together. How about that little greasy spoon where we used to meet for morning coffee out on West Colfax?" asked Jeff.

"That sounds fine to me," responded K.C.

"See you there in an hour."

Jeff entered the coffee shop and looked around. K.C. motioned to him to come over. He had arrived first and was sitting in the corner booth with his back to the wall. Ruling out sitting where there was a central entrance doorway or a plate glass window to his back, K.C. always tried to sit at tables where he could see everyone coming and going.

"Leaded or unleaded," K.C. asked.

"Leaded. I need my morning jolt, especially this morning for some reason," Jeff answered, as he pulled several folded pieces of paper from of his jacket pocket and flattened them out on the table before putting on his reading glasses. "Let me try to unscramble my notes. This guy you asked me about is supposed to be some kind of Information Technology guru. He's been retained by our bank as a computer consultant, contracted to examine the bank's computer operations as they relate to funds processing."

"Has the bank been having problems in this area?" asked K.C.

"Not that I know of, but you know the way top management is about security. They do and they don't want us to know certain things. Sometimes it's only after there's a big problem that we're told, and then they ask why we didn't do something to prevent it from happening. I guess they figure we'll eventually learn what we need to know through osmosis. Why are you looking at this guy?" Jeff asked.

"We just received some information that he might be up to something. We have only a preliminary opened for now," replied K.C.

"Maybe I'd better alert my bosses."

"I'd appreciate it if you didn't do that just yet, Jeff," K.C. responded. "We don't even know what he's doing, if anything. If he is doing something and is tipped off and disappears, neither the bank nor the Bureau may know for years what damage he's done."

"What about canceling his contract?" Jeff asked.

"If the contract were cancelled, there would need to be some kind of an explanation given, and neither of us has anything at this point," replied K.C. "Do you think you could get someone in there to work with him?"

"I don't know. Why? What are you thinking?"

K.C. answered, "Follow me on this and see if it makes any sense. Other than Kroft telling us, the only way we may ever know what he is doing would be to have someone in there working with him. I don't know if I can get it approved through the Bureau, but what I'd like to do is put an undercover computer agent in there to work with him."

Jeff raised a finger and temporarily interrupted, "I remember going to one of those early computer in-services. Maybe you could get somebody out of the Computer Unit at Quantico."

"I could try," responded K.C.

Jeff added, "We could introduce the undercover to Kroft as a person the bank has retained to assist in the implementation of any recommendations he makes."

"That might be the way to do it," agreed K.C.

"Also, K.C., I would probably have a better chance of selling the idea of an assistant to the bank's top management. Of course, the CEO will have to be let in on what we are really doing. I think that if I can show him there is no substantial risk to the bank in having the undercover agent there, he might be willing to go along with it."

K.C. added, "As we said before, the only way we may ever know if he has done something to your system is to have someone working with him."

"Good point."

"Who in the bank let the contract for Kroft?" K.C. asked.

"I don't know," answered Jeff.

"Whoever it is, we need to make sure he's not alerted, because we don't know how he fits into the picture."

"If, in fact, he does at all," responded Jeff. "I'll try to find out, and make sure we handle that appropriately."

"First things first, though. Let me see if I can get it cleared through the Bureau," K.C. answered.

"Okay, give me a call as soon as you hear anything."

CHAPTER THIRTY-SEVEN

Tom Wallace had managed to escape the weekly supervisors' meeting called by the SAC and the Assistant Special Agent in Charge (ASAC) unscathed. As he turned the corner to go into his office, he met K.C.

"Can I see you for a minute, boss?"

Wallace motioned for him to come in. "What's up?"

"You remember Jeff Brown?"

Wallace nodded that he did.

"Well, I just met with him this morning. He's now the Director of Security at First Westside National Bank."

"Good for him," Wallace remarked.

K.C. continued, "I met with him because we've learned that this guy, Darren Kroft, is presently doing a consulting job at First Westside. Not to bore you with the details, now, but do you think you could get an SA out of the Computer Unit at Quantico to come out here on a temporary undercover assignment to work with us on this guy, Kroft? That may be the only way we will ever be able to get a handle on what he is doing."

"Will the bank agree?" asked Wallace.

"Jeff will approach them on it once I can assure him that the Bureau will allow us to put in a UCA."

"Sit down, K.C. Let's give a call back to the Seat of Knowledge and see if they are meditating or actually working today."

K.C. laughed to himself.

"FBI Academy. To whom may I direct your call?" answered the operator.

"Nick Costigan, please."

"Hello, Nick. Tom Wallace, in Denver. Need to see if one of your Quantico brain trusts can help us humps out here in the field do some of the real work of the F.B.-One."

"You know our motto, 'We're here to help,' " Nick said in jest.

"Sure," Wallace countered sarcastically. "That's certainly the way it looks to us."

"Well, anyway, what is it we can try do for you, Tom?"

"It has to do with that Darren Kroft thing you called me about. K.C. Woodson is the case agent and he's here with me, now. I'll put our conversation on the speakerphone, so we can all discuss it. I'm turning it over to K.C. for now, since he's the one most familiar with the details."

"Nick, K.C. Woodson here. We would like to have one of Training Division's computer gurus come out here for a short-term undercover assignment. Our preference would be a younger agent who would work with Kroft under the auspices that the SA is new to Denver and has a background as a computer services contract employee. The bank would tell Kroft that they are hiring this person as a temporary employee, and once he is gone, this person will assist in implementing the recommendations he is making. We obviously hope in doing all of this that the SA will be able to figure out what Kroft is doing."

Nick responded, "Let me talk with the agents in the Computer Training Unit and see if they are lukewarm to the idea. If they are, we can see if the administration will approve it. In the meantime, send me something outlining all of the details."

"Will do," replied K.C. "I'll try to get that out of here today."

"Thanks, and we'll be talking," Wallace responded as he was hanging up.

From his office, Nick went directly over to the Computer Training Unit. Located near the ITU, in the bowels of the Academy, agents from both units worked closely together.

Nick briefly explained his conversation with the Denver Division to the unit chief, who decided it would be best if one of the instructors were in there with them when they discussed the details.

Shortly thereafter, Christine Smith stopped by the unit chief's office to report on the meeting she had just attended at FBIHQ. Before leaving, she was invited to remain for their undercover session.

Christine held an advanced degree in computer science, and although she had been an agent for only a few years, she had proved herself and her competency repeatedly in the field. She was bright, articulate, attractive, and recently married. Her husband was an Assistant United States Attorney who had been assigned to prosecute a computer fraud case for which she had been brought in as the expert witness. They were attracted to each other almost immediately, and shortly after the conviction, got married. Now living in a condo in Old Town Alexandria, both thoroughly enjoyed the culture and lifestyle that Washington had to offer.

Nick began by telling Christine of his earlier conversation with the Denver agents and explained that more detailed information would be forthcoming from Denver within hours. She expressed interest in the assignment, and as the three of them continued talking, the unit chief tentatively agreed to support her in it. He told her that it first had to be approved by both the front offices of the Training Division at Quantico and the Criminal Investigation Division at Headquarters. Denver would be forwarding requests to both Divisions.

In the meantime, Christine would contact the Undercover Unit to ensure that everything regarding her other identity was updated and backstopped so that she could be on the road as soon as everything was approved.

By day's end, Denver's fax requests for the undercover assistance, and K.C.'s summary of the case, had both been received by the respective Divisions and were making their way through channels.

CHAPTER THIRTY-EIGHT

K.C. was putting on his jacket when Marla Cross called his extension and asked him to come by her office before leaving for the evening.

When he knocked on the doorframe, Marla looked up from a stack of old closed case files covering her desk. "Come on in," she said. "Other than an indices reference from a closed money laundering case, we didn't come up with much on The Ruble Bar and Restaurant. What records we were able to dig up, though, show it to be owned by an offshore corporation that goes by the letters TFM."

K.C. nodded.

"My guess is it's an IBC," Marla added.

K.C. shrugged, "An IBC, what's that?"

"An International Business Company."

"Is that one of those types of companies that can hide behind confidentiality laws?" K.C. asked.

"Sometimes," Marla answered. "However, it depends on the particular offshore jurisdiction. In some countries they have been set-up in the names of local attorneys and nominee directors who serve to blur everything, so that the true owners can try to hide everything behind the veil of secrecy and confidentiality laws."

"What about that Miami team they mentioned at the In-Service? Could they help us?"

"You mean that team of agents and New Scotland Yard detectives assigned to work with the police down in the Caribbean Basin?" Marla responded.

"That's the one," K.C. nodded.

"I thought about them, too. When I was at Headquarters I got to know the Miami supervisor. I'll give him a call and see if they might be able to come up with anything. If it turns out TFM is one of those IBC or bearer share corporations, though, I wouldn't hold out much hope. With all of the secrecy and confidentiality laws, it could be months before we get anything."

"If ever," K.C. quipped.

CHAPTER THIRTY-NINE

One of the section chiefs from Headquarters called Nick to check on the request for Christine's temporary assignment to Denver. When Nick assured him that it was okay with the Academy, and that the front office had already signed off, he gave Nick the go ahead, and told him that they would be sending an approval to Denver within the next couple of hours.

Nick immediately went over to Christine's office and told her the news. He explained that it was still contingent upon the Denver bank's approval, but that she should probably start getting loose ends tied up, because once it was approved, things would move quickly.

His next call was to Tom Wallace, "Your request for the UCA has been approved by HQ."

"We'll get moving on it," Wallace assured Nick. "Let me transfer you to K.C."

When told of the Headquarters approval, K.C. was pumped and ready to get moving.

"Sounds great," K.C. told Nick. "I'll talk with the bank as soon as we finish so that things can be set up from that end. Before we hang up though, there is one other thing."

"What's that?" Nick asked.

"You have some Russian police contacts who work the Russian mafia over there, don't you?"

"I do."

"Could you ask them if they've ever heard of an off-shore corporation named TFM? I know it's a long shot, but that name has come up in this investigation as the owner of a local Russian bar and restaurant named, if you can believe it, 'The Ruble.' After tailing our man there, we had the white-collar guys do some checking and they came up with TFM as the owner."

"I'll give them a call. It'll have to wait 'til morning, though, because they're all long gone by now."

"I understand. Thanks Nick. In the meantime, I'll try to get things squared away with the bank."

As soon as K.C. hung-up with Nick, he called Jeff Brown at the bank.

Jeff's secretary told K.C. that he was out of the office, but she would beep him. She seemed hesitant to reveal any more, and K.C. knew better than to push.

Within a matter of minutes, K.C.'s phone rang. It was Jeff.

"That was quick," responded K.C.

"Well, your timing couldn't have been worse, K.C.," he said chuckling. "Just as I was in the midst of putting for my only birdie of the round, my pager vibrated. I missed the putt, and there went my chance to break ninety. When I saw your number come up, I knew it had to be important, though, so here I am. What's up?"

"Sorry about the missed putt, but it sounds like you're at least learning retirement priorities," K.C. said, snickering.

Jeff agreed, "Yeah, but I'm not sure the CEO would necessarily see it that way."

"Well, if he can't take a joke," K.C. chuckled, adding, "Some good news from this end. The Bureau has approved our use of a UCA, so you can now talk with your boss about buying into our proposal."

"Sounds good. I'll be back in touch soon, thanks," Jeff responded.

CHAPTER FORTY

Nick thought his best bet to learn anything about TFM would probably come from Vladimir. During that bitter cold ILEA Session, there had been several after-hour bull sessions, in the Buf'e, where he and Vladimir had discussed money laundering and the frustration the Russians were experiencing in tracing large fund movements to offshore islands, especially in the Caribbean.

Nick was in before six the next morning, and he called Moscow immediately. Fortunately, Vladimir was near his phone.

"Vladimir?" asked Nick.

"Yes."

"This is Nick Costigan, with the FBI at Quantico."

"Good to hear your voice, Nick," responded Vladimir. "How is everything at the FBI Academy and the ILEA?"

"Fine, as far as I know," answered Nick, "but, you must remember what I told you about us being like mushrooms down here where my office is. Remember, the only ones they have buried deeper are the behavioral scientists. How is everything going with you and Sergei?"

"We are doing fine, and still working together. We spend as much time as we can trying to find Matt's shooter. Just as we think we might be getting a little closer, something happens that puts us back to where we started. We will get whoever did it, though. I guarantee!"

"I know you will, Vladimir. I remember our talking in Budapest about some of the problems you were having with money moving out of Russia and your losing the trail on some far away offshore island."

"Yes, I also remember those conversations," replied Vladimir. "You were very helpful in explaining to me how this works. We are now taking a new direction in some of these cases."

"In your investigations, have you ever learned of an offshore corporation using the letters TFM as its name?" asked Nick.

"Yes, we have," answered Vladimir. "It is one of those corporations I was referring to at the ILEA when we were talking about large amounts of money disappearing into the Caribbean. Remember?"

"I do."

"Nick, I mean lots of money."

"Do you know what the three letters stand for, Vladimir?"

"No, and we have never been able to find out much about it. We are sure it is owned by one of Moscow's most powerful and vicious gangs, though."

"Have you ever heard anything about Moscow gangs operating in Denver, Colorado?" asked Nick.

"Nothing other than what Natasha overheard and passed on to Sergei for you," Vladimir replied. "It would not surprise me. They are getting footholds all around the world. Did that information from Natasha help?"

"We are still working on it, but nothing firm yet. It was from that, though, that we came up with TFM," replied Nick, as the static in the line increased. "Before we get disconnected, I know Matt will want to know how Natasha is doing. Do you or Sergei see her?"

Vladimir replied, "I can barely hear you, Nick, but I think you asked about Natasha. Sergei talks with her almost every day. She calls to see if we have heard anything from you two.

"Is she still working?"

"Yes, she still works at the social club and is our eyes and ears there."

"Has anyone tried to take her apartment from her?"

"Not yet. They must know we are just waiting for them to try. Can you hear me better now, Nick?

"A little, yes."

"That is good. How is Matt?"

"He seems to be almost fully recovered, and is getting back to being his old self. You and Sergei know how that is," Nick said with a laugh. "Seriously, he is doing well, and we were recently discussing how much we are looking forward to returning to Moscow to finish the course. That is, assuming you still want us."

"You know that you two are always welcome, and we want to see you as soon as you can come back."

"We appreciate that, Vladimir."

"It was good to talk with you, Nick, and be sure to tell Matt we said, 'hello.' "

"I will, and please give our best regards to Sergei, Natasha, and all of the others. We hope to see you all soon."

Later that morning, Nick called K.C. and relayed what he had learned from Vladimir regarding TFM.

During their conversation, K.C. told Nick that he had spoken with Jeff Brown shortly after the two of them finished talking the day before, and that Jeff would be calling as soon as he had an answer.

No sooner had K.C. hung-up from talking with Nick, than his phone rang. It was Jeff Brown.

"I just left the CEO's office. He was initially against the idea, but when I explained that our only chance to know of any potential damage prior to it actually occurring was to do it this way, he finally gave in. He made it clear, though, that it was my job on the line if anything goes wrong, and I told him that I understood."

K.C. replied, "I'll call Quantico as soon as we hang up, and let you know when the undercover will be in."

In the meantime, Nick returned to his office and started on some paper work. The phone rang. "Costigan," he answered.

"Nick, its K.C. No sooner did you hang up, than Jeff Brown called and said that the CEO of the bank approved the plan. When can the undercover be here?"

"I don't know for sure. The UCA will be Christine Smith. You might remember her by her maiden name, Christine Jackson. I'll talk to her today, and ask her to contact you directly to coordinate."

"Yeah, I know who she is," replied K.C. "She gave the investigative databases class at that OC In-Service. Tell her I'll be waiting for her call, and if for some reason I don't answer, to be sure and have me paged."

"Okay, K.C., we'll be in touch."

When Christine returned from class, she found the message and returned K.C.'s call. They quickly agreed that she would come to Denver the day after tomorrow. In the meantime, K.C. would have to find a place for her to stay and get her a car. Jeff would coordinate with his managers regarding her arrival at the bank.

By telling Kroft that Christine was moving to Denver, they would avoid having to do a lot of time consuming backstopping, since she would have virtually no history in Denver. Besides, even if suspicions did arise, Kroft's contract with the bank was a relatively short one, and there was little chance either he or someone inside Sasha's organization would take the time to do more than a cursory check. She shouldn't be there for more than a couple of weeks, anyway. They all hoped that would be enough time to learn what they needed to know.

CHAPTER FORTY-ONE

It was after 7:00 PM, and because the onslaught of afternoon business fliers out of Dulles had already departed, the lines were short. Fortunately for Christine, the check-in seemed to be going quickly and without incident.

As an armed FBI agent traveling on official business within the United States, the check-in always took additional time. There were identifications to present, multi-copy forms to complete, and once she had boarded, sticking her head in the cockpit to say "hello" to the Captain. This was all in addition to the security checkpoint, where she would have to be escorted around the metal detectors, so the security people could once again check her papers and identification, and log her into their records before she could proceed to the gate.

With the check-in completed, Christine and her husband, Michael waited near the security area. The two of them talked a little, but mostly held hands and looked at each other. This was the first time in their new marriage that Christine would be engaged in active FBI field investigative work, and even more than that, she was going into an undercover assignment. As an Assistant United States Attorney for the Eastern District, Michael had been working with FBI and DEA undercover agents for several years, and recognized the element of danger involved in these assignments. He was always concerned about the agents' well-being, but both he and the agents always knew that was part of the job. This was different, though. It was going to be his wife out there, and about all he knew was that it was related to a Russian mafia investigation.

Christine could tell this was bothering Michael. She tried to ease his mind a little by reassuring him that this was not her first undercover assignment, and that until her arrival at the Academy, her entire career had been spent working as a field agent. It was hard to tell though, whether she had been successful in convincing him not to worry.

Christine and Michael got up from where they were sitting, and he walked her over to the security checkpoint. As Michael kissed her good-bye, he didn't know if he could ever get used to her leaving on assignments like this. As he stood there, she turned a final time, waved good-bye and blew him a kiss, before disappearing into the shuttle.

This would be their first time apart, and Michael looked dejected as he turned and walked away. He thought to himself, this was going to be a short TDY separation and, although not happy, he could deal with it. But, what about the temporary duty assignments of longer duration that would more than likely be coming Christine's way in the future?

Also, there was the threat of those infamous "needs of the Bureau" transfers requiring them to pick-up and move around the country or even the world. What kind of a career path was going to be in store for him in trying to find jobs in any or all those new places? And, if all of that wasn't enough, he asked himself how children would fit into this picture.

These and other topics had been discussed before they agreed to get married, and they felt that, together, they could work through anything, but this was the first time they had to face one of those issues. Michael was going to have to learn to deal with these, and other obstacles if the two of them were to remain happily married and Christine was to continue her career as an FBI agent.

CHAPTER FORTY-TWO

K.C. met Christine at Denver's International Airport.

After gathering her bags at the baggage claim, they drove a half-hour from the outlying airport into the heart of the city and the Bureau's downtown offices located in the Federal Courthouse Building. There, Christine would pick up her car and follow K.C. to the place she would be staying.

Before parting for the evening, both agreed to meet early for breakfast, and at that time K.C. would bring her up to date on the case. After that, they would plan to meet with Jeff Brown. K.C. anticipated that Christine would begin her undercover work the following morning, assuming Jeff could complete the final details.

Everything from the out-of-state license plates on her car, to her out-of-state driver's license, to the supporting credit cards, and much more had been set up for Christine to ensure that her undercover was fully backstopped, and her true identity would not be discovered. She would be living in a hotel primarily catering to those engaged in apartment or house hunting, or awaiting their move into a new residence. All appeared to be in place.

With her body still on Eastern Time, Christine was wide-awake at 3:30 AM and could have been ready to go at least an hour before K.C. arrived. She had checked her e-mail and used her cell phone to talk with Michael for a couple of minutes before he had to leave for work. She would always use her cell phone for any calls made back home or to any Bureau people. This would ensure that their telephone numbers would not be identified on her hotel bill, should those with whom she would now be working decide to do a check on her.

As they ate breakfast, K.C. briefed Christine. "I'm sure you are probably already aware of this, but we got into this case by way of a call from Nick Costigan to two of our Denver supervisors, Tom Wallace and Marla Cross. I'll try to make sure you meet both of them before long." He paused to take a sip of hot coffee before continuing, "As I understand it, Nick received a call from one of his contacts at the MVD in Moscow, and after that, he called Wallace. Tom asked me to look into it and see if there was anything for us."

"What did the other squad do?" asked Christine.

"Marla's squad did some database checking and that's how we came up with Kroft's company. Once we had the name, I went to their offices. No one was there, but it was an impressive address in a nice hi-rise. The next morning we put a tail on Kroft, and followed him to First Westside National Bank and Trust. Later that same day the surveillance took us to a Russian bar and restaurant named The Ruble. It's located in Arvada, a suburb over on the west side of town. We think there is some link between The Ruble Bar and Restaurant and an offshore corporation, named TFM, but we don't know exactly what it is."

Christine interrupted, "I heard about that. Nick was able to spend a little time briefing me before I left Quantico, and he mentioned that offshore corporation. He said one of his contacts in Moscow told him the MVD had lost the money trail more than once when they got to TFM."

K.C. paused, "I wish I knew more but, as you can tell, we don't know a lot at this point. That's obviously where you come in."

"I understand," replied Christine. "With what Jeff can add to what you and Nick have been able to learn, we should have enough to at least get me started."

"I certainly hope so. This isn't going to be easy."

The two of them then got into K.C.'s car and drove to Boulder, where they would meet with Jeff Brown.

K.C. had called Jeff at home the night before and they decided it would be better for them to meet away from Jeff's office. Both agreed that the Bureau's Boulder Resident Agency (RA) office would be a good place.

By the time K.C. and Christine arrived at the RA, Jeff was already having coffee with the newly assigned Senior Resident Agent (SRA). He and the SRA had worked together for years at the Denver Headquarters, but since Jeff's retirement, most of their contact seemed to be limited to their playing a round together at the annual Colorado Peace Officers Golf Tournament.

K.C. introduced Christine to both the SRA and Jeff, and the three of them followed the SRA into the conference room. There, the SRA excused himself, closed the door behind him, and put up a placard "Interview in Progress."

Jeff began by explaining, "At this point it is only the CEO and I that know about the undercover. I spoke with him again early this morning and told him that we were ready to go. He will give a brief explanation to the staff regarding Christine's sudden appearance on the scene. It will be something to the effect that he received a call from a banker friend telling him that Christine was moving to Denver and had recommended her for a job. He'll explain that she helped that other bank in making some minor changes in their computer system, and that he thought it might be good idea to give her a try at helping the bank when it comes time to implement Kroft's recommendations. Also, by her being employed during the final phases of Kroft's contract, she'll get a better understanding of his recommendations and learn how to implement them. The bank's computer manager will be told that Christine is a temporary hire, and he, the CEO, will subtly imply that he is really hiring her as a favor to his banker friend."

"That sounds good to me," responded K.C.

"Me, too," replied Christine. "It doesn't sound like I'm supposed to know too much." She then gave him a sly look and laughed, "I wonder why that other bank CEO took such an interest in helping me out?"

Jeff smiled, "I can assure you that this CEO won't be putting any moves on you. After having suffered through a messy divorce and now having to pay a hefty alimony payment every month to his ex, he doesn't risk fooling around on this second wife."

Christine nodded, "I think we've all seen similar things happen to an agent or two, here and there."

Jeff continued, "The CEO will tell the manager overseeing the computer project that Christine will be reporting to work in the morning. He is to give her a desk and take her directly to where Kroft is doing his work. This manager will explain to Kroft basically what I told you, and that she will need to be briefed regarding changes to be made."

K.C. and Christine both nodded.

"Christine, you'll need to get to the bank at about 9:00 tomorrow morning. Go to the second floor and ask the receptionist to see Gary Martin. He's First Westside's computer and technology manager. He will have been told to have a desk for you and to introduce you to Darren Kroft."

"I'll be there," responded Christine.

"In the meantime, we'll drive by the bank, so Christine knows where it is, and take care of any other details," K.C.

said. "By the way, the CEO knows Christine by her undercover name, doesn't he, Jeff?"

"Assuming it hasn't changed," answered Jeff. Then, looking at Christine, he said, "Ms. Christine Scott, I presume."

Christine smiled and nodded, "You presume correctly, Mr. Brown."

Jeff told Christine, "If you need to get in touch with me, it might be best if you do it through K.C. I think that would arouse the least suspicion. Both the people in my office and others around the bank are used to the FBI calling for me. I know the Denver office can always contact K.C., and he can relay any messages directly to me. Since I've been having problems lately with dead areas on my cell phone, I'll be sure to also keep my bank pager with me."

"Sounds good to me," replied K.C.

"Since we all have things to do before tomorrow morning, I guess we'd better hit the streets. I'll be in touch," K.C. told Jeff.

While driving back across Rocky Flats, and passed the foothills toward where the bank was located, K.C. and Christine once again went over with one another what they had discussed with Jeff Brown.

CHAPTER FORTY-THREE

After a night of tossing and turning, Christine sat up in bed, wide-awake. Her mind continued to race as she mulled over a variety of concerns. Had they sufficiently backstopped her undercover identity? What would she do if word leaked out to someone outside Jeff Brown's inner circle regarding who she was and what she was doing? Would she be successful in finding the information they were after? She knew this was just the beginning. The stress would continue to build throughout this UC assignment.

After getting some breakfast at a nearby fifties style diner, and going over everything in her head, for now what must have been at least the fourteenth time, she headed out to the bank.

Gary Martin was already in his office sipping a second cup of coffee and working the crossword puzzle from the morning paper. As Christine stepped into the doorway and knocked on the door, Martin looked up, "You must be Ms. Scott."

Christine nodded her head affirmatively.

Stepping out from behind an imposing desk, Martin extended his hand, and invited her to be seated in a nearby chair.

"Welcome to First Westside," he said.

Christine returned the greeting and after shaking his hand, took a seat.

"Can I get you a cup of coffee?" he asked.

Already feeling a bit on edge, Christine told him, "Nothing for me right now. I'm fine, thanks."

Following the usual the pleasantries exchanged during a first meeting, Martin began his briefing. "When they first told me about your new assignment, I had a question about the need for it. But, after taking some time to re-think the whole thing, I concluded it would be a good idea."

"I'm glad to hear that," Christine replied, smiling.

"Too often, businesses retain consultants to prepare an analysis, and when it's completed, the report sits on a shelf for months or even years collecting dust. All that money spent and nothing is ever done with the end product. This way, we'll have you to help us when we start implementing Mr. Kroft's recommendations."

Martin cleared his throat. "I guess I had better back up. I mentioned Mr. Kroft. That's Darren Kroft. He's the consultant the bank retained to do a computer system update analysis. He really knows what he's doing. So far, I've been very impressed."

"That's good to hear," responded Christine.

"After you get a chance to talk with him, I think you'll be as impressed as I am with all that he's accomplished, not only here but also with other businesses and financial institutions as well."

Martin stood up. "Let me take you to meet Darren."

As they walked down the hallway, Martin continued to lay heavy accolades onto Kroft.

At Darren's office, he tapped lightly on the partially open door.

"Come in," a voice bellowed.

Extending his arm, Martin pushed the door the rest of way open and motioned for Christine to go in ahead of him.

"Darren Kroft, this is Christine Scott."

Kroft stood and extended his hand to Christine.

"She's the one I told you about."

"The one who's going to help implement my recommendations?"

"The very same."

Christine smiled graciously as she shook his hand.

Kroft invited them to be seated on the leather couch.

"For the time being, we're going to put Christine in that empty space next door," Martin explained to Kroft. "It's close, and since you're finishing up your final analysis, I thought that would be a good place. Convenient for both of you when you're going over your recommendations."

Christine nodded in agreement.

"I have been telling her how fortunate we are to have you here, and the great job you've done."

"To ad nauseam," Christine thought to herself, as she smiled and nodded.

Kroft returned the compliment to Martin. "I've appreciated the opportunity to work with you and the fine staff here at the bank. I believe we've got things well in hand." Now, turning his attention to Christine, he added, "And, I look forward to working with Ms. Scott."

As Christine and Gary Martin smiled graciously and nodded in Kroft's direction, Martin's beeper went off. After checking the number, he quickly excused himself.

"I guess that means it's time for us to get down to business," Darren said. "First, though, I think it might be helpful for you if I take a few minutes to tell you a little about myself."

Christine smiled. "I would appreciate that." Listening was always a big part of any FBI agent's job, and big egos had helped provide the noose for hanging more than one of her targets.

"I'm the CEO of my own IT consulting firm. Most of our work comes from the financial sector and, if I do say so myself, we have been quite successful," boasted Kroft.

"That sounds wonderful. How long have you had the business?" asked Christine.

"Since earlier this year. Before that, I was an executive with another computer-consulting company here in Denver. That job was okay, but I really wanted to be on my own. I didn't like the idea of the head guy always getting all the credit and taking big chunks of what I really made for the company. Besides, I knew more than he did," he puffed.

Christine smiled, "It sounds as though you made the right decision."

"No question about that! And, I've been able to put a lot of what I learned over the years to good use for my clients."

Christine nodded that she understood.

Kroft continued, "Let me give you an example. Do you remember hearing about the guy who worked in the data processing center of a company and inserted an instruction into one of the company's computer programs requiring periodic updating and maintenance or else havoc would be wreaked on the entire system?"

"Sounds vaguely familiar," she commented.

"Well, he got fired. And, when the time rolled around for this special program maintenance to be conducted, he wasn't there to do it."

Christine nodded attentively, again, indicating that she understood.

Kroft continued, "As a result, the company's computer system went ballistic." He began to systematically tick off the consequences with his fingers. "System malfunctions; memory losses; personal expletives printed into the executive board's reports; and so on. I think you get the picture."

"Kind of like a trojan horse or a logic bomb?" she asked.

"Or a time-delayed virus," Kroft answered. "You have the idea though. In that case it was an employee from within the company, and it's just one example of the kinds of issues I search out for my clients."

"O-o-o-kay," Christine responded.

In a patronizing tone, Kroft added, "But as we know, not all problems originate from employees within an organization. Over the years, there have been lots of situations where people from the outside have been retained and given total access to the object programs and computer source codes of an entire system in an effort make the system compliant or carry out special programming. When that kind of access is given, there's often no one, except those who actually did the work, who really know what was done. Information relating to changes and alterations made, or any trap doors installed, may be theirs and theirs alone."

Although Christine knew as much or more than Kroft did about computers, and was well aware of most everything he had mentioned so far, she gave the appearance of being awestruck as she hung on his every word. Her ploy was to appear relatively inexperienced and somewhat naïve in an effort to continue to boost his ego and get him to tell her as much as possible. Her lingering fear, however, was that some naïve question or response might make him suspicious.

"So, you're saying they might be able to later enter the system completely undetected?" she asked.

"Exactly," replied Kroft.

"And on the intruder's timetable?"

"Right, it could be years and years in the future. He will be able to read the files, copy, alter, do whatever he wants."

"And, whenever he wants?" she added.

Kroft nodded with a sly smile. "Even when things do happen, the users of most of the penetrated systems will likely never realize the true source of their problems. They'll just assume it was caused by a computer glitch and, unless there's a reoccurrence, that's probably where it will end."

"Sounds like the perfect scheme, but aren't these people afraid of getting caught?" she asked.

"Are you kidding?" Kroft chuckled. "Who's going to catch them? Some gumshoe? Hell, most of them are lucky to be able to turn on a computer and get their e-mail. Besides, even if they did look into it, how would they know who to blame? Sure, some of those who did the programming might be here in the U.S., but there are probably just as many, if not more, who live in other countries. Some are half way around the world. How would anyone know who did what?"

"And when?" Christine shook her head questioningly.

"That's where businesses like mine come in," Kroft explained. "We can look at, and test systems, and seek out flaws before something serious like that happens."

Christine nodded approvingly.

"Well, enough of that for now. I've got to get some things done if I'm going to get this contract finished on time."

Christine stood up. "I guess I'd better get going, too. I still need to get settled into my office. Thanks for the insight."

"Oh, Christine," Kroft said, handing her some papers. "Here are some of the recommendations I've made so far. You can start looking them over when you get a chance."

She smiled and thanked him for all of the help.

"By the way, Christine, I think you're just around the corner."

Christine's new digs turned out to be little more than a cubicle with an L-shaped modular furniture set-up. She now understood why Martin had referred to it as empty space, rather than an office. It was a stark contrast to the plush surroundings Kroft and Martin both enjoyed, but that was fine with her since she certainly did not want to attract any undue attention. Besides, this was more like she was accustomed to in the Bureau.

Settling into her new space did not take long, so she was soon looking at what Kroft had prepared. His findings so far seemed to be limited primarily to a few minor recommendations that had been puffed up to make them appear significant. She would continue to review these in more detail over the next few days. He was a pro, though, and whatever he was really up to was obviously not going to find its way into the final report.

Going back over their earlier discussion, Christine asked herself, "Did his ego get in the way, just enough, so that he revealed more to me than he had intended?"

She would be taking a long and hard look into what he had already said and what else she could get him to divulge in the coming days.

CHAPTER FORTY-FOUR

Pulling another late-nighter at the office, Sergei was finishing reports he had to get out by day's end, when his phone rang.

"MVD," he answered.

"Is that you, Sergei?" the muffled voice whispered.

"Yes."

"This is, Natasha. I can't talk very loud, because I don't want anyone to hear me."

"Okay, Natasha, I'm listening."

"I am at the social club, and one of those men I told you about who was talking about getting the FBI is back in here tonight."

"Is he one of those who shot Matt?"

"I can't be sure."

"Now just stay calm and continue your work. Act as if nothing unusual has happened," Sergei told her. "Vladimir and I will be there shortly."

Sergei called Vladimir at home and told him that he needed to meet him outside the social club, as soon as possible. In the meantime, Sergei would also call the MVD patrol station in that sector to alert the supervisor that they might be calling on them for some assistance.

The two MVD investigators arrived in front of the club at virtually the same time. Sergei motioned for Vladimir to drive down to the next block where they parked. Both wanted to make their presence as inconspicuous as possible.

When Natasha saw them at the door, she pointed to a table, making sure she didn't let on that she knew who they were. She did insure, however, that it was to one of the tables she was serving.

After they were seated, Natasha went over to take their order. She slipped Sergei a note identifying the guy she had called about. He looked at it and winked, indicating he understood. As they sat there, Sergei was able to pick up bits and pieces of the conversation going on a couple of tables away, where their suspect was sitting. So far, his talk seemed to be confined to boisterous bragging about how tough he was, and what impact fear had had on his last victim's bodily functions. This brought about a laugh from all at the table. No one mentioned anything about either the FBI or the attack on Matt, however.

As the evening progressed and the group became increasingly inebriated, they were also more obnoxious. On one occasion when Natasha brought them their drinks, the man she had identified earlier to Sergei grabbed her. As he was trying to pull her down into his lap, Natasha resisted. Sergei instinctively started to go to her aid. Fortunately, however, before Sergei could get over to their table, one of the Club's young thugs had already intervened. As Sergei eased himself back into the booth, he realized that his involvement would likely have associated him with her, and could have meant big problems for her when he left. This was one time he was happy to see these young guys hanging around.

The guy they had been watching finally decided to call it a night, and as he was leaving, they overheard his friends call him Georgi.

"So this scum's name is 'Georgi,' " Sergei muttered under his breath.

Sergei and Vladimir tossed rubles for their drinks and a tip onto the table, and quickly followed him out of the club and down the street.

They noticed an alleyway coming up on their right and decided that would be the best place for them to take him down. It would be out of the way, and no one leaving the social club would be apt to see what was happening.

The two of them started walking faster, and just as the suspect was about to reach the alleyway, Sergei yelled out, "Georgi!" as though he was calling a friend. As Georgi stopped to turn around, Sergei and Vladimir ran up, grabbed him, and whisked him into the alleyway.

After a brief struggle, they got him to the ground and cuffed. It had been so quick he hadn't even had time to unbutton his sport jacket. Jerking him to his feet, and throwing his face against the wall, Sergei stood with the cold metal barrel of his gun pressing against Georgi's temple while Vladimir patted him down.

Pulling a stainless steel pistol from the waistband of Georgi's trousers, Vladimir remarked to Sergei in a sly tone, "Look what I found."

"Yeah, I think we need to find out more about this, don't you?" Sergei smirked.

Vladimir agreed, "I think it is time for Georgi to be our guest for a while."

Sergei yanked Georgi back from the wall by the collar and whispered into his ear, "If you run or yell for help, I will take great pleasure in killing you, understand?"

Georgi nodded that he did, and offered no resistance as the three of them made their way to Sergei's black Volga.

Back at their MVD office, it was Sergei and Vladimir's turn. With no Miranda rights advisement required here, their tough, no-nonsense, interrogation tactics began in earnest.

The American TV viewer might have felt they were not playing fair, but the thought of fair play never seemed to cross Sergei's and Vladimir's minds. And, unorthodox or not, they had been effective in the past, and expected this time to be no different. Besides, if this was the sleaze who shot Matt, there was no way he was not going to pay.

Georgi was one of the new breed of Russian hoodlums. The old "thieves-in-law" were gone and now it was up to these new Russian mobsters to show who was boss. His cocky attitude, slick-backed, black hair, and cigarette hanging from his lips mirrored a thousand other young toughs just like him.

During the initial questioning, Georgi played the big man, not even acknowledging his first name, and shouting one expletive after another. Sergei and Vladimir had seen this happen a hundred times before, but as they pursued a systematic grilling and continued to make him more and more uncomfortable, his tough-guy facade began to show signs of cracking.

After finally admitting to extorting some small kiosk owners for protection money, and running money scams, Georgi again clammed up.

The Russian investigators decided it was now time to give it a rest and get some sleep. They booked Georgi into one of their local jails where he would reside for the foreseeable future. So far, he had denied everything when asked about anything related to threats against the FBI, or the shooting of Matt Kelly, and this would give him plenty of time to reconsider.

What Georgi didn't know, however, was that his gun was already at the MVD laboratory, and there, further examinations would hopefully confirm that the spent shell casings found at the scene of Matt's shooting came from that pistol.

The following morning, Sergei called Natasha to make sure that everything was okay.

"Natasha, this is Sergei. Any problems after we left?"

"None. What happened with that guy?" she asked.

"He's now residing in one of our fine jails," Sergei chuckled.

"Did he say anything about shooting Matt?"

"Nothing, but we are giving him some time to think about it. A few days in there might make him a little more cooperative."

"I wish I could be sure that he was one of those guys, but..."

"I know you would."

"Matt could identify him. I am sure," she responded.

"I plan to call him. I will also be taking his photo to Victor. He should be able to fax it to Matt."

"Will Matt be coming back to Moscow?" Natasha asked. There was a definite note of anticipation in her voice.

"I hope so," answered Sergei.

"Me too, and when you talk with him, please let him know that I am thinking about him."

"If you hear anything else or if anything else happens, you be sure to call me. If you have to leave a message, tell them it is an emergency," Sergei instructed Natasha.

"I will," she answered.

Sergei added, "And be very careful."

"I will do that, too," Natasha responded. "Thanks, Sergei. Bye."

Later that same morning, Sergei received a call from the MVD Forensics Laboratory. The examining technician knew this was a high priority case and wanted him to know the results as soon as they had finished their testing. They had a match. The shell casings came from Georgi's pistol.

CHAPTER FORTY-FIVE

At Quantico, Matt walked into his unit chief's office, "You wanted to see me, boss?"

"Yes, come on in and sit down. We received this photo fax from the LEGAT in Moscow. Look familiar?"

Matt carefully scanned the grainy printout. "It's a little tough to tell for sure because of the quality of the fax, but that looks like the guy who shot me."

"That's what the MVD thinks, too. They would like for you return to Moscow as soon as possible for a positive ID. They have him in custody."

"When do I leave?" asked Matt.

"Why don't you call the LEGAT and get the details?" replied his unit chief.

"Okay, but it will probably have to be tomorrow morning, since it's nearly midnight there. I'll let you know what I find out."

"That'll be fine. Just try to call them as soon as possible."

As Matt walked back to his office, thoughts of returning to Moscow began racing through his mind. It was a strange sensation. Although he had almost been killed there during his last visit, he now looked forward to the chance to return. The opportunity to see Victor, Sergei, and Vladimir would be good, but it was Natasha who unquestionably remained the real attraction for him in Russia.

Matt made sure he arrived at the Academy shortly after five the next morning. He didn't want to miss getting in touch with the Moscow LEGAT.

After speaking briefly with Victor, it was agreed that Matt needed to talk directly to Sergei. Whatever the two of them decided would be okay with the LEGAT.

Matt started off their conversation by telling Sergei that he had received the faxed photo and message from the LEGAT."

"Is that the shooter?" asked Sergei.

"The quality of the faxed photo left something to be desired, but I think you have the guy," replied Matt.

"When can you come to Moscow?" Sergei asked.

"When do you need me?" Matt asked.

"Whenever you can come," answered Sergei. "This guy is not going anywhere. We will hold him as long as is necessary. How are you feeling? Completely recovered?"

"I'm doing fine, Sergei. Everything seems to be as good as before it happened."

"That is good to hear."

"I'll need to make flight arrangements and get Country Clearance and a Visa. That will probably take at least a day or two. I'll call you back as soon as I can get everything arranged," Matt told him.

"That will be fine," responded Sergei. "You let me know when, and I will be at the airport to meet you. Oh, I almost forgot. Natasha wanted me to tell you she misses you."

"Thanks, Sergei. I will call you as soon as I have my travel plans."

"That will be fine, Matt."

Matt paused momentarily before exclaiming, "Sergei!"

"Yes, Matt, what is it?"

"Tell her I miss her, too."

"I will. We all look forward to seeing you, Matt."

Matt called back to the Moscow LEGAT office and relayed to Victor what Sergei had said. Victor told him he would take care of getting the Country Clearance, and insisted that Matt stay with him in the Embassy compound this time around. Although Matt didn't want to impose, that sounded like a good idea, considering all that had happened before.

His next call was to the International Section at FBI Headquarters, which would be responsible for getting the Russian Visa stamp for his Official Passport. In the meantime, the travel office would make his airline reservations.

Unknown to Matt, at this same time, Nick was busy making travel plans of his own, but going in another direction. A newly established ILEA was temporarily being opened in Panama and Nick had been assigned to instruct at the first session.

CHAPTER FORTY-SIX

It had been over a week now, and as Christine systematically worked her way through yet another series of Kroft's dull and boring recommendations, she remained uncertain as to what he was really up to. Nothing had jumped out at her, but she guessed that was to be expected. There was something missing, however.

Gary Martin had commented to her how pleased he was that Kroft showed so much interest in the security of all of their electronic funds transfer systems. He had expressed a special interest in learning as much as possible about the bank's wire transfer system, and since that was how the big money went into and out of the bank, Martin was eager to have his input. A significant failure in this area might cost him his job.

Martin told Christine that Kroft had meticulously gone over their entire system with a "fine-toothed comb." He met with personnel from the wire transfer area of the bank and listened to their concerns. Later, he assisted in testing many of the safeguards that they already had in place in an effort to insure that everything was working properly.

Not to her surprise, however, Christine noted there was an almost complete void in Kroft's recommendations when it came to those areas directly related to the wire transfer system. She had her own ideas as to why, but her experience in investigating white-collar crime had taught her that, and unfortunately, it might take a long time before the final tale would unfold.

Next, she checked some selected programs, paying particular attention to the dates and times identified in program updates and changes, and found those to be generally consistent with the recommendations and changes made thus far. Christine was certain that a pro like Darren Kroft, who knew his way around date and time identifiers, would only let you identify those date and time changes he wanted you to know about. Her only hope was that because of all the work he had been doing, he might have slipped up just once, and that slightest crack might be just the opening she needed. But so far, no such slip-ups had surfaced.

Working through the various programs, she suddenly noticed something strange occurring with one of them. When she checked the date and time notation, everything appeared to be consistent, but still there was something wrong. She re-examined the program as it appeared today, and matched that analysis against the same analysis she had done on that program the previous week. Being as familiar with computer program identifiers such as hash and cycle redundancy checks as most agents are with fingerprint and DNA examinations, Christine began her detailed analysis of the program. This comparison should tell her whether there had been any alterations or changes made to that program during the particular timeframe in question.

The program comparisons did not match. Even though the date and time notations reflected that there had been no program changes, she knew something was definitely amiss. The particular program in question had to do with funds transfers and it was now be up to Christine to find out what happened.

Warily, she began this most demanding and time-consuming task of examining both the object and source programming code to see what she could find.

After hours of tedious work, she suddenly stopped, finding what appeared to be a trap door. If it was, instant access might be granted to that part of the program, allowing intrusion into a particular group of accounts. Once penetrated, the money in those accounts could possibly be transferred out of that bank and into another at some future time. Since Kroft and his mafia counterparts would be after the big bucks, Christine assumed he would likely have chosen a point where he would have access to accounts with high six and seven digit balances. She would attempt to identify any accounts that might be targeted for penetration, and at the same time make note of other banks or accounts into which the funds could be transferred.

Christine was also going to have to ensure that she properly maintained and documented this program analysis, since the comparison would be needed for evidentiary purposes at the conclusion of the investigation. If confronted with the fact that there had been an alteration, Kroft could be expected to say, "See, I told you so," reiterating what he had forecast regarding programmers placing trap doors into programs and then accessing them anytime in the years and years to come. Christine still might not be able to prove that Kroft was the one who had altered the program, but at least she could show that it had happened within the past week.

If nothing else, she now had a good idea as to the type of things he had been up to in this bank. What she did not know, however, was whether this was his first effort or were there other changes that needed to be identified? Also, what about all of those other banks and brokerage firms where he had already worked? How much damage had he done there, and might they be eventually looted?

CHAPTER FORTY-SEVEN

Since there was a nearly incomprehensible number of lines of code making up the bank's numerous programs, Christine knew she was going to have to dramatically restrict her search. From those early days as a New Agent, she had been told to look for the repeat. The theory being, that until caught, criminals will tend to replicate their acts. This had been good advice in the past, and she hoped it would be the case again. Since the altered program was in the area of funds transfer, this appeared to be the logical place for her to start. It made sense, anyway, since those were the programs responsible for moving the money into and out of the bank.

As she looked up from her computer, Kroft peered around the corner and tapped on the modular wall.

"Good afternoon," he said.

"Good afternoon to you," Christine responded with a pleasant smile.

"Since my time here at the bank is getting very short, I thought that I would stop by and see if you would like to go for a drink with Gary and me after work today. This might be the only time for the three of us to get together and go out for a cold one."

This came as somewhat of a surprise to Christine, since Kroft had seemed to show little interest in socializing with her. For that she was thankful, although somewhat surprised. She was accustomed to having men hit on her and having to come up with new ways to dissuade their advances. The only man here, so far anyway, who had seemed to express any interest was Gary Martin.

"Sure," Christine responded. "What time and where?"

"We thought we would go after work today to this little out-of-the-way bar and restaurant I sometimes go to in Arvada. You can follow me over there."

"Okay," she agreed.

"Then it's set. We'll stop by and get you."

Christine continued to look through some of the other programs, but so far she had come up with no additional alterations.

Most of the staff had already left for the day, and as Christine heard Kroft and Martin coming in her direction, she turned off her computer. Now standing at the entrance to her cubicle, she joined them as they walked out to their cars.

The evening rush hour on Wadsworth Boulevard was about over, and Kroft's red Cobra Mustang was fairly easy to follow. Since Martin knew his way around Golden and Arvada, he had taken his own route, and would probably arrive there a little ahead of them.

There it was, The Ruble Bar and Restaurant, with Gary Martin waiting for them beside the front door. As the three entered the bar, they were directed to a large oval-shaped booth near the back. Traditional Russian music was playing in the background and the few patrons Christine saw seemed to be quietly conversing and appeared to be enjoying their evening out.

After they were seated, Kroft motioned to the waitress. She came over and placed a bowl of snacks in the center of the table. He asked Christine and Gary what they would like to drink, and after placing their orders, told the waitress to bring him his usual. She gave him an insincere smile and left, returning shortly thereafter with their orders.

Kroft declared that he was going to propose a traditional Russian toast. He went through a short litany, explaining how pleased he was that the three of them had been able to work together at the bank, and wished them all wealth and prosperity in the future. When they all raised and touched their glasses simultaneously, Kroft stopped them. He explained that the guest should always insure that the top of his glass touched below the rim of the host's glass. When the toast was completed, Kroft made sure he completely downed his double vodka in one quick gulp. After exhaling loudly enough for anyone within shouting range to hear, he let out with a disgusting burp and slammed his glass on the table. His actions not only got their attention, but also drew looks from almost everyone sitting at nearby tables.

Kroft again motioned to the waitress. Martin took Kroft up on his offer for a re-fill, but Christine declined, noting that she still had plenty left in her glass.

While Christine sat listening, Kroft and Martin continued to boast and monopolize the conversation. That was fine with her since she hoped something would be said that might help her piece together at least part of what had been going on at the bank. To her surprise, however, the next revelation did not come from Kroft.

"Mr. Martin, it is good to see you back with us," Sasha said, as he approached their table.

"It's been a while," Martin responded, as he tried to get up and stand between the bench and the table.

"Keep your seat," grunted Sasha.

Martin extended his hand. "It's good to see you, Sasha."

It was obvious that Martin knew Sasha. Christine was unsure whether he was reacting out of fear, or respect, but she had a good idea.

Sasha turned to Darren. "And, may I ask, who is this beauty that you have brought with you tonight?"

Kroft looked at Christine. "Oh, I should have introduced you two. Christine Scott, this is Sasha. He's the owner of this fine establishment."

"The Ruble is pleased to have you with us, Miss Scott. I hope you are enjoying yourself and that everything is satisfactory. If it is not, you be sure to let Sasha know."

"Thank you. Everything's fine," Christine assured him.

Sasha turned back to Gary Martin, "Did your teams fare well last weekend?"

"Not bad, for a change," responded Martin.

"Don't stay away so long next time, Mr. Martin. Let us hear from you."

"I'll be in touch, Sasha. You can count on that."

Then, smiling as he looked directly into Christine's deep brown eyes, Sasha remarked, "It was nice to meet you, Miss Scott. Please come back." He paused, and looked at Kroft. "You make sure that she does."

Kroft nodded in agreement, assuring Sasha that he would.

"Good, and all of you have a nice evening." Sasha motioned to the waitress, "bring this table some appetizers and another round of drinks. Put them on my tab."

"Thanks," the three of them said simultaneously.

While waiting for the appetizers and the next round of drinks to make their way to the table, a temporary lull in the conversation surfaced. Sensing they were expecting her to say something, Christine asked, "Do you guys have any suggestions on how I might get some more computer consulting contract work around here?"

"There doesn't seem to be any shortage of opportunities for work around Denver," Kroft replied. "The government agencies post their announcements and ask for bid submissions. The problem is those jobs usually require more than a couple of people, and as a result the small guy gets cut out. It's in small and medium sized businesses where the real opportunities lie. They usually need just one or two people, and often for only short periods of time. That's what got me the job at the bank."

"Speaking of the bank, may I ask what was involved in your getting a big contract at a place like that? My only association with contracts has been as a temporary employee."

"Let me answer that, Christine, since I was the one who let that contract in the first place," replied Martin. "I had heard about Darren from people at several other financial institutions in the area. He had done work for them, and since we had some similar concerns, I decided we needed to have him take a look at our system. I prepared a proposal and took it to the top management at our bank. The next thing I knew, they had agreed."

Looking in Kroft's direction, Martin added, "Let me say now that I couldn't be more pleased with the results, so here's a toast to you, Darren Kroft."

The three of them raised their glasses, and this time Martin joined Kroft in going bottoms up.

"I appreciate that," replied Kroft, "and now it'll be up to you and Christine to insure that everything is implemented properly."

She nodded and smiled.

As Christine tried to gracefully excuse herself for the evening, Kroft insisted on one more toast. Martin expressed some disappointment, as he had hoped to get to know her a little better during the evening, but he was certainly in no position to take issue with her departure.

At the conclusion of the toast, Christine politely excused herself and walked out of the restaurant and to her car.

There, she immediately placed a call on her cell phone to K.C. Woodson.

"Can you meet me at my hotel in about an hour?"

"I'll be there," he answered. "See you then."

CHAPTER FORTY-EIGHT

There was a tap at the door. As she peered through the peephole, Christine could see a distorted image of K.C. She quickly unhooked the chain, clicked open the lock, and pulled the door toward her. K.C. glanced in both directions and hurried into her suite as she quickly closed the door behind him.

"Did anyone see you?" she asked, as they sat down at the table in the kitchenette. "Can I get you anything?"

"I don't think so," answered K.C., to whether anyone saw him, and, "no, nothing for now."

"That's good, because there isn't much in this fridge, anyway. As I mentioned to you earlier, I went for a drink with Kroft and Martin tonight. You'd never guess where they took me," she said somewhat cynically.

"It couldn't be a bar and restaurant in Arvada with a name that sounds like money?" guessed K.C.

Christine smiled, "Surprise, surprise, and while we were there, guess whom I met?"

"Sasha?" replied K.C.

"Another surprise!" she exclaimed. "By the way, he's a real charmer," she said jokingly. "Something he said did tweak my interest, though."

"What's that?" K.C. asked.

"It may turn out to be nothing, but see what the Denver Division has on our man Gary Martin."

"You mean the geek at the bank?" asked K.C.

"The very same," answered Christine. "It turns out that he's the one who arranged the contract for Darren Kroft."

"Well, that would be expected, wouldn't it? He's the bank's computer guru, right?"

"Right, but there was something Sasha said that makes me think Martin might have a gambling problem. I just have the feeling that there might be some tie between his gambling and that contract Darren Kroft got with the bank."

"Okay, I'll run our indices first thing in the morning and see if I can come up with anything."

"I'll call you at the field office, tomorrow," Christine said, adding, "It'll have to be sometime when I can get away from the bank. If you're not there, I'll try paging you."

"Sounds good," K.C. told her. "I've got to get home."

CHAPTER FORTY-NINE

A late night meeting coupled with an early morning alarm left K.C. feeling as though he'd gone more than one day without enough sleep.

After managing to make it into the office and getting a cup of hot, black coffee in his hand, though, life was slowly beginning to improve. He began the first of several checks that he would be making regarding one Gary Martin. So far, the checks had not identified any cases in which Martin was a criminal subject. That was to be expected though, since he worked for an FDIC regulated financial institution. There were several references noted in the FBI files indices, but these turned out to be little more than his having been seen in the company of a local bookie, and even then it was just an association. He had never been arrested. There really wasn't much, but K.C. did recognize the bookie's name and decided to pay him a visit.

M. "Shades" Malone had been an active figure on the Colorado gambling scene for as long as K.C. had been in the Denver Division. As a kid, Shades started out as a numbers runner along East Colfax Avenue, and over the years moved up the ladder to where he eventually operated a very profitable book of his own. That success had not come without its costs, though. Shades came to the attention of the FBI's Organized Crime Squad, and in turn to Special Agent K.C. Woodson.

Getting busted once in a while seemed to go with the territory, so Shades had seen his share of courtrooms over the years. It was in connection with one of those busts that K.C. and Shades became much better acquainted. Things were not looking up for Shades, and, as a result, he saw the light and decided that it was in his best interest to cooperate.

A surprising side benefit of this cooperation was a tip that went a long way toward solving a gangland style execution that had been haunting the OC Squad for several years. As a result, K.C. met with the Assistant United States Attorney and a deal was struck whereby Shades got his sentence reduced, and the FBI cracked a cold case. Since then, Shades had become a valuable hip-pocket informant.

K.C. found Shades having his morning coffee at the same east Denver coffee shop he'd been going to every morning for the past 20 years. There he was, sitting on his favorite stool at the far end of the counter and playing grab-ass with Wanda.

Wanda Little had been working as a waitress at that same coffee shop for almost as long as K.C. had been going there for his meetings with Shades. He had been told that during her prime she was one of Denver's most recognizable exotic dancers and that her picture had been plastered across the local sports pages when seen in the company of a big-time sports hero. Later, alluring shots were inserted into advertising boxes of some of those same newspapers inviting "gentlemen" to come by and see her at the exotic club where she stripped. From what he could tell, she seemed to have loved all the attention and suspected that her stage name had likely included a "t" in place of the "d."

Even today, with the layers of caked make-up, thick deep red lipstick, and bouffant-style, bleached blonde big hair, covered with a generous topping of heavy spray, it wasn't much of a stretch for K.C. to believe what he had been told. Wanda's face and body both still looked pretty good to him. She always seemed to have a friendly, upbeat attitude; and furthermore, had proved to be a good street source for him on more than one occasion.

"Coffee, K.C.?" she asked, nudging up behind him and leaning over to give him a big kiss on the cheek.

"Regular," he said, as he started rubbing his cheek with the napkin. "Did I get it all off?"

Wanda reacted, "I'll never tell, honey."

"That's not what I'm worried about, Wanda. After the last time I was here to see Shades, I went back to the office, and guess what? Some of your lipstick was still on my cheek. It took me weeks to live that down."

"What, the FBI didn't believe you, K.C.?" she asked with a sly smile.

"What do you think? Besides, it wasn't the FBI that I was concerned about."

"Then who, my darlin'?" she teased, continuing to massage his neck and shoulders while at the same time leaning around to his side so he could see her big grin.

"The guys on the squad, who do ya' think? Once there is the first sign of blood, the squad bay goes into a feeding frenzy, like a group of sharks."

"Now, K.C., you're referring to your fellow FBI agents. They wouldn't do something like that to you, would they?" she laughed. "Here, give me the napkin, K.C."

She dampened it with some water from the glass in front of him and rubbed it against his cheek.

"Is it all gone, Wanda?"

"All gone, hon, but now nobody will know that you belong to me."

"That's what I'm counting on," he said smiling.

"Okay, if you want to be that way. I suppose you're here to see Shades, instead of me, huh?"

"You know you're always my first choice but, unfortunately, this time you're right. Next time, though."

"Promises, promises, that's all you ever give me, K.C."

When K.C. finished his small talk with Wanda, Shades spun around on his stool and pointed over to the booth in the corner. He picked up his coffee cup and K.C. followed him to the table. As they were both sliding into opposite sides of the booth, Wanda brought K.C.'s cup of coffee over to the table and set it down on a paper napkin.

Still poppin' her bubble gum, she gave him a smile and with a wink said, "No extra charge for the spill, K.C." Coffeepot in hand, she went off to the other end of the counter where one of the regulars was waving his cup in the air and calling for a refill.

Leaning forward and whispering in a low voice, Shades asked, "What is it, K.C.? I didn't do nothin'. I'm clean."

"It's not anything about you, Shades. I just need to know what you can tell me about a guy named Gary Martin."

"Man, that's a name out of the past. Haven't seen him for a couple of years. Last I knew he was working at some bank."

"Sounds like the same guy. What kind of a guy is he?"

"Well, if you mean did he like to put some money down here and there? The answer is, yes."

"A lot?"

"Yeah, sometimes."

"Why did you stop seeing him?"

"He was becoming a real pain, if you know what I mean."

"Tell me."

"Well, he thought he was some kind of computer wizard, and his computer was going to make him the winner of winners."

"Go on."

"The book didn't see it that way. Like you and me both know, K.C., there ain't nobody out there going beat the book day in and day out, computer or no computer, and he didn't."

"What else?"

"Well, when he kept losing, I needed to collect more and more often. There was always some reason why he couldn't pay up. I had to put the pressure on and you know me, K.C., I don't like to do business that way."

"So what happened?"

"I finally told him to go somewhere else. I couldn't carry him no more. He cried and bellyached, but that's the way it was."

"Have you heard anything from him lately?"

"Not directly, but funny you should ask. A few months ago word went out on the street that he was in over his head, big time. Fact was, wouldn't have surprised me if you guys had found him floating face down out in Cherry Creek Reservoir."

"So, what happened?"

"Well, the next thing I heard was that all was forgiven. This guy, Sasha, put that out, and from what I hear, he's nobody to mess with. You talk about somebody who'll do the job on you, he's it."

"Shades, do I hear you right? You're saying that Martin's entire debt was forgiven?"

"Strange, huh? But that's what word on the street was. Don't ask me why, 'cause I don't know no more."

"That is strange. Thanks, Shades. If you hear anything else, you let me know. Okay?"

"Sure, K.C."

"Stay in touch."

As K.C. was leaving, he heard a loud screech ring out from behind the counter.

"Don't stay away so long, K.C. Remember, I'm your first choice."

"You're the best, Wanda," smiled K.C., as he waved back at her.

"I'll be waiting," Wanda teased from behind the counter, as the glass door slowly closed behind him.

While driving back to his office, K.C. called Christine.

"Christine, this is K.C. We need to talk and soon."

"How about lunch in an hour? The same place we ate last week," she replied.

"The one just off C-470?" asked K.C.

"That's it."

"I'll see you then," he said.

This would give K.C. enough time to stop by the office on his way. Earlier that morning, he had asked one of the Denver Division's financial analysts to start running the databases on Gary Martin and he needed to know the results of that search ASAP.

Upon his arrival, K.C. went directly to the white-collar crime squad financial analyst who had been conducting the searches. "Anything?" he anxiously asked.

"Nothing of consequence so far, K.C., but you know me, I'll keep digging," the financial analyst assured him. "All of the searches haven't been completed yet. I still want to do some more checking with the analysts at the Regional Center, though."

"If you come up with anything that looks good, give me a page."

"Will do."

As K.C. entered the restaurant, he heard the hostess call, "Scott, party of two," and saw Christine motioning for him to follow.

"Glad to see you got here early," he said. "I'm not sure we would have gotten a table before dinner time with that crowd waiting."

After ordering, K.C. brought Christine up to date on what he had learned that morning from M. "Shades" Malone regarding Gary Martin's troubled gambling history and Sasha's mysterious forgiveness of a large debt.

"Did he seem to know any more about ties between Martin and Sasha?"

"No. In fact, he really doesn't even know Sasha. He's just heard stories and they're the typical tales that we hear day in and day out about the Russian Mob."

"The financial analysts are still running some searches, but, so far, nothing of significance has popped up."

"By the way, have you located anymore of those, um, uh. Oh, what did you call them?"

"Trap doors?" answered Christine.

"That's what I meant to say," K.C. smiled.

"No more, but that doesn't mean that there aren't more there. I haven't given up. Not yet, anyway."

CHAPTER FIFTY

When Jeff Brown returned to his office from lunch, there was a message on his desk telling him that he was to meet with the CEO at two o'clock.

Arriving with five minutes to spare, Jeff took a seat on the leather couch beside the receptionist's desk. He tried to engage her in conversation, hoping to find out what this was about, but she didn't seem to want to talk.

As the grandfather clock chimed twice, the receptionist opened one of the six-paneled doors leading into the CEO's office opened, and ushered Jeff in. The expression on the CEO's face told Brown that this was not going to be an enjoyable meeting.

Opening their meeting in a serious tone, the CEO remarked, "Mr. Brown, I haven't heard anything from you lately."

"I didn't want to bother you, Sir," Jeff replied.

"Well, let me get to the point, Jeff. I have become increasingly concerned about when this computer contract we let for our system will be completed and, also what has been going on with that FBI undercover agent."

"Oka-a-a-y?" Jeff replied questioningly.

The CEO continued, "I think I have an answer to my question regarding the completion of the contract. I spoke with Mr. Martin and he told me that the job should be concluded in the next day or two."

"That's my understanding, also," Jeff agreed.

"Now, Mr. Brown. My other concern is directed to you. What can you tell me about what the FBI has learned?"

"I don't know any specifics, but the Bureau is continuing to work on it."

"Mr. Brown, I can understand your not wanting to stick your nose into the FBI's case, but just keep in mind, you are no longer an FBI agent. As the chief of security for this institution, you have a responsibility to make sure that nothing happens to any of our systems that would put the bank's funds in jeopardy. If something is found, you and we must take appropriate action, immediately."

Jeff nodded that he understood.

"You must also remember Mr. Brown that we are not like the federal government. We must compete for our business. Our customers must have complete confidence in us and have no questions about the safety of their money. Otherwise, they may go somewhere else, and we certainly don't want that to happen, now do we Mr. Brown."

Jeff agreed that he did not want that to happen.

"The Board of Directors and I are always extremely concerned about image, and I don't want to have to explain our bank's name being tarnished as a result of all of this FBI stuff. Furthermore, I don't really care about any criminal prosecution. What I do care about is the possibility of word of this getting out, and our customers fearing that their money is in jeopardy. Do I make myself clear?"

Resisting the urge to say what he really wanted, Jeff answered, "Perfectly. I will keep you advised in the future, Sir."

"Make sure that you do. That is all for now."

Back in his office, Jeff seethed, mulling over that relatively brief, but certainly one-sided conversation he had just experienced with the CEO. He understood the CEO's concern about bad publicity, but Jeff had spent the better part of his life trying to get the bad guys off the street, and the CEO's attitude of being more concerned about image, than prosecuting the crooks and putting them in jail, was hard for him to swallow.

CHAPTER FIFTY-ONE

The door was open, but a slight knock on the frame caused Kroft to look up. It was Gary Martin. He looked concerned, and his voice sounded a bit tentative.

"May I see you for a minute, Darren?"

"Sure. Come on in. I'm putting the final touches on my report. It should be on your desk by day's end."

"That's great. We're going to miss you around here, though," Martin assured him.

"I appreciated having the job, and it was all thanks to you," replied a glad-handing Darren Kroft.

There was a pause, and Kroft could tell that something was bothering Martin.

Martin then blurted out, "The CEO called for me to come to his office. He asked me questions about what you had been doing and when the contract was ending."

"So, what's unusual about that? I would expect that he might be interested."

"You don't understand. When he asked, it was like there was something wrong."

"Did he say there was something wrong?"

"No, but it was the way he said it. You have to understand; he rarely shows much interest in what I'm doing or in our computer operations. He just wants everything to run smoothly and as long as it does, he leaves me alone."

"That sounds great to me."

"Well, it is, and it isn't. It kind of puts me out of the loop as to what's going on with the rest of the bank. He does, however, let me do and have virtually anything I need in order to get the job done. That's why I didn't have a problem getting your contract approved."

"Is that how you got Christine her job, also?"

"No, and funny you should mention her. That was one of the rare instances when he did get personally involved."

"How's that?"

"Well, after you had been here for a while, the CEO called and asked me to come to his office. He wanted to talk. When I got there, he made some small talk for a while and then asked me how things were going with your analysis. I told him that it was proceeding very well. There was some more small talk, and then he told me that a colleague of his at another bank, in some other state, I don't remember which one, had called and told him that Christine was moving to Denver. He said that she had helped their bank as a contracted computer consultant. The CEO then suggested that she might be able to help us in implementing some of the recommendations you are making."

"So what did you say?"

"I said 'fine.' I could tell that was what he wanted, and I was not about to question his reasoning. Besides, I thought then, and still do feel it is probably a good idea. Don't you?"

"It probably is," Darren agreed. "So, what was it in this recent conversation with the CEO that has been bothering you?"

"I can't exactly put my finger on it. It's weird. It was more than just a passing interest. More like he was very concerned, or suspicious that something might be happening. He wanted to know things like if I knew what you were doing and did everything look okay? Oh, one other thing, he seemed particularly concerned about when you would be leaving. I got the distinct impression that he hoped it would be sooner rather than later."

"Well, it's probably nothing to be concerned about," replied Kroft. "Besides, I'll be out of here tonight."

"Speaking of getting out of here, I'd better leave, so you can get back to work," Martin responded. "Otherwise, you'll be here all night trying to finish."

"I'll drop off the final report and my bank ID on your desk when I leave," Darren told him, "and again, thanks for everything."

"Thanks to you, Darren," Martin replied.

After shaking hands, Martin left and Kroft went back to his report.

This sudden interest of the CEO, however, could be cause for Kroft, Sasha, and the organization to re-think their plans. Since time might now be of the essence, they were going to have to quickly decide what to do and when. After all, who knows how long the money in the accounts might be accessible through the trap door?

Darren was going to have to meet with Sasha, and soon.

CHAPTER FIFTY-TWO

Matt was in the air and on his way back to Russia. He had departed from Washington-Dulles International Airport the previous evening, and welcomed the announcement that had just come over the intercom. "All passengers are requested to fasten their seatbelts, bring their seatbacks to an upright position, and secure their tray tables." They would be landing at Moscow's Sheremyetove International Airport momentarily.

The trip had gone well so far. The layover in Frankfurt had been relatively short, and other than suffering from swelled ankles and tired butt syndrome, he felt surprisingly good.

As Matt walked from the gateway, he heard his name called out in the dimly lit, quiet gate area. The voice was one he would never forget. With an unfiltered cigarette dangling from his lip, and a big smile on his face, Sergei greeted him with open arms and a traditional Russian bear hug.

"Good to see you, Matt."

"*Zdravstvuitse.* It's good to see you too, Sergei."

Sergei laughed at Matt's pronunciation of "hello," and asked, "You have heard of an expediter?"

"I have," answered Matt. "In fact expediters are most appreciated, and have assisted me on more than one occasion. I don't know if I ever would have gotten through some of those foreign airports if it hadn't been for them."

With his hands and arms extended, Sergei told him, "Well, here I am, Sergei Malkin, your personal expediter."

"*Horosho*," Matt responded in Russian.

"I am fine, also," replied Sergei, and they both had another good laugh at Matt's attempt at Russian. "It is the effort that counts, Matt. Russian is a hard language to learn. At least you try."

What a difference Sergei's preparations made. He had everything greased. Immigration, baggage claim, customs, everything had been set up ahead of time. Matt remembered the last time he processed through here and how it had seemed to take an eternity. In fact, this time Sergei had him moving so fast that he thought he might be in the midst of one of those rental car commercial filmings. But that was just fine with him. The faster they went, the better.

As they walked through the main terminal area, Sergei explained to Matt that the U.S. Ambassador had called a mandatory meeting for that afternoon. As a result, the LEGAT had called and asked Sergei if he could meet Matt and bring him to the Embassy compound. Sergei told Victor that he would have been disappointed if he had not asked him.

Since toting bags was not one of Matt's favorite pastimes, the sight of Sergei's black Volga parked nearby was indeed a welcome sight.

"I hope you don't mind, Matt, but a young woman asked if I would mind giving her a ride. I agreed. Again, I hope you don't mind."

"You know me, Sergei, the more the merrier. I just hope she's tall and very attractive."

"What else would you expect?" Sergei responded.

As they approached the rear of the car, Sergei stepped out ahead and popped the trunk lid. As Matt stood on the sidewalk with his bags, Sergei shuffled his coat, boots, protective vest, raid equipment, and a collection of old, stained coffee cups around the trunk to clear a space for Matt's bags.

As he opened the front door and looked into the backseat, Matt exclaimed, "You're right, Sergei. She is tall and ve-e-e-ery beautiful."

He quickly moved to open the back door so Natasha could get out.

As he held her tightly, tears came to her eyes, and she cried, "Matt, Matt, you don't know how much I have missed you!"

"Don't say anything, Natasha." Matt held her close and gave her a long and very passionate kiss.

Looking away and back several times, Sergei remarked, "I hate to break up this little party, you two, but as you Americans say, 'we have places to go and people to see.'"

"You are such a romantic, Sergei."

Sergei scoffed, "That is what the 'intimidator' says."

"Just because you're not loved, don't take it out on the rest of us," Matt responded.

Sergei added, "Who we really need here is Nick."

"You're right about that," Matt replied. "Since women don't seem to be falling head over heels for either of you, you two could cry in your vodka, and be good company for each other."

"Okay, we'll see what happens with you when you reach our age."

Matt smiled, "Remember, Sergei, I'll never be as old as you and Nick are."

"But someday, you will be our age."

"Thanks. I needed that."

"Anything to give your ego a boost," Sergei responded, as he gave out another of his patented, deep-belly laughs.

"Seriously, thanks for what you did here, Sergei. This is great."

Sergei smiled, "Even if I had tried, I don't think I could have kept her away. Once she heard you were coming, she called me two, sometimes three, times a day, for updates and any changes."

"I'm very happy to hear that." Matt said, as he looked into Natasha's eyes and kissed her one more time.

On their drive in from the airport, they passed the area where Matt had been shot. He was grimly reminded of how quickly things can change in one's life. One moment, he and Natasha were living a dream, a moonlit evening walk in the snow to a quaint little restaurant for an intimate dinner. Then, out of the darkness came a struggle for their lives. It all happened so fast, and had seemed like an eternity since they had been together. Matt pulled Natasha even closer as she remained silent, brushing her fingertips across his lips.

Now nearing the American Embassy, where Matt would be staying at Victor's residence, Sergei asked, "What time do you want me to pick you up for dinner?"

"You don't have to do that," replied Matt.

"I know that I don't have to, but I am going to anyway. At least on your first night back, I have no intention of letting you start out the evening just wandering around Moscow, either by yourself, or with Natasha directing you. We don't need anymore statistics. There are already more than enough of them to go around. Besides, look at it this way. At least one of us will have a gun."

"I appreciate your concern, but..."

Sergei interrupted, "No buts...I know, you are intending to spend time with Natasha while you are here. As you FBI guys are always saying, though, 'Trust me.' This will all work out fine. Since she has already arranged to get the night off from work at the social club, I thought we could all go to dinner together. Afterwards, I can drop you two off anywhere else you might like to go. We have a late night surveillance going on, but there will be plenty of time for dinner before I have to get back for that."

"Okay Sergei, that sounds great. Give me an hour?" Matt answered.

"An hour it is. Natasha and I will be here at the gate. Oh, and before I forget to tell you. Victor and I have set aside time tomorrow afternoon for the three of us to meet at my office regarding the shooter."

"I assume he is still in jail."

"You assume correctly. I don't see him going any-where, except possibly to Siberia," chuckled Sergei, "for at least twenty years."

As he was getting out of the backseat of the black Volga to go into the Embassy, Matt gave Natasha a kiss and whispered into her ear, "I can't wait for tonight. See you in an hour."

Natasha blew him a kiss as she smiled and nodded in agreement.

Sergei added, "Remember, you have my cell phone number, and I am only a call away. I expect to hear from you if you need anything, and I mean anything, at anytime. Understand?"

"Yes, Sergei," Matt smiled and nodded in agreement, "and thanks."

It had been less than an hour and Matt was already back at the Embassy gate where Sergei was having another cigarette, and Natasha stood anxiously awaiting his return.

The three of them went to dinner at one of Sergei's favorite spots, and afterwards he drove them to Natasha's apartment. As Matt and Natasha were getting out, Sergei once again reminded the two of them that they were to call him if anything should happen or they needed any help.

Matt smiled, and re-assured Sergei that they would.

With the exception of a sheet of black plastic now covering what had been a large hole in the drywall, the poorly lit stairs and hallway leading to Natasha's apartment was just as Matt had remembered. As they approached the door, Natasha handed him the key and Matt opened it. After switching on the light, and taking a quick look around, he took her hand and the two of them hurried inside, closing and locking the door behind them.

As Natasha gazed into his eyes, Matt pulled her to him and their lips met. She wrapped her arms around his neck and her foot instinctively raised and kicked back behind her.

"I missed you so very much," she whispered in his ear.

"No more that I missed you," Matt responded.

Continuing to hold her close, the two exchanged yet another passionate kiss.

Throughout their separation, images had been building in the minds of both as to what it would be like when they were reunited, and now that they were together again, the chemistry was even stronger than either had ever imagined possible.

Once released from his embrace, Natasha took Matt's hand and led him through the door into her bedroom.

As Matt sat on the edge of the bed, Natasha let the sleek, black sleeveless dress she was wearing slide off her smooth shoulders and firm breasts, and down the dark stockings covering her long, sexy legs. Now standing in front of him, she stepped out of her dress, and as Matt got up, she began unbuttoning his shirt and rubbing his chest. He pulled her to him, and as they passionately embraced, both began slowly slipping onto the bed.

Matt gently stroked her shiny, silky, dark auburn hair, and caressed her breasts, running his fingers along her soft smooth skin.

"You are wonderful," he whispered.

Natasha gave him a tender kiss and closed her eyes with a loving smile as he continued to caress her body.

"I never want this night to end," she told him as they lay there.

Matt responded with a loving kiss, and the look in his eyes expressed total contentment.

The incredible feelings each was sensing were fantastic.

CHAPTER FIFTY-THREE

This night at The Ruble Bar and Restaurant seemed unusually noisy. Darren Kroft looked around and spotted Sasha at his personal booth near the back. After squeezing his way through the crowd gathered around the bar watching the Rockies game, he arrived at Sasha's table. He had been waiting there since receiving Kroft's frantic call.

Sasha first gestured, and then commanded in his heavily accented voice, "Be seated, Darren."

Kroft nervously sat down.

"Now, tell me what the problem is," directed Sasha.

His voice shaking, Kroft blurted out, "They're onto us."

"What do you mean, 'They are onto us'?"

"I mean they know what we're doing, Sasha."

"Who knows?" Sasha pressed.

"The people at the bank. They know!"

"Now, be calm, Darren. Tell me exactly what you believe they know."

Kroft took a deep breath and began explaining what Gary Martin had told him regarding the CEO asking him what Kroft had been doing and when the job was to be completed.

"That does not sound unusual to me," replied Sasha.

"It didn't seem that way to me either, until Martin explained that it was very unusual for the CEO to ask him anything about the computer operations. Until now, his philosophy had been to leave Martin alone and let him take care of everything. The CEO just didn't want any problems, and as long as there were none, he let Martin do his job. I assume it was because of this latitude that we got the contract without any bidding opposition. Am I right?"

"You are right, Darren."

"Oh yes, one other thing. He also said the CEO seemed very concerned or suspicious that something might be happening."

"Like what?"

"He didn't say, and I don't think the CEO told him. Otherwise, he wouldn't have said anything to me about their conversation."

"Did you cover your tracks?" Sasha asked.

"Absolutely, and there is no way any of those bank employees will ever discover anything until long after we have the money offshore and under our control. While they are standing there, scratching their heads, I will be toasting vodkas with Catherine in some island paradise."

What about the woman who came here with you and Mr. Martin for drinks?"

"You mean Christine?"

"*Da*, she is the one, I think," answered Sasha. "She is some kind of a computer consultant, right?

"Supposedly, but I think she's clueless," answered Kroft.

"Just to be on the safe side, maybe we should remove her," suggested Sasha, in an effort to get Darren's reaction.

"That's kind of out of my area," Kroft responded somewhat tentatively.

"We will have to see. We certainly do not want some dumb broad falling into something that could end up costing us millions, now do we, Darren?"

"I guess not," Kroft answered.

Sasha gave him a disturbing look.

"I mean no, certainly not, Sasha."

"That is better," Sasha told him. "But first things, first. Are you saying you think we should move the money out of those accounts now?"

"I'm just saying that if the CEO is really suspicious about what I have been doing, the sooner we are able to get the money out, the better."

"Maybe the CEO should also be eliminated," suggested Sasha, as he once again laughed to himself, while observing Darren's reaction to such a thought. "How does that sound?"

"Well, uh, I-I-I'm not sure that's necessary," responded Kroft.

"What would you suggest, Darren?"

"I-I-I think that we should probably transfer the money out as soon as possible."

"Can you do that?" asked Sasha.

Kroft nodded, indicating that he could.

"Okay, then, do it."

"You mean, just like that?"

"I mean, just like that. Do I make myself clear?"

"Very," Kroft responded hesitatingly. Then, nodding his head, vigorously, he added, "Yes, yes. Very clear, Sasha."

"Okay, have the money put into that new account I gave you. You do still have the number?"

"Oh yes, I have it," Kroft assured him.

Sasha paused, noting a questioned expression on Kroft's face, "Is there anything else, Darren?" he asked.

"Who will be at the other end?" Darren questioned.

"I will be making some calls," Sasha answered. "You just let me know when you are ready to make the transfer."

"Okay, Sasha. I'll get things set-up," Darren nervously responded. "It should be within the next day or two. I'll call you when we need to start moving."

Gingerly sliding along the red leather bench seat of the booth, Darren quickly left The Ruble before any more of Sasha's wrath could be directed toward him. He knew Sasha was prone to violence, but he had never seen it portrayed quite as vividly as it was this evening. Sasha's total lack of regard for human life, when Christine and the CEO were mentioned, showed Kroft that he would not hesitate to kill anyone who got in his way.

Kroft's life as an up and coming CEO might be cut short if things didn't go as planned. It was up to him to make sure that they did. He was certainly glad there was a three-day holiday weekend coming up.

CHAPTER FIFTY-FOUR

Christine and K.C. agreed to meet for breakfast before she went to the bank. K.C. had met with Jeff Brown the day before, and he wanted to be certain that Christine was aware of everything that had gone on in the meeting between Brown and the bank's CEO, earlier in the week.

Christine had hoped to have this undercover assignment completed and be on her way back to Alexandria so she could spend the upcoming three-day weekend with her federal prosecutor husband, but that wasn't to be. It looked like she would be working the entire weekend, trying to get things wrapped up in Denver.

As the two of them sat in the restaurant, K.C. eating bacon and eggs, while Christine munched on a bowl of whole grain cereal and fruit, they began planning their next moves.

"I'll be meeting later this morning with one of the AUSA's with whom I do quite a bit of work," K.C. told her. "He's a good prosecutor."

Christine smiled, "I like how you said 'with whom you work.'"

"Why do you say that?"

"Not too long before my husband and I got married, we were working on a case together. At that time, he didn't know me very well, and I had overheard him referring to me as 'my agent' at least a half dozen times when he was talking with others. One afternoon, I had finally had my fill of it and, in a less than tactful manner, informed him that neither I nor most other FBI agents appreciated being referred to by Assistant United States Attorney's as 'my agent.' It took him aback temporarily, but he got the message and he never again referred to me as 'his agent.'" She then added with a chuckle, "Now, he just refers to me as 'his wife.' "

"Right on, Christine," agreed K.C. "And, he still married you, too!"

She smiled, and nodded her head.

"Before I meet with the AUSA today, we need to decide whether we want to execute any search warrants, and if so, upon whom and where. We are also going to have to decide who we're going to interview."

Christine replied, "I think our first interview should probably be with Gary Martin. He knows the bank's computer system inside and out. If we are going to be able to continue to monitor what's going on there, we'll need his cooperation. Right now, the only thing we can be sure of is that at least one trap door has been placed into one program, at one financial institution. There are very likely more trap doors at First Westside, and remember Kroft also had contracts at other banks and brokerages in the area. Who knows what he did while he was in their computers."

"As far as First Westside goes, I assume he will do whatever Sasha tells him to do. That is, unless he is willing to double-cross Sasha and their organization. Even as greedy as he seems to be, I somehow don't think he's quite that dumb," surmised K.C. "I think we both realize we can't risk interviewing either Darren Kroft or Sasha at this time, though."

Christine agreed.

K.C. continued, "I think that we're going to have to be prepared to execute search warrants at both Kroft's residence and on the business. Since time might be critical, I'll alert the AUSA to that, and prepare drafts for those affidavits so that they'll be ready to go, if and when we need them."

"That sounds good to me," replied Christine.

"Next, we need to decide how we want to handle the Gary Martin interview."

"I don't think we should tell him I'm an agent," Christine said. "Not quite yet anyway. Who knows, we might get lucky and he'll come in and start spilling his guts to me as soon as you leave."

"We should be so lucky," responded K.C. "I agree with your remaining a UCA at this point. Another agent and I should be able to handle that initial interview. That also allows you more time to keep your access to the bank's computers without suspicion arising, and as you said, to see if Martin says anything to you."

"First though, let me call Quantico. I have a message from my unit chief," Christine told K.C. "After I finish talking with him, I'll say 'hello' to Nick and a couple of the others, and then have them transfer me downstairs to the Behavioral Science Unit. They may be able to give me some suggestions regarding interview approaches to these guys. The agent I usually work with down there has given me some good ideas in the past."

"Okay, and in the meantime, I'll meet with the AUSA, and line up another agent to conduct the initial interview with me. I thought I would start off the Martin interview by talking to him about his gambling, and see where that leads."

"Sounds good to me," agreed Christine, "I'll give you a call after I talk to Quantico."

K.C. left the hotel and was on his way downtown when his cell phone rang.

"K.C., it's me, Christine. I just finished talking to Quantico, and it seems as though everybody with whom I wanted to talk is either in class, or out of the office on assignment. The only one I did reach was my unit chief and you know how it is talking to the bosses. All they ever want to know is, 'What have you done for me lately, and when will you be off of this boondoggle and back to the real work of the FBI?' I told him I didn't know, but things were beginning to get very interesting out here, and that I might be a while."

"I think 'interesting' might be an understatement," agreed K.C.

Christine added, "Oh, before I forget, my unit chief told me that Nick is down in Panama."

"What's going on in Panama?"

"He's there on a teaching assignment at the new ILEA (South)."

CHAPTER FIFTY-FIVE

"Matt, are you sure he is the one?"

"No question, Sergei. The fax photo made identification a little tough, but seeing him here leaves no question. He's the guy."

"Good. With your positive ID, and the gun, he's as good as gone for the next 20 years. I told you we would get him."

"You…with the help of Natasha," Matt quipped.

"And some luck," added Sergei, "but you know me, I would rather be lucky than good any day."

"That sounds like a Bureau line to me, Sergei."

"It is. That is where I first heard it. Nick said it in the class."

"So you did remember something from the seminar," Matt responded with a laugh.

"A little," Sergei smiled. "Not to change the subject, Matt, but how do you think Natasha is doing?"

"Outstanding!" Matt replied enthusiastically, "She's looking even better than I remembered."

"Now you know that is not what I mean," replied Sergei. "I may be a few years older than you, but my eyes are certainly not failing me. What I meant is, do you think she is getting along okay? As you know, it has been hard for her, and that place where she works can be tough on someone who looks like Natasha. She tells me she gets, as you American's would say, 'hit on all of the time,' and doesn't like it, but she stays there because the money is good and she needs the job."

"Yeah, I understand," Matt responded. "Natasha told me last night that there is a woman named, Catherine, at the social club who has seemed to be taking a special interest in her. She tries to help Natasha out from time to time. She told me how some big guy put his hands all over her, and tore her skirt. This woman, Catherine, stepped in and had several of the in-house thugs show him the door and points well beyond. Natasha could hear the guy crying out in pain, outside. So, it looks as though there is someone looking out for her there."

Sergei nodded. "That is good."

"Beyond that, though, I don't know," answered Matt. "When I took her home last night, her apartment seemed about the same as when I was in it a few months ago. It was clean, but there was still not much furniture. I'll see what else I can learn tonight.

CHAPTER FIFTY-SIX

Gary Martin was sitting at this desk, enjoying his morning cup of coffee, and thinking about what he was going to do over the upcoming three-day weekend, when there was a knock on the door.

"Mr. Gary Martin?"

"Yes."

"I'm Special Agent K.C. Woodson and this is Special Agent Mark Henderson of the FBI. We would like to speak with you, if you have a few minutes."

"Oh. Uh…Okay. Sure."

"Do you mind if I close the door?" asked K.C.

"No. Please do," answered Martin, as he gestured for them to be seated. "May I get you some coffee?"

"Not now, but thanks, anyway," replied K.C.

"I know the FBI investigates stuff involving banks, but you're the first agents I've ever met since working here. How can I help you? Is it about something one of my people has done?" asked Martin.

"It has to do with gambling," responded Mark Henderson.

"Somebody who works here?" asked Martin.

"Yes, it is, Mr. Martin. It's you," answered K.C.

Martin's face became flushed. "I-I-I'm all done with that. I'm clean. I've been away from that for years."

"That's fine, but we would still like to ask you some questions."

As Martin lowered his eyes and looked down at his desk, he softly responded, "Okay."

"Now, Mr. Martin, you said that you have been away from it for years. How many years are we talking about?"

Martin hesitated momentarily before answering. "Four or five, at least," he said.

"Are you sure?"

"Why do you ask?" questioned Martin.

"From what we hear on the street, you are into the book big time."

"Who says?"

"You know I can't tell you that," answered K.C.

"Well, just so you know, that's all been taken care of. I don't owe anybody anything, anymore."

"How did that happen?" asked K.C.

"I didn't rob a bank or anything, if that's what you're thinking, so why should it matter to you?" asked Martin.

"Well, as you put it earlier, 'The FBI investigates stuff that involves banks,' and we are especially interested if money is going out of banks that shouldn't be."

Martin slid his chair back and his face started turning red. "Now just a minute. Let's get the record set straight right now. I have never taken one red cent I wasn't entitled to out of this bank, or any other bank for that matter."

"Then, would you mind telling us how you managed to pay off the gambling debt?"

"It was forgiven. So there you have it," Martin responded.

"Now, Mr. Martin, I've been an FBI agent for over twenty years and have worked plenty of cases involving bookies. I have yet to meet my first bookie who goes around forgiving debts out of the kindness of his heart." K.C.'s voice rose as he stared into Gary Martin's eyes. "If it's forgiven, there is something expected in return, either now or in the future. So, what was it?"

"It was nothing really," Martin remarked. "In fact, it was a benefit to the bank."

"What was a benefit to the bank?" Henderson asked.

"The computer consulting contract," Martin responded exasperatedly.

"What computer consulting contract, Mr. Martin?"

"The one just completed by Darren Kroft."

"Darren Kroft is a bookie?" asked K.C.

"No, no. He's a computer consultant, and a damn good one, I might add."

"Well, then, we're back to how was the debt forgiven?"

"The bookie told me he would forgive my debt if I would get Darren Kroft a computer consulting contract with the bank."

"Now, why do you think he would do that, Mr. Martin?"

"I guess he wanted to help out a guy who was starting a new business."

"Who's he?" asked K.C.

"If I tell you, you can't let him know I'm the one who told you."

"Once again, Mr. Martin, who is he?"

"Sasha."

"What's his last name?"

"I don't' know. All anyone ever calls him is Sasha."

"Where do you meet with this Sasha?" asked K.C.

"The Ruble Bar and Restaurant in Arvada. He owns it."

"How much did you owe Sasha, Mr. Martin?"

"With the accrued weekly interest, it had grown to somewhere around $40,000. I was getting desperate."

"Now, I ask you again, why do you think Sasha would forgive a $40,000 debt, in return for your arranging for a computer consulting contract, especially if the consultant was doing a good job and helping the bank out, as you have suggested. Does that make any sense?" questioned K.C.

"It may not, but I swear to you, that is exactly what happened."

"Have you had a chance to take a good look at the work Mr. Kroft's firm has completed?" asked Henderson.

"Yes, I have, and it's outstanding. In fact, the bank has since retained a temporary employee, just to work on implementing the recommendations that Darren has made."

"Is there anything else you would like to tell us, Mr. Martin?" asked K.C.

"Nothing other than this has been a win-win situation for me." Martin paused, before adding, "Of course, that is up until now."

"Do you have any other questions, Mark?"

"Nothing, K.C."

K.C. looked Gary Martin straight in the eye. "In all likelihood, we will be talking again, Mr. Martin. In the meantime, I would like you to keep this among the three of us."

"You can count on that. I certainly don't want anyone else to know about this. Think of my job here at the bank. My reputation."

No sooner had the agents left his office, than Martin was scurrying down the hallway on his way to the restroom. The interview had caused him to suddenly become sick to his stomach.

Fearing that Sasha might somehow learn that the FBI was talking to him, and what Sasha might do to him if he thought he had squealed, Martin got on the phone.

"Sasha, it's me, Gary."

There was no response.

"You know, Gary Martin over at the bank."

"Sure, Mr. Martin. I recognize your voice. How are things going?"

"I just want to let you know," Martin paused.

"Let me know what?" asked Sasha.

Martin spewed out his guts at an almost machine gun pace, "The FBI was just here, and they were asking me questions about gambling."

"Now slow down, Gary, and tell me what you told them?"

"I told them that I wasn't gambling anymore."

"Is that all they wanted to know?"

"Well, not exactly," Martin answered.

"What does that mean?" asked Sasha. "Tell me. Exactly what was it they asked you that prompted this call?"

"Well, they asked me about you, bu…but…I didn't tell them anything. I promise."

"You didn't tell them anything?"

"Nothing, Sasha. You know me, I would never say anything at all. I just wanted to let you know."

In a low, but very authoritative tone, Sasha said, "Thank you for the call, Mr. Martin. I would like to talk to you some more about this. Maybe we can meet, let's say in an hour."

"Where?"

"You remember the place where we used to get together from time to time."

"You mean out toward Morrison?" asked Martin.

"Yes," answered Sasha. "I will see you there in an hour. Please don't keep me waiting."

"No. No, Sasha, I would never be late. You can count on seeing me there in an hour."

They both hung-up. Within seconds, Martin was up from his desk and heading around the corner to the cubicle where Christine was working.

CHAPTER FIFTY-SEVEN

As soon as Gary Martin hung-up, Sasha was back on the phone. "Darren, this is Sasha."

"Yes, Sasha."

Leaving no question in Kroft's mind that this was a directive, rather than a question, Sasha said, "You will have the money moved from the accounts as we discussed?"

"Yes, of course. Is there a change?"

"No change. I want to make sure that if I call the bank where the money is being transferred I will be told the monies are there in the account."

"I can assure you that, if you were to make such a call, you would be pleased with the result. I have already gone into the accounts and issued the transfer instructions. In fact, the money might already be there. Why don't you call down and check? Then let me know. I'll be waiting in my office."

"I like your attitude, Darren. I think I'll just do that." The line went dead.

Within a matter of minutes, Kroft's phone rang, again.

"Darren?"

"Yes."

"Darren, you did well. Now that I know the money is already there, I have decided to make a surprise visit to our friends at that sunny Caribbean bank."

"Have a good trip, Sasha."

"I will. Women, vodka, millions of dollars, what else could I want?" Sasha replied. "What are you going to do, Darren?"

"I'm going to finish things here at the office, so I will be ready for our next job. Whenever that is."

Sasha laughed, "*Da*, when-never," and abruptly hung-up on Darren.

Sasha's closing remark certainly had not left Kroft with a warm, comfortable feeling. As he sat mulling over what Sasha had just said, Kroft asked himself, "Am I ever going to see a dime of that money I just transferred from the accounts at First Westside?" He concluded that the answer was probably, "No." He had already heard more than enough about what Sasha had done to others, so why should he expect things to be different for him?

It was beginning to look like all of that money laundering reading and research he had been doing was going to finally payoff. For months, he had worked to prepare an alternate course of action, just in case something like this happened. Now was his chance to see if what he had read about in theory was going to work in practice. His future and his life might literally depend on how much he had learned.

CHAPTER FIFTY-EIGHT

Gary Martin told Christine, "I am going to be out for a while. I don't know exactly when I'll be back."

Noting a tinge of nervousness in his voice, she asked, "Is something the matter?"

"Oh no, it's just something that came up, and I remembered we had talked about getting together today to go over some of those recommendations, but it doesn't look like that's going to be possible. Why don't you continue to look over Darren's report and jot down any questions you have."

Expressing concern, Christine responded, "Okay, but is there something I can do to help?"

After a brief hesitation, he looked down and replied, "I really appreciate that, but no. It's a personal matter. But, thanks anyway," and he turned and hurried back down the hallway.

Since there was no time to get any of the surveillance units in place to put a tail on Gary Martin, Christine grabbed her purse and walked quickly out of the building. Martin was just pulling his emerald-green, four-door Explorer out of its parking space when she arrived at her car.

As Martin left the parking lot and pulled out onto the highway, Christine kept him in sight, following at a distance. Martin was driving just about the speed limit and didn't seem to be up to anything out of the ordinary.

Christine thought to herself, "This tail is a piece of cake." It certainly could not be characterized as a typical FBI surveillance where the bad guy is constantly making unpredictable u-turns and other dangerous maneuvers in an effort to "dry clean" himself.

As the two of them continued along the highway, Christine pressed K.C.'s extension on her cell phone. There was no answer, and after getting his phone mail was transferred to the squad secretary. There, she left a message for him to call her ASAP. K.C. had gone downstairs to see the Assistant United States Attorney. The squad secretary would beep him.

Christine could now see a large drag-racing complex with its high bleachers and advertisers' billboards spread along the landscape in the distance. Next, came a narrow, winding roadway. Finally, she followed him into a large parking lot that stood at the foot of a large and very beautiful, red rock outcropping. There, Martin drove directly to an area near the front and parked his green Explorer in the first open spot that was not reserved for handicapped.

Christine hung back and drove over to the side of the lot, where a couple of motor homes, a large van from a local recreation center, and several other cars were parked. They would block her car from his view.

While she was sitting in her car, her cell phone rang. It was K.C.

"I just got an urgent message to call you. What's up?" he asked.

"Not long after you and Mark left the interview, Martin came to see me. He seemed pretty upset, and told me that he was going to have to leave for a while. Things just didn't seem right, so I decided to follow him and see if there was something going on. We're now parked in a large lot that sits at the foot of a huge outcropping of red colored rock. I think that the sign said something about an amphitheater."

"It sounds like you are out on the hogback at the Red Rocks Park Amphitheater. On your way to Morrison?"

"That's it, K.C. There were signs that said Morrison, and it wasn't very far, according to the mileage signs."

"Does anything seem to be going on?"

"Nothing so far. He's just sitting there in his Explorer. I'm over on the side, mixed in with some other cars and motor homes. Wait. He's getting out and it looks like he is walking in the direction of a paved pathway. I've got to go."

"Christine, be careful. I'm going to start heading out there. Give me a call if anything happens, or if you need anything in the meantime."

"Will do, bye."

Christine had planned to run after work, so she grabbed her running shoes from her gym bag, in the backseat, and quickly slipped them on.

Martin walked along the long pathway that led to a huge amphitheater, majestically set into the towering sandstone rocks. He entered the amphitheater and walked down the steps to one of the lower-level seating areas toward the far side, and sat down. Other than two or three couples holding hands and walking near the stage, the complex was nearly empty.

Christine was going to have to be careful to stay outside the confines of that area if she wanted to remain undetected. Fortunately, she was able to find a place to position herself so that she could observe Martin, while at the same time managing to stay out of his line of sight.

After watching for only a couple of minutes, Christine noticed a dark-haired white male, probably in his late 20's or early 30's, walking up the long stairway on the far side toward Martin. He walked with a slight limp and was wearing black slacks, a burgundy colored leather sport jacket, and sunglasses. From a distance, she could not tell for sure whether Martin recognized him or not, but since they were the only two in that entire area of the amphitheater, it was a good guess that they would soon be meeting.

The guy sat down next to Martin, and even though the two did not appear to acknowledge one another's presence or shake hands, there was a clear indication that something was happening.

While trying to remain concealed and concentrating intently on what was going on with Martin, Christine was suddenly startled. Turning, she caught a glimpse of a group of elementary school age children running behind her on a pathway toward another giant outcropping of red rocks. They appeared to be playing a game as they chased one another along the pathways and trails located around the numerous rocks and crevices.

Suddenly, she heard a pop. Christine whirled around to look where Gary Martin and the other man had been sitting. She noticed Martin slumped to his side. The guy with the limp, who had been sitting beside him, was now walking rapidly along the row and toward the lower exit area. His right hand, concealed under the opening in his jacket, appeared to be holding something.

Christine drew the 9mm pistol from her handbag, and yelled, "Halt! FBI!"

The man turned, extended his arm, and fired two rounds in her direction, before quickly ducking into an exit area.

Beyond this opening were huge sandstone outcroppings. One ran along the entire seating area on the far side of the amphitheater. Where he had retreated to was unknown.

Fortunately, both rounds went astray, but with the children in the area, Christine did not want to risk anymore gunfire at this time. She got back into the semi-concealed position from which she had been observing the two and took out her cell phone.

Since K.C. was already on his way, she wanted to alert him, knowing that he knew the territory and that he would bring in all of the necessary assistance. Even though it had been only a couple of seconds, it seemed like it was taking an eternity for K.C. to answer.

"Hello."

"K.C., it's me, Christine. We've had shots fired and Gary Martin is slumped over on his side on one of the bleacher seats here in the amphitheater. The shooter got off a couple of rounds in my direction and has moved into the rocks. Everyone will have to be very careful. There's a group of kids playing in the area."

"Are you okay, Christine?"

"Yeah, he missed."

"Christine. You keep your phone line open to me. I'll use my radio to get help."

"Headquarters, we have an emergency. There have been shots fired. An agent needs assistance."

As the air went silent, a chill went through every agent who was in earshot of his or her radio. The radio operator responded, "All units, we have an emergency. Leave this channel open. Go ahead, K.C."

"We have shots fired at the Red Rocks Amphitheater. There is a UCA on the scene. The UCA is all right and I'm on my cell phone with her. There is at one least victim down, and we need an ambulance, immediately. Tell them the only information I can give about the victim is that his name is Gary Martin, and that he is a white male, thirty-five years of age. Further details regarding his condition are unknown. The shooter is believed to be hiding in the rocks."

"We are calling for the ambulance now," replied the radio operator.

"Any available units are requested to meet me at the main parking lot at Red Rocks Park, ASAP."

Several FBI units radioed that they were already en route.

"HQ, I need you to contact Tom Wallace. Have him and our SWAT team proceed to the scene as soon as possible. Also, call the Jefferson County Sheriff's Department, and the Denver and Lakewood Police Departments, and advise them of what has happened and request their immediate assistance and SWAT Teams, if available. Tell them we will meet in the main parking lot. Request that uniform patrol units close off all entrances and exits to Red Rocks, and try to get everyone out of the Park area so that it can be secured. Oh yes, one other thing. The UCA said to be sure and tell everyone that there are young children running throughout the area, so everyone needs to be extremely careful."

"K.C., I'm going to try to get over to Martin. I'll see if I can do anything," Christine told him.

"Be careful. Help is on the way. Do you see any sign of the shooter?"

"Not right now, but I think he may be in some high rocks that run along the far side of the amphitheater or in the rocks down behind the stage. I don't know for sure, though."

With her heart pounding and the adrenaline flowing, Christine was ready to make her move. She crouched low in the walkway and was moving as rapidly as she could to where Martin's body was slumped on the bleacher seat.

There appeared to be at least one bullet hole in his head, and blood was pooling on the bench seat. Christine first took his wrist, and then pressed her fingertip to his neck. With the cell phone line still open, she gasped, "K.C., he's been shot in the head. I can't find a pulse."

"Keep a low profile, Christine. Help should be there shortly."

"Okay, but in the meantime, I need to find those kids who were running around here, and get them out of the area."

As dispatchers from the local Sheriff's and Police Departments aired the situation to their units, Christine could hear sirens blaring in the distance. As far a she was concerned, though, their arrival couldn't be too soon.

Since there was nothing she could do for Gary Martin, Christine quickly moved back to where she had last seen the children. As she moved in the direction they had been running, she heard a child scream. Had her worst nightmare just occurred?

Shortly thereafter, a group of children came running toward where Christine and two other women were now standing. She had noticed these women walking around the amphitheater area earlier. They were wearing khaki shorts and collared shirts with a local recreation center logo embroidered on the front pocket. Both appeared to be with the group of children that had startled her earlier. As the children got closer, Christine could hear the children yelling and crying, "It's Jonathan! It's Jonathan!"

Gathering around the other two women, the children all seemed to be trying to talk at the same time. Christine asked, "What about Jonathan?"

Several of them blurted out simultaneously, "He fell! He's hurt!"

"Okay," she said, gesturing and trying to calm them down. "I'm an FBI agent. Now, one at a time, tell me where he is and what happened."

A little girl spoke up, "We were playing on the path around the rocks, and a man came running toward us. He had a gun. When we started running away, we yelled for Jonathan to come down. He had gone up onto one of those big rocks over there."

"I told him he would get into BIG TROUBLE if he went climbing on the rocks, but he wouldn't listen to me," interrupted another little girl who was standing in front of one of the workers.

"Shut up, tattle-tale Sarah!" yelled several of the boys.

"That's enough of that from all of you," one of the workers said sternly, and they all stopped. "Now, tell us what happened to Jonathan."

Others followed, one at a time, "He slipped trying to get down!"

"I guess he couldn't hold on!"

"We couldn't see him moving!"

Christine looked up and pointed in the direction of a long strip of towering, angled rocks separated with long, narrow crevices, "Those rocks up there?" she asked.

"Yes. Yes," several of them anxiously answered.

Pointing in that direction again, Christine continued, "He's in those rocks?"

"Yes, those are the ones."

"And he wasn't moving?"

"No."

"Did you see where the man with the gun went?"

"He's somewhere up in there too, I think," responded the first little girl.

Christine asked the leader, "Are all of the rest of the kids here?"

The leader quickly looked around and nodded, "Yes."

With her 9mm still in hand, Christine turned to the two women, "Take the kids, and run as fast as you can down the pathway to the parking lot. When you get there, get the children to crouch down beside the motor homes and van. The police are on their way. I'll go and see what I can do for Jonathan."

"K.C., can you hear me?"

"Loud and clear now, Christine. What happened? I could hear some kid's voices in the background, but they were muffled."

"A group of children ran this way, and told me that a boy named Jonathan has fallen. It sounds like into a crevice. They said he's not moving, and thus his condition is unknown. I'm heading in that direction, now. The children and their recreation center leaders are on their way down to the parking lot. I told them to stay down beside the motor homes and van until the police arrive. You might want to get on the radio and warn everyone who is responding, one more time, about children being in the immediate area.

"I'll do that, and at the same time I'll have them alert the hospital's emergency flight team that a child has fallen and he is reported to not be moving. In the meantime, you be careful."

"Okay."

In a solemn voice over the radio, K.C. reported, "Headquarters, be advised that a child has fallen, and he's reported to not be moving, so his condition is unknown. He is believed to be in the vicinity of the shooter. Alert the hospital's emergency flight team, and tell those responding they need to seek out and secure any of the children who are now gathering in the parking lot."

"Ten-four."

As Christine continued making her way up the trail and through the rocks toward the crevice, she could only hope and pray that Jonathan was still alive.

Crouching as she ran, and moving from one point to another, she suddenly tripped, catching her pant leg on a prickly shrub. She pulled until the material ripped loose, and then moved ahead to a point where she could see Jonathan lodged on a small ledge between the rock walls. From her vantage point, however, she could not tell much about his condition, but she didn't notice any movement.

"K.C., have you heard from the chopper?"

"They are in the air and on their way. It shouldn't be more than a few minutes. Also, I just got word the first patrol officers are now on the scene. I'm turning the corner into the park entrance and should be there shortly."

In the meantime, two of the first police officers on the scene had managed to work their way up to where Christine was. Her position offered some concealment and also allowed her to observe Jonathan. Within a few minutes, K.C. arrived. Crouched beside the rocks, they could hear a helicopter approaching, and more sirens screaming as additional units responded.

The sheriff's deputies sealed off the Park and called out over the loud speakers of their patrol cars. "This is the Sheriff's Department. Red Rocks Park is closed. Return to your vehicles immediately."

By asking those at each vehicle in the lot, they learned that everyone had complied. When the recreation center leaders were asked about the children, they responded that all had been accounted for...except Jonathan.

The FBI SWAT Team and hostage negotiator, and SWAT teams from both the sheriff's department and one of the police departments arrived on the scene. Officers from the Denver SWAT team were unable to respond due to an earlier incident involving a now barricaded robbery suspect.

As the last of the remaining SWAT team members filtered into the area, the three team commanders and the FBI hostage negotiator gathered and formulated plans. Because all of the teams had considerable experience in working on joint operations, this initial planning session moved along smoothly.

With assignments made and their gear in place, the teams moved out of the command post area, and into where they believed the shooter was now hiding. As they cautiously moved through the rocks and crevices, calls for him to surrender were blasted over a loudspeaker.

"This is the FBI. Come out with your hands up."

There was no response.

Suddenly, one of the FBI agents spotted movement in an elevated outcropping of rocks directly ahead of his position. At about that same time, the shooter must have also realized that he had been sighted, because the next thing the agent saw and heard were flashes and pops coming from the muzzle of a weapon. "Are you okay?" the agent heard in his earpiece.

"A round hit my vest, but I'm all right."

The shooter was positioned for maximum cover, but he could not remain completely protected.

While the negotiator tried to get the shooter to surrender, the SWAT Teams began to move. First, it was the Sheriff's Department whose team included several experienced mountain rescue officers. They had been assigned to get themselves into a position to rescue the boy. As that team was re-positioning itself, the shooter rose up from his position and fired in the direction of the deputies. When he did, a sharpshooter from the police SWAT team took aim and fired. The shooter could be seen slowly falling backward into the rocks and popping off several more rounds into the air.

With the shooter now out of sight, members of the FBI team began their slow, methodical descent. When they climbed over the rocks surrounding the shooter, they saw no activity. It appeared that he had slid down the rock and ended sitting-upright, with his head tilted toward his right shoulder and drooped downward.

While other team members drew a bead on the shooter, in case he should try something, one of the agents jumped down into the basin to see if he were still alive. There was no pulse.

In the meantime, deputies from the sheriff's SWAT team made their way to the crevice where the young boy remained lodged. The small ledge upon which he was now lying had hopefully served not only to break his fall, but also to save his life. Had he dropped farther into the crevice, his small body might have been tightly sandwiched between the giant rocks, making a rescue even more difficult.

With his ropes secured, one of the deputies was lowered into the crevice. Mountain rescues had become a way a life for these specially trained deputies. Even so, they could never take anything for granted. A slip, a loose knot, a wrong move, anyone of these or a thousand other things could mean instant death or permanent disability to either the rescuer or the person being rescued. Being held from above, the deputy stopped at the ledge and reached over to take hold of the young boy's hand. His eyes were closed, but there was a pulse.

The deputy started speaking to him, first, telling him who he was, and then asking him what his name was.

The boy gave a weak reply, "Jonathan," he said.

There was considerable blood on his face and head, and the deputy still had no idea as to the extent of any fractures or internal injuries, but at least he was alive.

That information was immediately relayed to those now waiting with the medical chopper in the parking lot below. One of the police officers who had been in the rocks above the boy quickly made his way back down to the pathway so he could assist the medical crew, leading them back up to Jonathan.

As soon as the hospital's emergency flight team members with their on-board stretcher could make their way to Jonathan, they would attempt to lower the stretcher, along with a medic, to see if the boy could be lifted out that way.

"Jonathan, we're going to get you out of here," he was assured by the deputy.

With tears streaming down his cheeks, Jonathan looked up at him and smiled.

"We'll be strapping you onto this stretcher and the people above will be lifting you out. Okay?"

"Okay," Jonathan quietly responded.

"Can you tell us where you hurt?"

"All over, but 'specially my head and my arm," he told them.

Jonathan winced with pain, as he was carefully strapped onto the stretcher. Slowly, those above lifted him out of the crevice. When the stretcher reached the top, the crew checked his vital signs and carried the stretcher to the helicopter.

One of the medical team crewmembers who remained behind to finish packing up a bag was asked by Christine, "How is he going to be?"

She was told, "His vitals are good, considering, and the bleeding seems to have stopped. He's conscious and talking. The next couple of hours should tell us a lot."

In the meantime, the other two SWAT teams had finished securing the area. When the "all clear" was given, the crime scene investigators and personnel from the coroner's office came in to do their jobs.

On their way back down, K.C. and Christine went over to where the shooter's body was lying. As K.C. stood there looking down, Christine asked, "Do you recognize him?"

"He looks like one of thugs I saw with Sasha at The Ruble. In fact, he might be the guy the police have been looking for in connection with several unsolved homicides. They appeared to be mafia style hits, and witnesses have said that the last guy they saw in the area walked with a slight limp. It's obvious that this guy won't be any help, though."

"No. I think that's a certainty," Christine agreed.

CHAPTER FIFTY-NINE

Until Sasha landed at Miami's International Airport, he had almost forgotten about this being a long weekend for most Americans. There, he found himself caught up in a long security check line for flights destined for the Caribbean. It was beginning to look like he might not make his scheduled departure to Antigua. Not known for his patience, Sasha watched for a break anywhere and when he saw another security checkpoint was opening, quickly rushed over to it. After completing the screening, he ran down the concourse, arriving at the gate just as they were calling for final boarding. He had made it.

Once on board, he stretched out in his first class seat, sipped a glass of champagne, and began dreaming about what might lie ahead. The women, the booze, and the fun in the sun would all be fine, but his big dream was the money – millions waiting for him at the other end. Soon, he would be receiving his single biggest payday, ever.

During this time, Darren Kroft was also carrying out travel plans of his own. Sitting in a gate area located outside a string of pay telephones at Houston's International Airport, he had just finished talking with an officer at the bank in Antigua. This was the same bank where the newest TFM account Sasha had given him was located. That call resulted in his successful execution of yet another wire transfer.

Now, the money was out of that bank, and shortly before the bank's books would be closed for the weekend.

CHAPTER SIXTY

While K.C. and Christine were waiting for their dinner to be served, she took a minute to call the hospital to see what she could learn about Jonathan. The nurse at the intensive care station would only tell her that his condition had "stabilized," and that he seemed to be resting comfortably. That sounded like good news to Christine, considering all that he had been through.

Dinner arrived as she and K.C. were rehashing the day's events and making plans for their next steps.

"I'll get going on the Sasha end of this thing," K.C. told Christine. "What's your next plan of attack?"

"I need to go into the bank and check on a couple of things. Would you let Jeff know, so that he can make arrangements with security for me to get in tomorrow without a hassle? Oh, and also ask him if someone from the wire transfer department can meet me there sometime in the morning."

"I'll call him now. What time do you plan to be there?"

"Let's make it fairly early, say about eight."

K.C. made the call, and after talking for only a couple of minutes, seemed to have everything arranged. "Eight it is. Jeff said that he'll make sure everything is cleared for you. As far as a person from the wire transfer department coming in, he said he'll call you at the bank in the morning."

Feeling a little sorry for herself, since it was now clear she was going to be spending her entire three-day holiday weekend working in Denver, instead of being with her husband, Michael, Christine remarked, "Well K.C., I guess you know where you can reach me."

"Yeah," laughed K.C., "Same here."

The following morning, Christine was up early and standing outside the bank's side entrance at five till eight. She flashed her bank ID to the guard, and signed in at the entrance register. On the way to her cubicle, she noticed that Gary Martin's office door was slightly ajar. He must not have closed it when he left in a rush the day before. She pushed the door open and walked in. Although she had been in there a number of times and nothing appeared to be out of order, there was still something eerie about being in there now. Wanting to verify that the last outgoing call Martin made from his office phone was to whom she had expected, Christine picked up the receiver and punched the re-dial button. There were four rings, and then a recorded message clicked on, "You have reached The Ruble Bar and Restaurant. Our hours are 11:00 AM until 2:00 AM, daily, except Sunday." That was just as she had expected.

On the way back to her desk, she stopped to fix a pot of coffee, and see if anything had been left in her mail slot. There was no mail. With her coffee cup in hand, she arrived at her desk as the phone was ringing.

"Yes, Jeff," she answered.

"And just how did you know it was me?" he replied.

"The FBI knows everything, didn't you know that?" Christine replied, as laughter came from the other end of the line.

"I want to let you know that someone from wire transfer should be in between nine and ten this morning."

"Thanks, Jeff. I'll be waiting."

Knowing the big money usually goes into and out of a bank by wire transfer, Christine had made it a point to get to know the employees who worked with the wires, and had taken time to look over the daily wire transfer logs each day since her arrival. That was, with the exception of yesterday, when she was out at Red Rocks Park. Up to this point, she hadn't detected anything out of the ordinary.

Shortly after 9:00 AM, Susan Anderson from the wire transfer department came into Christine's cubicle. "Isn't that terrible about Mr. Martin? I heard it on the news as I was driving over here this morning."

"It certainly is," responded Christine.

"Shot at Red Rocks they said on the news. I can hardly believe it. We were just there recently for my little sister's high school graduation."

"It's hard to understand things sometimes, Susan."

"It sure is," she agreed, as she looked down. Then, looking back up at Christine, asked, "How can I help you this morning?"

"Would you get yesterday's wire transfer log for me, so that I can take a look at it."

"Sure. I'll be back in a minute --- or three, maybe."

Moments later, Susan rounded the corner, log in hand. "Here it is, Christine."

"Thanks. Now would you take a look at it and see if any of the transactions seem out of the ordinary."

"Certainly," said Susan, as she started running her finger down the page, not stopping until she came to an entry for $9.8 million. "This one," she pointed. "I don't recognize that account at all." She continued down that page and onto the next one. "That looks like the only one."

"Did any particular problems, or funds' shortages come to light yesterday?"

"No, not that I remember. No one said anything, anyway."

"Okay. Would you pull a copy of the actual wire transmitted and the account information for this $9.8 million transaction?"

"I'll see what I can find and be right back."

In the meantime, Christine went back to the area in the computer program where she had found the trap door to take another look.

Susan returned with the papers in hand and gave them to Christine, "I think this is what you want."

As the two of them looked over the transaction, they noted the $9.8 million was sent from the First Westside account of TFM to another TFM account, which appeared to be at an offshore bank, located in Antigua and Barbuda. Christine immediately suspected that this and other TFM accounts had been established in secrecy and confidentiality havens around the world, and that money was regularly transferred from one account to another in an effort to disrupt any tracking of the paper-trail by authorities.

Flipping to the next sheet and looking at the account information, Susan exclaimed, "This can't be! This just can't be!" On the sheet was little more than the name TFM and an account number assigned by the bank. Most of the other portions of that sheet, and other sheets relating directly to the TFM account, were missing information, except where necessary, in order to execute a wire transfer. Somewhat indignantly, she said, "I don't understand how this could have happened. There must have been some kind of computer input error; that is, unless," and she paused, "unless someone was able to get direct access to our system." She shook her head and said, "No, that's impossible. In fact, Mr. Kroft told us as much. After all, he spent all of that time with us. We went over everything in detail with him, step-by-step. No, no," she reiterated, "It's impossible for someone to get into our system."

Christine smiled and nodded.

"Anyway, we didn't come up short yesterday," Susan said. "We can take a closer look at this next week, when everyone is here. I'm sure there is some logical explanation. It's probably just some computer glitch that occurred when the information was being keyed in. I'm sure everything is okay."

Christine once again smiled and nodded.

"Well, anyway, if there is nothing more you need, Christine, I have to get back home. I'll see you next week."

"Before you go, there's just one more thing, Susan," Christine added. Would you please pull up that account and check the deposits recorded during this past week?"

"Okay. Is there anything special I'm supposed to be looking for?" she asked.

"Not that I know of. I'm just curious."

It wasn't long before Susan returned, looking perplexed as she held the papers in her hand.

"What is it?" asked Christine.

"Until yesterday that account had only a few dollars more in it than was required to keep it open." Susan paused, "I assume it must have been early yesterday morning..."

"What must have been early yesterday morning?" Christine asked.

"It must have all happened then. There were a number of different deposits totaling a little over $9.8 million transferred into that account. The funds were transferred internally. As a result, they were made available to the TFM account immediately. It was most all of the $9.8 million that was wire transferred to the bank in Antigua."

With that deposit information, it was time for Christine to take a look at the accounts that could be accessed through the trap door that Kroft had created within the program. Sure enough, all of the accounts from which money was moved into the TFM account came from accounts that could be accessed through that trap door.

"Susan, I don't need anything more from you right now, but would you jot down your home number for me, so I can get in touch with you in case there is something else that comes up."

"Here it is, Christine, and I'll call you if I'm going to leave."

"Thanks, Susan, and have a nice weekend."

"Okay. Bye." She turned to leave.

"Oh, Susan, one more question."

Stopping in her tracks, Susan turned around, "Yes."

"Can you think of any reason why the amount transferred was $9.8 million?"

"None other than the fact that we have several internal procedures set up to run additional checks and approvals on transfers greater that $10 million."

"Mr. Kroft was aware of that $10 million limit?"

"Certainly, and as I mentioned earlier, he took time to go through all of our procedures with us in great detail."

"Thanks again, Susan."

"Call me if you need anything else, Christine."

"I will."

No sooner had Susan departed, than Christine was on the line with K.C.

"K.C., he did it. $9.8 million to Antigua."

"$9.8 million. Are you sure?"

"As sure as I'm talking to you."

"Do you know how, Christine?"

"It looks like it was all done through the trap door I mentioned to you, earlier. He stole different amounts from accounts he could access through it. Put those monies into the TFM account he created. Then, transferred it all to a haven bank offshore. Pretty slick, huh?"

"Everything's beginning to fit into place."

"Why do you say that, K.C.?"

"Well, after dinner last night, I called Mark Henderson, and the two of us decided to pay a visit to The Ruble. I asked if Sasha was around and was sternly told he was not. Later, a guy who seemed to be running the place came over to where we were sitting and said he had heard we were looking for Sasha. I told him we were, and that we needed to talk with him about some business. The guy said that Sasha was out of town and he didn't expect him back for at least a week. I asked if there was somewhere I could call him, and the guy said, no, he had gone on a trip out of the country."

"Did he say where?"

"No, but Mark and I got on the horn with a couple of our airline security contacts out at DIA, and bingo. Sasha's name came up on the manifest of a flight that left DIA yesterday afternoon for Miami. After a change of planes there, he went on to his final destination of St. John's, Antigua, arriving sometime in the evening. Three guesses what he intends to do there, that is other than party, and the first two don't count. In the meantime, I'll give Marla a call and ask her to alert the Caribbean unit that operates out of the Miami Division, that we have something going on that may require their immediate assistance."

"Do you know if Kroft is with him?" asked Christine.

"No, we had them check those two flights for his name, also. Nothing came up. I assume he must still be around here. Why don't you call his home and his office just to be sure, though?"

"I'll do that right now and call you back, K.C."

"Okay, and after I talk to Marla, I'll freshen up the probable cause on those search warrant affidavits."

"You mean the ones for Darren Kroft's residence and his business?"

"Yeah. I'll meet with the AUSA, so we can get them issued and executed before sunset. The squad is going to love me when they get called in on a three-day weekend. But, as we say in the Bureau, that's why we get the big bucks."

Christine chuckled, "Yeah."

K.C. hadn't been off the line five minutes, before his phone rang again.

"K.C., I called the numbers and got the answering machines at both. Do you think he's gone?"

"We should find out this afternoon, assuming I'm successful in getting the warrants run through today, but this being a three-day weekend, it might not be so easy. Some good news, though. I did get in touch with Marla Cross and she is going to work on the Caribbean end, through our unit in Miami. I told her you would give her a call and fill her in on what you have. She said she would be coming into the office shortly."

CHAPTER SIXTY-ONE

His mind racing with an incessant lust for Catherine and anticipation that the two of them would soon be together again, Darren Kroft placed a call to the Moscow social club.

"Catherine, please," Kroft commanded.

There was a short pause, followed by a muffled comment he could not understand relayed in the background.

"This is Catherine," she answered.

"Catherine. It's me, Darren. I must see you. It's very important!"

"Where are you, Darren?"

"I'm in Panama."

"Where?"

"Panama. You know, where the Panama Canal is."

"What are you doing there?"

"It's a long story, but I'm here for us. You and me."

"Okay, but why? What is going on?"

"I'll explain it all to you when you get here. You have to trust me."

"Now, Darren, you know I cannot leave Moscow just because you call and say to come to Panama without giving me an explanation. You must tell me what is going on."

Kroft pleaded, "You have to understand. I love you and I need you here with me. Now!"

"Just tell me what is going on, Darren. You know how I feel about you."

"Okay, but promise me that we will be together. Please promise me that, Catherine."

"I promise," Catherine responded, her voice reflecting a slight agitation. "Now, tell me what is going on."

"I'm here in Panama to pick up $9.8 million dollars. This is money from some of the work I was doing with Sasha."

"Okay?" Catherine questioned.

Continuing to speak more rapidly as he got more and more excited, Kroft continued, "I thought we were all in this thing together. You in Moscow, and Sasha and me in Denver. All of us together. But, after I told Sasha I'd gotten the money transferred, he scoffed, and told me he was going down to Antigua to get it. I could tell by the way he acted and what he said, that he intended to keep all of it for himself." Kroft paused briefly to take a breath, before adding, "You and I were never going to see a dime of it! Do you understand, Catherine, nothing! I had to do something!"

"I still don't understand, Darren. Why are you in Panama? I thought the money is in Antigua."

"It was, but not anymore!"

"Then where is it?"

"That is what I am trying to tell you. It's here in Panama. It will be safe until you and I can make our withdrawal early Monday morning."

"How did this happen, Darren?"

"The money that was transferred to the bank in Antigua remained there for only a few hours before I had it transferred on to Panama. That was just before the banks closed for the weekend."

Fearing that she might lose their connection at anytime, Catherine continued, attempting to learn as much as she could about what was going on. "Darling, does anybody else know about this?"

"Nobody, it's just you and me. Don't you see, that's the beauty of it."

"Are you sure all of the money is there, Darren?"

"Yes, yes. After making that second transfer, I called the bank here in Panama and they confirmed that the $9.8 million had arrived."

"That is wonderful, lover, but I am curious. How did you know to do it this way? Did someone tell you?"

With that bit of encouragement, Kroft was beginning to feel more confident and cocky. "No, nobody," he responded. "Just things I've managed to pick up here and there. This is how some of the big-time money launderers around the world do it. The only difference between them and us is that they usually run the money through a lot more offshore bank accounts than I did. I guess they think that layering will cover the paper-trail, or something. This worked for us, though. Besides, I didn't have time to set up all of those different accounts in other countries. That would have also meant transferring the money between more and more banks and kept us apart even longer."

Patronizingly, she responded, "You're so smart, Darren. But, what about Sasha?"

"Don't give him a second thought. He won't even realize the $9.8 million was transferred to Panama until he tries to make his big withdrawal at the bank in Antigua. And, by the time they get through the paperwork with him there, we will be out of here and on the way to our own island paradise."

"Where we can lie on the beach and drink piña coladas?" Catherine asked.

"Exactly, and, where no one will ever find us," answered Kroft.

"How did you manage to get this all done so quickly, darling?"

"It really wasn't that quick. Since I was always a little worried that something like this might happen along the way, I contacted an attorney down here in Panama, a couple of months ago. He filed the necessary papers for incorporation, and set up a bank account for me, all well in advance. Looking back, now, I'm sure glad I did. Otherwise, there might have been nothing out there for us. That is, other than those special things we do best together. Remember?"

"How could I ever forget?" Catherine responded, in her most seductive voice.

"When can you be here?" Darren anxiously asked.

"I'll try to be there by Sunday night. If not then, I should be there by early Monday morning. We will take up from where we left off in Moscow."

In an increasingly excited tone, Darren responded, "I want you so much, Catherine. It seems like an eternity since we were last together."

"Where are you staying?" Catherine asked.

"Near the airport. We can have drinks by the hotel pool, and maybe even take a moonlight plunge, before going back to our suite to practice some new and different positions I recently found in a sex book."

"I can't wait to see you, Darren," Catherine once again replied, in a tone of seductive charm.

"Me either, Catherine! I'll call you later, there at the social club, and you can give me your flight information. I will be at the airport to meet you and from there we can go directly to our suite."

"Your voice is fading, Darren. I think we are losing our connection. Bye for now."

After hanging up, Catherine immediately went upstairs to pass along what she had just learned to Boris. "I just got off the phone with Darren Kroft."

"Your lover, huh," grunted Boris, as a broad smirk spread across his face.

Reacting indignantly, Catherine responded, "No Boris, what you meant to say is that I heard from that pompous, sniveling, obnoxious, overweight, computer jerk. The one I had to play bedtime with here in Moscow, so that you, I, and the rest of this organization could all hopefully get in on some big time scores."

"Of course, Catherine. You know that is exactly what I meant to say," he said laughingly. After a brief pause, Boris became serious and asked, "Why did he call?"

"To tell me that he had stolen $9.8 million from a Denver bank, and was successful in wire transferring it to one of our TFM accounts in Antigua. When he told Sasha what he had done, he said that Sasha immediately left for Antigua, and was going to withdraw the full $9.8 million, and cut the rest of us out of it entirely."

"That does not sound like something Sasha would do to us. He might short your Mr. Kroft, but he knows better than to not give us our share."

"I agree, and we can't worry about that at this point, even if it is true. Especially, since the money is no longer in that Antigua bank, anyway."

Startled, Boris asked, "The money is not there?"

"No, that is why he called here. He later transferred the entire $9.8 million into a bank account in Panama, and plans to withdraw it all, early Monday morning. He wants me to meet him in Panama tomorrow, so we can run away together."

Boris snickered and nodded approvingly.

"In his dreams," she laughed.

"We have always said that you are the best, Catherine!"

"The things I do for this organization," Catherine responded shaking her head. "One more night in bed with him and I think I would throw up."

"Now, where and how are you supposed to meet him when you arrive in Panama?" Boris asked.

"Remember, I am NOT arriving in Panama," she responded.

Boris smirked, and corrected himself. "I meant, IF you were going to meet him there."

"That is better. He is going to call me back, here at the club, so that I can tell him when I will be arriving. He said that he will meet me at the airport, and from there we will be going to the hotel where he is staying. It is supposed to be somewhere near the airport."

"Okay, Catherine. While you are waiting for him to call back, check on the available flights, and make three reservations on a flight that will arrive there, tomorrow. Also, find out when the next flight would arrive, after the one you have made the three reservations for."

"Is he going to be in for a big surprise!" she grinned.

"You are right about that," agreed Boris.

CHAPTER SIXTY-TWO

As the dance music played in the background, Matt and Natasha held one another tightly, and gazed into each other's eyes. Their time together was fleeting, and those enchanting moonlit walks, dancing, and candlelight dinners would shortly be coming to an end.

Natasha was not prepared to have him taken away from her, again, and would likely never be, but she knew that was not her decision to make.

At the same time, Matt had also found himself struggling with how he was eventually going to have to say goodbye to her. It was going to be harder than he had ever imagined.

With tears in her eyes, Natasha asked, "Have they said when you are going to have to leave?"

"Nothing for sure," answered Matt.

His departure could be as early as tomorrow or the next day, but Matt didn't want to say anything that might upset her more than she already was.

For several days, Sergei had been trying to get a decision from the prosecutor's office. He needed to know what, if anything additional was going to be needed from Matt before he could leave Moscow and return to Quantico. Matt had already given them his complete statement and made his eyewitness identification. As far as Sergei was concerned, that evidence, coupled with the positive forensics on the shell casings, and the pistol they had should be enough.

Matt had not been complaining about having to stay on, though. As far as he was concerned, the more time he could spend with Natasha the better.

Returning from the dance floor to where they were seated, the two quietly continued to gaze into each other's eyes. As they held hands across the tabletop, Natasha slipped off her high heel and gently ran her foot up and down the side of Matt's leg. His heart began beating faster.

Suddenly, a pair of hands grabbed his shoulders from behind.

Startled, Matt quickly jerked his hands away from Natasha's.

"Sergei," Natasha cried out.

Matt stopped and looked up.

"As you Americans would say," Sergei smiled, "Gotcha!"

"Yes, and I would like to thank you for that, Sergei," Matt responded. "Maybe someday I will be able to return the favor. Just watch your back, if you ever get to Budapest and I happen to be over there teaching at the ILEA. You will be in the grasp of one of those beautiful Hungarian women, and all of sudden, surprise!"

"Sorry about that, Matt, but I need to see you, and thought I might find you here with a very attractive Russian woman."

"Not just any very attractive Russian woman," Matt replied, as he looked into Natasha's eyes and smiled, before temporarily excusing himself to take a walk with Sergei.

"What's up?" he asked.

"One of Vladimir's top snitches called him tonight and said several of our local wiseguys are on their way to Panama to pick up $9.8 million. His first thought was it sounded like some of the money laundering Nick had talked with them about at the ILEA. After talking to the snitch a little more, though, it sounds like there's more to it than just the money laundering."

"Why do you say that?"

"It looks as though an execution is also being planned. Remember Nick's 'old friend,' Darren Kroft?"

"Sure, how could any of us ever forget?" Matt smiled, "Especially after that story about Nick seeing a knockout blonde hanging on his arm. I think it really bothered him to see Kroft with a woman who looked like her."

"And not with Nick?" added Sergei, with a sly smile.

Matt chuckled, "You've got it, Sergei. I guess some of us have it, and some of us just don't."

"Wait until I tell Nick what you said."

"What? That he never gets hit on by beautiful women," Matt smirked.

"Could we add those who are, not-so-beautiful also to that list," smirked Sergei.

"We could," agreed Matt. "In fact, let's just say I've never seen any women trying to hit on Nick."

"Well, enough of that, anyway, it seems that our Mr. Kroft is in Panama waiting to pick up the money for himself."

"And cut the wiseguys here out?" questioned Matt.

"That is what it sounds like, and they are not happy about it. As you Americans would say, 'Mr. Kroft is not expected to live long enough to ever spend a dime of it.' "

"Did the snitch tell you anything more about the $9.8 million? Whose it is? Where it is from? Anything else?"

"No, just that there is $9.8 million in a bank in Panama. And, oh yes. Something about the money arriving there after it had been moved through another bank in the Caribbean. That is what first made us think of money laundering."

"Uh-huh," Matt agreed.

Upon their return to the table, Matt stood behind Natasha and rubbed her shoulders with his fingers, "Well, Sergei, you certainly know how to put a damper on my love life, don't you?"

"Only doing my job," laughed Sergei. "Besides, trying to keep you out of trouble while you are here in my city is almost a full time job."

Matt paused, "But do you need to try so hard, Sergei?"

"You know me, Matt. I do not believe in doing anything 'half-assed.' "

"Yeah," Matt reluctantly agreed. "Now, turning to this business at hand. Can you get me to the Embassy right away, and then take Natasha home?"

"Certainly, no problem," answered Sergei.

Leaning down to Natasha, Matt made it clear that this was not the way he had intended their evening to end and that he would be making up for it.

Natasha first stuck out her lower lip and then smiled, giving him a kiss on the cheek indicating that she understood.

CHAPTER SIXTY-THREE

"Denver FBI," answered the weekend duty clerk.

"Is K.C. Woodson there? This is Quantico calling with a patch call from Moscow."

After receiving no answer on the call transfer, the clerk switched on the in-office page and called, "Agent Woodson, line two."

"This is Agent Woodson."

"K.C., it's Matt Kelly from Quantico."

Before Matt could get in another word, K.C. started giving him a bit of harassment. "Matt Kelly, huh. Are you sure? Headquarters agents are supposed to be home. This is a three-day weekend, remember?"

"Well maybe, if I were back at the Academy."

"Where in the world are you?" K.C. asked.

"Moscow."

"Moscow! What's happening in Moscow that would cause you to call me here in Denver? Somebody going to get killed?"

"Something like that, K.C."

"Are you serious? Who? What's going on?"

"Word's come through an MVD informant that there is $9.8 million down in Panama and that it is to be picked up by that computer guy, Darren Kroft."

"You said $9.8 million, as in a nine, an eight, and five zeros?

"That's what the snitch said. He didn't know if the money was being laundered or exactly what is going on, but he did say guys from the Moscow mob are on their way to Panama as we speak. Once Kroft withdraws the $9.8 million from the Panamanian bank, they will grab the money and kill him."

"Did they say anything about an Antigua connection in all of this?" K.C. asked.

"Not exactly, but you know they have about fifty offshore banks located on those islands."

"Yeah, and some probably without vaults and tellers," chuckled K.C.

"Maybe even located in a building on the second or third floor, above a bakery or hair salon, in a single room with a telex on the floor and a 'brass plate' on the door," Matt added.

"Nothing would surprise me," answered K.C. "And, with the shades pulled down, too?"

"Of course. What would you expect?" Matt continued, "There was something about the $9.8 having first gone through a bank somewhere in the Caribbean, and then being transferred to Panama. That was what made the MVD investigators initially suspect money laundering."

"Did the informant identify which Russians are on their way to Panama."

"No, but the investigators we are working with here are seeing what they can find out. There's a good chance they won't get it in time, though."

"If you hear anything else, be sure to let me know. In addition to working with the locals on shootings we had here, I've been trying to get search warrant affidavits drafted for Kroft's residence and business. Since it doesn't sound like he's in the area now, that should give me a little more time. In the meantime, I'll see what I can do about getting in touch with the LEGAT in Panama City."

"You might also call Nick Costigan," Matt added. "Last I knew, he was teaching one of our programs at the new ILEA which is temporarily located in Panama. Call the switchboard at Quantico. They should have his number."

"Okay. I'll do that."

"I'll let you know if I hear anything more, K.C. Also, you can reach me through our LEGAT office here at the Moscow Embassy."

As soon as K.C. finished his conversation with Matt, he called Christine to tell her what he had just learned. Since most of the activity now appeared to be focusing on Panama, there was going to have to be some quick re-prioritizing of their efforts.

"K.C., I'll meet with the wire transfer people again and see if by chance they had any wire transfers going directly to banks in Panama within the past week. If not, this should pretty well confirm for us that this is the same $9.8 million. Are you going to contact the LEGAT in Panama and Nick?"

"I'll get in touch with both of them, and I'll also tell Marla that she can tell the Miami agents it doesn't look like we will have to be interrupting their weekend after all."

K.C.'s next call was to the FBI LEGAT in Panama City, but got only the answering machine. A check with the U.S. Embassy staff's weekend duty official revealed that the Legal Attaché was out of the country, and not expected to return for about a week.

A call to Nick's downtown hotel room brought no answer, either. K.C. left an urgent message with the hotel's switchboard operator for Nick Costigan to call him in Denver as soon as he returned. He hoped that Nick had not gone away for the weekend.

CHAPTER SIXTY-FOUR

"Catherine! It's me, Darren."

"I have been anxiously awaiting your call, lover boy," she responded seductively.

"I'm glad to hear that," Kroft replied. "I was surprised to hear you answering the phone, though."

"I could not risk missing your phone call, so I have been answering all calls for the past couple of hours. Fortunately, there were only a couple of them."

"When will you be getting here?" Kroft asked with anxious anticipation.

"Tomorrow, on Flight 422. I am supposed to be arriving at 5:32 PM."

"That's great!" he shouted.

"Do you promise to be waiting for me?"

"Nothing could keep me away! I'll be standing as close to the customs exit as I can get."

"I will see you then, lover boy," she said, blowing him a kiss over the phone line.

"You know I can't wait, Catherine," Kroft responded, excitedly.

The line went dead.

Rushing to report what she had learned to Boris, Catherine advised, "Everything is set. He will be standing outside the Panamanian Customs exit at about 5:30 PM."

CHAPTER SIXTY-FIVE

After re-examining the daily logs for the past week, Susan Anderson found no other unusual wire transfer activity to report to Christine. In addition, there were no wire transfers of any kind, going directly from First Westside to any banks in Panama. That was still no assurance, however, that Kroft would not try to transfer more money out of First Westside accounts, later. It was certainly possible he had created other trap doors in the computer programs. Christine would continue to search for new clues at the bank, until it came time to execute the search warrants on the computers at both Kroft's residence and his office.

With Sasha out of the country, and shooting teams from the local police and sheriff's departments finishing their investigations at Red Rocks Park, K.C. sat at his desk, nervously tapping his foot and fiddling with his pen.

K.C. kept asking himself. "Did the Panamanian hotel operator give Nick the message? When is he going to call?"

Finally, the phone rang. It was Christine, "Anything more from Matt? Have you talked with Nick, yet?"

"Nothing from either. All I can do is make sure I remain available, and wait," K.C. sighed.

"The waiting game often seems like the worst part of our jobs, doesn't it?" she remarked.

"Yeah. I'll be sure to call you if I hear anything from either of them."

K.C. waited a few more minutes before getting up to get a cup of coffee and take a walk around the office. He alerted the switchboard to page him if he didn't answer his phone.

Shortly thereafter, he heard, "K.C. Woodson, you have a call."

He hurried back to his desk. It was Nick.

"Are you ready to go to work?" K.C. asked.

"What do you think I've been doing down here, K.C.?"

"No, I mean real FBI work," jabbed K.C.

With a note of sarcasm and a chuckle in his voice, Nick responded, "Oh, that! Sure, but it's been a long time. I might have to work my way into it. Gradually."

"That's what I was afraid of."

"What's up, K.C.?"

"It's your buddy, Darren Kroft."

"What's he up to now?"

"He's there in Panama with you."

"What?"

"Yeah, Nick. It looks like he's trying to get himself killed."

"Okay, I guess you'd better fill me in, K.C."

"It looks like he stole $9.8 million from the First Westside National Bank, here in Denver, and wire transferred it through a bank in Antigua, and on to another bank there in Panama."

"Do we know what bank here in Panama?" asked Nick.

"No, because the records here only show it going as far as Antigua. From there, he initiated a new wire to take it on into Panama. He did his homework."

"Sounds like it," Nick agreed. "You also mentioned something about his getting killed, K.C.?"

"Yeah, there's more. It seems as though while doing this, he's also at the same time ripping off his Russian mafia buddies."

"That doesn't sound too smart to me."

"Me, either, but as you well know, some of these characters we deal with get some strange ideas, and this is one of the strangest.

"Sounds like it might get him killed.

"Yeah, that is, if we don't get to him first."

"This came from Matt?" Nick asked.

"Yeah. Sources in Russia are telling him that the mob is sending some of their guys from Moscow into Panama to get the money, and probably eliminate Mr. Darren Kroft in the process."

"That should make things interesting."

"To say the least," agreed K.C.

"Do we know where he's staying down here?" asked Nick.

"No, but I thought you might be able to contact the Panamanian police and see if they will help."

"There are several Panamanian officers in the ILEA class I've been teaching. I'll call them and see if they can check the country entrance records which all non-residents turn in when they arrive at Tocumen International. That record might show us where he's staying. Anything said about guns or weapons?"

K.C. answered, "Nothing, but I imagine the Russians will use whatever they can get their hands on. I'm sure they have some good drug contacts down there. How about you, Nick? Will you be okay?"

"I hope so. I'll get some help from those Panamanian officers I mentioned. As far as a gun for myself, I'll have to see what I can do. The LEGAT is out of the country, but I should be able to scrape up something from either the Embassy or the police. I'm sure one or the other of them will have either a pistol or an old .357 around that I can use. Then, I'll need to get a quick temporary authorization to carry it."

"Also, just so you know. There is paper backing this up. An AUSA here in Denver is already in the process of getting an arrest warrant issued for Mr. Kroft. We're charging him with Bank Fraud, Conspiracy, Fraud by Wire, and Money Laundering."

"While you're at it, K.C., you, and the AUSA need to call the Office of International Affairs in Washington, so they can complete the paperwork for Kroft's timely extradition."

"That's already in the mill. The faxes should be on their way shortly. Is there anything else you can think of that we need to do now?" asked K.C.

"Nothing comes to mind," Nick answered. "I'll be getting in touch with my police contacts here to see if I can find out where Kroft is staying."

CHAPTER SIXTY-SIX

With the MVD informant information now passed along to K.C. the previous evening, Matt was back in the LEGAT office early the following morning and on the phone with Sergei.

"I gave Denver Division what you told me, and they're running with it. Any messages from Natasha?" he asked.

"Only that she was disappointed she was not able to say goodnight to you in a proper fashion when I dropped her off at her apartment last night," Sergei chuckled. "I told her to go ahead and just give it a try on me, but she declined, only saying thanks and giving me a ladylike peck on my cheek. Can you believe that?"

"Sounds like she did exactly right."

"Yeah, that's easy for you to say. You don't live with the 'intimidator.' "

"Anything new from Vladimir's guy?"

"Nothing. Vladimir's been trying to meet with him, but he cannot find him."

"I know how that goes. We have the same problem with some of our informants. We sometimes refer to that as being 'out of pocket.' Have you ever used that expression?"

Sergei laughed, "Not exactly." He paused before continuing, "Some good news, or maybe not so good news, Matt. I was just getting ready to call you."

"What's that?"

"I talked with the Prosecutor's Office this morning and you're not going to have to testify. Your signed statement and positive ID, along with the lab evidence was enough to do the job. Georgi is on his way for a long stretch in Siberia."

"For how long would you say?"

"Probably twenty years, if he behaves himself."

"Good job, Sergei."

"Unfortunately, this means you will have to leave us, shortly?" Sergei concluded.

"Yeah, probably so," Matt agreed.

"That is not so good news."

"No, it isn't. I'll have to check with the travel office at the Embassy and see when I can get a flight out. Maybe they'll be all booked up."

"And then you could spend more time with Natasha?"

"That's what I'm counting on. It's going to be tough to say good-bye to her again."

"But you will be returning to Moscow to see her?" asked Sergei.

"I certainly plan to," Matt responded.

"Be sure to let me know when you are leaving. I want to take you to the airport."

"Will do, and thanks again for everything you have done, Sergei."

CHAPTER SIXTY-SEVEN

The first flight out that Matt was able to get booked onto was leaving the next afternoon. In the meantime, he would help Victor finish up several short deadline leads that had come into the LEGAT office overnight, and then... he needed to make a call.

"Natasha, it's me. Sergei got you home all right?"

"Fine, no problem," she assured him. "But saying good-night to Sergei was just not the same."

"That's good to know. I would have been disappointed if you had felt otherwise. Speaking of good-night, how about our getting together tonight?"

"I was supposed to be at the club, but I will call and tell them something has happened and that I will not be able to work."

"Will it be a problem for you?"

Noting a sense of urgency in Matt's voice, she responded, "No, don't worry. They have a waiting list of girls who want to come in for my tips. Why, is something up?"

Matt paused, before sadly replying, "I have to leave Moscow tomorrow afternoon."

There was silence on the line.

The realization that Matt would be leaving tomorrow hit Natasha hard. When he returned to Moscow, she knew this day would come, but that still didn't make it any easier.

"Natasha?" Matt asked when he did not hear her voice.

With a cracking voice, she whispered, "Yes, I'm still here."

"That's good! Remember our first dinner together and trudging through the snow from your apartment to the restaurant?"

"How could I forget?" she responded, her voice a little stronger now, as she wiped away a tear and began to smile, remembering those tender moments.

"Let's go back there for dinner tonight. How does that sound?"

"Wonderful!"

"Seven o'clock at your place?"

"Or as early as you can get here, I'll be waiting," she assured him.

They both quietly returned the receivers to their cradles before giving their emotions a chance to take over.

Attempting to re-focus on the deadline paperwork still lying in front of him was difficult, but Matt had promised Victor he would try to get it completed before day's end, and he still intended to make it.

CHAPTER SIXTY-EIGHT

Outside the Embassy gate in front of the red brick reception area, Matt flagged down a taxi. Leaning his head into the taxi, Matt addressed the driver in English. The driver shook his head and waved his hand, indicating he didn't understand. Matt stopped talking and pulled a slip of paper from his pocket. He showed the driver Natasha's address. The driver looked at it and nodded that he understood and knew where this was. It was for times like this that he kept slips of paper with names or addresses of places he was going, business cards from those with whom he was working, and the hotel where he was staying. The business cards often had the information in the native language on one side and English on the other, which made it quite easy. If not, he made sure that the information he needed was in both languages somewhere on the card or piece of paper.

Matt opened the back door and slid into the taxi. As the taxi pulled away from the Embassy gate and the driver made a couple of quick turns, Matt noted that they were at least starting out in the right direction. Moscow's inner-city was clogged with its usual congestion, but as they went farther out, the traffic improved. The closer they got to Natasha's apartment complex, the more buildings and landmarks Matt recognized.

He tapped the driver on the shoulder and pointed to a young girl selling flowers.

The driver nodded, acknowledging that he saw her.

Matt motioned for him to pull over and stop.

He had bought flowers from her before, and she recognized him immediately. During an earlier visit to her stand, he noticed her interest in learning a few words of English and she seemed to want to try using them whenever she got the chance.

"Flowers for your lady?" she asked, smiling.

"Yes," answered Matt as he nodded and pointed to some long-stemmed red roses.

She gathered them from the canister, and after wrapping, held them out to him. "Pretty?" she asked.

"Very pretty," he replied.

As was done for most foreigners who did not speak Russian, she then wrote down the amount on a piece of paper and handed it to him.

When he gave her the money, she responded very distinct and correctly, "Thank you very much."

Matt smiled and responded, "Thank you!"

A big smile crossed her face. She was very proud of herself; she had spoken English. Matt waived good-bye to her and jumped back into the taxi.

Finally arriving at the apartment complex, Matt leaned over the front seat, and the driver wrote down the amount on a piece of paper. From the right front pocket of his trousers, Matt pulled out a wad of rubles he kept bound with a heavy rubber band and peeled off the amount the driver had written down, plus a tip. The driver nodded that the fare payment and tip were satisfactory, and Matt got out of the taxi. He was thankful the ride had gone without incident.

As he walked through the entryway and toward the stairway leading up to Natasha's, his feelings for her and the fact that he was going to have to be leaving shortly were slowly beginning to sink in. Being the All-American playboy that he was, Matt had enjoyed numerous opportunities to spend time with any number of very attractive women over the years, but Natasha was not just another woman. She was something very special.

He knocked on the door and heard Natasha's voice, "Just a minute," she anxiously replied.

The door opened and there stood Natasha, as beautiful and enchanting as ever. Matt handed her the long-stemmed red roses and pulled her close to him. Lifting and holding her tightly, he gave her a kiss that he hoped would remain in their memories for an eternity. Once both of her feet were back on the floor and she had a chance to catch her breath, she took Matt's hand and led him into the apartment, closing the door behind them.

After putting the roses into a vase, Natasha rushed over to snuggle beside Matt on the couch. Gazing into his eyes, she lifted his chin toward her and gave him a kiss. Matt reacted passionately, and as their lips met and their bodies pressed against one another, they both experienced an incredible sensation and feeling. Continuing their embrace, each began stripping clothes off the other and their lust quickly moved them off the couch and into the bedroom.

"You are wonderful," he told her as he placed one lingering kiss after another across her body.

Natasha closed her eyes and smiled, as she savored every moment and an incredible feeling of satisfaction.

Matt continued caressing her breasts and slowly ran his hand along her long, smooth, silky leg as it gently rested on his.

Finally, after gazing into one another's eyes for several more minutes, Natasha gave him a mischievous look and kiss before whispering, "If we are going to make it for our late evening dinner, I need to get ready."

Smiling contentedly, Matt would have preferred that the two of them remain just as they were, but that was not going to be, since the time for them to be at the restaurant was quickly approaching.

After reluctantly giving in, Matt gave her a lingering kiss and returned to where his clothes were strewn across the floor, next to the couch. Natasha remained behind and closed the door leading into the bedroom.

Wearing high heels, dark stockings, and a perfectly fitted, dark burgundy dress that followed her bodylines flawlessly, Natasha emerged from the bedroom as striking and captivating as Matt could ever remember seeing her.

"New dress," he commented, while at the same time smiling approvingly.

"You like it?" she said.

"Very much," Matt answered.

"This is one of the benefits of working at the social club. They give us clothes and insist we always try to look attractive, or as they put it as appealing as possible for the customers."

"That's no problem for you. No matter what you are wearing, or for that matter, not wearing," Matt slyly commented, "You always look fantastic."

Natasha blushed.

As they were leaving the apartment, Matt told her, "Better get your jacket. Would you like to take a taxi, or should we walk to the restaurant?"

"A walk would be nice," Natasha replied, giving an appealing and delightful smile. "My jacket is hanging up over there, but first let me put on more comfortable shoes. I'll take my leather shoulder bag. I can put my heels in it."

Matt rolled his eyes back.

"Don't worry. I'll change them once we get there."

"I would never worry. Your legs look great to me no matter what shoes you are wearing."

Natasha laughed, "I knew there was something I liked about you," and she gave him another lingering kiss.

"There are a lot of 'something's' I like about you," Matt replied, as he helped her on with her jacket.

When they got to the street, Natasha held out her hand for Matt. "It's supposed to be a nice evening, and just think, there's no snow for us to slip on and fall down into."

"Yeah, that's really too bad," Matt said with a wink.

"Seriously Matt, that was a wonderful night. I just wish that we could live it over and over again."

"Me, too, but this time I guess it will have to be without the snow." He smiled and still holding her hand pulled her into his arms for another kiss.

As they walked, Natasha asked, "Do you remember what kind of a moon there was that first night?"

"I do, it was a bright orange harvest moon, right?"

"Right, that is very good," agreed Natasha. "And, what kind of a moon do we have out tonight?"

Looking up, Matt gave a cocky response, "A round moon?"

She gave him an exasperated look, and smiled.

"Okay, a full moon," he added.

"But not just any full moon," Natasha replied. "This is the second full moon this month."

"A blue moon," Matt responded.

"A what?" asked Natasha.

Matt repeated, "A blue moon. The second full moon in the same month is called a blue moon. In the U.S. we sometimes use the expression, 'Once in a blue moon.' "

"I guess," responded Natasha, having never heard the expression before, and looking a bit perplexed.

"It means something that does not happen very often," explained Matt.

"Oh, I see," nodded Natasha.

"Well, I think that's very appropriate, since I know that this is one night I will never forget."

"Me, either," Natasha agreed, as she looked at Matt, and blew him a kiss.

"Isn't this about where you slipped and fell? A ploy so you could pull me down into the snow with you and rub my face in it?"

She looked back and saw her apartment complex in the distance. "This is about where it was, but I don't remember it happening exactly that way. As I recall, you were the one trying to lure me when I slipped."

"You're probably right, but you couldn't blame me for trying."

"What do you mean 'probably?' You know I am right," corrected Natasha, laughing. "And, no, I don't blame you for trying. In fact, I don't remember my putting up much resistance, either."

"Much resistance, Miss Federova?"

"All right, Agent Kelly, no resistance."

"And let me tell you I appreciated that," responded Matt.

Recounting some of those earlier incidents had made the time fly by, and now they were at the front door of the restaurant.

Inside, things looked about the same as Matt had remembered. The lights were turned down, and there were candles glowing on each table. Most of the stools at the bar were occupied, and from the way each of the waiters, cocktail waitresses and violinists were hustling around, it appeared that business was good.

After a brief wait, they were escorted to the same table they occupied during their earlier winter visit. Being near the fireplace was obviously not so important this time, however. Their chairs were pulled back and once seated, linen napkins were placed on their laps. When the leather bound menus were handed to them, Natasha laughed as Matt acted as though he were giving it a thorough reading. As far as she could tell, however, his Russian language skills had not substantially improved since his earlier visit.

Matt lowered his menu and looked across at Natasha. "Okay, but do you think I fooled any of them?"

"Probably not, especially when they return for our orders," she laughed.

"What are we going to have, Natasha?"

Running her finger down the menu, she suddenly stopped. "How about the tripe?" It was not really on the menu, but she had heard that most Americans would not even look at it, much less eat it, and she wanted to see Matt's reaction.

Seeing the expression on Matt's face made her wish she had a camera. "Um... uh. What else do they have?" Quickly recovering, he added, "The bear we had here the last time was good."

She laughed, "I was just testing you."

"I had tripe one time in the Caribbean and that was enough for me," Matt commented. "It's strange how just one taste, one time, can make you remember certain foods. I guess many people like it, but it's not for me."

"If you really liked the bear, we can have that again," Natasha responded.

Matt gave a quick sigh of relief, "That would be great!" Then, with vivid memories from their earlier visit continuing to linger in his mind, and a feeling of wanting to be able to re-live as many moments from that night as he could, Matt added, "In fact, let's see if you can remember exactly what we had the last time."

Natasha nodded that she could.

"Let's order the same thing."

"Again? You do not sound very adventurous tonight."

"Well, not when it comes to food; however, if you have something else in mind?"

Giving him an alluring look and a wink, she teased, "I am not telling."

The waiter returned and Natasha gave him their order. "We will start with an appetizer and bottled water. We would then like a kettle of borscht soup, followed by a bear meat entrée and potatoes."

"*Spasibo,*" Matt thanked the waiter.

"What did you order, Natasha?"

"You'll see," she told him with a sly smile.

A while later, their appetizer arrived, and as dinner progressed, Matt commented, "You remembered everything. Right down to the borscht soup and the bottled water. I didn't know what to expect after that look you gave me."

"Good," she smiled.

After they finished their entrée, Matt asked, "Are you up for the same pastry dessert we had the last time?"

"With a cup of cappuccino?" added Natasha.

"Sounds good to me," Matt agreed.

"Then, to use one of your Americans expressions, 'let us go for it.'"

Throughout most of the evening, their conversation had been light-hearted. Neither was ready to broach the subject of Matt's leaving tomorrow, and the thought that the two of them might somehow never again be together seemed incomprehensible. Those thoughts and any passionate good-byes were going to have to wait until later, when the two of them returned to Natasha's apartment.

It was getting late. With the check paid, and their waiter and the violinist generously tipped, it was time for the two of them to be on their way. Would their next stop be a hot Moscow nightspot or would they go back to Natasha's and listen to music? It would be up to her.

Natasha waited between the bar and coatroom, while Matt walked over to gather her jacket. As he was returning, two men got up from the bar and walked toward them. They had spotted Matt earlier, when he told Natasha to wait for him there, while he made his way to the coatroom. The two were talking loudly, in Russian, and Matt had heard one of them say something that sounded like it had FBI in it, but he couldn't be sure. Natasha had understood every word, though, and as she started toward Matt, so did the two Russians.

Reaching out to him, she cried, "Matt, they recognized you! They are going to kill you!"

One of the two men then pointed at Natasha and yelled, in Russian, "You, the bitch from the social club! The FBI snitch! You are dead, too!"

The two confronted Matt and Natasha. There was no time for their escape. One of the men thrust his hand under his sport coat and to his waist. He pulled out a shiny pistol and yelled in Russian, "This is for Georgi! You two are dead!"

Matt gave a karate block to the guy's hand, knocking the gun to the floor. As the gunman dove for it, Matt kicked it with the side of his foot, causing it to slide across the floor, where it remained out of everyone's reach under a heavy, ornate base that supported a large, tall cabinet.

The other guy lunged toward Matt. As he did, Matt gave him a sidekick to the knee, causing him to cry out in pain as his leg buckled and he dropped to the floor, unable to walk. In the meantime, the guy who had pulled the gun was now back on his feet. Matt spun around and delivered a roundhouse kick to his groin. The guy doubled over. Matt followed that with a front kick to the jaw, sending him backwards and onto the floor where he hit his head.

With all of the commotion, and not knowing for sure how many other local thugs might still be hanging around the area and coming to the aid of their downed comrades, Matt knew he and Natasha had to get away. With her coat in his left hand, Matt grabbed Natasha's arm with his right hand and the two of them rushed toward the door. As they did, the guy who had been left on the floor nursing what could very likely be a torn ACL and broken kneecap yelled, in Russian, "FBI snitch bitch."

Natasha then heard him clearly yell, "He may go back to America, but there is no escape for you. We will find you bitch. You are dead!"

Natasha and Matt escaped out the door.

"Which way to the subway?" he asked.

Natasha pointed left.

As the two of them raced in that direction, Natasha kicked off, and picked up her high heels.

At the station, they quickly made their way to the long underground escalators, and upon stepping onto the loading platforms, Matt asked, "Which way now?"

"Where are we going?" Natasha frantically responded.

"Good question. We can't go back to your apartment, that's for sure. Do you see a phone?"

Pointing, she told him, "There should be one down there at the other end."

Taking her hand, he responded, "Let's go in that direction. As we walk, I'll tell you what I have been thinking. I think we should try to get to Sergei's office. Can you get us there?"

"That should not be a problem, but he is not there at this time of night."

"Yes, I know that. That's why we need to get to a phone. By the way, what did that guy say to you as we were leaving?"

"Oh, he was just talking."

"No, Natasha. I know that he said something that scared you." Matt stopped in mid-stride and looked Natasha directly in the eye. "The way you grabbed me when he spoke told me that it was more than just talk. Now tell me exactly what he said!"

She gripped Matt's hand more tightly and said, "He called me the 'FBI snitch bitch.' "

Sensing that was not all, Matt told her, "Go on, tell me all of it."

Tears started streaming down her cheeks. "He said that you may go home, but that I can't escape, and that they will get me and kill me."

Matt put his arm around her and pulled her to him. "I don't want you to worry."

Her head nestled tightly against his chest and shoulder, and with her voice cracking, she asked, "But what will I do? They can find out where I live from someone at the club."

"We'll work out something," Matt replied, rubbing her shoulder with his hand as he held her. "Have you seen either of them before?"

"I think the one who yelled at me was in the group I told you about that was in the club."

"The one talking about getting the FBI?" Matt asked.

Natasha nodded yes.

"That's probably right since they seemed to know you worked at the social club."

"Did you recognize either of them, Matt?" she asked.

"I think the one who pulled the gun might have been in the group that surrounded us the night I got shot, and maybe the other guy, too, but I can't be sure about either of them. It was Georgi that I was positive of."

Looking ahead and pointing, "Hey, there's a phone. I'll call Sergei. You watch for the train that we need to catch."

Matt stood with the phone to his ear, waiting nervously and listening to the ringing. Once, twice, three times. There was no answer. He continued to let it ring. Finally, on the tenth ring, Matt heard a groggy sounding, "*Zdravstvuitse.*"

"Hello. Sergei, it's me, Matt."

"Do you know what time it is, Matt?"

"Yes, Sergei. I know it's late, but this is important."

"Have you been drinking, Matt?"

"No, Sergei. I'm with Natasha."

"Where are you?"

"In a subway station not far from Natasha's apartment. We need to see you, Sergei. It's really important."

Noting the sense of urgency in Matt's voice, Sergei told him, "I will meet you two at Natasha's apartment."

"No, no! We can't go there. I'll explain later."

"Then where?" asked Sergei.

"Is it okay to go to your office?"

"Yes, I will meet you there."

"Okay Sergei, gotta go. Natasha just gave me the high sign. We'll see you as soon as we can get there," his voice trailing as he quickly hung-up the receiver.

Natasha was now motioning frantically. In the distance, she had spotted one of the guys from the restaurant. He was almost to the bottom of the escalator, and it looked as though there were at least two others trailing close behind. By this time, Matt had made his way to Natasha and the two of them slipped aboard the subway car. What remained a mystery was whether that group of thugs had seen them and, if so, had they boarded another car further back.

As Matt and Natasha sank into a seat toward the rear of the otherwise empty car, he tried to re-assure her, telling her everything was going to work out.

With Matt's arm firmly around her and feeling a bit more secure, Natasha wiped a tear from her cheek and asked, "Did they teach you to handle those guys the way you did at the FBI Academy?"

"Some of it, but there's a group of us who continue to train in karate every week. We also have fun teaching some of the FBI kids on Saturday mornings. You should see some of them in action. It's been good for me."

"I'd say that it's been good for both of us," she said, resting her head on his chest.

As they came to a stop at the next station, both the front and rear doors slid open. Matt and Natasha watched intently for any new faces, but it appeared that no one was going to board.

Suddenly, one of the three guys Natasha had spotted at the previous station yelled back to the others, and the three of them burst into the car. Matt and Natasha jumped to their feet and dashed through the double door opening in the rear of the car. Seeing Matt and Natasha exiting, the three thugs stopped in their tracks, turned and darted out the front door of the car and onto the loading platform. The three looked around, as Matt and Natasha quickly slipped back into the car. There was only a split second before the doors would finish closing, but that proved to be long enough.

One of the thugs tried to catch the door as it was coming together, but was too late. As the train emerged from the station, the three thugs ran beside the car yelling threats.

Matt flashed his gold FBI badge against the window and smiled.

To this, one of them gave the international salute and another showed a fist, as the train sped into the darkened underground toward the next stop.

Shaken by the events of the evening, Natasha sat down on a nearby bench. Looking up at Matt, she patted her hand on the seat beside her and he eased into it. On this night that was to have been filled with love and passion, danger had struck once more, and suddenly the two of them were again thrust into a nightmarish struggle for survival.

"How many more stops 'til Sergei's office?" Matt asked.

Natasha looked across to the subway map that was posted on the opposite side of the car. "I think three or four, but I can be sure when I see the sign at the next stop."

The next stop was coming up shortly. As the car pulled into the station, Natasha looked at the sign. "Yes, it's three more from here."

There were no new boarders at this stop, but considering the hour, that was to be expected. Trains were now running much less frequently, as passenger loads decline during these late night hours of operation.

At the next stop, a well-proportioned lady of the night boarded and caught her three and one-half inch stiletto heel in the door guide. She tried unsuccessfully to pull it out with her foot. When she took her foot out of the shoe, and started struggling to kneel down in an extremely tight and very short mini-skirt, Matt jumped to her aid. He twisted and pulled, managing to remove the shoe from the doorway just as the signal was activated indicating the doors were closing.

Standing up and handing her the shoe, she smiled and spoke to him in a soft, seductive voice. Even though Matt didn't understand the words, he had a pretty good idea what she had said. Matt smiled, and returned to his seat beside Natasha. The other woman made a point of sitting down on the corner of a bench, several rows forward. She extended her shapely legs into the aisle, and stretched her arms back, as she turned, ensuring Matt got full benefit of at least some of her wares.

Natasha nudged him and asked quietly, "Do you make a habit of helping out women in distress?"

"You mean like ones wearing lots of make up, low cut blouses and short skirts?"

"Very short skirts," she corrected. "I can see that you help them, but what about others?"

"I help them, too." He paused, as he smiled, and added, "Occasionally."

Natasha reacted, giving him a disapproving look and a gentle kick with the side of her foot.

"What was that for?"

"A love tap. What do you think?" She gave him a kiss on the cheek. "Do you know what she said to you?"

Trying to look surprised, Matt answered, "No," then grinned, "She probably wanted to know what time it is."

"Not quite, lover boy. She offered to treat you to a good time and invited you to get off with her at the next stop."

"What should I tell her?"

Natasha snuggled up a little closer and again gently nudged him on the side of the leg with her foot. "You tell her nothing. You're mine."

As they approached the next to the last station before they would be getting off, this well endowed, leggy, lady of the evening stood up. As she did, she wiggled and tugged to straighten her tight fitting skirt and stretched a little more. She looked back at him and winked. When he was sure Natasha was watching, Matt winked back and Natasha reacted, as he had expected, with another "love tap" to his shin. Matt laughed, and as the woman started to go through the doorway, she turned and motioned for Matt to follow. Matt turned to Natasha and she gave him a glaring stare. He smiled back at the woman and shook his head.

Natasha told him, "Now that's what you were supposed to do," and gave him another kiss on the cheek.

While the train was pulling out of the subway station, Matt watched through the window as their fellow passenger strutted off toward the escalator, trying to make sure that anyone watching got full benefit of her every curve. That was until Natasha saw what he was doing and put her hand up in front of his eyes.

The subway station at the stop for Sergei's office was so deserted it was eerie. No one else had gotten off, and other than a couple of people sleeping on the benches, there appeared to be no one else on the platform. As they made their way to the escalator and started up toward the street, they passed a couple of young lovers going the opposite direction, but as Matt looked both ahead and behind, he could see no one else on their side. On the street, there was a little activity, but nothing approaching what Matt was used to seeing when going to Sergei's MVD office.

Sergei was waiting just inside the main entrance when they arrived.

He opened the door. "Come in. Come in."

While following him into his office, Sergei asked Matt, "What is the matter? You sounded upset."

"They're trying to kill us, Sergei."

"Who?" Sergei asked.

"Some of those same thugs. I'll be okay. I have the embassy to go back to and besides, I'm scheduled to fly out of Moscow in a few hours. It's Natasha I'm worried about. She has nowhere to go. By now they have probably found out where she lives and are probably standing outside her door as we speak."

"What happened?" Sergei pressed Matt for more details.

"We had finished dinner and were leaving one of the local restaurants. It's fairly close to where Natasha lives. There were a couple of thugs sitting at the bar and at least one of them must have recognized me. He may have been part of the group that jumped me the night I was shot. Anyway, two of them got up and came toward us saying something in Russian."

Natasha spoke up, "They said they knew who Matt was, and that they were going to kill him."

"That wasn't all. They know who Natasha is, too."

Sergei looked at Natasha, "How is that? What did they say to you?"

Visibly shaken, Natasha responded, "At least one of them recognized me from the social club. They called me the 'FBI snitch bitch' and said they were going to kill me, too."

"What happened then, Matt?"

"One of them pulled a gun. I struggled with the two of them until Natasha and I were able to get away. On the way here, we met up with several of them again. This time it was on the subway, and once again, we were lucky. We left them a few stops back."

"It sounds like you two were very lucky," agreed Sergei.

Natasha nodded her head.

"So as you can see, Sergei, our problem is keeping Natasha safe and protected. I doubt they would let me take her into the Embassy compound, and as I mentioned before, those thugs who were after us probably already have her place staked out. If not, they will certainly find out everything about her and where she lives, from some of the guys at the social club, by tomorrow at the latest."

"Right, Matt, and once the club learns she's an FBI informant?"

"I don't even want to think about what they might do," answered Natasha.

"There's only one answer," Sergei told her.

Natasha looked at him questioningly.

"You will stay with the 'intimidator' and me. That is if you can put up with the 'intimidator.'"

That quip brought a smile to Natasha's face. "I am certain that I can, as you say, put up with Mrs. Malkin quite easily. It is you that I am worried about," she said in jest.

"Then it is done. Matt, I will take you back to the Embassy and I will take Natasha home with me."

As they rode to the Embassy, Matt held Natasha close and kept re-assuring her everything was going to work out. At this point, though, he didn't know exactly how.

At the Embassy gate, Natasha threw her arms around Matt and gave him another lingering kiss. While catching his breath, Matt held her tightly, and although he didn't want to let her go, he had to.

Looking to Sergei, Matt gave him a Russian bear hug, "Thanks, good friend. I'll talk with Victor and we'll get back to you in the morning."

After pausing briefly, and shaking his head in disbelief regarding all that they had been through, Matt continued, "Be sure to take good care of her for me."

"You know I will," Sergei assured him.

CHAPTER SIXTY-NINE

A light mist covered the runway as the afternoon flight carrying Yuri, Mikhail, and Leonid touched down at Panama's Tocumen International Airport. It was on time, and that meant they would have a couple of hours to complete their arrival processing, gather their baggage, and clear customs, before Flight 422 was scheduled to arrive at 5:32 PM.

Since Leonid was proficient in Spanish, as well as Russian and English, it had been left up to him to get the trio through their various stops. So far, so good. Everything had gone smoothly. Recently, he had made use of his language skill when he accompanied several of the Russian bosses to Colombia, where they managed to hammer out additional agreements with the reigning drug lords.

Not wanting to risk even the slightest chance of being late, Kroft got to the airport well ahead of Catherine's scheduled arrival time. While in the terminal, he checked the board identifying incoming flights. Much to his dismay, he noticed that Flight 422 had been delayed, and there was no estimated time of arrival posted.

Kroft decided to go to the bar and have a drink while he waited for an update. The bar was noisy and very crowded, but with a smile, and a little bump here and there along the way, he managed to work his way toward the back, where he found a small table beside a partition. A waitress finally came over and took his order for a piña colada.

While he waited for the waitress to return with his drink, he fanaticized about Catherine, and how it was going to be when they were together again. He asked himself why was it that her flight had to be one delayed. He could hardly wait to see her.

Continuing to sip his drink in the midst all of the commotion and noise, Darren suddenly picked up on familiar sounding voices. Not only were the voices familiar, but also the language. It sounded like they were speaking Russian.

Trying not to be too obvious, he peeked around the partition. There, several rows of tables away from where Kroft was sitting were the three guys he met with at the hotel bar in Moscow. What were they doing in Panama?

He was relatively sure this was not mere coincidence.

Had they somehow heard about what he was up to, and were there to intercept him and Catherine?

If so, he was going to have to get the money and act quickly to get the two of them out of there and on the way to their paradise hideaway, before those three guys could react.

Continuing to watch, he noticed Leonid, the guy who spoke English and had interpreted for them in the Moscow meetings, get up and go over to a pay phone located on the back wall. In the meantime, Kroft lowered his head and shoulders, trying to remain as inconspicuous as possible.

Leonid returned to the table, and Darren listened intently to see if he could get an inkling of what the three of them were talking about. Unfortunately, it all sounded like Russian to him, but then, what else was he to expect.

After one more piña colada, the arrival of Flight 422 at Gate 4 was announced.

Before moving, Kroft watched to see what those three were going to do, if anything. Sure enough, they got up and made their way through the crowd, to the entrance of the bar.

Kroft followed at a distance. He knew he needed to get to the area outside the customs exit to meet Catherine, but first, he needed to learn where that trio was going.

As he followed, however, it appeared that they, too, were making their way to the customs exit. When they got there, the three of them stopped and lit their cigarettes. They positioned themselves near a pillar, so as not to be too conspicuous, while at the same time being able to see anyone exiting through the doors.

Darren hung his head and stayed back even farther, appearing to be part of a large crowd of tourists gathered there awaiting transportation. From there he could see the three Russians and the door, too. What action he would take when Catherine came through the doorway, he had not yet decided.

Kroft watched as planeloads of passengers passed through the doors. He saw a number of passengers carrying bags with tags from flight 442 attached, but there was no sign of Catherine. He began to wonder if she was even on the flight. There would be one way he could possibly find out. That would be to call the social club. He located a telephone and placed the call.

"Yekaterina," he asked, with the best Russian inflection he could manage.

Something was said in response that Kroft could not understand, but since the line had remained open, he would wait to see what happened next. Shortly thereafter, he heard footsteps, and a voice came onto the line.

"Zdravstvuitse."

It was Catherine. Not quite knowing how to respond to the fact that she was still in Moscow, Darren opted to say nothing, and immediately hung-up the receiver. He now knew Catherine wasn't coming. What he did not know was why, or what had happened. They must have done something to her, he thought. After all, she felt the same way about him as he did about her, didn't she? Maybe she would be able to sneak away, once he re-settled. For now, it was all up to him, though.

Taking things one step at a time, he had to first make sure that the three Russians did not find and follow him when he picked up the money from the bank, and later made good his escape from Panama.

When Darren returned to the area of the customs exit, he noted that the Russians were still standing there, puffing away, and talking. Time to get out of here, he thought, and immediately slipped away, catching a taxi back to his hotel.

Once there, Nick Costigan and two of the Panamanian police officers from his ILEA class were waiting, observing virtually every move Darren made. In a little more than an hour after Nick had called for their help, these two officers had Darren Kroft's hotel identified, and were sitting there awaiting Nick's arrival. In the interim, they had also reviewed Kroft's hotel registration information, and identified several locations from which they could monitor comings and goings of hotel guests without being spotted.

As Nick watched Kroft, he noticed that Darren seemed to be nervously looking around, as if he thought he was being followed. Why he was acting this way, Nick didn't know, but he was certainly glad that they had managed to find a location that was generally out of the public view.

Walking over to the elevators, Kroft got on. No one got on with him, and Nick watched as the lights flash on the identifier located above the elevator door. The elevator only made one stop before returning to the lobby, and that was on twelve, the floor on which Kroft's room was located.

CHAPTER SEVENTY

Outside the wide double doors leading back into the customs area at Panama's Tucumen International Airport, the three Russians continued to look puzzled as they scanned the crowd for Darren Kroft. After all, it wasn't as if they were trying to identify some guy they had only seen in a photograph. All three knew exactly what he looked like. They had all been with him on at least two different occasions in Moscow.

They told themselves there was no way they could have missed him standing in front of those double doors, as he had told Catherine he would be.

Had Catherine for some reason had a change of heart though, and alerted him?

They suspected not, but if that did happen, they would deal with her upon their return.

With both Darren Kroft and Leonid's Panamanian contact coming up as no shows, things were rapidly deteriorating. Leonid had called his contact from the airport bar and was assured everything was set. The man was to meet the three Russians near the customs area and from there they were all to follow Kroft.

Leonid rushed back into the nearest airport entrance and finally spotted a pay phone on the wall of a walkway. Two people were in line ahead of him. Since they use both Panamanian balboas and U.S. currency in Panama, Leonid had earlier exchanged rubles for U.S. dollars at the airport currency exchange. He waved one of his $20 bills in front of the caller now on the phone and showed additional ones to each of those ahead of him for his chance to get the phone now. The elderly woman now talking took the $20 and quickly hung-up. The others in line followed suit, snatching the two remaining $20's from his hand and motioning for him to go ahead.

Leonid pulled a piece of scrap paper from his pocket and punched in the numbers.

"*Hola,*" the person called answered.

"¿Cuchillo?" Leonid responded.

"*Sí.*"

"*Este es Leonid.*"

The two of them had first met in Colombia when Leonid was tasked with interpreting for the Russian mafia bosses. Leonid knew him only by the nickname, "Cuchillo," and was told that he was the Panamanian enforcer for one of the largest cartels. When this problem with Darren Kroft came up, Leonid's first call was to his strong-arm comrade.

As the two of them continued their conversation, Cuchillo told Leonid that he was once again on his way. The police had set up a checkpoint not far from the airport and he had been caught in the delay. He was now within a couple of minutes of the main terminal. Leonid was to look for a new, black, four-door luxury model SUV with gold trim, chrome wheels, and dark tinted windows.

Cuchillo was in turn told that the three of them would be waiting beside the 'arriving passengers' walkway.

Shortly thereafter, the black 4 X 4 pulled up and Cuchillo slowly lowered the dark tinted driver's window. Leonid walked over to the side and looked in. Cuchillo's black shoulder-length hair, piercing, cold, dark eyes, and pockmarked face made him appear even more intimidating than Leonid had remembered. His nickname, translated

"Blade," seemed to fit perfectly, and Leonid was relatively certain that it had something to do with the long, jagged scar that extended from a high, protruding cheekbone near his eye, to a point halfway down his neck.

It was obvious to Leonid from what he had heard and seen that Cuchillo was definitely not someone to confront.

Leonid nodded to the others and the three of them got into the SUV. Leonid sat on the passenger side in the front, while Yuri and Mikhail ducked into the rear. As they departed the airport, Leonid again briefly explained the circumstances surrounding their rapid dispatch from Moscow to Panama City, and the importance of their finding Darren Kroft. All they knew was that he was supposedly staying at a hotel in the vicinity of the airport.

Cuchillo nodded that he understood.

"Did you bring the guns," asked Leonid.

"Sí," Cuchillo answered, as he headed toward one of the local cartel owned bar hangouts. There, they would all have some drinks, be introduced to some hot women, and Cuchillo would put the word out to his snitches. A thousand dollars would go to the first one to come up with the hotel where Darren Kroft was staying.

All that was left now was for the four of them to sit and wait for Cuchillo's cell phone to ring. In the meantime, he would continue to try to show the trio of Russians a good time. So far, that hadn't been too difficult. Several of the local working girls had already taken his hint and were making the rounds lap dancing with the three.

Cuchillo snapped his fingers and the girls quickly gathered up the Russians and escorted them out to the SUV. As five of them squeezed into the rear, things were a little tight, but Mikhail and Yuri weren't about to complain.

It wasn't long before the 4x4 approached a walled complex.

"What is this?" asked Leonid.

Cuchillo replied in a deep and menacing tone of voice, "It is a surprise."

That response was not at all encouraging. In fact, it was right down intimidating, and sent a chill down Leonid's spine. Not being one to challenge Cuchillo on his home turf, though, Leonid sat back and stared straight ahead, not saying another word. All the while, heavy breathing, and squeals continued to come from those confined to the backseat and rear compartment. From what Leonid could tell, Yuri and Mikhail were totally caught up in the moment and remained oblivious to anything else going on outside. Furthermore, he suspected that they didn't really care.

Cuchillo pulled into the walled area. In every direction, there were garage doors. There must have been forty of them in all. As he drove past one garage door after another, Leonid became increasingly nervous. He didn't know exactly what Cuchillo had in mind, but whatever it was, he hoped it would be over soon.

When he did finally stop, Leonid felt a sudden lump in his throat, and his heart skipped a beat. Cuchillo lowered his driver's side window and reached out to push a button. The garage door directly ahead slowly opened. Not knowing what to expect next, Leonid quickly peered through the SUV's darkened windshield, and much to his relief saw nothing more than a completely empty garage.

Cuchillo drove forward, and once inside pushed another button, and the garage door closed behind them.

Now, picking up on his earlier comment about "it is a surprise," he turned to Leonid and added, "but I am sure you will be pleased."

Even with that subtle re-assurance, Leonid remained uncomfortable.

"Okay, if you say so," Leonid warily responded.

As they were getting out of the SUV, Cuchillo directed everyone's attention to a door located near the front corner of the garage. One of the micro mini-skirted party girls was already there, and after opening the door, she flicked on a light switch with one hand and pulled Mikhail in behind her with the other. It was obvious that she had been there before. Once inside, she wrapped both of her arms around his neck and drew him to her. As he held her tightly, she hopped up, stretched her legs around his, and locked her ankles behind, while at the same time giving him an arousing kiss.

By this time, Yuri and one of the other girls had gotten themselves untangled and out of the rear compartment of the SUV. They followed the rest of the group into the dimly lit room. It was taking everyone a few seconds for his and her eyes to adjust. Strobe light beams reflected off a revolving mirrored ball and giant mirrors hung directly over two king-sized waterbeds. The crimson walls were accented with ivory décor, and music played as the water bubbled from the jets in the sunken hot tub. There was a bar area and a small dance floor over to the side where the guys would watch the girl's strip and then join them in some passionate grinding.

Leonid looked over to Cuchillo and nodded his approval.

"What do you call this place?" Leonid asked.

"It is called a 'push-button,' " responded Cuchillo.

Leonid looked at him questioningly.

"All you do is push-a-button. The garage door opens and then closes. Nobody knows who comes in. Nobody knows who goes out. No cars parked outside. No registration. No receipts. No credit cards. Cash only."

"No one knows you are here, huh?"

Cuchillo gave a sly smile and nodded to Leonid, confirming that he now had the picture.

"See that slot in the door?" Cuchillo asked.

Leonid nodded his head that he did.

"I shove the money in there. They charge by the hour."

Reflecting on his experiences in Colombia, Leonid laughed and said, "Great for a nooner?"

Cuchillo nodded with a sly smile, "I see you remember."

"How could I forget?" smirked Leonid. "I did not know if I would ever recover."

Cuchillo laughed, "But if you had died, it would have been with a smile on your face."

This evening at the "push-button," however, proved to be even wilder than any of those afternoon sessions in Colombia ever were, and until now, Leonid never predicted that could have been possible. Here, the party girls made sure that nothing was left to the imagination, and the more everyone drank, the more obscene their actions became.

As late evening wore on into early morning, Cuchillo became increasingly anxious. He had still not heard anything back from the word he had put out on the street. As he was about to start finding out why no one was responding, his cellular phone rang. It was his top snitch asking if the money was still on the table. When told that it was, he gave Cuchillo the hotel name and room number.

"Time to go, guys," yelled Cuchillo. "You whores, get your clothes on!"

Cuchillo slid the room payment through the slot in the door, and then peeled off some more bills for the girls. They would be left up to their own devices to find a way home.

The four men jumped into the 4x4 and headed out for the hotel. During this early hour, traffic would be light, so it wouldn't take them long.

Once at the hotel, the four of them fanned out. Since Cuchillo didn't know what Kroft looked like, he would stay near the SUV, while the three Russians positioned themselves in and around the lobby and hotel grounds. This way they should be able to monitor Darren Kroft's activities.

With their not seeing Kroft at the airport, however, they remained concerned as to whether he had been tipped-off by Catherine. Warned or not, though, they still didn't want to alert or take him down before he went to the bank.

Their primary objective had not changed. They were there to get the $9.8 million, and until Kroft got the money from the bank, and they, in turn, got it from Kroft, their job in Panama would not be finished.

As the early morning hours wore on, Nick and the Panamanian officers noticed several others also hanging around the hotel. They certainly did not appear to be locals, and Nick suspected they might be the Russian contingent sent from Moscow. For the time being, he would just keep an eye on them, and see if he could figure out what they were up to.

Long nights on surveillance tend to wear any body down, so the sight of a brilliant orange fireball rising on the eastern horizon was a most welcome sight for Nick and the police officers. Even though it was already starting to get hot and very muggy, he counted on this daybreak rush to give him a second wind, especially since it looked like he was going to be in for another long day.

Nick was fairly certain Kroft would not leave the hotel until it was close to time for him to go to the bank. Since most of the banks were not even open for a couple of hours, this seemed like a good time for him and the Panamanian officers to take turns freshening up in a room the hotel security offered to let them use, and also grab some coffee and a quick bite to eat at the hotel restaurant.

Another hour passed before they spotted Kroft getting off the elevator and going into the restaurant. One of the Panamanian officers followed him in, while Nick and the other officer remained concealed in a location where they could observe anyone coming or going.

About forty-five minutes later, Kroft emerged from the restaurant and returned to his room.

Shortly thereafter, he returned to the lobby, and while walking toward his car, suddenly stopped and took several long looks around. Not seeing anyone taking an interest in him, he felt relieved.

Even though Kroft had not spotted them, the Russians had definitely drawn a bead on him. They were now sitting in the black SUV, awaiting his next move. They hoped that he would lead them directly to the bank.

In the meantime, Nick and the two Panamanian officers got into their vehicles. Since Nick would be driving the LEGAT's car, the Panamanians loaned him one of their portable radios so everyone would be able to communicate on the same frequencies. In addition, the police had also arranged for one of their helicopters to be overhead and monitor Kroft's movements from the air.

When Kroft, the Russians, the police, and Nick all emerged from the hotel parking lot there was no indication from Darren that he had detected any of them.

"So far, so good," called out Nick, to the Panamanian officers over the radio. "Let's make sure we stay with him."

As the FBI agent / police team moved along the highway and began to gradually close in on the central part of

Panama's three-cities-in-one, the driving was becoming evermore challenging, and it unfortunately appeared that the traffic and congestion were only going to get worse.

Currently passing a string of towers and walls that remained standing amidst the brown stone ruins of Old Panama, they would shortly be entering the central section of today's modern Panama.

There, numerous colorful buses loaded with daily commuters would pack these central thoroughfares. These brightly painted buses, sporting decorated windshields and roaring, glass-packed, chrome exhaust pipes had become synonymous with Panamanian transportation and on this particular morning, it seemed as though there were even more of them on the roads than Nick had ever remembered seeing before.

Suddenly, one of the buses pulled out directly in front of him. The tires on Nick's car squealed and smoked as he slammed on the brakes and swerved, barely missing another car and several pedestrians standing in the nearby median.

Taking a deep breath, and shaking it off, he told himself, "Get a grip, Nick."

Now boxed in behind two buses pouring out streams of black smoke, and engaging in what appeared to be the race of the tortoises, a slightly shaken and frustrated Nick Costigan was back on the move, but there was no sign of his subject.

Where was Darren Kroft? Had they lost him?

CHAPTER SEVENTY-ONE

"Are you okay?" came the call over the radio.

"Yeah, I'm all right," answered an exasperated Nick Costigan. "Is your air unit still on our guy?"

"Sí," responded one of the Panamanian police officers.

"Thank goodness for that chopper."

"Nick," the other officer called, "the chopper reported a black SUV staying with us since we left the hotel. Any ideas?"

"I guess it could be the Russians," Nick concluded. "I haven't seen it yet. Have either of you?

"No," both responded, simultaneously.

"We'll have to see if that SUV stops when we reach the bank."

Both Panamanians double clicked their mic's acknowledging that they understood.

"We just got a break," Nick added, "I've passed the buses and Kroft is directly ahead.

Their tail continued.

A few more minutes passed and Nick was on the radio, again. "He's making a right turn into the parking garage of a high-rise building straight ahead. This must be the bank."

The Panamanians again double-clicked their mic's.

One of the police officers remained on the street, near the garage exit, while Nick and the other officer followed Kroft's car inside. They parked several rows away and followed him up a stairway and into the bank.

As Nick peered into the lobby, he looked for a place where he could remain inconspicuous while at the same time being able to watch Kroft. This could be difficult, as the building was old, with large open areas, glistening marble floors, and huge round pillars that rose majestically to a sculptured ceiling. There were security guards strategically located in the vicinity of each entrance and exit, and all of them appeared to be armed with automatic weapons.

To his left was a group of impressive looking offices that had been set aside for the private bankers, and directly ahead were at least fifteen female tellers, all neat, attractive, and well groomed, and dressed in matching light blue tailored business suits with colorful silk scarves. They stood in the line of teller cage windows that backed up to the vault area, near the rear wall.

Nick moved around until he finally located a spot where his profile was obscured by one of the large pillars. He watched as Kroft made his way to one of the teller windows. At that window, he opened his briefcase and handed the teller a piece of paper.

"A bank robbery?" Nick chuckled to himself.

Surely Kroft didn't travel all the way to Panama to pull a "note" job.

Those thoughts quickly disappeared after the teller took a look at what had been written on the piece of paper. There was no panic, and after exchanging what appeared to be brief pleasantries, she made a telephone call. As she talked, she looked toward the group of offices located on the side. Nick concluded that she was probably talking with a secretary for one of the private bankers.

A call came into his earpiece from the officer who had remained outside. He reported that a black SUV stopped outside the bank. Two of the three guys they had seen hanging out around the hotel earlier that morning, got out and headed into the bank. He could not tell if they were armed, because each was wearing a Panama style shirt, which hung loose and covered his belt line.

In the meantime, the conversation between the teller and the secretary concluded, and one of the private bankers headed in Darren's direction. As he approached, the private banker greeted Kroft with a smile and a handshake. After he looked at the sheet of paper Darren had presented to the teller, the banker said something and the two walked back across the lobby toward the banker's office.

As he crossed the lobby, Darren caught a glimpse of Yuri and Leonid. Unfortunately, for Kroft, they also spotted him at virtually the same time, and as their eyes met his, Kroft's world turned upside down. It was panic time.

Even though he had not succeeded in making his $9.8 million withdrawal, his priorities had suddenly changed from being rich, to staying alive. With his briefcase in hand, he started running toward the garage door entrance.

Yuri immediately gave chase.

Leonid noticed that several of the security guards had raised their automatic weapons and decided it was time to make himself scarce. He quickly ducked out of sight and headed for the nearest exit.

Nick got on his radio to make sure the two Panamanian officers were aware of what had just gone down. The officer who had come into the bank with Nick acknowledged he had also seen it, and was on the move toward Nick. The officer who had remained outside double clicked his microphone, acknowledging that he understood.

By this time, all of the commotion had caught the attention of additional bank security guards, and when Yuri pulled a chrome-plated pistol from his waistband holster and began waving it in the air; Nick knew that Yuri's demise was imminent.

One of the security guards yelled in Spanish for him to drop his weapon and raise his hands. Instead of doing as he was ordered, Yuri spun around, pistol in hand, and pointed it in the direction of the voice. When he did, bursts from several automatic weapons hailed upon him. Yuri reacted, spraying rounds high into the ceiling and down the wall, as he first dropped to his knees, and then collapsed onto the floor.

While going over some of the arrest options earlier that morning, Nick had considered the possibility of showing a gun if and when they made the arrest at the bank. Once they arrived, though, and he saw all of the automatic weapons, he concluded that would not be the prudent thing to do, especially, when the guards had not been briefed on what was happening. After seeing what had just gone down, there was no question they had made the correct decision.

Kroft had now reached the door leading back into the garage.

Shortly thereafter, Nick made his way to the same garage exit. By the time Nick reached the level where they had parked, Kroft was already in his car and speeding toward Nick. As he did, Nick pulled the borrowed .357 revolver from his waistband with one hand, and with the other waved for Kroft to stop. When Nick saw that wasn't going to happen, he quickly jumped to the side and yelled, "Stop! FBI!"

Kroft sideswiped the car next to where Nick was standing and sped out the exit.

While continuing to run toward his car, Nick used the radio to alert the Panamanian officer who had remained outside.

"He's coming your way. Try to stay with him," Nick told the officer.

The officer responded with a double-click affirmation.

As the tires on Kroft's car squealed out of the parking garage and onto the crowded avenue, two tails picked up on him almost immediately. First, was the Panamanian officer who had remained outside, and not far behind was Cuchillo's black SUV.

Weaving dangerously in and out of traffic, Kroft's panic level intensified as he entered what could easily be described as the race for his life. His earlier movements that morning had been memorized, and he had felt confident. He had taken time over the weekend to make several trips between his airport hotel and the city bank from which he would be making the $9.8 million withdrawal. Everything on those trial runs had gone without a hitch. But, now he found himself venturing into unfamiliar territory. He had no idea what would face him around the next corner or crossroad, as he followed traffic along the Bay of Panama.

In the meantime, Nick and the remaining Panamanian officer had reached their cars and joined in the chase.

It was only a matter of time before Kroft would be making another crossroad decision. On his right, were the Panama Canal's Miraflores locks and what now remained of the old U.S. military installations located near there. To his left was Colonial Panama, and rising in the distance directly ahead was the elevated Las Americas Bridge linking North and South America.

As Kroft veered off to the left, Nick ran his mind through a quick mental "good news - bad news" scenario. The "good news" was that Kroft's movement would now be much more restricted. With the old narrow streets and a dead end at the Pacific Ocean, this car chase would likely end soon. The "bad news" was that these streets were more than likely to be very crowded, making both driving and the possibility of gunplay extremely dangerous.

Colonial Panama sits on a finger of land forming one side of the Bay of Panama, and much of its architecture seems centuries removed from the glistening, shiny glass high-rises that tower just across the way. Within an arm's reach of its narrow brick streets are rows of pastel-colored buildings with wrought iron balconies and painted roofs.

When Nick had been in Colonial Panama on a previous visit, he had been reminded of Bourbon Street in New Orleans. There did seem to be several differences, though. He hadn't seen any women showing off bare breasts and there hadn't been anyone throwing strings of gold, green, and purple beads down on him, as was the case during Mardi Gras. What he had noticed, however, was a large number of merchant seamen partying throughout the area, but that was not surprising since this might have been their first time in port after a long trip across the vast Pacific.

It was also near here that he had sat on the sea wall and watched as the huge ships passed in both directions. Many had been lined up waiting to pass through the canal's Miraflores locks, while others coming from the opposite direction had already made their way through these locks and were now being piloted eastward toward the Gatun locks, and the Colon Free Trade Zone, and on into the Caribbean. It had definitely been a sight to behold.

As Kroft raced down the narrow red brick streets, a very bright sun reflecting off windows and shiny metal roofs made it hard to see. The rental car's cracked and pitted windshield was not helping, either.

All four of his pursuers' vehicles were still in the chase. The closest, being one of the Panamanian officers who was only two cars behind Kroft. A brightly painted red and yellow bus separated that officer and the black SUV carrying Cuchillo and the two Russians. Nick and the other Panamanian officer were gradually gaining, but continued to remain several cars behind the SUV.

Suddenly, a ball rolled in front of Nick's car. A small boy darted out from between two parked cars and into the street after it. Nick slammed on his brakes, and slid to a screeching halt. As he jumped out of his car, a woman, screaming hysterically, ran from one of the row houses that sat almost on the street. He could see no sign of the child, but did hear a whimpering cry. The Panamanian officer who had been following Nick managed to also stop in time, and he, too, rushed to the front of Nick's car. As Nick and the officer knelt down beside the boy, the officer asked the boy if he was hurt. He pointed to his knee. Fortunately, it appeared to be just a scrape from sliding on the bricks. He had fallen as Nick was braking toward him, and had slid under the bumper, miraculously untouched by the car. Thankfully, his tears seemed to be more a result of the narrow escape and scare than any serious injury.

Seeing that the boy appeared to be okay, the woman stopped screaming. She picked the boy up and gave him a hug, consoling him as she walked away.

Now back into their cars, the Panamanian officer honked and Nick looked into his rear view mirror. The officer motioned for Nick to turn left at the cross street just ahead. Nick complied as directed. As he slowed after turning, the officer came up beside him.

"Nick, go to the next street and turn right. It will meet up with the street we were on in just a few blocks. There should be less traffic."

There was less traffic, and as Nick moved through the intersections, he glanced over to his right to see if he could tell what was happening. Traffic seemed to have slowed considerably.

Suddenly, he spotted the rear panel of a black SUV clearing the same cross street intersection. If that was Cuchillo and the two Russians, he was getting close.

A call came over the portable police radio.

"Nick, the traffic has stalled."

It was the Panamanian officer, who was now sandwiched between Kroft and the SUV.

"One of the Russians!" the officer shouted. "He just came by my car looking for Kroft."

Before Nick could say anything, the officer was back on the air.

"Kroft saw the Russian. He is getting out of his car. He is running toward the French Plaza! The Russian is a half block behind!"

Nick and the Panamanian officer who had been following him both pulled their cars to the curb and jumped out on the run. As they rounded the corner, they spotted the other officer who now joined them in the chase.

In the meantime, Darren Kroft and the Russian had both been slowed by a large group of Japanese tourists now congregating around a signal at an intersection. That timing had allowed Nick and the Panamanians to gain ground and keep them in sight.

When they approached the French Square, Kroft stopped to bend over, in an attempt to catch his breath. Slowly turning to see how far his pursuers were behind, Kroft saw Mikhail, and before he could do anything, the Russian was already upon him, grabbing his arm.

With a pistol in one hand and Kroft's arm in the other, Mikhail turned and spotted Nick and the Panamanian officers closing in. He fired several shots in their direction and the three of them ducked for cover. At the same time, Kroft jerked, and pulled his arm away, escaping Mikhail's grasp.

After pausing briefly to catch a glance of Kroft as he ran up the wide stone stairway leading to an elevated panoramic view of the waterfront, Mikhail continued firing in Nick's direction.

Instinctively, Nick dropped to one knee and, bracing his hand against a tree, raised the .357 to eye level, took careful aim, and stroked the trigger twice.

Mikhail jerked as each round hit. Falling, he twisted and popped off three more rounds toward the stairway. All of them missed Kroft. The Russian mobster went down on his back and his blood spread rapidly over the walkway.

Nick and the Panamanian officers continued toward the stairway where Kroft had fled.

When Kroft arrived at the top of the stairway, he realized, too late, that he was at a dead end. Jumping down to the sea wall and into canal waters was not an option. His only escape was back into the path of his pursuers.

Nick yelled, "Darren Kroft, this is Nick Costigan, FBI."

Kroft immediately stopped and threw up his hands.

Nick ordered, "Keep your hands up, and start walking back down the stairs toward me,"

"Don't shoot! Don't shoot! I'm coming," Kroft yelled in a panic.

Hands up, Kroft began making his way down the stairs. Suddenly he tripped and stumbled.

"Don't shoot!" he yelled, again.

"Stand up. Hands up, and keep coming," Nick bellowed.

"Okay," Kroft said tensely. "Just don't shoot," and he cautiously made his way back to the street level walkway.

Nick yelled out, "Now get face down on the concrete. Keep your arms and hands extended, and legs and feet spread eagle. Don't make any quick movements."

Keeping his hands over his head, Kroft dropped to his knees and then to his chest. He spread his hands, arms, and legs out just as Nick had directed. He was sure he would be going to jail, but he was not about to end up with his face lying in a pool of blood the way Mikhail did, not if he could help it, anyway.

"Now stay there and don't move a muscle until I tell you that you can. Do you understand?" Nick told him.

"Yes, I will. Just don't shoot me!" Kroft responded.

As Kroft lay prone on the walkway, one of the Panamanian officers rushed over to handcuff him.

Nick carefully approached Mikhail, and while tightly gripping his revolver in his right hand, he slowly knelt to check for any signs of life with his left. There were none.

As Nick's solemn face dropped, he found himself feeling totally drained. The adrenaline rush that had kept him going for much of the past twenty-four hours was beginning to ebb, and signs of exhaustion were slowly settling in.

The Panamanian officers got Darren Kroft to his feet. They had already called for additional police to respond to the shooting scene, and a unit to handle the body. Sirens could be heard blaring in the distance.

From a concealed location across the street, Leonid had been observing everything going on. When the shooting stopped, and Nick rushed to capture Kroft, Leonid dashed back to the SUV where he flagged down Cuchillo who was already making his move out of the area.

CHAPTER SEVENTY-TWO

Wearing an FBI snitch jacket for a label, and unable to return to either her job or her apartment, Natasha had run out of options. In the meantime, Sergei was making sure she was protected for now and his intentions regarding her future security were good, but with no real witness protection program available, Natasha, and the others realized that this was, at best, only a temporary solution. She needed to be taken to the U.S.

At the American Embassy, Matt had been successful in delaying his return to Quantico, and was now busy assisting Victor as the two of them took on the bureaucracy.

First, they had to get FBIHQ involved, relaying the circumstances surrounding Natasha's peril to those at the State Department in Washington. Headquarters would explain how she had unintentionally become a vital Moscow source for the Bureau and now had to be protected, as her life was in extreme danger. The Bureau would also work on securing employment for her, hopefully as a translator and interpreter in the D.C. area.

Next, there was all of the red tape associated with visas and immigration, and getting Natasha out of Russia and into the U.S.

Although this exercise was challenging, surprisingly, everything appeared to have rapidly fallen into place. Now, all that remained was the wait.

CHAPTER SEVENTY-THREE

The phone rang in Victor's office, and after getting off the line, he came out to where Matt was sitting. "Good news!" he exclaimed. "A translation service in Washington has come through with a job for Natasha."

"That's great!" Matt stood up and gave Victor a high-five. He then paused before asking, "But, what about all of the other bureaucratic paperwork?"

"It's been approved!"

There was a big smile and another high-five. "Yes!" he said. "Let me call her."

"Oh, one other thing, the translation service said they would help, but it sounds like they are expecting you to do the legwork on finding her a place to live and getting her settled in."

"Can do!" replied Matt. "Did the Embassy say when she can leave?"

"As soon as you can arrange for the airline tickets."

Matt immediately called Natasha to give her the good news. "It's been approved! We'll leave together!"

He could hear the excitement in her voice. "Are you sure?"

"When do you want to leave?" he asked.

"Would tomorrow be too soon?" she answered, hesitatingly.

"Not for me," Matt answered. "Let me see what I can do about getting us ticketed."

He stopped at the Embassy travel office and, to his surprise, there were still plenty of seats available on a flight scheduled out early the next morning. There would be a four-hour layover, en route, at Frankfurt Main, but after that, it should be a straight shot into Washington-Dulles.

He called Natasha back. "You're sure you are ready?"

"I am sure!" she anxiously responded.

"I hope so, because we will be leaving on the early morning flight to Frankfurt. From there we will fly to Washington, D.C., and have dinner at a quaint little seafood spot near my place."

"I can hardly wait!" she told him.

"In the meantime, I'll talk to Sergei."

"Sergei, this is Matt. Good news! Natasha's on her way to the U.S. We'll be leaving early tomorrow morning."

"What time do you want Natasha and me to pick you up?"

"Victor will take me. Let's plan for the four of us to meet at Sheremyetove International. We can have some coffee and say our good-bye's there. How would that be?"

"Fine. What time?" asked Sergei.

"Five-thirty."

"See you and Natasha then. I will have the tickets and her paperwork with me."

Before Matt could hang up the receiver, however, he heard Sergei yell, "Matt, wait! There is something else."

"What's that, Sergei?"

"I think we found the guys who contracted Natasha's apartment and murdered her grandmother."

"That's great, Sergei! Have they copped out to it?"

"Not to us."

"Not to you?" Matt questioned.

"No. Not much conversation goes on at the morgue, jested Sergei. "My guess is they talked to somebody, but did not give the right answers."

"Does the MVD know what happened?"

"No details yet, but it looks like it occurred several days ago. I understand that the stench in the area where the bodies were found was beginning to get bad. Our people said it was a bad scene. Blood everywhere. Slit throats. Faces beaten so badly you could hardly tell who they were."

"Any idea who did it?"

"Ideas, but no hard evidence. A couple of apartment contracts were found on the bodies, but not the one for Natasha's grandmother."

"What about prints on the contract I found in Natasha's apartment. Any matches with these guys?" asked Matt.

"The lab is still checking."

"If you learn anything more, Sergei, let me know."

"I will."

"Remember, early tomorrow morning. Don't oversleep, Sergei."

"Never, the 'intimidator' will make sure of that."

"See you then, Sergei." Matt hung-up and called back into the other office, "Victor, I have to go and pick up the tickets and then I need to get some packing done. See you later."

Shortly after Matt left, there was a knock at the door leading into the main office of the LEGAT. It was one of the Marine Security Guards. Victor recognized him from one of the recent parties put on by the Moscow Embassy Marine Guard detachment.

Victor motioned for him to come in. He rose from his desk and shook the corporal's hand. "Have a seat."

"Thanks, but I can't stay long. I have to get back for a meeting the sergeant called."

"Okay. How's it going?" Victor asked.

"About the same," the corporal responded. "That is, other than the fact I'm getting short."

"How much longer are you here?"

"Twenty-seven days and a wake up, but who's counting?" replied the young Marine with a smile.

Seeing an envelope in the corporal's hand, Victor asked, "What's up?"

"This was dropped off for you, at the front gate. We ran it through the security scanner and nothing suspicious came up, so I thought I'd bring it up."

"Do you know who left it?" asked the LEGAT.

"I don't know her name, but I sure remember what she looks like. She was some kind of babe. A little old for me, but still mighty close to a 'ten' on anybody's scale."

Victor raised his eyebrows. "Did she say anything?"

"Just, 'Please see the FBI gets this,' and 'Thank you.' Then she got back into her PHAT ride and was gone."

"Fat ride?" Victor repeated, giving a quizzed look.

"Sorry Sir," shot back the corporal. "P-H-A-T, Pretty Hot And Tempting. You might have called it a hot red sports car in your day, Sir."

"Okay, enough of that 'in your day, Sir,' " answered Victor with a smile. "Did she say anything else?"

"No, Sir," replied the corporal, as a sly smile gradually spread across his face. "You really don't know who she is, do you, Sir?"

"I'm afraid not, but from your description, it sounds like I wish I did."

"You should," the corporal agreed.

"Thanks for the information and letter, anyway," Victor told him.

"No problem, Sir."

Again, with the sly smile, the corporal commented as he was about to leave the room, "She was sure one fine lookin' honey. Are you sure you don't know her? She's probably somewhere around your age. Maybe a little younger."

Victor shook his head and smiled, "No."

After the Marine corporal left, the LEGAT stared at the envelope and asked himself, "Who left this and what's in it?"

Victor couldn't believe he would not have remembered meeting the woman described by the Marine. The outside of the envelope was marked with only the three letters "FBI." Victor held it up to the light and then slit it open only to find another like it inside. Printed on the second envelope was, "FBI, please give to Natasha Federova."

The LEGAT curiously asked himself. "How could this person know Natasha had a tie to the FBI?"

He carefully opened the second envelope and found a single sheet of rose-colored stationery and a third plain white envelope. The handwritten contents were in English, and when Victor finished reading them, he set the letter aside.

It would be left up to Matt to determine the best time to give Natasha the envelopes.

CHAPTER SEVENTY-FOUR

The phone rang in the LEGAT office, "Matt, it's for you."

"Kelly," Matt answered.

"Matt, this is Sergei. How would you like to go for a ride?"

"Is this some kind of set-up?" Matt chuckled.

"Now would your old Russian friend do that to you," quipped Sergei, as he let out with one of those boisterous laughs that had by this time become so unmistakable.

"Seriously, Natasha needs to get some things out of her apartment before she leaves in the morning. Vladimir and I are going to take her. Would you like to go with us?"

"Sure, when?"

"We will pick you up in front of the Embassy in one-half hour. Okay?"

"Fine, I'll be waiting."

"I'm meeting Sergei at the front gate," Matt yelled back as he was leaving the LEGAT Office. "I should be back in a couple of hours."

Within minutes, Sergei's black Volga rolled up. Vladimir got out of the front and opened the rear door for Matt. Natasha smiled, and reached her hand out to Matt as he quickly slid into the backseat beside her. Vladimir closed both doors, and Sergei was off, weaving his way through the traffic in his usual international grand prix competition mode.

As the two of them talked, Matt took the envelope from his jacket pocket and handed it to Natasha.

She looked at him questioningly, and asked, "What is this?"

Matt shrugged, "It was left for you at the Embassy gate."

Natasha pulled the already opened envelope apart. Inside was a single sheet of rose-colored stationery and a second envelope.

Unfolding the single sheet, she read:

Dearest Natasha,

By the time you read this, I hope you will have safely escaped from Moscow.

This is very hard for me to write, but I want you to know the truth. My decision to desert you as a young child was for the lure of power and nothing else. As I sit here writing this today, I can make no excuses for my choices and can only hope that someday you might find it somewhere within your heart to forgive me. You and your grandmother were the best things that ever happened to me, and I have only myself to blame for our separation. Although I gained power and money, I still did not have you, and I was not there for your grandmother, my mother, when she needed me most. I cannot bring back either our lost years or her life and for that I am very sorry.

One more thing, Natasha. Your are in great danger! One of Moscow's most violent gangs has placed a contract to have you killed. They say that you are an FBI informant, and it is because of that claim that I have tried to reach out for you only in this way.

I tell you, my dear, be very careful and do not attempt to return to either your job at the Social Club or to your apartment at this time. They will be looking for you in both places.

You have grown into a beautiful and wonderful young woman, and, although I will probably never see you again, you will remain in my thoughts forever.

I am very sorry for everything.

I love you.

Your mother,

Catherine

P.S. In the other envelope is the contract your grandmother signed for the apartment. No one else any longer has a right to it. The apartment is yours to return to, whenever it becomes safe.

Elena's death has been avenged!

Teary eyed and clinging tightly to the letter, Natasha shook her head as she sat there quietly, pondering. Matt put his arm around her shoulder and said nothing.

When they arrived at the apartment complex, Sergei leaned back to Matt and said, "You stay in the car with Natasha while Vladimir and I take a look around."

Going in opposite directions, they checked up and down the street. When both returned, Matt rolled down the dark tinted window and Sergei stepped up.

"We saw nothing. Matt, you hold onto Natasha. Vladimir and I will stay in front of and behind you two."

Natasha handed Sergei her key as they approached the main entrance. He would lead the way up the stairway and into the hallway where Natasha's apartment was located.

As the four of them slowly eased their way down the hallway and reached her door, it was immediately evident that one or more uninvited visitors had arrived ahead of them. The door was unlocked, but closed, and splinters from the wood frame were lying on the floor. Someone must have tried to pry it open, before managing to get it unlocked.

With pistols drawn, Sergei and Vladimir stood on each side of the doorway.

Vladimir pushed open the door and yelled, "MVD!"

There was no response. Leading with their pistols, they entered the apartment.

So far there was nothing, no sign of anyone.

Matt remained in the hallway with Natasha while Sergei and Vladimir continued their sweep.

Finally, Sergei yelled, "All clear!"

Although there was no one inside, Natasha's belongings were strewn everywhere. When she walked in, Natasha could hardly believe her eyes. Closets, drawers, clothes, everything she owned had been trashed.

Thinking things couldn't get much worse, she entered the bathroom. In bright red lipstick on the mirror, someone had drawn a large circle, printed the letters FBI in it, and then struck a slash through the circle. She reached out for Matt.

Grasping and holding her tightly, he whispered reassuringly into her ear, "It's going to be all right," but Natasha couldn't help but wonder what might be next.

From the other room Sergei called, "Natasha, it is time for you to start gathering up what belongings you need so we can get out of here."

He didn't want her to be exposed to any more danger.

Natasha opened a bag and in it put several pictures, some clothes, and a few personal items, and handed the bag to Matt.

"Time to go!" Sergei announced to everyone.

Vladimir led the way out of the apartment, with Natasha and Matt following him down the stairs.

Sergei remained behind working to get the damaged door secured. The splintered frame was giving him more of a problem than he had anticipated.

As Matt was going down the final flight, the strap on the bag he was carrying for Natasha broke, and he bent down to see what he could do about repairing it.

When Vladimir and Natasha stepped outside the main entrance, a lone gunman was waiting for them. His sudden appearance frightened Natasha and she screamed. He fired several shots in their direction before Vladimir could turn and get a round off. As the bullet from Vladimir's pistol found its mark, the gunman slumped to the ground.

When Matt heard the gunshots, he dropped the bag and ran toward the partially open doorway. Getting only a glimpse of Natasha lying on the ground, he finished shoving the door open.

Seeing Matt, Vladimir kicked the gun from the assailant's hand and toward him. Matt reached down, grabbed the pistol, and rushed to Natasha. Kneeling down beside her, Matt took a quick look around to see if anyone else was in the area.

He spotted no one.

To their rear, Vladimir and Matt could hear Sergei approaching, as he came flying down the stairway toward the open doorway.

When Sergei arrived outside, he found Vladimir standing over a motionless body sprawled on the ground a few meters to his left, and Matt straight ahead, holding Natasha in his arms.

"Are you all right?" a stunned Sergei asked Vladimir.

"I am fine, but you must get an ambulance for Natasha!" yelled Vladimir.

Grabbing the cell phone from his pocket, Sergei started pushing buttons.

"They are on the way!" he yelled back.

Noticing that she was losing consciousness, Matt shouted, "Look at me, Natasha! Look at me!"

She looked into his eyes and smiled. Matt gave her a gentle kiss on the forehead and stroked her hair. She smiled once more, and then there was nothing.

Matt gently shook her, crying, "Natasha! Natasha! Stay with me! Stay with me!"

There was no response.

Pulling Natasha to him, and holding her tightly, Matt's eyes began to water and tears began slowly rolling down his cheeks.

"Why Natasha? Why not me? It's not fair! It's not fair!" he cried out.

Unable to respond, Sergei lowered his head and put his hand onto Matt's shoulder. There was nothing he, or anyone could say or do.

CHAPTER SEVENTY-FIVE

As Sergei drove, Matt didn't say a word. He was beating himself up with "what ifs." If the three of them hadn't gotten separated. If the strap on Natasha's bag had not broken, if, if, if...

"Do you want to go somewhere and get a drink?" Sergei solemnly asked.

"No, why don't you just drop me off at the Embassy gate. I'll maybe have something there. I would just like to be alone for a while."

When they arrived at the Embassy, Matt got out of the Volga and told Sergei, "Don't worry about seeing me off at the airport in the morning. I won't be leaving tomorrow."

"Is there anything I can do?" asked Sergei.

"Nothing, I'll have to work it out myself," answered Matt.

Sergei nodded that he understood and replied, "I will call you at Victor's office, tomorrow."

Matt stepped out of the car, still numb from what had transpired.

"Thanks, Sergei."

As the black Volga sped away to a local MVD watering hole, Sergei asked Vladimir, "What happened?"

"It was all so fast," Vladimir answered. "Natasha was behind me when we came out of the main entrance. As we started toward the car, the guy jumped out from where he was hiding behind some shrubs next to the building. Natasha screamed, and he started shooting. He had already gunned her down before I could get a round off. She didn't stand a chance."

"She was between you and him?"

Vladimir nodded affirmatively.

"Where was Matt?"

"I don't know. He was following us, but we must have gotten separated in the stairway. He got outside only shortly before you."

"Any idea who the guy is?"

"None," answered Vladimir.

"Did you see anyone else?"

"Nobody, my guess is he was some mope trying to make a name for himself."

"And a bundle of rubles at the same time," added Sergei.

"Yeah, but at least the scum will never collect," responded Vladimir.

Sergei nodded his head in agreement, as they rolled up to the local MVD hangout where the two of them would try to drown their sorrows in vodka.

CHAPTER SEVENTY-SIX

The phone rang, "Office of the Legal Attaché," answered the secretary.

"Matt Kelly, please. Tell him this is Sergei."

"Hello, Sergei," Matt answered somberly.

Sergei could tell by the tone in Matt's voice that all was not well.

"Are you alright, Matt?" he asked.

"About the same. I can't get what happened out of my mind."

"Me, either," agreed Sergei.

Choked up, and having trouble getting anything out, Matt replied, "She should be leaving Russia with me."

"I understand," responded Sergei. "Do you want to get together?"

"Yeah, I guess," answered Matt.

"I will meet you at the Embassy gate in one hour. We can get some coffee."

"I'll be there waiting."

Vladimir was with Sergei when they picked-up Matt. They could tell that it had been an even rougher night for him than it had been for the two of them. Several cups of very strong coffee would be required when they arrived at their usual morning coffee spot near the MVD office.

"Any word on who that guy was?" asked Matt.

"We got an ID this morning. On the street, they called him... I think you would say in English, 'Stray,' " Vladimir answered.

"Stray?" questioned Matt.

"I guess he had no home with one of the gangs. He must have heard about there being a contract out on Natasha and thought he could make some quick money."

Matt shook his head in dismay.

Sergei added, "We also got an answer back from the lab on those prints on the contract."

"Did they match?" Matt asked.

"One of the guys did," answered Sergei.

Matt shook his head, and then asked, "Have any arrangements been made for Natasha?"

"The 'intimidator' is working on that, as we speak."

"Sergei, you are going to have to stop referring to your wonderful wife that way. She's a delightful woman."

He smiled. "I guess you are right. She would have to be to put up with me for all of these years."

Matt returned the smile and nodded in response, "You're certainly right about that, Sergei. Please tell her if there is anything, and I mean anything I can do, to let me know. I am willing to pay for any of the costs for the funeral, or do whatever is needed."

"I will tell her, but it is my understanding that everything has been taken care of."

"Like what happened with Natasha's grandmother?" asked Matt.

"Exactly," answered Sergei. "A mysterious benefactor."

"Interesting."

"Will you be here for the funeral, Matt?"

"I will," he replied. "I will be staying at Victor's until then."

CHAPTER SEVENTY-SEVEN

The sky was overcast and a light mist fell on the small group of mourners gathered at the cemetery for the graveside services. In addition to the priest and those responsible for handling the funeral, the only others in attendance were Sergei and his wife, Vladimir, Matt, a couple of residents from the apartment complex, and a few parishioners from Natasha's church. Victor had been called out of Moscow on an urgent assignment.

The service was short. The priest made a few remarks and a couple of the parishioners said something, but that was all. Matt wished he could have understood what words the priest and other mourners said about her, but that was not to be.

At the conclusion of the service, Matt remained behind and told Sergei he would be staying there for a while. Sergei offered to wait, but Matt told him to go ahead. He would take a taxi back to the Embassy.

Considering the fact that taxi's were not readily available at cemeteries, and that this might present an ideal opportunity for the mob to deliver a fate similar to what had happened to Natasha, onto Matt, Sergei insisted on remaining behind. He, his wife, and Vladimir would stay close enough to keep an eye on Matt until he was finished.

Matt nodded, and thanked him, "I'll be okay."

Sergei refused to leave.

Matt was to take as long as he wanted, and whenever he was ready to leave, he was to return to their car.

As Matt knelt beside her grave, he closed his eyes. Memories of Natasha began flashing through his mind.

There was that initial glimpse of innocence and her stunning beauty as she peered out from behind the apartment door. The magic he felt when he held her hand on their first moonlight walk, and her pulling him down into the snow beside her after she had slipped and fallen.

He was also reminded of her loving tenderness, her kisses, and those streams of gentle tears he had been told about by Nick that came rolling down her cheeks as she remained at his bedside after he was shot. There were the intimate dinners they enjoyed at their favorite restaurants. Their embraces, his gazes into her enchanting, beautiful eyes and of course the unbelievable passion the two of them shared.

Finally, there was his holding her in his arms when she took her final breath. Those and others were all moments Matt would cherish forever.

Although they had known each other only a relatively short time, there had never been anyone like Natasha in Matt's life before, and he doubted there would ever be again.

Suddenly, the sound of footsteps brought him back to the present. Looking up, he saw a tall, middle-aged woman dressed in black and wearing a dark, mesh, veil approaching. When she got to the gravesite, the woman paused to drop a single, long-stemmed, red rose onto the casket.

Matt continued looking up at her.

The woman remarked, "You must have thought a great deal of her."

Matt's eyes were watering as he nodded his head, and his response said it all, "I loved her."

"I could tell she felt the same about you," replied the mysterious woman.

Matt looked at her and smiled appreciatively.

"You made her very happy. I am very sorry that it had to end this way," she added, and then turned and walked away.

Stunned by her remarks, Matt remained kneeling and watching as the mystery woman slowly disappeared into the heavy mist.

"Who was she, how did she know?" he asked himself.

As tears began streaming down his cheeks, Matt continued to gaze at the casket and the single red rose that rested on top of it. The shock and finality of her death was now truly sinking in.

His dealing with the loss of Natasha was going to take time, and there was nothing he or anyone else could do to lessen its impact.

CHAPTER SEVENTY-EIGHT

Within twenty-four hours of the recovery of the money, arrangements had been made for the entire $9.8 million to be returned to the same Colorado bank from which it had been stolen. Each account had been fully re-credited, and all of this accomplished without any First Westside customer ever realizing that his or her account had been fleeced. This was truly one for the good guys.

Extradition proceedings were already well under way. It took only one night in a Panamanian jail before Kroft was yelling from his cell that he wanted to talk with someone from the American Embassy.

Nick went to see Kroft and told him the Office of International Affairs, at the Justice Department, in Washington, had been in contact with the Panamanian government in Panama City, and that, as long as he cooperated, it shouldn't take too long.

"I'll sign anything," Kroft told Nick.

"We'll have to see what is needed," Nick answered.

Nick then looked Kroft squarely in the eyes and said, "You know that you still don't have to talk to me, but I would like to know if you have any more trap doors out there."

Kroft just grinned and smugly responded, "I'm the least of your worries, Mr. FBI agent. I'll be in jail until it's time for you to get your pension. It's those other guys out there with the millions and billions they can get to that you need to worry about. Who knows, some of their trap doors might even lead straight to your money and you'll never know it. That is until it's gone." He began laughing, "It could happen next month, next year, or even five, ten, twenty years from now."

Nick grimaced at the thought, before briefly pausing and trying one more question.

"What can you tell me about TFM and those accounts?" Nick asked.

Kroft smugly replied, "Not much, other than what TFM stands for."

"Okay, let me have it," responded Nick.

"Trail From Moscow," Kroft blurted out with a chuckle, adding, "Why, what did you think it meant?"

CHAPTER SEVENTY-NINE

Following the conclusion of their investigation, Special Agents K.C. Woodson, Christine Smith, and Nick Costigan were summoned to an emergency meeting at FBI Headquarters in Washington, D.C. Others in attendance included officials from the Department of Justice, the Federal Reserve, the Office of the Comptroller of the Currency, the FDIC, the Treasury, and of course the FBI.

The Topic:

"TRAP DOORS – How many are out there?"

As the meeting opened, a deafening silence hung over the room. No one knew the answer to the looming question, but all realized the potential for dire financial consequences in the coming decades, should these menacing trap doors continue to lurk in cyberspace, and not be identified and removed.

EPILOGUE

Special Agent Christine Smith returned to her Quantico assignment, where she has remained an instructor on the staff of the FBI Academy's Computer Training Unit. She and Michael are expecting their first child.

Jeff Brown, Special Agent Ret., resigned his position as Director of Security at the First Westside National Bank and Trust to become a part-time starter and greens keeper at a local golf course, and travel with his wife.

Special Agent Victor Gorski completed his 2-year assignment as the LEGAT in Moscow, and retired from the FBI shortly thereafter. He subsequently formed his own investigative business, and as a private contractor is now conducting background investigations in the Metropolitan Washington, DC area.

Boris has since moved up and recently gained total control of one of Moscow's most powerful Russian mafia gangs.

Special Agents Tom Wallace and Marla Cross were both transferred to FBI Headquarters where scuttlebutt recently reported that their career development program "blue flames" were in the midst of being re-ignited.

Sergei Malkin continues to work with Vladimir Panilov and the two of them remain assigned to the MVD's elite anti-mafia unit. Both have barely escaped death on several occasions. Sergei finally received his wish to attend the ILEA in Budapest.

Special Agent K.C. Woodson took to heart much of what Jeff Brown had told him about life after the Bureau and opted not to chase the dollar. After retiring from the Denver Division's Organized Crime Squad, K.C. stays busy with his family, and doing church and volunteer work. He was recently spotted on the slopes of the Colorado Rockies teaching at-risk youth from the inner-city to ski and snowboard. K.C. is said to be very happy and have never looked back.

Yekaterina "Catherine" remains active in the hierarchy of the Moscow mob and the operation of several of their Social Clubs.

Georgi, sentenced to twenty-years of confinement, is now residing in one of the coldest and toughest prisons in all of Siberia. He refused to cooperate with the MVD in identifying any of the other attackers.

Sasha never returned to Denver. Once word reached him in the Caribbean regarding what had happened in Denver and Panama, he went on the lam. He is now believed to be hiding out somewhere in Ukraine. Warrants have been issued for his arrest and extradition.

Leonid made good his escape to the Colombian border, and with the help of Cuchillo, returned to Moscow, via Bogotá.

Darren Kroft was extradited back to Denver, where he faced a variety of Federal charges ranging from Bank and Wire Fraud, to Conspiracy and Money Laundering. Upon his conviction, he agreed to take a polygraph and "tell all" in an effort to get his sentence reduced. When asked by the examiner about his placing additional "trap doors" in the programs of banks, brokerage houses, and other financial institutions, for which he had acted as a consultant, he showed deception. Refusing to further address the issue, his sentence remained intact. He is currently confined in a medium security Federal correctional facility located in Alabama.

Special Agents Nick Costigan and Matt Kelly continue to work internationally and remain assigned to the faculty of the FBI Academy at Quantico.

ABOUT THE AUTHOR

Ron Cleaver served more than twenty years as an FBI
Special Agent and he is currently a writer and international advisor. During his FBI career, he investigated
and supervised complex criminal investigations and was
a member of the faculty of the FBI Academy at
Quantico. His international assignments with both the
FBI and as an advisor have taken him to over forty
countries around the world.